James Phelan is the bestselling and award-winning author of twenty-nine novels and one work of non-fiction. From his teens he wanted to be a novelist but first tried his hand at a real job, studying and working in architecture before turning to English literature, spending five years at a newspaper and obtaining an MA and PhD in literature.

The ex-CIA character of Jed Walker was first introduced in *The Spy*, which was followed by *The Hunted*, *Kill Switch*, *Dark Heart* and *The Agency*.

James has also written five titles in the Lachlan Fox thriller series, and the Alone trilogy of young adult post-apocalyptic novels. A full-time novelist since the age of twenty-five, he spends his time writing thrilling stories and travelling the world to talk about them.

To find out more about James and his books, visit
www.jamesphelan.com

Follow and interact with James
www.facebook.com/realjamesphelan
www.twitter.com/realjamesphelan
www.instagram.com/realjamesphelan
www.whosay.com/jamesphelan

ALSO BY JAMES PHELAN

JAMES PHELAN

KILL SWITCH

CONSTABLE • LONDON

CONSTABLE

First published in Australia and New Zealand in 2015 by Hachette Australia,
an imprint of Hachette Australia Pty Limited.

First published in Great Britain in 2018 by Constable

13 5 7 9 10 8 6 4 2

Copyright © James Phelan, 2015

The moral right of the author has been asserted.

A CIP catalogue record for this book
is available from the British Library.

ISBN: 978-1-47212-718-1

Typeset in Simoncini Garamond by Bookhouse, Sydney
Printed and bound in Great Britain by CPI Group (UK), Croydon CR0 4YY

Papers used by Constable are from well-managed forests
and other responsible sources.

MIX
Paper from
responsible sources
FSC® C104740

Constable
An imprint of
Little, Brown Book Group
Carmelite House
50 Victoria Embankment
London EC4Y 0DZ

An Hachette UK Company
www.hachette.co.uk

www.littlebrown.co.uk

KILL SWITCH

PROLOGUE

Fade in.

It's an interior shot. Dark. The camera finds a man on a seat. He is slightly to the left of frame. We see him head to toe. He is slouched. Not big, not small. Average. His hair is longer than short, blacker than brown. He wears wire-framed glasses. The scene is poorly lit. We cannot see his face in detail.

The scene changes. The lens or camera moves towards the seated man. It's centred on the figure, from the waist up. The lighting is better now, the focus too. He is in his thirties. Fine lines around his mouth and eyes. Two days' stubble. Sweat beads on his forehead, then slides down onto his nose. His glasses slip. A lip is swollen and cut.

The man pushes his glasses back to their position on the bridge of his nose. His nose is straight, never broken, but the viewers will not take much notice of that.

They won't, because they've just seen something else.

His hands. They moved together, as one, even though he only used one finger to push the glasses back.

They moved as one because they are connected at the wrist, by handcuffs.

It's then that the man's outfit makes more sense, and those watching will make the connection.

He is wearing an orange jumpsuit. A prisoner.

But this man is no prisoner of the law, and all of a sudden the audience gets it.

They have seen footage like this before. From Syria and Iraq and other places where nothing good comes of such an image.

This is a hostage situation. Propaganda. The audience will now know that the man seated is there not of his own volition. He is captive. But what will happen next? Should they look away? Will they see the captors? Will there be a beheading?

No. It's not like that.

This man? They're making him *do* something.

And he is about to talk, to the camera. There are unseen people around him, those who must be forcing him to do this, those who gave him that fat lip and the bruise coming up on his cheek. That's what the audience at home will think, that's what the world media will say: this poor guy has been worked over and they're playing with him.

But it's worse than that. It's worse because as bad as it seems for this man, it's going to be just as bad for those watching. What this scene is about today? It will take up all the air time for the next thirty-six hours.

Because what the captive man is about to say, what and who he is, will irrevocably change the world. All within the next day and a half. Forever.

1

Walker exhaled. *Inevitability . . .*

The CIA taught Jed Walker how to travel. How to remain inconspicuous. Avoid capture. Prior to that, military service taught Walker how to kill a man with nothing but his bare hands, and that's all he had at his disposal right now, having just passed through airport security at LAX. *Well, that's not exactly true*, he thought, in hindsight, watching the two men approach. He had his small backpack, which contained a change of clothes and toiletries. A few items would do. A toothbrush through the eye socket into the brain. The straps of the backpack could be used to choke a man. He had a paperback novel in there with an orange cover that he'd found in his hotel room that morning – and from the few pages he'd read during the cab ride to the airport, it could probably bore them to death.

A few decent options, but none was a good one right now.

He made a mental checklist of the possibilities around him. Steel-framed chairs. Laminated, sharp-edged tabletops. Metal stands in gift shops. Any number of items from said gift shops. The overpriced food from the restaurants. The fast food – he could force-feed these two guys a couple of foie-gras geese and watch them have coronaries. Gavage, it was called, but in France they used feeding tubes and corn and fattened the geese up for seventeen days then slaughtered them at four months. Funny how the Europeans had such strict laws for some things. At any rate, Walker didn't have seventeen days, let alone four months. A glass beer bottle to the temple would be quicker. A twist of a neck.

But not now. Inevitability, and all that.

For Walker, a life on the outer had honed his thinking. Improvising. Making do. Surviving. To use what was at hand and to adapt on the fly and do whatever it took to see one more day.

He knew from the scene in front of him that he only had seconds of freedom remaining. Maybe thirty. He was trapped and he had little choice but to take what was coming.

Walker knew that none of his evasion training would come into play today. It would not help, because today he was a target. Not randomly selected. Not pulled aside for conspicuous behaviour. The men who came for him knew who he was. They had purpose. A singular goal.

His detention.

So. Cut and run, or stand and fight? Neither option good. Not here. Not against two uniformed TSA officers. One had his hand on his holstered Glock. The other had a taser drawn in his dominant hand, hanging by his side. They only had eyes for Walker.

It was inevitable.

2

The two men dressed as TSA officers found Walker with ease. They knew what he looked like because they had seen a photo of him. They knew what he was capable of because they had read a brief summary of his physicality and experience. They had both served in Special Forces units, but their target today had done that too – and then some. They knew it was him because he was six-three and 230 pounds and he moved with the physicality of a pro athlete. He was thirty-nine years old and in his physical prime; statistically, he'd never be faster or stronger than he was now. They knew he had about twenty years' experience with the military and CIA doing special ops work. Rated beyond excellent in hand-to-hand combat and the use of firearms. Capable. A man not to be underestimated. Which is why they had their weapons ready. Their orders were simple: apprehend and render him to another country.

•

Hands on holstered weapons made it clear to Walker that these guys were not here to chat. They were not sent to relay a message or warning about his mission. They were here to detain him.

And he had a plane to catch.

Walker was in LAX's terminal six. He had already passed security, so turning back wasn't an option. And there were cameras everywhere.

Locked doors and security up the wazoo. So, running for it was not an option either.

Damn.

But he remained calm, because that was his general disposition and because Buddha once observed that inward calm cannot be maintained unless physical strength is constantly and intelligently replenished. Walker had not read much of Buddha, and his mental image of the deity wasn't exactly the symbol of physical peak conditioning, but he'd heard that titbit from a member of the Gurkha Regiment, and they were among the toughest soldiers he had ever met. The remark had come after the soldier, serving in the British Army, had disarmed two insurgents trying to gain entry to Baghdad Airport. Neither insurgent survived the encounter, or kept their head. Walker learned never to pick a fight with a Buddhist.

With running ruled out, Walker was left with two choices.

The first was to fight. Put these two guys down and run; hope to get away. But these TSA officers were ready for him, and back-up would be on hand within seconds. LAPD and the TSA's own heavily armed response units would be minutes away, tops.

He could see the cafe just twenty paces ahead, where he had planned to wait for his boarding call over a couple of strong coffees, and maybe even read the newspaper. The paper could wait, but the caffeine he needed. Long night. Long week. Big days and weeks ahead.

Walker sighed. Relaxed his shoulders. Decision made. No point fighting.

Which left one option.

Give himself up to detention.

So, Walker relaxed and took what was coming. It was inevitable. He watched the two federal officers approach, a few yards apart and coming at him from the side. He put his backpack on the floor by his feet and kept his hands in clear view, his arms loose and hanging by his sides. One of the TSA guys, the one with a hand on a taser, kept approaching while the other, with his hand on the butt of his service-issue Glock, slowed and took a step to Walker's side.

Five seconds of freedom remained.

Whatever this was, Walker was certain that he would miss his flight, which was boarding in twenty minutes. How often were the flights to Alaska? He had no idea. Every couple of hours, he figured, tops. With oil and gas prices so low, he saw no good reason for workers to be flooding into the state. Lumber and fishing crews would be year-round or seasonal, not some kind of fly-in-fly-out types with any regularity. That left tourism and those visiting family and friends, and there couldn't be much call for that, especially just as winter had so recently ended.

Walker was confident that he could be out of here within two hours. Three, tops. He would phone a friend, and that friend would place a call, and then more phone calls would be made down the chain until word filtered down to these two front-line guys. The officers would apologise, he'd be issued a new plane ticket and retrieve his papers and backpack and be on his way. He'd board a flight to Alaska, where he had plans to avert a terrorist attack. Call it two to three hours, beginning to end.

But it still didn't feel right, and he still wanted coffee, and a good fight *would* wake him up good and proper, that's for sure.

The TSA officers slowed as they neared, watching Walker with intense curiosity. The one with the hand on the Glock looked around. No-one batted an eyelid as they passed, regular people wheeling their carry-on baggage, drinking coffee from styrofoam cups. In their eyes, just another random stop-and-search. Thank 9/11 and the Boston bombing and recent events in New York and St Louis for that. A couple of wars and the Patriot Act played a part too. Just another day at LAX.

The two uniformed officers stopped just short of arm's reach from Walker.

'Josiah Walker,' the taser wielder said. 'Place your hands on your head. We're bringing you in.'

3

Walker weighed it up.

Still no good option. These two guys had to be the cream of TSA officers, big and tough, near to zero body fat and muscles that bulked out their uniforms. Each was just the other side of thirty. Definitely ex-military. And that he'd been called Josiah, which was fine because it was on his passport and driver's licence, but no-one called him that, aside from his mother, and thinking of her made him a little sad, just for a half second, then that turned to anger and frustration at the delay, and that ticked him off.

Walker said, 'Can I at least get a coffee first?'

No answer.

Walker was led towards a blank door that simply stated: 'Unauthorised access prohibited'. He ran through a list in his mind, the CIA paper he'd helped draft a long time back for operatives being taken to security screening at airports – how to evade such scrutiny, and, when taken to secondary screening, how to get out with your cover identity intact.

Confirmed or suspected government or military affiliation almost certainly raises the traveller's profile. Walker's passport and papers had none of that – they were new, organised by the Vice President not long ago, replacing the counterfeit ones Walker had commissioned in Croatia. *Airport officials receive advance information on arriving passengers from airlines through an advance-passenger information system and passenger name records. APIS information, which enables an advance check against watch lists, includes passenger name, date of birth, sex, passport details and secondary contact information.*

Any red flag there and you would be in for closer scrutiny, secondary screening. Walker could see the door to those rooms, clearly marked, as they shepherded him away. *Referral to secondary screening could occur for concrete reasons, such as a watch-list match or discovery of contraband, because of random selection, or because the inspector suspects that something about the traveller is not right. Behaviour, dress and demeanour also factor into an inspector's decision . . .*

LAX is a major international airport, but Walker was in terminal six, Alaskan Air. Officials at US airports on average send about one in thirty foreign tourists and business travellers to secondary screening, although particular airports may impose higher percentages for certain groups. But he was travelling within the country, so he didn't have to declare any purpose for flying, he didn't have to pass any kind of immigration.

He knew how to avoid suspicion and close scrutiny because he had helped craft that version of the CIA's training manual on how to travel. He knew that and yet here he was . . .

Part of him wondered how quickly word got filtered through systems about watch lists; the kind of list maintained by security services that can also include names of confirmed or suspected intelligence officers, as well as people under surveillance or suspicion by security agencies.

Walker had been on such a watch list run by the Department of Homeland Security and Interpol until barely a month ago. A slight misunderstanding, it had eventually been ruled. He'd been on plenty of lists run by other nations, allies and others. The fact was, every nation on earth tried to keep tabs on each other's spies. He'd spent more than a year on the US watch list, when he'd been forced to go off the grid and work solo to bring down corruption within the

CIA, and it had forced him to avoid major transportation hubs and all legitimate airports.

He had since been cleared, though, his records cleaned up by the White House. But maybe these guys hadn't got word. Maybe their databases flagged watch-list people for a set period of time in case there was a stuff-up and a terrorist was let through. Better to err on the side of caution.

So, while this shouldn't be about his name ringing any alarm bells, he was prepared for that to be the case.

Maybe it wasn't that. Maybe they *were* getting a message to him, from Bill McCorkell, about the Alaska op.

No. This was not a message from McCorkell – he'd use a plain-clothed FBI agent from the LA Field Office.

This was something else.

Random selection? Not with the intent these officers were showing.

No. This was a problem.

He had no time for problems, but there was little chance of evasion now that he'd passed security. A dash for an exit, triggering a fire alarm, blending in with the masses . . .

No. He had to stay on mission. Which meant he had to bluff and lie his way out of whatever was coming.

Walker knew it the second he saw the glance between the TSA officers. It was brief, but it was definitely a look. He now had a big problem. Because he was on no watch list, and he knew how to travel. He knew TSA procedures. There was no reason for them to take him to secondary screening.

The ticket was booked via McCorkell's office. The national security expert's involvement would not raise concerns in internal travel within the United States.

As he was led towards the secondary-screening rooms, Walker ran through what he had on him. A backpack. No firearms, nothing that triggered security, though he had to pass through the scanner twice but there was nothing unusual about that. His pack held a phone charger, two sets of clothes, toothbrush and shaving kit. No computer, nothing for them to spend hours pulling apart.

His cell phone was near new, a pre-paid on which he could contact McCorkell, and be contacted. That's all he'd planned to use it for. That's who he'd need to call, once given the chance to make a phone call.

The combination of procedures available in secondary screening, a stressful experience for any traveller, may pose a significant strain on an operational traveller's ability to maintain cover . . . Not Walker. He could get out of anything these guys could dish out – but he couldn't afford to miss the next flight, or the one after.

This was a set-up. But to what end? Ordered by whom?

Ahead of him was a corridor. White walls and ceiling, grey tiled floor.

A TSA officer was before him, the other after. The one in front had Walker's pack over his shoulder and still kept a hand on his Glock.

They walked in silence, past the secondary-screening rooms. They then passed storage rooms and change rooms and doors and corridors that led to building services and plant rooms. Finally they got to a door that opened up to a staircase that led outside, onto the tarmac. A car was waiting; an airport-labelled Jeep.

Walker was shoved into the back seat and pushed across. The taser man climbed in next to him and pulled a black sack over Walker's head. His world went dark, but not just because of the material – the hypodermic needle that entered his neck had injected etorphine. He was out.

4

The hood was pulled off at the same time as a needle entered his arm.

Walker blinked away darkness and sucked in air. He was seated, cuffed to a chair, his arms behind his back. His head rolled about as he looked around, his equilibrium slowly returning as the drugs wore off, vertigo being a side effect of the cocktail of barbiturates. As his head tilted to the side it felt heavy, like a hundred-pound kettle bell atop his neck; his brain couldn't make sense of it and his neck muscles couldn't fight it, it was pulling him down and down, round and around, but he didn't fall over, he didn't tip, because his chair was bolted to the floor. His eyes could not find focus. He blinked. Wondered how he got here, but the concept of here and there was too abstract. For now it was all about survival. Of regaining his faculties. Of fading into the now. He closed his eyes and let the spinning and tugging just happen. There was nothing he could do about that, but he focused. The question *Where am I?* could not be answered, not like this, not now. There was a precursor to that question, and he felt that the answer to it was within grasp, if he could just manage to focus.

How did I get here . . .

•

Five past ten am Pacific Standard Time was five past one pm Eastern Standard Time.

12

An executive secretary, a second lieutenant in the Air Force, rapped his knuckles on his boss's door and entered. It was the first time he'd had to barge in quickly and to the point, and he didn't relish it. He was the General's fifth secretary in as many months. Her temper was legendary. But this couldn't wait.

'Ma'am, you've gotta watch,' the executive secretary said. He turned the TV on. 'It's on all news channels, live feed.'

General Susan Christie, US Army, head of US Cyber Command, looked up from her laptop. Her hair was a neat crop of silver-flecked red, and she had the poise of someone who always worked hard to keep fit and capable.

The television showed a man in an orange jumpsuit. The tagline was 'Breaking news – live'.

Christie said, 'Where is this?'

'No idea, ma'am.'

'Who is it?' Christie asked. She leaned forward, watching, listening as her aide turned up the volume. 'Have they identified him?'

He said, 'Just listen, ma'am.'

5

Through the fog of the drugs and vertigo, two things were now clear to Walker: he had been rendered some place, and it was some place from which he would not readily be liberated. Whatever was coming, it would be up to him to find a way out of it, at any cost. He closed his eyes and focused.

More correctly, it was *extraordinary* rendition.

Rendition meant he had been taken from one location to another. *Extraordinary* rendition was what happened when the CIA wanted you transferred to somewhere with fewer laws concerning how a prisoner could be treated. Syria and Egypt used to be popular spots. As an old Agency friend would often say, if you want them to be tortured, you send them to Syria; if you want them to disappear – permanently – you send them to Egypt.

So, this rendition meant a couple of things. With each passing minute, Walker's vertigo was abating. Some nausea remained around the edges but he'd never been one to give in to that, no matter the circumstance.

Rendition. From LAX to here . . . by TSA officers.

No, by guys posing as TSA officers.

The cream of the TSA. Fit, strong, muscles bulging out clean pressed uniforms.

CIA? Guys like those he used to train.

14

Why? There was no reason. He was on the outer but on good terms with the Agency. They would take him back in a heartbeat, give him a choice of postings. He could be deputy director of operations if he wanted to, driving the operatives in the National Clandestine Service, the branch that did all the hands-on spy stuff.

No. They were not CIA. Ex-CIA.

Walker fought to keep his head steady, the vertigo tug drawing him to the left, as though his head were ten times its usual weight.

Unless . . . they had been compromised. They may think they're on a legitimate rendition. Or had their orders been compromised? Activated by their superior, but masked through someone else.

Time on the outer had honed Walker's cynicism towards what a country owed you when you had bled so much for it. He well knew to look at all the possibilities, to whittle them down to those most likely. He'd been burned by the Agency before. It was easy enough to get orders through to guys like these: compromise someone above them; use leverage – the kind of leverage that would tear a family apart, destroy lives – to get them to place the rendition order; get the guys down the chain to carry it out without question. Walker knew all about it because aside from being wary of it happening inside his old organisation, he'd been on the other side. He'd used all kinds of leverage against foreign nationals to get the information deemed in the best interests of the United States.

Okay. So, either two serving or two ex-CIA operatives had rendered him. They knew the protocols, the channels, the aircraft and crews to use to make sure that it stayed secret – the days of reporters and Congress being able to track aircraft IDs back to dummy CIA corporations were long gone, thanks to far too many stuff-ups – the downing of a CIA rendition aircraft in 2007 carrying seven tonnes of cocaine into Mexico had been the final nail in the coffin. Since then, total secrecy had been obtained. Agency aircraft now either ran counterfeit IDs on flight numbers or were entered into logs doctored after the fact.

So, these two were either a legit op, or doing their own thing on the side for an extra pay cheque. A legit op he could talk his way out of, but guys in it for cash could only be stopped by brute force. And these operators were clearly ex-Special Forces, and when those guys encountered hand-to-hand combat, it was for keeps.

Walker knew he'd need to wait until his faculties fully returned, and that he'd need to make the most of every tiny opportunity. Fight or flight. Waiting.

The vertigo stopped. Walker opened his eyes. His world was steady. Colour had returned. Sounds. Smells. Taste. Touch. He flexed his fingers, his arms. Felt the blood pumping in his heart. Listened to his rhythmic breathing. In and out. Calm. Steady. Ready.

Go time.

He looked around. The room was dark but for arrows of bright light spilling through gaps in boarded-up windows. His vision was still blurred. He couldn't make out anyone in the room, but he felt a presence: the two guys were behind him.

And they could see that he was now alert.

That much was clear because the cuffs were undone. A knife was used to cut through two sets of cable ties.

Walker let his arms drop to his sides and paused. The contact to his wrists was unexpected; it wasn't the action of someone on a legit CIA op – they would have kept him secure until he was manoeuvred into whatever position was next: interrogation, or water-boarding, or to a cell. He rubbed his wrists and settled a little in the chair, hands on his thighs. Relaxed his shoulders. Felt his resting heart-rate settle close to normal, maybe ten per cent over.

The vestibular system in his inner ear was still disrupted in its solution from the nerve agent buzzing through him, the antidote chasing it away, whispers of disturbance ghosting through him. His senses checked in with what he could take in. The room smelled damp. He felt beads of sweat running down his neck. It was warm, more humid than LA had been that morning. His watch was gone – he had no way of telling how long he'd been out. His shoes were gone too. And his belt, his phone and his wallet. He breathed through the last remnants of the sedative, and settled, feeling almost normal.

Almost, but angry. Pissed. Furious. Not an ounce of fear – it was all blind fury.

Walker looked up and to the side and, squinting against the gloom, raised a hand against a shaft of daylight. His eyes adjusted and focused as he scanned the room.

Seated opposite, was a figure facing him, in the shadows. A few metres between them.

Walker tried to make the person out.

A man. Similar size to him. Sitting still. Watching. Waiting. He leaned forward, into the light. The sunlight cut across the man's face.

His father. David Walker.

6

'Walker's gone.' The speaker was FBI Special Agent Fiona Somerville. Tough, professional, no-nonsense, a rising super-star in the Bureau. Bobbed blonde hair, short and compact, eyes alert and probing. The listener was her boss, Bill McCorkell. A veteran of national security, he headed a secret unit within the UN that looked into global hot spots no-one else would touch. He was late sixties and in demand on think tanks and foreign-policy groups, but rather than the allure of prestige and good money, he'd decided to head up this new outfit at the UN. Officially they were called Special Rapporteurs, which was a cover. What he ran was an intelligence company known simply as Room 360, named after its office number in the United Nations office in Vienna, and its members were on loan from the world's best intelligence and law-enforcement agencies. Several investigations were ongoing, and each month he briefed the permanent members of the Security Council on what they were up to. Zodiac was their current top priority.

Fiona Somerville was the lead on the Zodiac case, now that her colleague, FBI Special Agent Andrew Hutchinson, was on medical leave to recuperate from injuries suffered in the line of duty. She had good reason to keep track of her freelance colleague Jed Walker.

'He was at LAX, picked up his ticket, never arrived in Anchorage,' Somerville said. 'And I checked with the airline – he didn't board.'

'So, he's still in LA?'

'Maybe.' She handed over her iPad. It showed a still image of Walker being apprehended by TSA staff.

'That's from LAX, half an hour before he was due to board,' she said.

McCorkell looked at the shot. Two uniformed TSA officers had Walker by each arm and were escorting him. To where?

'There's no footage of him leaving,' Somerville said. 'They escorted him down a hallway that led to staff areas and the tarmac. Then they took him down to the tarmac. Then they disappeared.'

'How can that be?'

'Inside help. He was made to disappear. The cameras outside terminal six were down, for five minutes. That was their window.'

McCorkell looked back to the image. To Walker's face.

'He doesn't seem concerned,' he said.

'He wouldn't,' Somerville said. 'He's trained not to.'

'Right.'

'I spoke to the head of TSA there. Showed them this shot.'

'And?'

'Those guys aren't his,' she said. 'He's triple-checking, but they're not showing up as TSA from any place.'

'Best guess?'

'Could be anyone.'

'What's your gut say?'

'Okay, best case, they're working for Walker's father. Some kind of ex-specialists that he got to do a snatch and grab or escort.'

'Sounds plausible . . .' McCorkell thought about the ramifications. About Zodiac. About what was coming next. He knew David Walker was involved in Zodiac's originating. And maybe more. Likely more. McCorkell didn't like unknowns, and didn't trust what he didn't know for certain was legit. And Zodiac, with David Walker's faked death, was on the nose. And what didn't add up was on McCorkell's problem list until he knew better. 'What's your worst case for Jed?'

'Worst case is that they're not from David – that Walker was intercepted at LAX and has been taken by the next terror cell.'

'No.'

'No?'

'Well, maybe no. I hope not. It'll be David. He's deceived us on this.'

'You think he may have sold us out on what was next?' Somerville asked, reading her boss. 'Why?'

McCorkell nodded. 'Think, no; of course he did. There was nothing happening in Alaska. He got that tip to us because he knew Walker would move there, fast. And we'd move assets.'

'Want me to get Hutchinson in?'

'No, not yet, let him recuperate or we're going to burn him out.'

Somerville nodded. McCorkell could tell that she was thinking about her fellow FBI agent, a good operator he'd met more than ten years ago and had been working alongside almost constantly since. Hutchinson was starting to show the signs of falling apart; after sustaining serious injuries in the New York Stock Exchange bombing, the event that had put Zodiac in motion, he'd gone straight onto the net terror cell before being sidelined by McCorkell. This will be a marathon, not a sprint, McCorkell told his troops in their tri-weekly briefings. Keep sharp. Keep fresh. Reach out if you need help. Hutchinson had pulled rank, being McCorkell's 2IC, and powered through to work on the St Louis situation – but it had proved too much. The fact was, Hutchinson would be a good mind to have around, even at the office, but McCorkell had seen many staffers burn out too fast and too soon by pushing the envelope.

'Sir – the television,' Zoe Ledoyen said, entering the room and pointing to one of the three blank screens on McCorkell's wall in the New York office. She had worked for fifteen-years for the French intelligence agency Direction Générale de la Sécurité Intérieure, and via a past op that had impressed him, was now that country's liaison with McCorkell's UN outfit. She switched on the television, which immediately showed an image of a man wearing an orange jumpsuit.

'What channel is this?' McCorkell asked, reaching for a remote to turn up the volume.

Zoe said, 'All of them.'

•

'Where am I?' Walker looked at his father, his gaze steady.

David said, 'Mexico.'

'Where, specifically?'

'A house. In Rosarito.'

'Why?'

'Because we need to talk.'

Walker leaned forward, his elbows now on his knees, weight shifted. He could spring up, but even though he felt his mind running at close to a hundred per cent his body was lagging, the drugs lingering. More than that, he'd been in a still, seated position for what must have been at least two hours. He moved his feet forward. They felt heavy. The sense of pins and needles ran up his calves and through his quads and hamstrings. Not good. They were seventy per cent, maybe. Seventy per cent reaction time for Walker would be about the same as a regular guy, but it wouldn't be enough, not for here, not for now. He glanced behind at the two guys who had previously been in TSA uniforms and were now dressed in casual short-sleeved shorts and khaki pants. One still held a taser in his hand.

Walker said, 'So, talk.'

'How are you feeling?' David asked.

'Why are we here?' Walked looked to his father. 'We're close to the border, but not in the US.'

David Walker replied, 'You know that I have to be careful.'

Walker stared at him. 'Why?'

'You know why.'

'Because in America you're a dead man.' Walker watched for a reaction. None come. Back home, his father was listed as deceased, two years back. He'd gone into the woodwork and Walker was still trying to figure out why. It had everything to do with an operation labelled Zodiac. But he could not be sure what function David Walker's 'death' was serving – to help him avoid US authorities, or whoever had instigated Zodiac? Was he part of the problem, or part of the solution? Was there a difference?

'Why did you do it like this?' Walker said, motioning to the guys behind his father.

'Because we had to talk.'

'You said that.'

'I needed to talk to you, face to face.'

Silence hung in the air.

'So,' Walker said, 'There's this thing called FaceTime. Or Skype. Why like this? Needles and hoods and weapons and all?'

'One can't be too wary with technology.'

'A phone call wouldn't have killed you.'

'You don't know that.'

'You could have met me in Alaska.'

'No.'

'No?'

'That would be a waste of time.'

'But you had time to drug me and fly me here – what time is it?'

'Just after ten am. And you needed to hear this from me, and it had to be in person, and this was the nearest solution to meet both those needs.' David bent to his side, picked up a water bottle and gave it to his son. 'And here, in Mexico, you're closer to your objective.'

'Closer?' Walker held the bottle, which was cool and wet to the touch, and thought of Alaska. 'Why don't you tell your guys here to relax?'

'I can't take chances.'

'You think I'd kill you?'

'You've had that look in your eye before.'

'My point exactly. You're still here.'

'Jed, listen to me. I can't ever go back to the US. Not with what I know. Not until all of this is over. And until you know what I know. I need to take every precaution.'

'What *do* you know?'

'I know what's coming next.'

'And how exactly is that?'

'Patterns.'

'Ahh. And they pointed to Alaska, right? And yet here we are, detouring south of the border, in the completely wrong direction to where I need to be headed.'

David Walker shook his head. 'And how do you know that you needed to get to Alaska?'

'*You* told us Alaska was next,' Walker said. '*You* told McCorkell that's where the next Zodiac attack would occur.'

David Walker nodded, said, 'And I *had* to tell him that.'

Walker paused, said, 'A misdirection. Why?'

'Inconsequential. After you hear what I have to say, you need to get back to southern California.'

Walker watched his father for a moment, his anger building. 'Your tip-off to head to Alaska was, what, a ruse?'

'Ruse, misdirection, whatever you want to call it. We had to get your UN colleagues, and whoever is watching *them*, out of the picture –'

'Why?'

'Or they'd shut you out of this before you even began.'

'*We* had to?'

'Me, and you.'

'You think we're a team now?'

'Aren't we?' David leaned forward. No more than two feet between father and son. 'Who got you into this?'

Walker remained silent.

'Look, Jed, to get near this next Zodiac terror cell? You have to go dark. I'm talking *completely* off the grid. That's *no* comms – no emails, no calls – and don't let *them* make you,' David Walker said. 'You have to work alone and become a ghost, or you'll never get close enough to stop it in time. And what's happening? It's already begun. We're on the clock and there's less than thirty-six hours until the main event. Drink your water.'

Walker looked at the bottle a moment, as though taking it would be like sealing the alliance. But there was little option but to hear his father out and move in a new direction. He knew that David Walker was telling the truth, at least about being the one to filter information to Walker. But the trust and faith he'd had in his father his whole life had eroded over the past two years. The man he'd known growing up, a professor of international studies and senior policy advisor to every administration since Nixon, had become . . . What? A traitor? A liar? A manipulator – that was for certain. But why? That's where he had to start. The *why*.

Walker drank the water, then said, 'So, what is it? What's in southern California?'

'What do you know about the Internet?'

Walker looked at him briefly. 'Something to do with computers, isn't it? Like, FaceTime and Skype and a whole other bunch of stuff you seem to know nothing about.'

David matched his son's stare. 'It makes the world go around. Without it there would be chaos.'

'Without it?'

David nodded.

'Right,' Walker said. 'And your point?'

'It's about to be switched off.'

7

McCorkell, Somerville and Ledoyen watched the news feed in silence. Listened to Jasper Brokaw's speech. Stared at the screen as it cut back to the news anchors.

'That's our next Zodiac cell right there,' Ledoyen said.

McCorkell looked from her to Somerville, who nodded that she concurred. He said, 'What are the chances David Walker got a different tip-off to his son?'

'You think he lied to us?' Somerville said.

'It's possible.'

'But why?' Ledoyen said. 'Just because he wants Walker working separately to our unit? Or because David himself is running Zodiac. A puppet master of chaos.'

'Maybe,' McCorkell said.

'Maybe to what?' Ledoyen asked.

'All of the above.' McCorkell couldn't yet see the trees for the forest. All the answers would be there. Could they figure it out within the thirty-six hours that this captive, Jasper Brokaw, just mentioned? Would they find Walker in time?

'Why?' Somerville said, then looked to Ledoyen. 'You're right. We need to know the *why*.'

'He lied to us, and he's taken Walker,' McCorkell said, letting that possibility hang in the room.

'I'm not so sure,' Somerville said. 'I've seen Walker hesitate – in England, remember?'

'A lot has happened since then,' McCorkell said. 'And that's not like Walker – he'd reach out and tell us, right?'

Ledoyen said, 'Maybe he didn't have a choice.'

'You really think his father picked him up and put him on this new threat?' Somerville said. 'Told him to keep us in the dark?'

McCorkell looked at the screen and shook his head.

'I don't know.'

•

Walker watched his father. As a kid he could remember thinking of him as a towering man. He recalled riding on his shoulders. Passing footballs and baseballs in the backyard in Houston. As a teen they'd moved to Philly so his mother could be around her extended family as her dementia worsened. Walker Snr had to travel a lot for work and had always kept an apartment in DC, to be near his government work and his Alma Mata, Georgetown, where he was an emeritus Professor, but he was home as much as he could be. That's when, as a young man, Jed took the measure of his father as a man. He perceived his father to be an honest man. Someone who never skirted from a fight or argument to set things right. Hard working. Consistent. Appreciative.

The man looking back at him now: Walker wasn't sure what he saw. The man who'd left Walker's mother in a nursing home to die, her mind long dead before; even he was gone. This guy before him was an enigma. A former professional academic specialising in global affairs, who had guided all kinds of administrations in the way they shaped their foreign policy and intelligence doctrines, had packed up and faked a death and disappeared and was now either the key to unlocking Zodiac, or the driving force behind it. Either way, he knew more than he let on. Either way, Walker couldn't trust him, but he had little choice but to take the chance, because he was the only link he had to Zodiac . . .

Zodiac. A program of terror cells that David Walker had developed in a DC think tank tasked to dream up worst-case scenarios that could damage, degrade and destroy the United States – a program that had in the past two years gathered a life of its own, perpetrators unknown, each terrorist attack initiating the next unlinked terror cell. So far Walker had succeeded in averting wide-scale damage during the first two attacks, but according to his father, ten more would follow.

And David was the key. A key that would not be decoded. Not here, not like this.

'That's the next terror event?' Walker said. 'Switching off the Internet?'

'Yes,' David replied. 'That's the goal. But getting there is going to be the nightmare – the journey there are the attacks.'

'Cyber attacks?'

'Yes.'

'Against critical infrastructure?' Walker said.

'That'd be the best bet. The quickest way towards chaos. But we don't know, and you have to work to find out.'

'How?'

'You look. Listen. Do what you do.'

'Where do I start?'

'Think of all the hacks we've seen lately,' David said. 'A few years ago we were hearing about General Dynamics being breached, the Chinese gaining access to plans to our new fighter jet. Then the Home Depot hack that exposed more than fifty million credit-card accounts. Sony. The Pentagon. Remember when someone hacked the Twitter feed of AP and reported a bomb had gone off at the White House and Obama was wounded?'

Walker nodded.

'A hundred and fifty billion dollars wiped off the economy in the three minutes it took them to broadcast it as a hoax,' David said. 'We've seen major cyber criminal intrusions as front-page news – and that's just what makes the news. With the world as connected and reliant on the Internet as ours is, everything is vulnerable. Everything is porous. And you realise there's very little that can't be hacked. Someone's going to try to work their way into our networks and wreak as much havoc as they can over the next thirty-six hours.'

'Where do I start? I look at everybody on the planet who has a fast enough computer and the skills?' Walker said. 'Hell – even kids are taught programming in elementary school.'

'True. But your focus will be narrowed.'

'Because of where the attacks are coming from? A nation state – Russia, China?'

David shook his head, said, 'Inside the US.'

'By a US national?'

'Yes, although he's held by someone – a group, maybe a foreign party.'

'They're forcing him to hack us?'

'Yes.'

'Who's running the counter-attack, NSA?'

'Homeland Security will be tasking elements of NS and FBI as first responders, but this will become military-led, fast. We're in a different world now.'

'What do we know?'

'The first cyber attack is the data breach. The next is threatened to occur inside of six hours; more to follow over a thirty-six-hour period. But . . .'

'But?'

'It won't get that far.'

8

General Christie's phone rang. Her exec answered it, then passed it to her.

'It's the Director of NSA,' he said.

'Yes, I'm watching it,' she said into the phone, turning down the volume of her television. 'Is it legit, because he sure talks like it. Who is he?'

'Checking specifics now,' the Director of NSA, an Admiral on the same campus at Fort Meade as Christie, his office half a mile down the military road, said. 'But he's NSA. Was Army. He's worked on all our best stuff.'

'That's . . . unfortunate.'

'That's an understatement.'

'What's next?'

'I'm headed to the White House to brief the President, then front the press room as the Homeland Sec doesn't have the lingo to answer all the tech questions that will arise.'

Christie paused, then said, 'Want me to tag along?'

'Not yet. Let me take the President's temp on this. I've already been told I'm running in the background. This will be driven by Homeland Security all the way.'

'You sure about that?'

It was the Admiral's turn to pause before speaking. 'No,' he said after a moment. 'Not really. Not if this starts playing out and the bills start piling up. I'm betting at the hundred billion in damages mark we'll be called in.'

'I'll call it at fifty.'

'You're on. What are we betting?'

'Street cred.'

The Admiral laughed.

'This is scary, isn't it?' Christie said, looking at the television screen, watching a replay of Jasper. 'That we're so vulnerable. That it's too easy to work a human angle like this and bring us to our knees.'

'It's terrifying.'

'Get him,' Christie said, her voice detached as she watched the screen. 'Bring him home.'

'On it. FBI have already called me. They're on it.'

'Have his team brought in. His co-workers. That'd be my first move. See what they know, what they're working on. Who they may have recently come into contact with.'

'Yep.'

'Double-check, then check again.'

'Ah, I'm Navy, remember? Talk soon.'

'Anything you need to get these SOB's, reach out.'

'Thanks, but I told you we're off this. It's become a federal law operation. I'm there to advise and pick up the pieces and give background.'

'Give it time.' Christie ended the call, turned up the television.

•

Walker said, 'Why won't it get that far?'

'Someone will stop it,' David replied. 'Someone has to.'

'Who? Me? You?'

'Someone. Maybe the President will give an order that can stop it.'

'Then why doesn't the President do that right now?'

'That will be a last resort. It will have devastating consequences, but, perhaps, it will be the better of two terrible outcomes.'

'Okay. So, you say there's six hours to the next cyber attack,' Walker said. 'That's it? We don't know the target?'

'That's it.' David stood and went to the boarded-up window. He peered through a slot between the rough-hewn planks, the sunshine making a line across his eyes. The eyes were still. Watchful. Regretful. 'When I ran the Zodiac war-game in DC, we worked up a lot of worst-case scenarios about potential cyber attacks. The worst was an escalating series of events that got worse until demands were met. It spread resources for a response, created mass panic, and it was loud enough and big enough to force the President to make moves that would not normally be considered.'

'Like?'

'Martial law. National Guard on the streets. Turning off the Internet. Fun stuff like that.'

'Has this group made demands?'

'In a sense.' David turned and leaned his back against the window, his arms crossed over his chest. 'When we gamed it, we mapped out a total field of targets, everything from personal-data breaches to total infrastructure compromise. Water, sanitation, power grids, cell towers, traffic signals, airports, the GPS system – anything and everything that makes the world go around can be attacked from a computer, anywhere, any time.'

'That's a huge list. You're talking anything automated. Anything connected to the Net – which is most things nowadays, from a nuclear plant in New York to missile silos in the Dakotas.'

'Yes. And it's even worse now than when we theorised it. But the fact remains that the perpetrators can turn these targets off, they can reprogram them, they can destroy them – they can *completely own them*. They can use malware that overwrites and wipes out data so that it can't ever be recovered after the event. Think back to Sony in 2015. They stole data and released it publicly – that's embarrassing to some people, sure, but it was wiping all the data that was the kicker. Imagine that on a federal government level: wiping data from the IRS or the Fed Reserve.

'Major cyber breaches and attacks occur every day,' David continued, pacing. 'We're always worried about hackers who will hurt critical infrastructure such as the electrical power grid, financial systems or transportation networks. That's the sort of scenario that some policy-makers are most concerned with. An attack could cause large parts of the country to lose power by overpowering transmission systems – big lumps of iron that transmit our electricity, and if one is destroyed, there's no spares and each one takes nine months to build. Remember Obama's *Wall Street Journal* op-ed, offered an example of train derailment, since many transportation systems rely on computer networks to function?'

'I missed that one,' replied Walker. 'How worried should we be?'

'Worried – but let's not get too paranoid. These are doomsday scenarios. Experts agree that it's a definite possibility but not the easiest or most likely way someone would try to inflict damage. The simple repetition of the worst-case scenarios tends to make people think it's the most likely, which isn't true. But does that mean we shouldn't prepare for it? Hell no.'

'Do you think this group has perpetrated some of those, as proof of concept?'

'It's possible.'

'And a threat has just been made?'

'You'll see a tape of it in a moment.'

'This threat is enough to make you believe that this is the next Zodiac cell?'

'The person making the threat *will* be taken seriously and this *will* play out unless they're stopped.' David shifted so that he was leaning against the wall with his shoulder, his arms still crossed. 'So, yes. This is it; the next Zodiac cell. And it's going to activate the next.'

'And on we go . . .'

'And on we go.'

Walker drank some water; condensation dotted the bottle from the humidity. There was a watermark a couple of feet up the walls of the room, along with patches of black mould, as though the house had flooded in a climatic event. Walker felt sweat running down his back. He was wearing a navy blue cotton shirt, the sleeves rolled up, over a black T-shirt. Black jeans. Walker welcomed the sweat, specifically, the sensation of it – he reckoned that his senses were now fully online. The only hold-up would come from his legs and back and arms having been stationary for so long that he wouldn't be as quick as he could be. But adrenaline would play its part, if called upon.

'Switching off the Internet has to be impossible,' Walker said. He took off his shirt and used it to mop his face. 'There are servers all over the place; the Internet is an entity with no master – and certainly no master switch to turn it off. An earthquake here, a tsunami there, grid failures – it survives those things. Maybe not in spots, but as a whole.'

'There's a way. There's always a way.'

'What are we talking – some kind of super-virus?'

'Nope. Like you said, the Internet's too spread out for that. Programmers could take steps to stop it before it reached world-wide proportions. And you're right that the Internet is an entity unto itself. It's like a living organism – a brain, with synapses firing through pathways that are able to duplicate and find new ways of transferring and directing traffic.'

Walker wondered if his father thought of his mother when he gave that brain analogy. How her pathways got muddled, blocked off, shut down. How, in the end, as complex as the brain is, it can be turned off. He searched his father's face but the man had shifted again, his hands now on his hips, his feet spread apart.

'A big virus like an updated Stuxnet,' David Walker said. 'Sure, it might crash a whole range of networks or servers, but it can be stopped. Servers can be disconnected, the virus purged; the Internet would slow significantly in the meantime but it would find a way to keep going.'

'But you're saying that there's a way to literally switch it off?'

'Yes.' Walker Snr paused to make sure he had his son's undivided attention. 'It's called the law.'

9

'What's our response?' General Christie asked the Director of the FBI's Cyber Crime Division, after waiting five full minutes for the call-back.

'We've got a team on it. Big team – I just retasked five hundred agents here and in Atlanta and New York.'

'This Jasper Brokaw,' Christie said, watching the news scenes. 'There were no known threats against him?'

'Nothing telling. And the guy was a star at the NSA. Super-nova bright. Never flagged a follow-up in security clearances, aside from the usual stuff when posted overseas. He's as clean as they come. Cleaner, actually, with pedigree background. But we're shaking trees and rattling bushes or whatever it is that we're doing.'

'I read his file,' Christie said. 'He used to be Army.'

'We've just spoken to his superiors – old Army COs as well as his NSA department head. Brokaw is good at what he does. Among our best, they say. Certainly capable of attacking critical infrastructure.'

'Where's Homeland on this?'

'They're planning for the worst while hoping the sky doesn't fall so that they might actually have to do something real.'

'Those guys . . .'

'I know. There's simply too much to protect and they're still green. This kind of thing is out of their league.'

Christie leaned forward on her desk, said into the phone, 'You're briefing the White House?'

'Half-hourly. We've got a team set up in the Situation Room. They're keeping the President informed. I'm across this, believe me.'

Christie smiled, knowing what that meant: we're making sure that Homeland Security is kept in check, and we're ready to use our gravitas to intercept ineptitude.

'POTUS is in Hawaii?'

'And he's staying put,' the Director replied. 'Either there or on Air Force One, until this is over. The VP is in the Sit Room. Congress isn't in session, and the Hill's largely deserted, so that's one security headache we don't have in the face of however many cyber attacks are headed our way.'

'We might need them on the Hill to make decisions.'

'The President has all the power he needs.'

General Christie smiled again. *He sure does.* 'I'll connect in to the next Sit Room briefing, patch into the video con.'

'You're expecting to be called in on this?'

'If the President needs us, we're ready and willing to act.'

'God, I can't fathom it will get to that.'

'Plan for the worst, right? It's happened before.' 9/11. Pearl Harbor. She didn't need to say it. They both knew what destruction looked like. *Plan for the worst . . .*

•

'There's a law that says they can turn off the Internet?' Walker said. He stood, moved to the plastic bag of cold water bottles and took another. Neither TSA guy moved, but they both watched him. He passed them around, saying to the two big guys, 'No hard feelings.'

'Sure are laws, a whole load of them, in fact.' David sipped his water. 'Here and in most other countries. But we're not just talking China or Iran or Syria or Russia turning off their Internet to stop people talking online to prevent civil unrest in those autocracies. Look,

Jed,' David continued, still standing but shifting positions again, 'this is about switching the Internet off in North America and among our allies around the globe. What's left will be a ghost network, cut off from the world, small pockets here and there.'

Walker nodded. 'Effectively all that's left would be intranets and local-area networks in far-flung corners of the Middle East and Africa.'

'That's right.'

'Who enacts this law here – the Supreme Court?'

'The White House,' David said. 'A raft of laws have been passed since 9/11, probably the most pertinent to this being the Cybersecurity and Internet Freedom Act.'

'Don't you like how they put "freedom" and "patriot" in bills through Congress so that they sound all rosy?'

'Whatever works.'

'And why will the White House enact these laws?'

'The coming events will force the President's hand.'

'Over the next thirty-six hours.'

'Yes.'

'At what point? At events that we don't even know are coming . . . they're going to have to be catastrophic.'

'That's the unknown, the multi-trillion-dollar question,' David said, pacing. 'What will come, where, when . . .'

'Say the Net *is* shut down for a period of time,' Walker said. 'That will do what – stop more cyber attacks only until it's switched on again? To put up bigger walls of defence.'

'Maybe. In theory.' David Walker exhaled. 'Maybe it will buy the time to find this guy and those who have him captive and put a permanent stop to it. But there's more to it than that – it won't be that simple. It can't be.'

'I've always heard it's much easier to attack than defend in cyberspace . . .'

'Correct. But what we're talking about – enacting this law – won't happen easily. I mean, this is not like the President has a literal button or switch to shut off the Net; orders have to be given and papers served and lawyers across the globe briefed, and all the while the world's biggest companies will challenge at every turn to save their very existence. Even if the Net is down for an hour, or two, or six, can you imagine the shock to the global economy? Let alone all the systems that rely on the Net, from personal-safety to a national-security point of view.'

'I'm more worried about getting to that point of the President's decision,' Walker said. 'Nothing happens fast in Washington, so shutting down the Net inside of thirty-six hours may be a moot point. The President will have to deliberate with the National Security Council, Congress and the Senate will have to be recalled and they'll be arguing – it's going to take time, and we're going to see what these events are, and that's all going to happen before we see any private-sector push-back.'

'But there are laws in place, and a few executive orders, that authorise him to direct the Department of Homeland Security to shut it down, fast.'

'To prevent further attacks . . .'

'That's right. They sold it as a what-if scenario. Like, what if a terror group were using cell networks or wi-fi to detonate bombs around the country – how do we stop that? How do we make sure it's all shut down?'

'How are they going to know the attacks are from this group?' Walker said. 'That they're different from the thousands of cyber attacks on US networks every day?'

'Because a credible threat has just been made. We've under six hours until the next cyber attack, and it will involve all US government personnel.'

'That's vague. That's it?'

'I'm afraid so.'

'Who knows about it?'

'It was on the news two hours ago.'

Walker checked his watch. 'That's after you picked me up and brought me here.'

'Yes. I moved fast.'

'You had advance warning.'

'No. I was watching for signs. I told you: patterns.'

Walker nodded. That's what his father was known for, how he'd been so in demand as a professor who specialised in global security and foreign policy.

Walker said, 'What can I do?'

'I'm not certain. But you won't be working with the NSA or FBI or DoD. Nor your friends in the UN.'

'Why?'

'Because they're all going to be looking into this the wrong way. They're on defence, remember?' David looked at Walker, and in his eyes was something that wasn't there before: pity. 'And they don't have what you have.'

'What's that?'

'A connection.'

10

Walker's connection had watched the news, and she now sat with her father in the sitting room of his home. The air was humid and heavy. Neither father nor daughter had spoken for five minutes. Nervous tension arced between them. The house was dark, because all the curtains were drawn. Not for any reason other than practical safety. The coffee table before them held a jug of iced tea, two glasses poured, neither touched. Her father's face was flushed. Anger, she figured. Anger that was soon replaced by a feeling of impotence, of being on the sidelines, of not being allowed to interfere. It wasn't just that he was retired from military service. It was that this was not a military affair. That, and they were being watched.

The watchers were in the form of two Special Agents from the FBI, one in the kitchen and one seated in the hallway. There was another security presence, outside, where two police cruisers from the San Diego PD sat parked at each end of the residential street, screening all those who came and went. A quiet street, mainly retirees and a couple of military families.

We're here to ensure your safety, the lead FBI agent had said upon arrival. *You're to stay here, under our supervision, until we hear otherwise. The assistant SAC from the LA Field Office will be here soon to discuss the matter further. In the meantime, you are to cease all communications – for your safety, of course, and that of Jasper, whom we are doing everything we can to locate and rescue.*

So, this was what it felt like to be captive. Inside the house, sitting on a couch next to her father, Monica Brokaw felt numb. She'd seen the news feed and had not spoken since. Within twenty minutes the police had shown up, and five minutes after that, the FBI agents. She sat next to her father and watched the news. The volume was down because her father, hard of hearing from decades in the Air Force near fast jets, preferred to read subtitles. The newscasters were analysing and dissecting what had been demanded in the face of a pending cyber attack. Experts were being questioned. Hypotheticals were being thrown about. None of them knew what they were talking about.

Monica glanced out the open doorway to the agent sitting in the hall. *For our protection?* she thought as the agent looked from the front door to the television, and back. *Then why do I feel like a prisoner? I might as well be the one in the orange jumpsuit. And that won't do. Not at all.*

•

'A connection?' Walker said.

'I'll get to that,' David replied.

'Time's ticking, right?' Walker said. His father was silent. 'Do we know the first target at least? A clue, something to go on, besides the fact that it will involve all government employees?'

'No. That was it.'

'Do we know who's making the threat?'

'Partially.'

'China?'

'No.'

'If you're going to tell me it's some nerd in a basement—'

'No. This is quite real.'

'One person can really do this?'

'An insider can.'

'An insider? Like, an NSA guy or someone?'

'Exactly like an NSA guy. He's hostage, his captors unknown and unseen.'

'And he's on the news?'

'Yes. They've dressed him in an orange jumpsuit and all. Apparently he's been through the ringer a bit.' Walker watched his father stretch out against the window frame. The old man had always had a bad back, the result of a childhood accident on the family farm outside Amarillo, and had suffered through multiple surgeries over the years. He'd heard his father claim that the injury was caused by a slip on a hoodoo in Palo Duro Canyon and Walker had vowed one day to get the truth. But not today. 'You might know him, actually.'

'The NSA guy?'

'His name's Jasper Brokaw.'

Walker thought about the name. Nothing. 'No.'

David turned around. 'You sure?'

'I don't know the name at all. I've only ever met a handful of guys from the NSA. It sounds like this guy's at the tech end, and aside from a couple of guys attached to a high-profile-target cell-phone tracking unit in Baghdad, I haven't met any others. Certainly no Jasper. I'd remember that name. Friendly ghost, right?'

'Okay,' David said. 'What about Brokaw?'

'Common enough name,' Walker said to him. There was silence for a moment, and Walker added, 'You look tired, worn out.'

'So do you.'

'I've been busy.'

David merely nodded. Walker wondered how much his father knew about who was behind Zodiac. It was not that long ago that he'd been the one standing over his father, whom he had captured, in England. Now this. Could David Walker prevent all the Zodiac terror threats that he admitted to helping brainstorm years ago, when he was part of the intelligence system? Or was this it – doing whatever it was that he could from the shadows and directing his son to do the point-work?

'So, in the scheme of things, what's the big deal with shutting down the Net?' Walker said. 'I mean, turn it off, we switch it straight back on, right? Threat's over. Close the guys out and prevent whatever threats they're making. Use the opportunity to track them down.'

'It's not that easy.'

'Can't be too hard if the President has the power to do it,' Walker said. 'Having no Internet for a minute or two will be annoying, sure, it might cost billions of dollars to the global economy for every second it's off. But that's it – turn it back on, freeze whoever it is out, right? We use the full powers of the NSA and global partners to track down those doing the hacks. Problem solved.'

'It won't be that easy,' David repeated. 'I can't be . . .'

Walker could tell his father's mind was elsewhere, trying to catch up and piece together the threat.

'You wonder how I knew this was happening before anyone else?' he said, returning his gaze to his son. 'How I had all this in play before you got to the airport?'

'Either someone told you—'

'No-one told me.'

'Patterns? You've been watching them everywhere and you noticed something before anyone else? I don't buy that. You're not in the game any more – you don't have the resources.'

'Well, that's what it is, buy it or not. I've spent a lifetime making contacts, building networks of watchers and listeners. I've had feelers out, and a line was tripped. Like a tripwire. Or more like a tsunami warning. I detected the tremors and can see what's coming. Not specifically, but enough to predict that this is certainly the next Zodiac attack, and that it's the real deal.'

'I want to see it. The tape of the hostage.'

'Two minutes. Two minutes and you will.'

'What happens in two minutes?'

'I leave. And you have a job to get on with.'

'Where are you going?'

'Look, Jed, this terror cell? This isn't a series of hacks driven to infiltrate high-value political, economic and media locations in the US. It's not going to be about attacking us and hurting us for the sake of it. I have to do what I have to do, and you do what you do. This certainly won't be an escalation of hacks that have been going on for years out of China and Russia. This will be undertaken for one reason: to shut the Internet down – and to keep in down. It's the end game, the worst-case scenario, and to get us there, there will be unimaginable chaos and costs.'

'No,' Walker said. 'Not unimaginable. Because *you* imagined it. In your Zodiac war-game. You and countless other security boffins holed up in some ballroom in some hotel on the beltway. Someone there thought this up, and now look at where we are.'

'We must prepare for what might happen.' David shook his head. The guy looked so tired he might just keel over and sleep, right there. 'That was the entire purpose of Zodiac.'

'In designing Zodiac, you didn't prepare for *hypotheticals*. You designed a *map* to destroy the world. Can't you see that?'

David sighed, said, 'And you're missing your connection.'

11

'Madam Secretary,' Christie said.

'General, I've got one minute before briefing,' the head of Homeland Security replied. 'Have you got something for me?'

'I want to offer our assistance and the full resources of the—'

'Thank you, General, duly noted and filed away.'

'We can help.'

'Right. At any rate, our hands are tied until the attacks unfold. At the moment we're calling everybody in and looking at every possible target that we can. This is a matter for law-enforcement agencies. Not the DoD. Certainly not the Army.'

'Remember, ma'am,' Christie said, her hand tight on her phone, 'if this becomes catastrophic enough, we take over.'

'Well, we have to make sure that it doesn't come to that now won't we.'

'Seems out of your hands.'

'What you're suggesting is tantamount to martial law, General. You're a military outfit. Posse Comitatus Act etcetera – removes the Army from domestic law enforcement.'

'If we're protecting America, it is what it is.'

'Try telling my boss that.'

'The President? He's my boss too. By its express terms, the Posse Comitatus Act is not a complete barrier to the use of the armed

45

forces for a range of domestic purposes, including law-enforcement functions, when the use of the armed forces is authorised by an Act of Congress—'

'Which isn't in session.'

'Or the President determines that the use of the armed forces is required to fulfil the President's obligations under the Constitution to respond promptly in times of war, insurrection, or other serious emergency – like we did in Katrina.'

'Look, I do enjoy your little hypotheticals, but I must go.'

The call ended. Christie leaned back and wondered: what would it take? Six hours? Or twelve? Sooner or later, they will ask for her help. Then we'll see what's what, and who's who . . .

•

'I need to know what you know,' Walker said to his father. He stretched his legs and shook his arms, feeling almost back to normal.

'You know it. I've just told you.'

'That I have a connection to this?'

'That's right.'

'And you were tipped off because of patterns.'

'Yes.'

'What patterns?'

'Right now the FBI are running a global operation to find fourteen missing persons,' David said. 'They were all abducted over the past twenty-four hours. And the only reason to do that would be as a precursor to this attack.'

'Who are they?'

'They represent ICANN,' David said. 'They are the fourteen people in the world who have password-controlled electronic keys to restart the Internet in the advent of a catastrophic failure. They've been the same fourteen people since the Internet began. They meet four times a year to generate new electronic keys, which last three months; at the three-month mark, the keys expire and error messages spread across the Net. Overnight, all fourteen have been abducted. Vanished. Without them, the Internet will be useless – all Web addresses will be invalid.'

'So, now you're saying that if the Internet is shut down, it can't be restarted?'

'Not quickly.'

'How quick?'

'A month?'

'There has to be another way. It can't be reliant on a few people.'

'There are seven back-up people, with back-up keys . . . but the back-up keys contain only a fragment of the code needed to create a new master key, and it takes time to piece it together for authentication. These people are only needed when the Internet goes down – they're the ones who are able to reboot it. And sure, we can select other key-masters. Rebooting the security matrix and making complete new sets of keys will take a few weeks – in theory, because it's never been attempted – and that's if the safes containing the back-up keys are kept . . . safe.'

'So, if it's shut down – it's down for up to a month.'

'Maybe longer. Probably longer. We're dealing with hypotheticals and worst case, because it's never been tried.'

'The world in darkness for a month . . .'

'Yes.'

'I don't understand what I can do about this,' Walker said. 'The FBI will handle the abductions. The White House will be working on a response to the threatened cyber attacks. What am I missing?'

'The connection to Jasper Brokaw.'

'But what can I *do*? They could be holding him anywhere on the planet.'

'He was abducted four hours ago; the FBI have a witness to the snatch, from his home in Palo Alto. The lead's gone cold. The vehicle was switched and torched twenty miles west of the scene.'

'This was in Silicon Valley? Four hours ago – that doesn't mean he's still stateside, not for sure. Anywhere with a computer and high bandwidth could be used, right?'

'He's in the US. It makes sense. The only alternative to fit such a short time span would be to move him by plane, but that involves too much risk.'

'He could be in Central or South America now. They could have transported him like you did to me.'

'All flights have been checked,' David stated.

'You got me out.'

'All flights have been checked,' David repeated, his tone unwavering.

'Fine. So, assume you're right and he's still in the US. How can I find him?'

'Do what you do best – investigate it. Run it.'

'The FBI and Homeland Security will be all over it.'

'They don't have what you have.'

'The connection? To what?'

'Brokaw.'

'I told you I don't know the name.'

'You know his father.'

Walker just shook his head. Couldn't think of a Brokaw he'd ever worked with.

David said, 'He was the Air Force Academy's commandant back when you were a cadet there.'

Finally it clicked. 'General Brokaw. That was almost twenty years ago . . .' Walker trailed off.

'And you have a connection – not just to him.'

Walker sighed.

12

Walker said, 'Monica ...'

'That's right,' David said.

'I – how do you know ...'

'You told your mother.'

'I did?' Walker thought back. He'd been twenty; Monica a year older. The commandant's daughter, a psychology major at Cornell. They'd met at the Academy gym at the start of the July Fourth weekend, then caught up later that day and spent the three days holed up in a hotel in Boulder, Colorado. Close to the Air Force Academy in Colorado Springs but far enough away from the prying eyes of fellow cadets and staff. And her father. 'Mom told you?'

'Yes.' Walker thought about his mother's condition back then. She was lucid, but that was around when it had started, when he'd moved out of home. He'd called her every other week and each time he'd noticed it a little more. Dementia.

He looked at his father. 'How did they pick Jasper for this?'

'I don't know.'

'Because of you, and me?'

'No. It can't be that. I swear I have no idea. It's because of Jasper's skills set. Nothing more.'

'This is linked back to you, it has to be.'

'There's no way of knowing that.'

'Whoever is running this Zodiac cell, whoever took this guy hostage, they know of the connection.'

'When I created Zodiac you were in the Air Force, in Iraq, your first overseas tour. I looked at his record – Jasper had nothing to do with cyber stuff then. There's no way this goes back to me, to you.'

'Maybe. Maybe not.'

'I don't like coincidences.'

'Me either. This could be connected to us. Of course it could. Because you started Zodiac, and they're working backwards, not forwards, and they have the benefit of hindsight.' Walker looked at his father. Watchful. 'Whoever they are.'

'Well, this is happening, so you have to deal with it for what it is. Look into Jasper. Go find Monica, talk to her, see what she knows and what she thinks. Find a way in.' David's watch beeped. 'That's it. Time to go.'

'Where are you going?'

'I've got my work, you've got yours.'

Walker held his father's eye. 'You really think Monica can help?'

'It's a lead. Pull at the thread and see where it goes.'

David Walker handed over an iPad from one of the guys standing sentry.

'Her father's address is on there. She's with him. The video of Jasper too. Look at it and leave the tablet behind – it's not secure.'

Walker looked at the screen, the address pinned on a Google map. Riverside Drive, Palermo. 'The General lives in San Diego? That's why we're meeting here?'

David nodded. 'It's close to here. Watch that movie file. Look up Monica and then leave. Toss the tablet out the window a few blocks from here. Someone will pick it up, and with any luck it might take some NSA resources off you – because once you find her, you'll be a person of interest to them.' David stared at his son. 'Stay off the grid, Jed. Completely dark. You know how the NSA and FBI will be working this. This is happening real time, which means you have to get out there, on the road.'

Walker nodded.

David said, 'They're not looking for you yet but as soon as you make contact with Monica Brokaw, they will be. They'll voiceprint you and – well, you know the rest.'

Walker did know. They'd have him tagged. Any time he spoke on a phone the government would have him identified and his position located within a minute. Then it would be a matter of how quickly they could get a team to him. Local police could be minutes away. But they'd likely have their own people, mobile forward units deployed to his last known addresses, ready to pounce.

And there was more to it, too. For several years the NSA had mapped the movement of every cell phone in the world by monitoring MAC and IMEI addresses: the unique identifiers emitted by each cellular and wi-fi device. The phone didn't even have to be turned on. It was harder to do in countries where they had to tap into local cell towers, but in the United States, it was as easy as giving the order to target the phone or tablet.

Walker said, 'What will you be doing?'

'What I have to.'

'Can you stop this?'

'No, I really can't. Neither can your friends in the FBI and UN. This will be up to you.'

'It can't be that simple.'

David Walker headed for the door, putting a hand on his son's shoulder as he passed. The hand was heavy. Warm. Walker remembered those hands. They'd held him and picked him up and comforted him more times than he could ever count or fully appreciate. The hands of a stranger became the hands of his father again. 'No, it won't be simple. But you can do it. I've always believed in you.'

'You didn't say where you're going,' Walker said. 'What are you going to do?'

'What I've been doing for years,' David said, continuing to the door.

'Running?'

David stopped. His head tilted down towards the floor. Shame? Hard to tell. He turned and faced his son.

'I helped make this,' David said. 'I have to do what I can to take it apart.'

'Are you any closer to finding who started Zodiac off?' Walker asked. He knew it could have been taken and started by the rogue CIA guys he'd dealt with a while back, who'd hatched a plot to privatise the CIA via the assassination of the Vice President. But Walker felt that there was more. There had to be. 'Someone is steering this. Linking the cells. Giving them their activation signal.'

For his part, David Walker was silent as he stood in the doorway, his security men waiting outside.

Walker opened his hands in a gesture that said, *Give me something. Anything.* His father shook his head, then tossed Walker a car key on an old NASA key ring, along with a folded piece of paper. 'You'll be needing wheels. And, well, let's call it a letter of transit, to expedite you at the border. Good luck.'

He was gone without another word. The two heavies too. Walker stood by the window slats and watched them depart. Saw his father and the two guys drive away in a blacked-out Suburban. One car remained outside.

'Oh, you're kidding me . . .'

13

Walker stood and stared.

The car was a 1971 Plymouth Hemi Barracuda; the Cuda. The car was older than Walker and just as banged up. Shiny black once, now a dull matt finish from decades of sun and rain and wind and grit. The panels had a few dings and scrapes and bad repair jobs. California plates.

It was a thing of beauty.

There were no feminine curves like on an old Porsche or Ferrari or Bugatti. This was a beast. Old-school American muscle. It was something he had wanted as a teen, desperately. He'd had a poster of it in his room in Philly. His friend's father had owned one, bright yellow, which they'd snuck out in a couple of times, cruising the streets like kings.

He walked around it. The fat tyres were near new, plenty of tread front and rear. Sixteen-inch things with mid-sized walls, none of these modern sports car types where the rubber wall was only an inch high and you felt every bump like it would rattle your teeth loose.

Walker popped the hood. The engine was clean and tidy. Not gleaming new like in some kind of *Transformers* movie, but an engine that had been taken care of, probably overhauled recently by someone who cared. He checked the oil. It was honey-coloured and to the full line. Coolant was as it should be. He closed the hood and looked around. Nothing doing. He got in the car and put the key in the ignition. Under a hundred thousand miles on the odometer. Nicely run in for a big engine like this, over such a lifespan.

Walker told himself he'd spend five minutes online, then watch the movie file and then ditch the tablet a few blocks away. The camera had black tape over it so that those tracking any search hits on keywords such as 'Brokaw' and 'NSA' and 'hacking' and so on could not take his picture or video feed. Tape covered the microphone too, but he wouldn't be talking. But they could still geo-locate him, so time mattered. Ideally he'd search Monica on a different device, in a different location, so that anyone analysing the Web-traffic would not make a connection, but there was no time.

First, he Googled Monica Brokaw. She had a lot of hits, mainly social-media pages. She looked good. She'd looked good at twenty-one, but now she was a woman and had lived in her skin, and it suited her. Google images brought up a raft of shots, almost all of them business related, at events and public talks. Her blonde hair was pulled back into a tight ponytail in all of them. She had a tan. She appeared the same height and physicality as he remembered her: five-nine, athletic. She was slightly curvier now. A woman.

Walker gave himself another couple of minutes. He had her father's address in San Diego written down in his father's handwriting. He wanted to know as much as he could about Monica inside of a minute on the Net.

Her Pinterest page was the only one of the social-media pages to show her personal side, her likes and dislikes outside any business thoughts or motivations. She liked home and decorating design, Cape Cod–type places, green gardens, wide open rural spaces, beaches with breaking waves. Her LinkedIn profile gave her CV. Currently joint director of Brokaw Jennings & Associates, a human resources company. She'd previously worked at Yahoo and at an executive recruiting firm in LA, the latter going bust in the GFC. She held a Bachelor of Science in Psychology and a Master of Arts in Communication. He couldn't find any confirmation of a partner or family. Her Twitter page had more than a thousand followers, all of whom seemed business related, and there were no Brokaws among them.

Walker then Googled Jasper Brokaw. A million-plus hits in the results. He clicked on the news search, and the gist of the reports showed that every news outlet was taking this seriously. The first dozen pages were American sites, the remainder a mix of global news sites and then pages of chatter. Reddit was in overdrive with users discussing the possibilities of the coming attacks. Walker could spend hours scrolling through them.

He'd already blown through ten minutes, carried away by what was being discussed.

Time to go.

He turned the ignition. Life. The sound was awesome. A thrum and a roar, the whole vehicle vibrating.

He checked the map to General Brokaw's house on Google Earth. Zoomed in on the local streets. Memorised them. He was good with maps; from hiking with his father to years in the military.

Time.

He clicked on the video file of Jasper Brokaw's appearance. It went for two minutes three seconds. It was date and time stamped: just on two hours ago. Walker pressed play.

'My . . .' Jasper looked up, off camera. As if looking to someone. He hesitated, then continued reading the prepared speech in his hands. 'My fellow Americans. My name is Jasper Brokaw. Until yesterday I was an employee of the NSA. I'm a programmer, a coder, a hacker. I'm one of the best, working for years in the shadows to defend our nation – and by the time this has aired, you will all know my name.' He paused, swallowed. 'You will know my name, because my employer, the United States government, will go into turmoil. They will go into a state of panic, and then distress, and then anger and vengeance. Finally, they, and you, will be on the other side of this. And it will be better. This will all occur not just because of what I have to say, but for what – for what, for who, I am.'

Walker watched the feed, headphones in his ears.

'As of this moment,' Jasper continued, 'those who hold me captive are requesting that the US government shut down the Internet. How this will play out is entirely in the government's hands.' He looked up to the camera, said, 'They have the power to act, to stop what's coming. I – they – suspect that it will take time. That the government, as usual, will drag their feet. They will argue and—' He looked back to the speech '—and they will bicker and talk in circles. But this isn't up for negotiation. It's inevitable. The timer is set. We've made our move, given you warning. Now it's time for you to make your move. You've got thirty-six hours. You've seen our first data breach, and you will feel its effects. Our next cyber attack will occur in six hours. It will involve every federal employee. The next attacks will become more frequent, and more . . . threatening. How this ends is up to you.'

The movie file ended at a black screen.

•

Captain Cam Harrington, US Army, stood with the five soldiers in his six-man team and waited. He was nervous. They were nervous.

They'd never met the General before.

They were a rag-tag group. The Dirty Half-Dozen, some called them behind their backs. It was apt for a couple of the members in his team, Harrington figured.

Each man was dressed in head-to-toe black tactical gear. Their Kevlar vests and communications equipment and weapons were already stowed on the plane, a US Army Gulfstream V.

A car rolled in. A single star. Brigadier General. Everyone just referred to her as The General. Some, far, far behind her back, called her Ice Queen.

Harrington stood at attention and watched as the General's lap-dog second lieutenant got out from behind the driver's seat and went around and opened the door of the Army-spec town car. General Christie emerged and walked over to Harrington, looking the line of his team up and down.

'We haven't met,' General Christie said.

'No, ma'am,' Harrington replied.

Christie was silent, watching, appraising.

'Have your men board the aircraft,' she ordered. 'You and I need to talk.'

14

Walker turned the tablet off. He stared a moment at the black screen, imagining a time when the hyper-connected world could be dark for a month or so. He'd been through high school without much of the Internet, before it was the beast it was today. He'd survived. His parents hadn't had it at all – his mother had emailed a couple of times in her life, maybe. To lose it now would be a big deal, no doubt, but the world would adapt – but not within a month of darkness. It would take time. But by then it would be up again. Unless the chaos created was such that others tried to use it as the means of a major terrorist attack. This was potentially so much easier than replicating a 9/11-type event. A geek or bunch of geeks with laptops and fast Internet connection could wreak havoc. What was the collective noun for a group of geeks – a quark? A basement?

The Cuda's engine thrummed. Walker worked the clutch, selected first and took off, the back tyres spitting up loose chips of bitumen and stones and debris from the broken blacktop, then they grabbed purchase and flung him down the road. Soon he was in second, and then third, before he eased off and dropped into neutral to coast until he used the brakes to slow to a stop. He placed the iPad on top of a little VW Beetle, a copy of the original that continued to come out of a factory in Puebla until the early 2000s, then he sped off in a cloud of vapour and debris.

Ahead was the drive to San Diego. He'd show his passport at the border, where they would see the Mexico entry stamp that David or the guys posing as TSA officers had put in there, along with a bogus letter from the Department of Homeland Security for expedited transit at the border crossing; he would cross and be at the Brokaws' inside of an hour. Maybe the letter was genuine; his father still had reach, and friends, even if he was a ghost in the United States. Either way, Walker would soon be on target.

Though what use Monica or her father could prove to be remained to be seen.

Outside Rosarito, Walker let the car open up. The 1970 Hemi Cuda was one of the most sought-after of the small E-Body platform that Dodge stuffed their massive Hemi engine into. This was a '71, Walker knew, because it was the very poster he'd had. What denoted it visually from other Hemi Cudas was the front grille, with four headlights rather than two, and a six-inlet design and fender grille louvres. Fewer than a thousand were built. He started to wonder how he could keep this. Where he'd keep it. He eased off the gas and coasted in neutral for a mile. The sound of the engine idling and the wind whipping in the open windows and the muted roar of warm tyres on the highway. He dropped it into third and pressed the accelerator.

With 390 brake horsepower and a 440 V8 engine, the Cuda could go from zero to sixty in 5.8 seconds and the quarter-mile in fourteen seconds at 102 miles per hour. He went into fourth gear. Walker felt that someone had tinkered with this big block. Feathered it. Bigger air intakes, richer fuel mix. He put the number closer to five flat. And then, in 1972, the Clean Air Act came in and the government and EPA kicked the muscle car in the arse with emissions regulations and ruined everybody's fun. After that time, no more Hemi, no more big block models of any make could be ordered. Engines became smaller, more efficient.

Progress.

The car was headed north and the March sun was rising over his right shoulder. The highway between here and Tijuana was clear but for mid-sized trucks headed both ways.

Walker thought of the last time he'd been in a version of this car. His high-school friend's father had one in their garage. He spent a lifetime obsessively rebuilding it, driving it a little every other Sunday. Walker had learned via his mother that the friend had taken it out during college break and wrapped it around a tree. Walker had been in Colorado then, the Air Force Academy. His mother had called him with the news early one morning. Neither the friend nor the car survived the wreck. He had been Walker's first close friend to die. In Iraq and Afghanistan, he lost dozens more.

This car was a message, from his father. A token, an apology, making some tiny amends. Or . . . a warning? Watch where you're going? Don't be corrupted by the past? Did David even know of Chad's death? Did his mother and father talk much then?

Probably not. Not like that. But possibly . . . it *was* something that had involved him, and he'd been more than halfway across the country in his first year at the AFA. And his mother had told David about Monica, two years later.

Walker dropped to third to overtake, then slotted fourth and settled in front of a three-truck convoy, the vehicles soon dots in his wake. He was skirting around Tijuana. A place largely deserted by tourists now, because of the drug crime and other options that lured the American tourists and kids on spring break.

Progress.

Walker eased off the gas pedal as he noted his guard already lowering, with only a couple dozen miles behind him.

Losing the Internet for a while before getting it back . . . what would happen to the reliance on the Net as a resource? Would local real-life networks become more vital again, be appreciated, take up some slack? Would older technologies like analogue radio regain popularity? Snail mail?

Walker flicked on the radio, turning the dial to tune in to English-language news. They were replaying Jasper's message while talking heads chimed in with opinions. Walker's hands on the Cuda's wheel. The border crossing loomed ahead. This side was choked up, all four lanes. Coming in was far easier, a small stream of trucks and a few motorhomes. A good hour's wait, maybe two, without that piece of paper. Walker headed for the official's booth, wound down the window, passed his ID and paper over. The guard took them, while two others went about searching the car. A cursory examination, the papers passed over, the boom gate lifted, and he was on his way.

The gas tank had been full and was now at three-quarters. He hit the accelerator and headed north.

•

Harrington looked to his right, to his senior non-com, a guy named Hank, and that's all that needed to happen. All five soldiers moved in formation and climbed the steps of the aircraft and disappeared inside, one having to go in sideways for the width of his shoulders.

'How long have you been stationed here in Fort Meade?'

'Two months, ma'am.'

'Where were you before this?'

'Alpha Company, third battalion, 1st Special Forces Group, ma'am.'

'And your team?'

'They're pulled from all over, ma'am.'

'They're capable?'

'Yes, ma'am.'

'Look at me, Captain Harrington,' General Christie said.

Harrington took the command and stood at ease and met the General's eye.

'You've seen the news this morning.' It wasn't a question.

'Yes, ma'am.'

'The lead agencies on the case are currently the FBI and Homeland Security, because the FBI trumped other federal agencies with regard to hostage situations, and, well, Homeland is Homeland. And the NSA can't be seen to be investigating one of their own where there were so many unknowns at play. But I expect all this to change as the day wears on.'

'Ma'am?'

'If I had it my way, I'd have the President do what Lincoln did and suspend Habeas Corpus and declare martial law throughout the country until the threat to the union abated.' General Christie watched Harrington's reaction. He was stoic. 'What do you think of that?'

'I follow orders, ma'am.'

'Good. That's good. You've watched it all? The news?'

'Yes, ma'am.'

'And?'

'And it seems a legit threat against the nation, ma'am.'

'You've researched the guy they have?'

'Yes, ma'am. And we were briefed just before your arrival.'

'Then you know what he's capable of.'

'Yes, ma'am.'

'What are we going to do about it?'

'What is it you want me to do, ma'am?'

'Make this go away. At any cost.'

Harrington hesitated, but only for a beat. 'You're activating us to operate on US soil, ma'am?'

'I just got off the phone to the National Security Advisor to the President. I'm headed to the White House now. This is being seen as the largest cyber threat our nation has faced. We have to beat this thing before it becomes all that it can be. Therefore, you have been activated.'

'I need to have it in writing,' Harrington said. 'Ma'am.'

'Sorry?'

Harrington looked forward, at attention. 'I need you to authorise the use of deadly force on US soil, against US citizens. Just like my unit did when we operated in Katrina.'

'Go read the Patriot Act, Harrington.'

'I have, ma'am. And, all the respect in the world, but you know who this team is, and why we're here. One more slip-up from any of us means Leavenworth at best, ma'am. I'd feel more comfortable with an order on this in writing.'

'Or, how about you just do your job and follow an order, or I find another team who can.'

'My team's ready to rock. I just need to give them the go order. In writing. Please. Ma'am.'

A pause.

'My secretary will have it to you while you're in the air.'

'Thank you, ma'am.' Harrington paused, then said, 'Can you tell us our objective, ma'am?'

'This is a clean-up operation,' General Christie said. 'Starting with Jasper Brokaw's sister. Find her, detain her, await further orders.'

'Yes, ma'am.'

15

Walker pulled up to the police cruiser. He could see another at the end of the street. A pair of San Diego's finest on station in each. He was glad to see them there, because it meant that the government was taking this seriously, and that the Brokaws would be safe should anyone or anything threaten them. For the first time Walker realised that they may be being protected from the general populace. Jasper's name was out there, and surely by now some news outlets were reporting that his father was a high-ranking general in the US Air Force, and pundits would be saying, *How did this happen?* and *Maybe the father knows something,* and *Why don't we go talk to the old guy and see what's what.* Walker had been around long enough to know that crazy people did crazy things, and there was no shortage of crazy when things started to fall apart.

It was like what he saw so many times in Afghanistan, in the big villages. Where the locals, initially a mix of the jubilant and those sceptical of the soldiers who had booted out the Taliban, soon lashed out at anything in a uniform when things went wrong. The United States, NATO, the coalition forces, the Afghan Army – it didn't matter. It's not that the Afghanis wanted the Taliban back, it's that they were frustrated and desperate and angry, and anyone in a uniform became a symbol of their problems. The small villages were a different story, as the power vacuum invited local warlords, many of them ex-Taliban, to fill the security role. And around and around it went.

Walker showed the local police his Homeland Security letter and his ID, and was directed to park his car halfway down the street – in case it contained explosives, Walker figured. One SDPD officer followed him on foot, then patted him down and checked the vehicle over in a cursory search. He motioned onwards and ghosted Walker shoulder to shoulder to the house, the whole time keeping a hand on his side-arm and the other on his radio, into which he spoke quietly and listened intently.

The General's house was storybook Spanish Colonial. The American flag was on one post, the clasp holding it at sixty degrees; the blue Air Force flag on the other, with its coat of arms, thirteen white stars representing the original thirteen colonies, and the Air Force Seal.

The door opened as Walker's foot touched the first hardwood step leading up to the porch.

An FBI agent in a suit, jacket open, badge ID on his belt to the side, service automatic next to that, nodded to the cop, who took his leave.

'You here to talk to the General?' the agent asked.

'Yep,' Walker said.

The agent looked him up and down.

'ID?'

'I already showed the cop.'

'I'm not that cop or any other cop.'

'That makes two of us.'

The FBI man smiled and put his hands on his hips, signalling that their little dalliance was over as it began. 'And where'd they say you were from, exactly?'

'The General knows me,' Walker said. 'We go way back.' He gave the agent a stare that he used to use for junior soldiers and recruits who needed to learn a lesson in obeying the chain of command, and flashed the piece of Homeland Security paper. He'd learned through a life in the military and intelligence worlds that being direct to those subordinate usually expedited things. He was slowly adapting to a life on the outer where his status was not immediately apparent.

'Right,' the FBI guy said, handing the paper back, having thoroughly read it over. 'This way.'

The agent paced down a wide, open hallway. There was a cloakroom and a hatstand and a wall of family photos: the General, his wife, Monica and Jasper, all on holidays, the General never in uniform. Walker figured that there would be a study, perhaps upstairs in a spare bedroom, that contained all of the General's uniform photos. His 'Me Wall', they called it. Pictures of the General at various stages of his career, mostly those when he held command posts or was posing with heads of state and Capitol leadership.

The hallway opened up to a bright kitchen at the back of the house, where another FBI agent stood by an island bench, a stool showing where he'd been seated before Walker's arrival. But Walker and his guide didn't enter the kitchen, instead they had stopped seven paces down the hall at an open doorway to the right, where Walker saw two overstuffed couches, a couple of armchairs and a large television next to a gas fireplace. News was on the television; Jasper's picture was in the bottom corner.

Walker saw the General, but no Monica.

'Sir,' the FBI agent said to General Brokaw. 'This man, a Mr Walker, to see you.'

'Can you leave us a moment?' Walker asked the agent.

The agent looked to General Brokaw, who didn't respond.

'Integrity First, sir,' Walker said to General Brokaw. 'Service Before Self, and Excellence in All We Do.'

The General's eyes softened a little, then he looked to the agent and motioned him away.

Walker headed over. General Brokaw stayed put. Walker could see why when he got there – a set of crutches lay on the floor to the side of the sofa.

'Walker, right?' General Brokaw said.

'Yes, sir,' Walker said. 'Class of ninety-nine.'

'What rank did you leave the Air Force?'

'Lieutenant Colonel, sir.'

'You got the Air Force Cross.'

'Yes, sir.'

'And multiple Purple Hearts.'

'Three, sir.'

'Yes, I remember.' He looked to the television. 'I had to check in on you, occasionally, for my daughter.'

Walker was silent. He didn't know what to say. Monica had kept tabs on him all this time? Just to be sure he was okay? How that may have sat with the General seemed moot in light of current circumstances.

General Brokaw said, 'You know where those Purple Hearts came from?'

'Sir?'

'They were made during World War Two,' said the General. 'We made about a million of them, figuring that we'd be invading Japan and that we'd need them. The bomb fixed that. And they're still giving out those medals; have been in every war and conflict since.'

Walker was silent.

'What are you doing here?' General Brokaw asked.

'I want to help.'

The General looked to Walker, who was standing to attention in the middle of the lounge room.

'At ease, Walker, and sit down,' the General said. His voice was low and gravelly, the result of years of cigars and whisky, Walker could see from the bar in the corner and the glass on the side table by the sofa and the stubs of cigars in the crystal ashtray and the smell in the air.

Walker sat on the closest armchair.

'Where you at now?' General Brokaw asked.

'Freelancing, sir.'

'Ditch the sir crap. Last I heard you were at the CIA.'

'I was.'

'Didn't suit?'

'For a spell. Near on a decade.'

'I read that you saved the Vice President last year.'

'I was there.'

'I didn't vote for the guy, let alone his boss.'

'Unbiased duty, and all that.'

'I'm too old and cranky for that shit now. But sure, good job.' The General stared at Walker. Almost a minute passed. There was no volume on the television, only subtitles. The General's eyes were red and wet, not with sadness but with anger and despair. 'What can you do to help?'

'I can talk to Monica.'

'That'll help?'

'I believe so.'

'How?'

'I won't know until I talk to her.' Walker looked from General Brokaw to the empty space next to him, a blanket curled in the corner of the sofa as though a person had been seated there in the cold hours of the morning and since departed. 'Where is she?'

The General looked back to the television as he said, 'She's gone.'

16

'Monica left half an hour ago,' General Brokaw said.

'Where to?'

The General didn't take his eyes off the screen when he said, 'LA, where she lives.'

'They let her go?' Walker motioned to the FBI guys, out of sight, one in the hall and one in the kitchen, covering the front and rear doors.

'Yes,' the General said. 'The assistant SAC from the LA Field Office came to brief us on all they're doing to try to locate Jasper. Monica asked to be at home, agreed to the same kind of FBI and police presence there, and she left with him.'

'Can I have her address?'

General Brokaw looked to Walker. 'What for?'

'I need to ask her some questions.'

'The FBI Assistant Special Agent in Charge asked us about Jasper. If there's anything we suspected, of him being in danger, any threats, any associates that may have wanted to do foul by him.'

'And nothing was gleaned?'

'Nothing. Monica mentioned some of his late career Army stuff, something he worked on, but that was it.' General Brokaw looked at the image of his son on the television screen. 'Besides, Jasper's never been much of a figure to have close friends and associates. Nor family, for that matter.'

'Never married.'

'No. Never close, to my knowledge.' He chewed at his lip, then added, 'Never close to anyone in the family. Out the door at eighteen and seen maybe once a year. Didn't matter to me. His mother was upset.'

'Sir, your wife?'

'Passed. Four years back.'

'I'm sorry. I didn't know.'

'Not yours to know. How's your family?'

'My mother died a couple of years ago.' Walker hesitated, then added, 'My father too, not that long after.'

'I'm sorry for your loss, son.' General Brokaw looked at the fireplace. 'So, tell me, Walker, what do you think you can do that the FBI can't?'

'All that I can, sir.' Walker knew that adding the honorific of *sir*, when told not to, gave his statement credence that only military men could and would understand; it carried with it the weight of oaths and sacrifice and respect and said, *I will move heaven and earth to help in any way that I can because we are in this together: we are family.*

'Why don't you help me to my office,' the General said.

Walker got the crutches and helped the General to his feet. He offered to aid him but the older man moved with practised rhythm. Walker couldn't see any obvious reason for the crutches and didn't ask about it.

In the hallway, the FBI agent stood from his chair, appropriated from the formal dining room opposite, but the General growled at him and he resumed his position.

'Meet you at the top,' General Brokaw said to Walker. 'No point you watching my arse all the way up. This ain't the damned Navy.'

Walker humoured the old guy with a chuckle and waited for him at the landing.

Ascending the stairs was slow going for General Brokaw. The carpet runner had wear marks in it from frequent such journeys. Walker wondered how long he had been like this; if it was long enough to make wear marks in the carpet like that, then why didn't he get one of those mechanical chairs installed on a rail to get him up and down? Or move house to a single storey? Pride, and memories, Walker figured, that's what kept him doing this, and doing it here. But the guy was late sixties, and while overweight he didn't seem so out of shape or beyond it that he should be in this physical situation.

Even the best and brightest break down, even those we care about most, his father had once said on hearing the diagnosis of his mother. It doesn't mean it's fair, or that it's for any reason other than damned stupid luck, he'd added. That was as much as David had ever spoken of the matter with his son.

'Here,' General Brokaw said, turning left at the landing and heading through a door to a dark-wood-panelled office. There was the obligatory Me Wall, just as Walker had pictured. There was a photograph of a previous Vice President, who'd been in office when Walker was a cadet. He remembered the visit to the Academy, and the Vice President's address, all chest-beating stuff about how the war on terror was being won because of brave men and women like those assembled.

'Shut the door,' General Brokaw commanded, interrupting Walker's thoughts.

Walker did so. The study was a corner room and two walls had picture windows with padded seating built in to the deep bookshelves, stacked with reference books and trinkets from a life served around the globe in the armed forces.

'Sit,' General Brokaw said.

Walker sat in a chair opposite the desk. General Brokaw leaned his crutches against the desk and sat on the edge of it. The hulk of old mahogany didn't protest.

'No BS,' General Brokaw said. 'Lay it out. What can you do?'

'You heard what I did at the Stock Exchange, the thing with the Vice President,' Walker said. 'Before and after that, I've been working on a long-term assignment with a specialist investigative unit. This is a part of the deep op we're working on. And while the FBI and NSA and all those guys may well find your son, I'm here to do whatever it is I can to help you and your family and avert what is planned in these cyber attacks.'

'Okay . . .' General Brokaw said. 'Do you have any leads? Do you know who has my son?'

'No.'

'And you really think Monica may have some more ideas?'

'Yes.'

'Why?'

'Maybe Jasper was more forthright with her,' Walker said. 'Maybe he told her things that he couldn't tell you.'

The General looked at Walker for a long moment, with something behind his eyes that Walker couldn't read. Then General Brokaw looked away.

'I doubt that.'

17

'Tell me, Walker, what does cyber warfare mean to you?'

'It's another language,' Walker said. 'Or, rather, it's a new weapons system. Something I'm not current on. I see it for the awesome power it can wield, but I can't deploy it myself.'

'You're part right, it is awesome.' General Brokaw was silent as he got up and moved around to the other side of the desk, hobbling without his crutches but always with a hand on the desk top. He sat in a worn leather chair. 'But don't think of it as a weapons system. Think of it as a whole new branch of warfare. It's asymmetric to the square root of we're screwed, if you get my meaning. My final couple of years were at the Pentagon. Cyber's the next big thing, and it has a lot of brass scared.'

'State and non-state actors can cut us down to size,' Walker said. 'And we have to think about the reality that we are fighting opponents who are as well armed and informed as we are – and this is the only battle space where that's the case.'

'Why?'

'Our hands are practically tied up with all kinds of laws.'

'And that's the rub, see? There's no rulebook here, no global set of standards or defined combat space. There's no Hague or Geneva conventions putting restraints on cyber warfare, or treaties governing the number of nukes we can have or even some kind of informal understanding of mutually assured destruction to keep these young punks from pressing their damned keys. It's a mess. I mean, hell, we don't even know what an act of cyber war is, do we? It ain't defined any place I can think of.'

'Do you think this is the first shot in a cyber war?'

'I think those shots were fired a long time ago, by all kinds of parties. We're fighting this on all fronts.'

'How do we respond to a serious act of cyber war?'

'Exactly. What is our response going to be?'

'Depends on the attacks.'

'Sure. What if someone wipes off a trillion dollars from our economy? What if they melt down a nuclear plant or two near a populated area? What's that worth? What do we do about it? Send in the tanks and carriers and B52s? Where does that response start – and where does it end?'

'We would have to think about our first line of defence, and what's beyond that. Guys like your son,' Walker said. He sat forward with his elbows on his knees and his hands together. He remembered a few conversations like this with the General. It was a test. To see if the person was worthy of greater respect, and a reward – usually in the form of being chosen for a special assignment on or off base. Conversations like this had changed after he'd spent that time with Monica. Not that he let the General know, but it changed things, within Walker, that knowledge. And the General sure did know now. And the way in which Walker participated in this conversation would dictate whether he would earn the reward. 'There are laws in place to react, but what do they mean, in practice? What does it mean to take over civilian infrastructure, when over ninety per cent of the US military communications travel over public networks?'

'You think they'll force Jasper to attack civilian targets?'

Walker shrugged.

'The writing has been on the wall about this for a long time,' General Brokaw said. 'And we've done far too little about it in terms of gettin' prepared.'

'We've got a Cyber Command.'

'Sure, but we need better than that. Something with teeth. Bigger. See, Walker, in the Gulf War, a new military revolution emerged. A transformation, from the mechanised warfare of the industrial age to the info warfare of the information age. Information warfare's a war of decisions and control, a war of knowledge and intellect. Is that how you see it?'

'Yes,' Walker said. 'And it's changed since then.'

'How?'

'Information warfare has gone from preserving oneself and wiping out the enemy, to preserving oneself and controlling the opponent. At least, that's what other state actors like China and Russia and Iran have in their mindset. Electronic warfare, tactical deception, strategic deterrence, propaganda warfare, psychological warfare, network warfare, structural sabotage. They want to vanquish, conquer and destroy – as deviously and pervasively as possible.'

'We don't do that?'

'Not on the scale that they do.'

'Why?'

'All those laws I was referring to before. And because we're more about building up our defence and preparing for retaliation, being on the back-foot. Plus there's the talent pool – we should have the best experts in the world available to us on this, but the military will never compete with Silicon Valley salaries in attracting and retaining talent.'

'But it can appeal to recruits through its national-service ethos and its proximity to the action, like it did with Jasper.'

'Sure. And all that said, we've been good at scooping up electronic and signals intelligence. The best.'

'What makes us the best?' General Brokaw prompted.

'We have the best gear to do it. The NSA practically hoovers up every written and spoken word on the planet, and they can decrypt past any protections. We can hear every conversation we want to. We have the biggest eyes and biggest ears.'

'Yes,' General Brokaw said. 'But we're the ones spending the most in R and D on weapons systems across the spectrum, so these other actors think "Why bother doing that – why not just steal the plans for fifth-generation fighter jets?"'

'Which they're doing.'

'Which they're doing.' Brokaw leaned back in his chair. 'What will it take for us to change our playbook – to be able to act like them? To start attacking their servers on a daily basis and stealing all the data that we can get our hands on.'

'A Pearl Harbor,' Walker said, matter of factly. 'A cyber Pearl Harbor, and we'd be there. The country would rally. The landscape would change. It'd be like when Roosevelt said we'll build fifty thousand aircraft for World War Two.'

'And how many did we build?'

'Three hundred thousand.'

'Three hundred thousand,' the General repeated, although Walker knew he already knew the answer. The old man looked as though he had come to a conclusion. 'Walker, do you care for my daughter?'

Walker paused, just a moment, thrown a little by the question. 'Yes.'

'Yet you hesitated just now.'

'Sir – I – a lot of time has passed. But of course I care for her. And I'll do all I can to get your son to safety.'

'You won't put my girl in unnecessary danger to achieve that?'

'No.'

General Brokaw neither spoke nor moved for a minute. He was weighing up options. In the end, perhaps he figured: what's the harm in someone capable wanting to help? At least, that's how Walker read the response when General Brokaw said: 'You really think you can find something out from talking with her? Something that will help find Jasper?'

'You said yourself that she knew about his Army work,' Walker said. 'What was that?'

He said, 'You can ask her about that yourself.'

'You'll give me her address?'

'You dim or hard of hearing or both?'

Walker smiled. The General did too, the first Walker had seen. He opened a drawer in the desk and looked at its contents, hesitated, then retrieved a small book, flicked pages and read out an address.

'Got that?'

'Got it,' Walker said. He pointed to last year's edition of a Rand McNally California road atlas on the General's desk. 'You mind?'

'Go for it.'

Walker checked the address, memorised the route, closed the book.

'You going for a long drive north?' Walker said, seeing that the General had marked the section along the Oregon coast.

The General nodded. He showed an older version of the map book, again with marked pages. 'I had long planned on the drive with my wife, but we never got to do it. So, I'm seeing what's still there, and I'm, well, I hoped I'd do that drive later this year. We'll see.'

'You'll do it. This will work out. I'll find Jasper.'

General Brokaw appeared pensive, then said, 'So, are you working on this alone?'

'Yes,' Walker said.

The General gave him a measured stare.

'Because of the nature of this investigation,' Walker said, 'because the FBI and NSA will be watching and listening to and reading every communication related to your son and the attacks, I'm working on my own.'

General Brokaw didn't react. After a moment he said, 'You last served in the 24th Tactical, right?'

'Yes.'

General Brokaw nodded. Then he reached into the desk drawer and pulled out a black plastic box, which Walker recognised, because he'd been issued something similar once but had not been allowed to keep his.

'See this?' General Brokaw said, opening the clasp and pulling out the service automatic. It was an M1911, a Colt .45, the official side-arm of the US military for seventy-five years until the mid-eighties. 'You have use for this?'

Walker met the General's eye. 'Yes, sir.'

18

Walker had a hundred miles of the black ribbon of the Interstate 5 ahead of him.

He kept the Cuda near-on ninety-five miles per hour. The limit here was seventy; he was driving fast enough to get booked at the highest rate, but not so fast as to get arrested and have the car impounded. He didn't care about racking up tickets, but he couldn't lose hours in a police cell, and couldn't lose the car. Well, he could get a new car. But he liked this car.

It was a Saturday afternoon and the traffic was light. The overtaking lane was empty and when it wasn't he either flashed his lights to force a slower car to move or he wove around them. The speed needle never moved from ninety-five. Over a hundred and fifty kilometres per hour. Walker preferred metric, given the choice. It was simpler in its description of accuracy, and as someone who had called in all manner of ordnance in the mountains of Afghanistan, often dropped from fast jets in what he would describe to them as a *danger close* situation, with friendly forces within the kill box, accuracy was *everything*.

Walker wondered about the choice of days for these cyber attacks. A regular weekend. The main events would play out tomorrow, a Sunday. A day of rest for most. A time of worship for many. Either way, not many people would be at work in offices. Did that mean anything? Or was today just an opportunistic time for the people who snatched Jasper?

And today. Saturday: people shopping, kids at sport. Saturday night: busy, people out, bars and clubs and restaurants packed.

The possibilities of targets for the cyber attacks seemed limitless.

Walker's plan was to get to Monica, question her, take her to Jasper's house where the abduction had gone down and see what he could put together. Maybe she knew people who wished him harm, or something secret from his later Army career. Maybe she had some further insights into her brother, insights that could lead to something, anything.

Walker turned up the radio news. A Senator was calling on the press not to publish any salacious details of people's inner lives that had been laid bare in the first attack, or whatever was coming next. Walker couldn't care less.

He was worried about what was coming next.

19

Monica's neighbourhood was Abbot Kinney and Venice Boulevard. Down side streets were framed views of the beach. Boats. Cafes serving gluten-free organic everything. Walker had to navigate through a street blocked off for a farmers' market and side streets lined with food trucks. A lot of yoga pants on display and upscale frozen yoghurt in hand. Old rich guys wearing velour in a non-ironic manner. People with laptops at outdoor cafes running their start-up ventures and looking for shared studio space to run said start-ups out of, as though if only they had said space then their ideas would really take off. Shops that stocked the fancy things that hipsters didn't yet know they liked.

He parked around the corner from Monica's place, on a hill that ran four blocks down until it petered out. He locked the car and pocketed the key ring. Looked around. The afternoon was warm. The air had a tinge of gold to the particulate in the Los Angeles air. He headed to Monica's street on foot.

Walker liked the LA weather, but he preferred defined seasons. He'd grown to like Colorado in his three years there, but some said it had twelve seasons, where in winter you would have an eighty degree day and the next there'd be a blizzard. He didn't miss Houston summers, and that place had but two seasons – hot and less hot. It was the Philly weather that always felt like home. And every place he'd lived in across the US all trumped the time he'd spent in Iraq, where he'd been during the 2004 summer.

The scene on Monica's street was different from that on General Brokaw's. There were no marked police cruisers at either end. In fact, there were no uniformed cops nor police cruisers in sight. There were cars parked along either side of the street. Walker figured there must be either FBI, or plain-clothed LAPD officers in unmarked cars. Probably the former, given the FBI's involvement in running this. He scanned the windows of cars as he walked, searching for faces.

The cars seemed empty, no cops. Residential area. Cars belonged to those still home or those who commuted to work some other way; while LA was no doubt born and raised and matured as a car town, this neighbourhood was the type that looked as though communal car pooling was the vogue thing to do, driving around in their electric Toyotas or bio-diesel Mercedes, using some kind of app to organise who was driving who to where on any given day.

He counted down the houses. Monica's would be the seventh on his left, going by the street numbers.

He was two houses away when he saw motion. A guy, emerging from a hedge, a house before Monica's. There was a flash of something shiny. A badge. A plain-clothed cop. A young guy, in casual jeans and polo shirt, bulge at his hip, showed an LAPD badge and put a hand out to Walker to signal he was to halt like traffic. Walker stopped. The cop glanced around, making sure that Walker was alone.

Walker said, 'I'm a friend of Monica's.'

'She can't see friends today. Move along please, sir.'

'I just came from her father's. She needs to see me.'

'I'm sorry sir, no visitors. Come back Monday.'

Walker looked up and down the street. 'There may not be a Monday.'

'Excuse me?'

'You haven't seen the news? You know what they've got Monica's brother doing?'

'Sir . . .'

'Just knock on the door, and you'll see that—'

'You have to leave, sir. No visitors. That's my orders.'

'I'm just here to—'

'I'm gonna count to three.' The cop reached to his hip opposite the gun and returned with a weapon – he flicked out an extendible carbon fibre baton.

'You ever serve?'

'What?'

'You heard me.'

'Navy. Four years.'

'I won't hold that against you. I was Air Force. Monica's father was a General. He's sent me here to check in. You can verify that.'

'You have to leave.' The cop held the baton out. 'Last warning.'

Walker sighed.

'No,' he said, looking down at his feet, his voice low. 'You're either knocking on that door and seeing that all is well with me being here, or I'm going to shove your badge up your nose, and the baton up your butt.'

The cop smiled, said, 'One.'

Walker didn't wait for three. Or even for two. He reached out, spun the cop and put him into a one-handed choke hold that had both the cop's hands fighting at the grip, the baton falling to the ground. Walker used his free hand to field strip the cop's Glock as he marched him onto Monica's property and dropped the weapon into the potted plant at the top of her steps. He then used that hand to take the cop's badge and held it under his nose, building the pressure there to the point where the cop, when they were at the door, went to stand on his tiptoes to try and alleviate the pain. Walker relaxed the grip on the guy's larynx and said into his ear: 'Who's in the house?'

'Monica.'

'Who else?'

The cop was silent. Walker increased the pressure.

He said, 'You want me to go get the baton?'

The cop replied, 'One officer.'

'Okay. You knock on that door, gently, three times,' Walker said. 'Don't try being stupid. Don't think. Just do this and you'll see that all's right in the world.'

'You're making a big mistake.'

'You made the mistake. You weren't listening to reason. You were provoking me. And you let me get too close. And you sure as hell don't have enough security out here.'

The cop knocked on the door, a big old green-painted thing. *Tap-tap-tap* with the brass knocker.

Silence.

'Yeah?' said a voice from behind the door. Male. Similar tone and timbre to the cop he had in the hold.

'It's me.'

'Can I help you?'

'Tell them you need the restroom,' Walker whispered into the cop's ear.

'I need the restroom,' the cop called.

'Hold it in,' the other voice said.

'Tell them you can't.'

'I can't.'

'Piss in the gutter. Or a shrub.'

'It's not that,' the cop said.

Walker smiled. He quite liked this cop. He had spunk. He would learn lessons from this encounter and be better for it. Navy always were a little slow at learning. Quicker on the uptake than Army though.

'Okay,' the cop on the other side of the door said. The door hardware shifted: a bolt, a chain, then two key locks.

The door opened.

Walker applied more pressure to the choke hold and rushed the room, pushing his cop into the other and pinning them against a hallway wall.

'Don't move!' Walker said to them.

The other cop, uncertain as to what was going down, and what the intruder was armed with and how his colleague had been subdued and used, raised his hands and didn't fight.

'Monica!' Walker called out. 'Monica!'

A head appeared from around a corner. Monica Brokaw. She looked at Walker and did a double-take, as though she were seeing a ghost. That's how it felt for Walker too. A face he'd not seen in so many years. Similar but different. Familiar but foreign. Even from here, her light blue eyes took him back to memories of shared intimacy.

'Monica,' Walker said. 'Tell them I'm here to help you.'

'But . . .' There was hesitation in her eyes as she stayed in the doorway at the end of the hall.

'Your father sent me,' Walker said. He kept his attention on the face in front of him, the back of the head and the two bodies, a few hundred pounds of LAPD flesh pressed against a wall. 'I left there just over an hour ago. Tell them it's okay. That I'm here to help.'

Monica looked at the scene. She could see that the cop pinned against the wall was slowly moving his hands down, his right hand to his hip holster.

Walker noticed it too, and he shook his head at the guy.

'It's okay,' Monica said. 'It's okay. This is a friend.'

Walker released some of the pressure. His eyes were locked onto those of the pinned cop who, Walker could see, was computing that he hadn't seen a firearm on this intruder and that both his hands were holding his comrade.

'It's okay,' Monica said, moving towards the three men. 'I know this guy. He's okay. It's all okay.'

20

Walker watched the cop he'd used to get into the house; the guy rubbed his neck and headed back outside, where he retrieved the pieces of his service automatic from the potted plant and blew the dirt and dust out before reassembling and departing down the steps to the street, where he picked up his baton. The other cop shut and locked the door and stood there, looking back at Walker, professional humiliation in his eyes. Walker thought about chastising him, telling him he had one job here – one job, to protect Monica at any and all reasonable cost – but he figured the guy had already learned—

'What you lookin' at?' the cop said.

'You had one job,' Walker said, holding up a finger – his middle finger. 'One.'

'This way,' Monica said, getting between them and steering Walker away.

Walker followed her up the hall, past the stairs. The floorboards were dark-stained timber, the walls stark white. The woman in front of him was a ghost. A memory. A person he'd not seen in the flesh in almost twenty years. Her appearance and voice were the same but different. Grown up, lived in. She was wearing dark blue pants and a tight white top and her body was as he remembered but she had a walk now, a way of moving that she'd not had before, a practised motion. It was beyond a woman walking to attract attention. Walker had studied body language, as useful to those providing security at airports as it was to any intelligence or law-enforcement personnel in reading a person's capabilities, training, intentions, their physical and mental state. It told Walker that whatever life Monica had lived over the past twenty years, she took care of herself, she had grown used to being watched, and she made the most of it. No motion or movement was wasted. Every action had a purpose. Everything was calculated.

She glanced back. Her eyes connected with Walker's and she looked away. They were headed to the kitchen.

They passed a bag in the hall. A square carry-on, with wheels, the handle up. Her bag from her father's. Now here, still packed and ready to go. She'd left San Diego forty-five minutes before Walker, but he'd sped the whole way, faster than the FBI Assistant SAC had driven, or his driver had driven, Walker was sure. They'd been home anywhere from twenty to thirty-five minutes. She'd left her bag there and done what? Watched the news?

They entered the kitchen. Monica moved around the other side of a long black-granite-topped bench with stools on Walker's side.

'Where's the FBI?' Walker asked.

'Excuse me?' Monica said. She looked at him, as if it was rude to talk business straight off the bat. But she couldn't help herself. Her eyes searched his face, then glanced up and down his body.

'Your father said that the Assistant Special Agent in Charge out of the LA Field Office personally brought you back here,' Walker said. 'Where is he? And he didn't leave any agents here – but he did with your father?'

'She,' Monica said. She poured two glasses of water from a tap, a tiny tap, next to the main faucet, filtered water. Her hands trembled as she set them down on the long bench. She kept one glass near herself, and the other she slid across to Walker. Her hands didn't shake violently, not spilling the content, but there was vibration there. Nerves and being wired and bugged-out by the situation with her brother. 'The Assistant SAC is a she. And she's back in the office, working with her people, to find my brother. And I didn't need FBI agents here – I insisted. I can be quite persuasive. Two cops is more than enough. I'd rather the Bureau allocated their resources where best needed.'

Walker glanced down the hall and saw the cop still looking his way, watching, all kinds of embarrassment running through him and being replaced by anger and thoughts of revenge against the man who had so easily entered the house without any kind of weapon. Walker didn't doubt that they could fight, nor that they could fight and shoot well. He was disappointed that they didn't pat him down, even after the okay from Monica; her father's .45 was tucked into the waistband in the small of his back, hidden from view by his untucked shirt and jacket. But he knew they'd learned a valuable lesson and that they'd now be on their toes for any kind of threat. He hoped. They'd probably accost the postman, he figured. Good. Better to err on the side of over-kill when on protective detail. But still, two guys did not a protection detail make, not in a suburban setting like this, not with a big house with all kinds of points of entry.

'You might be a target,' Walker said.

'I doubt it.'

'They may need leverage to force your brother's hand to do something he refuses to do.'

'Like what? Make him leak some more social-media accounts?'

'Like melt down a nuclear power plant near a civilian population.'

'Is that why you're here, after all these years?' Monica said. 'To protect me from harm?'

Walker drank half his water and set the glass down.

He said, 'I'm here to help.'

'How?'

'Any way I can.'

'Who are you working for? Not the Air Force. My father told me you left that behind, nearly ten years ago. Then you good as disappeared.'

Walker didn't answer. He didn't know how to answer. Instead, he tried a different tact.

'You look good.'

'Really?' Monica said, her tone that of a woman shooting down a guy's advance. Her demeanour changed. There was the slightest nod of her head and the corner of a smile. She took a step back from the bench that was between them, and then she paced a little in the kitchen. 'Is that why you're really here – you saw this on the news, and you thought, what, you decided to reach out to me? To make contact, after all this time? For what – just to *see* me? Is that what this is? Not really appropriate timing, don't you think?'

Walker shook his head. 'It's not like that. I'm here because I just had a good chat with your father.'

'Why would you do that?'

'Because we have to stop what's coming. And we need to find and save your brother.'

Monica stared at him. Her eyes were still, locked onto his. After about ten seconds, she looked away, picked up her glass of water, sipped it. Her hands were now steady. Walker fought the desire to talk about the past. They had to keep moving forward. He needed her to be in the present, to shed any kind of light she could on her brother.

'I'm working on this thing, have been for a while,' Walker said. 'An operation. Anti-terror.'

'Terror?'

'Terror cells. Cut-outs. Linked. Triggered by other terror events.'

'For who?'

'That's . . .'

'Complicated?'

'Yes.'

'Try me.'

Walker bit his lip, thinking, then replied, 'Myself.'

'No.'

'No?'

'You're not a plumber. You're not a PI. You're not even a gun for hire. So, no sole-contracting work for you.'

'What am I?'

'I'm trying to figure that out. But I haven't got the time. I really haven't got the time. And I don't need your protection, despite what my father may have said to you.'

Walker looked up the hall. To the bag. 'You're leaving?'

'Look at you, being all observant,' Monica said. 'Yes, I'm leaving. A hotel. A big one, in Beverly Hills, a place used to looking after big names and keeping things quiet – in case the press shows up, here or there. They're bound to find me, sooner or later, like you have. By sunrise, probably, to broadcast it on the morning shows – they love a little drama, right? Then it will be a zoo. And who knows what else may happen – human nature, right? People know where I am, who I am, and they may want to harm me for what my brother is being forced to do. Rotten, isn't it? People . . .'

'When?'

'They're moving me at midnight.'

Walker looked down the hall at the cop, who was still staring at him. Walker considered giving him the finger again, to reinforce the one job the guy had . . .

'Look,' Monica said. 'Walker?'

He looked at her.

'I think you should go,' she said. 'There's really nothing you can do here. Nice to see you, though. Another time, perhaps? Say, another twenty years from now?'

There was a moment of silence between them, then Walker said, 'You know I had a hand in what happened at the New York Stock Exchange.'

'I saw that. Are you trying to impress me?'

'And St Louis.'

Monica paused, her hand on her glass of water, which she was looking at, and then she let it go and crossed her arms across her chest.

She said, 'That was you?'

'I helped out,' Walker said.

'For who?'

'Us.'

'Us?'

'All of us. I'm doing what I was paid to do by the US government for nearly twenty years. This is all connected.'

'It's really been that long, hasn't it?'

'We're getting old. But you're missing my point.'

'That this thing with Jasper is connected to New York and St Louis? How?'

'I'm working on the how. But yes, it is.'

'Who pays you now?'

'No-one.'

'Bullshit.'

'No-one,' he repeated. 'I could cash a pay cheque, I guess. If I wanted to, if I said yes.'

'Yes to whom – a cheque from whom?'

'The UN.'

'The UN?' Monica uncrossed her arms, her fingertips on the bench. 'They've got no money. And they don't have people like you on their so-called payroll.'

Walker shrugged.

Monica said, 'Why are you here?'

'I'm here to help.'

Monica turned and looked out the window that looked into her backyard. Her arms crossed across her chest again, as though a shiver of cold had run through her. She looked fragile, in that moment. Walker wanted to hold her, but it wasn't the time. She seemed distant. Resigned. Exhausted – not from today, but from memories of long ago, dragging her back, wearing her out.

She said, 'You can't help.'
'I think I can.'
'How?'
'Tell me about your brother.'

21

'Heads up,' Harrington said over comms in the hangar at Los Alamitos Army Airfield just outside LA. Two cars, big black Suburban SUVs, loaded with three men each, began to pull out of the building. 'This is the op.'

His teammates were silent.

He passed around the printed photos. The three in the other car would be doing the same. The guy in the back seat glanced at them and went back to his screen and joystick. The drone he was piloting was high above, already on target, doing big slow circles and beaming the footage down.

'Target is Monica Brokaw, the captive's sister. She's being protected by two members of LAPD's finest. Currently at her home address, which is where we will pick her up.'

'Cops going to be a problem?' the soldier driving asked.

'They're getting orders to leave,' Harrington said to them. 'Remember, this is *not* a training op. We are to get Monica at all costs and render her to a safe location.'

'Where's that?' the big guy asked.

'We've got three options, depending on how it plays out. Call signs are Tango, Whisky and Mike, and the GPS location of each is in your comms pack should anyone become separated. We are to get her there, keep her put, await further instructions. We good?'

The men applied in the affirmative.

'Then let's do this. And remember, comms will go dark once we breach. You all know what to do. And no harm is to come to this woman.'

•

'I don't know what you want me to say.'

'I think you can help me find Jasper,' Walker said. 'Your father thought as much too, that's why he helped me get here. So, just tell me what you think is pertinent, about Jasper.'

Monica paused, her eyes searching his, then she said, 'How? How, *exactly*, could what I know possibly help you find my brother – my brother who the news is saying is being helped by criminals or terrorists or whatever. What could I *possibly* know that could help find him?'

'Tell me anything that you think can help.'

'I could talk about my brother all day. You want to narrow it down?'

'He was taken from his apartment in Palo Alto.'

'That's been reported on the news, you don't need me for that.'

'Did the FBI tell you anything more?'

Monica paused, then said, 'There was a witness. A passer-by, who saw either three guys and one blacked-out SUV, or possibly six guys in two SUVs and something big being loaded, something that could have been a body. That person thought it was odd and called the police, who arrived an hour later. Apparently the car or cars and the men had vanished. Nothing. That's not much to go on, right? One person as a witness to something nobody can find any evidence of. And that's it – that's all I know.'

'Have you been to his apartment?'

'In Palo Alto? No.'

'He has another apartment?'

'The FBI told me that he's been based on the east coast. Maryland. They put up unmarried NSA staff in apartments there.'

'They told you? You don't know where he lives?'

'We're not close.'

'He's your only sibling.'

Monica was silent.

Walker said, 'How close does a sibling have to be to know the other's address?'

Monica shrugged.

'What was he doing back on the west coast?' Walker asked.

'I don't know.'

'Best guess?'

'It's the weekend. Maybe he goes home some weekends. But that's just speculation on my part.'

'What did the FBI say?'

'Nothing.'

'You didn't ask?'

'No. Mine is not to question why. Does it matter why he was on the west coast?'

'It might. You don't want to know why?' He watched her closely. Nothing showing, but there was something there.

'I just wanted to know what the FBI were doing – are doing – to help him. To find him. That's it.'

'Do you want him found?' Walker asked her, looking her straight in the eye.

'Of course I do. Why would you say that?' Monica paused, then something in her voice changed as she said, 'What – what did my father say to you?'

'He said to talk to you about it.'

Monica appeared wary. She seemed nervous. Standing a little different. Her mouth stayed open slightly, as though she was breathing faster than usual.

'He said to ask you about Jasper's time in the Army. Something from late in his career?'

Monica didn't look convinced, as though her father had shared more with Walker and she was playing catch-up.

Walker said, 'You didn't ask the FBI who may have Jasper?'

'They asked that of me.'

'And?'

'I know nothing.' Monica looked down at her hands, as though they were again betraying her with a near-unseen tremor of worry. 'And asking it over and over isn't going to change that, so I really don't see the point in talking like this, not with them, certainly not with *you*.'

'Certainly not *me*?'

'They're an organisation with thousands of staff and billions of dollars behind them, agents and assets all over the place. You're . . . I really don't know what you are, other than a ghost from my past.'

'I'm the guy who can help your brother,' Walker said. 'But I'll need your help to do it. Your father believed in me enough to send me here. Do you?'

'Do I what?'

'Believe in me?'

'I . . .'

Walker felt himself being appraised. He was dressed in a jacket. Black. Over a shirt, unbuttoned to midway down the chest, black T-shirt under that. Not his usual outfit, which was jeans and a T-shirt and a jacket of any colour, but it had been purchased for him in haste at St Louis and had been laundered yesterday at his hotel on Sunset Boulevard and it fit well and he hadn't had the time to shop for anything else. On reflection it made him feel invisible. Just another guy in a dark suit jacket. At least that's what he'd thought when he'd first entered LAX this morning.

'I've really got nothing to say,' Monica said. 'Just as I told the FBI earlier.'

'Your brother's in serious trouble,' Walker said. 'I know that, better than those at the Bureau know that.'

'Because you have a connection to it.'

Walker nodded.

Monica remained silent. She went to a small coffee machine, put in a capsule, pressed a button and it hissed and steamed a brew into a cup.

'We can find him,' Walker said. 'We can end this.'

'How?'

'We follow any lead you can think of. The apartment. Any friends or associates. The Army thing. Any threats you may know of.'

'Who's we?' There was a noise at the back door. A sleek grey Persian cat slunk into the kitchen through the plastic cat flap and rubbed up against Monica's legs.

'You and me,' Walker said.

Her cell phone rang. Walker knelt down and held out his hand to the cat as Monica answered the call. The cat wandered by him then brushed against his hand. Unafraid, inquisitive of the stranger in its house. Walker picked it up and it started to purr. It seemed old, weary, wary. It had a tattoo in its ear that denoted it had been de-sexed and micro-chipped. Walker looked to Monica, at the cell phone to her ear.

'Right, that's fine,' Monica said into the phone and ended the call.

She had her coffee in one hand, and she scooped up her cat in the other. They both watched Walker.

'That was the FBI,' Monica said. 'They're going to move me to the hotel, not these cops. And they're moving me at eleven, not twelve. And from that time they'll be taking over from the LAPD in my protection. Thanks to your arrival – one of these guys must have called it in. Happy?'

'A little.' Walker glanced down the corridor. The cop in the hall was looking at his phone, as though reading something.

'So, Jed, you have a few hours of my time.'

'I can live with that,' Walker said. 'Do you have the address of Jasper's apartment in Palo Alto?'

'I'll write it down for you.'

Walker nodded. He looked down the hall, to where the LAPD officer was leaning against the wall, still looking down at his phone's screen. Maybe checking messages or playing a game. Or reading an update. Or any number of things. The front door was oversized, timber, thick. Two locks, heavy-gauge steel in big barrels going into a steel plate screwed into a hardwood doorjamb. Walker looked to the back door. It was nothing, in comparison. A bolt and the chain, light-weight stuff, more of a placebo than anything concrete in keeping out intruders. It had a timber frame painted the same shade of white as the house but in gloss, with double-glazed panes of clear glass but for the small plastic cat door. The small garden out back was a walled-in space, the walls brick, eight feet high. Topiary hedges, a small patch of grass, a steel-framed seat setting around a round table. There was no gate out there leading to an alley, which meant that the house backed onto the backyard of another, which he could see had a light on upstairs. All kinds of deep shadows out there. Better that she was being moved from here, to the type of big hotel with cameras and security and keycarded floor access.

'When's the last time you saw your brother?' Walker asked as Monica started to sort through a stack of unopened mail from the bench and then went through it while absently inserting a coffee capsule into the machine and pressing the button, refilling her cup and then making one for Walker.

'A while,' she said, pushing the mail aside once she'd flicked through it all and evidently saw nothing of note or out of the ordinary. She passed Walker his cup of coffee, her hand moving away before his reached it. She wrote an address in Palo Alto on the back of an envelope, and slid it across to him. 'I fail to see what you can do about my brother that the FBI can't, but give it your best shot.'

'It's not what I can do,' Walker said, pocketing the envelope and sipping what turned out to be a strong flat white. It was some kind of hipster coffee blend, complex and nutty, and the milk was probably some sort of organic gluten-free fat-free protein-rich and vitamin-boosted non-dairy concoction. 'But what you can tell me.'

22

Monica showed Walker photos that the FBI had left behind, of Jasper's apartment in Palo Alto, in case Monica looked again and noticed something. There were near-on a hundred digital files on her tablet.

He flicked through and saw a spartan flat. Nothing. A futon mattress on the floor, sheets rumpled. A folded blanket and pillow in a wardrobe. Diet sodas in the refrigerator. Pot noodles in the cupboard. A tin of coffee and a drip-filter machine and one mug. A tiny television on the bench. Bare white walls except for one that contained built-in bookshelves stacked with books. That was it.

Walker said, 'Do you think the FBI took anything?'

'This is how he is.' Monica looked at her coffee. 'He never hung on to anything of his past. Always moved forward.'

'He's living like a college student.'

'He was hardly ever there, as far as I know. From what they said.'

'So, why keep the apartment at all?'

'Maybe he was keeping a toe in the commercial world, being near Silicon Valley.'

'He wanted out of government work?'

'That was just a guess. I don't know. But he gets restless.'

Walker looked through the pics, back and forth. 'No computer?'

'Laptop, I suppose. There's a router in one of the pictures. Cable Internet, the FBI said.'

'No storage devices on show. The world's smallest TV.' Walker flicked back through the pictures. 'A couple of long-life meals in his pantry, no bag of clothes – no clothes hanging up.'

'The absence of something doesn't mean anything.'

'I think it can, and I think it does.'

'How?'

'He wasn't there to stay. Where's his stuff, even for a short trip? If he was going there for the weekend, he'd have a carry-on bag, right? With a couple of T-shirts and a toothbrush at least, because there's none of that there. There's nothing there. The wardrobe's empty.'

'You think the witness was lying, that he took his bag and went some place?'

'Or they took his bag. Maybe it had his computer in it.'

'Maybe he's gone all hikikomori.'

Walker looked at her, wondering if she was trying to make a joke. He remembered that face. Those eyes. Those lips. A happy time. Long past.

'It's a thing in Japan,' she continued, matching his look with her own, taking in his blue eyes, his mouth, the lines of his jaw and neck. 'People who, ah – they withdraw from the world. There's more than a million of them in Japan who don't leave their rooms, or apartments. Not ever.'

So, she wasn't joking. Hikikomori. 'I've heard of it,' he replied, 'but do you really think your brother's like that?'

'He may be. I told you, we're not close.'

'But you're perceptive, Monica. You're a professional at this. You know people. You'd know if your brother was like that.'

She sighed. 'I think he has the tendencies. I mean, look around, right?'

'But that's it. He has a job and he travelled on a plane from the east coast to here, so he's not withdrawn from the world.'

'What, then?' she countered. 'He comes here to enjoy a monastic lifestyle.'

'Perhaps.' Walker looked at the FBI pictures that showed the view out the apartment's windows. The sight lines. It was a corner apartment. There was a car park and apartment buildings opposite the bedroom side. Taller buildings in the background. A street to the other side. Apartments beyond. Nothing telling. But Jasper could have been observed, watched, by someone out there.

23

'I told the FBI everything I could think of,' Monica repeated.

Walker said, 'I don't want to know what they wanted to know.'

'Why?' Monica looked puzzled. 'Why wouldn't you want to know the same things as them?'

'Because I know their type, I work with them,' Walker said. 'They would have asked you when you last saw him, if you've had anyone contact you about him, if you've noticed anything out of the ordinary. They're working all those angles.'

'And they're wrong?'

'No. But they're handling it from those angles.'

'And how many kidnappings do they handle a year?'

'A lot.'

'Right. And you?'

Walker was silent.

'See my point?'

'They're doing what they do,' Walker said. 'I'm doing what I do.'

'Fine,' Monica replied, coffee in her left hand, the index finger of her right hand tracing a line across the granite bench top as though drawing an imaginary line through dust. The house was spotless. Designed and decorated with everything in its right place. 'What do you want to know that can help my brother? Hmm?'

'Anything that can help me in knowing your brother,' Walker said. 'Start with your thoughts of him.'

'It's that simple?' Monica walked away from the bench, looked outside, settled by the sink, turned, said, 'I've got nothing.'

'Start at the start.'

Monica's eyebrows raised. 'That's a long Q and A session. Are you building a profile so you can find him through some kind of spiritual medium?'

Walker paused, looked around, then said, 'You don't seem too worried about him. He's being held by some dangerous people.'

'I've never worried about something happening to Jasper,' Monica said, and she looked out again over the kitchen sink to the small garden of hanging plants and flowers, an espaliered pear tree across the back wall budding with new shoots, as the shadows of the LA night fell.

'They're going to force him to do terrible things.'

'So?'

'*So?*'

'Walker . . .' Monica said. She looked at him. There were tears welling in her eyes. 'My brother? He has always done terrible things.'

24

She began with their childhood. Jasper was two years older than her. They'd bounced around Europe as military brats with her father's Air Force career, the most time spent in Germany, which was West Germany for most of that time. She was fifteen when they'd returned to the United States, and they'd been posted in Florida for two years, then a year in North Dakota, and then the General took up the spot at the Air Force Academy and Monica had gone to college.

'Tell me about Florida,' Walker said. When she'd said it, he'd noticed something. She'd sped through it. Said it really fast – Germany, Florida, North Dakota and then onto Colorado Springs and the Air Force Academy. Florida. Three syllables, but said in the same time span as one regular syllable. Like she spat it out.

Monica looked at him. There was pain there, visible beneath the veneer of the smart, successful, capable and striking woman. Vulnerability. Memories she didn't want to dredge up. But her eyes held Walker's gaze and she didn't look away when she told her story, which seemed to occupy most of those two years in Florida when she was fifteen and sixteen, and her brother had been seventeen and eighteen.

Walker listened, took it all in. He didn't make notes, didn't need to. This was all background. Maybe useful. Definitely it told him about the type of character that Jasper was, and why the relationship was distant between the siblings. It painted a picture he'd seen a few times. Friends at school and at the Air Force Academy who'd opened up to him like this. Stories that as a young man had made him mad, and now, as a guy who'd seen the worst that wars and war zones had to offer, didn't have much impact. Sad for the victims, sure, but life went on. There was therapy and drugs and all kinds of avenues to help deal with it in America. Sure, he felt a pang of anger because he'd known this woman once, really fell for her for a few days, but what would that anger do now? There was nowhere to direct it, and he had to keep her talking. Hours were going by and he could see she was exhausted. He had to know all he could.

What had that meant to Jasper, abusing a younger sister like that? What did it mean now? How did that get skipped in his psych profile for the Army?

'It was post 9/11, and we were fighting in two unpopular and seemingly never-ending wars,' Monica said, as though sensing what he was thinking. 'The Army needed front-line meat. Screening standards were relaxed, especially in an outfit like the Rangers. The Army welcomed him with open arms. My dad put in a good reference for him. That was that.'

She didn't say if her parents ever knew. Walker pictured some kind of moment years later where the General found out, maybe from the mother who'd known from earlier – perhaps from Monica confiding in her, or reading Monica's diary – and there being a tussle and the General somehow getting unbalanced in the act with the younger man and tumbling down some stairs and needing the crutches ever since.

'Do you hate him for what he did to you?' Walker watched her, for what she didn't say as much as what she did. He kept his voice gentle but his questions on point. He couldn't change what happened to her, he couldn't offer comfort, but he could show her that what she had told him was important, and that he would use the information to help her family now.

'I did. For years. After being scared faded away, sure, I hated him. Then, after that, I guess I felt sorry for him. It's like a sickness, doing what he did.'

'Can I ask you something?'

'Why stop now?'

'Are you glad he's been taken captive?'

'Part . . . part of me is indifferent to it, I admit that.' Monica paused, said, 'But, ultimately, no. I don't want harm to come to him.'

'Did he ever apologise?'

'No. I used to want him to, to apologise and take penance and admit his evil depravity to everyone who'd listen but then, when I forgave him in my mind . . . I think now that if he ever mentioned it in any way I'd just hate him all over again.'

Walker nodded. He'd not known that about her but it made sense now as he remembered back to that July Fourth weekend; how in a couple of the quiet times she'd flinched when he'd gone to kiss her, to touch her. It must have been raw back then, and he felt a rising anger at the guy despite himself. He breathed in and out, heavy. He didn't buy that it was a sickness. As far as Walker was concerned, if you hurt children, and Monica was a teenage kid back then, a child really, and family, well – he had no objection to guys like that being dropped off en masse into the middle of the ocean. *Sink or swim, sickos, don't mind the sharks.*

Monica had stopped talking. She was watching a news bulletin.

He saw the television. Monica un-muted it. It was a profile on Jasper, since the news outlets had nothing else to go on reporting other than, in just over an hour another cyber attack may or may not occur, and all kinds of security experts had weighed in with possible scenarios.

There were pictures of Jasper. One from the Army, when he'd been discharged from the Rangers with a medical condition that was the result of a training accident.

'What was the injury?' Walker asked.

'Amputation,' Monica said. 'He'd been pegged for Special Forces and was training with the Rangers at Camp Merrill when his Black Hawk clipped a tree in the mountains of Georgia. It went down hard. He broke both legs and developed a clot and now has a prosthetic below the left knee. After that, the Rangers were out.'

'Then the Army Cyber Warfare came knocking.'

'Cyber Command pounced on him. He could have left with a payout and medical pension, but he saw it as an opportunity. He was always deep into computers.'

'So, he went to work in Fort Meade.'

'That's right. He was there a short while, then he was lent out to the NSA when it was evident what he could do with a computer.'

'Hacking foreign networks?'

Monica nodded. 'His high-school and college hobby had become the new black in military circles. They're desperate for recruits – they're still running at less than half the manpower of what they're aiming at.'

'Because of Silicon Valley.'

'Mainly. Why work on computers for the Army when you can do it for Google and play ping pong all day and earn a whole heap more.'

'What sort of work did he do?'

'He never said. It wasn't long, that first NSA posting. He was dragged back to the Army and tasked to an assignment with the MPs; 110th, some kind of special investigators.'

'I've heard of them. They're good.'

'Well, that op spelled the end of the work he could do with the Army, because it made him a target.'

'How?'

'It was law-enforcement stuff.'

'For the Army?'

Monica nodded. 'More coffee?'

'Sure, I'll give my kidneys another sharp punch.'

She put another capsule in the machine, then pressed the button. As water steamed, the smell of freshly brewed coffee filled the air. She seemed content to be busy, happy to be talking of something other than what her brother had done to her.

'Jasper started out helping the MPs investigate rings of Army units that were doing . . .' Monica trailed off, absently watching the coffee stream into the cup. 'They were attacking women, degrading them.'

Walker's eye twitched. *More guys to be dumped at sea.* 'Like?'

'Jasper never told me about it, but I heard, later, from – well, I guess you'd call him a mutual friend,' Monica said. 'He came in on the tail end of a three-year operation that would be the Army's biggest bust for sex rings and sexual harassment. Army guys would rate women in uniform, not just how they looked, but what they were like in bed. Details were shared around. About Army wives and girlfriends, too. Local bar staff and other women. It led to rapes and other sex crimes being committed against women who had rated highly but evidently got sick of all the attention from men in uniform. Over a hundred Army personnel were booted out for that. A few are doing time in Fort Leavenworth. And a huge number – up to a thousand, I heard – were reprimanded for accessing the footage and data.'

Walker nodded slowly. 'That's interesting.'

'Interesting?' Monica's voice raised a little.

'The guys busted out. They'll be pissed. At Jasper. When was this?'

'Seven, eight years ago.'

'It's motive. I mean it could be, right? Some of those guys would harbour a hell of a grudge against him. And you said yourself he had to leave the Army because of ongoing threats.'

'That's what he said to me. Well, to Dad, and Dad told me. But I'd say those guys wouldn't know of Jasper's involvement. His focus was on collecting the data, running the hacks on the computers and networks and phones that these creeps were using. He never faced them in court, and his name wasn't on any documents.'

'You sure?'

Monica nodded. 'That's the first thing Dad did this morning: he rang the Pentagon and called in favours. They confirmed that the guys Jasper helped bust were never aware of his involvement, and his name isn't recorded any place. The 110th MPs are good like that.'

'I bet those guys could find out, if they really wanted to. Army is a close-knit circle. People know people. Friendships run deep. A guy like Jasper could be seen as a traitor, in their warped eyes – worse, to those who got caught and were bumped out of the Army. They're probably still looking out for one another, furious about losing not only their jobs and pensions and all that, but their little side project too. Maybe it took them seven or eight years to find out who exactly he was. They made him, and now they've got him.'

'Does that fit with your linked cells of terror attacks?'

'It might.'

'You really think they could play a role in this?'

'Maybe. It has to be considered.' Walker caught her eyes. 'That's when you forgave him – when you heard about that work?'

Monica nodded. 'I thought it was his way of making amends. Catching those criminals and depraved a-holes.'

'So, they have form. They could be the ones who've taken him.'

'It's just . . . Okay, let's say you're right. What do we do? Track down every last one of them in the next twenty-four hours?'

'Leave that to me.' Walker sipped his fresh coffee. 'What did Jasper do after that?'

'He was doing that op for a couple of years. When they did the big bust, he got a Silver Star for his involvement, as well as a promotion to Captain, and was given his choice of roles.'

'What'd he choose?'

'To leave. To go to the NSA, full-time. He'd worked so long looking inwards, he wanted to deal with foreign-only interests. He felt the Army and the Cyber Warfare outfit were crap. So, he transferred to the NSA for good.'

'How do you know that?'

'Because, he . . .' Monica again looked out her back window into the darkness. 'He asked my advice.'

'And you gave it?'

'Sure.'

'Did that happen often between you?'

'Asking for advice?'

'Asking, and receiving.'

'No. No, it didn't. Ever. That was literally the first time.'

'Why then?'

'Because . . . because I wanted him to move away. Out of the country. A posting some place, for a few years, maybe more. I wanted him to do something that would make him even more valuable to the government.'

'You were protecting him?' Walker asked gently. 'Because of the Army investigation?'

'Maybe.' Monica nodded. 'I think. I don't know. That Army investigation did have him spooked. They'd given him access to all military communications. *All* communications. Emails and phone recordings. There was a General involved – that's how high it went, some scumbag in the 101st. He never said, and I've not heard anything to confirm it, but I've wondered – what else would he have seen and heard when running those communications through keyword programs to hunt out these creeps? I honestly think he left the Army because he was scared that someone may have thought he'd seen something else in there.'

'Like what?'

Monica shook her head. 'No idea. That's just my thinking. It's like the Snowden files, you know? How Snowden cherry-picked and only took this and that, then left breadcrumbs behind for investigators to see exactly what he took and what he didn't, showing he'd touched some files but not taking them because they were too explosive and damaging.'

'But the powers that be are terrified that Snowden took it all, or looked at things that are thermo-nuclear in content, too explosive to be laid bare to the world.'

'Right? That's what I figured with Jasper. They may think he saw even more than he reported.'

Walker filed that away, said, 'What did Jasper think of Snowden?'

'We never spoke about him. The last communication I had was that conversation about leaving for the NSA posting, just over two years ago. He'd got in touch because he'd heard of my divorce, from Dad. We chatted and met up and then all he talked about was his work. No, actually, just before he left, he sent me a letter. Snail mail. Not-hackable. He said he could get my ex, if I wanted him to. "Sort him out," he'd said. "Finish him."'

'Kill him?'

'That's not how I took it. Not at first. At first I assumed he meant finish him online – hack his accounts, wipe data, post things that would incriminate him somehow, destroy his career and reputation. But who knows? Jasper was weird like that, always talking in riddles, the result of never fully trusting communication, whether in that letter or when it's verbal and face to face, in a Barnes and Noble cafe like we were that day we last caught up.'

'Why'd he write that?' Walker said. 'After years of no communication between the two of you, why would he suddenly act like he cared?'

Monica closed her eyes. They may have been wet. A tear ran down her cheek.

'Because. At the end of the day, he's my brother. For all his faults, he loves me.'

25

'Did Jasper have friends?'

'Not really,' Monica replied. 'No-one that I knew about, not since his school and college friends. I never met any of his Army buddies, if he had them.'

'Any close friends from ages back, a best friend?'

Monica shrugged. 'That's another story. A long one.'

'I'm listening.'

'I really don't think it's related.' Monica gave him half a smile. 'Though you'll think otherwise.'

'Let's talk about it and see.'

'They'd had a fight.'

'About?'

'It doesn't matter. But the upshot was that things were said, things happened, they fell out. That was, oh, fifteen years ago and that guy has moved on. Jasper too – that's when he up and joined the Army, after college.'

Monica fell silent.

Walker finished his coffee, then rotated his head slowly to work the kinks out of his neck. He checked his watch.

'Okay,' he said, 'what did Jasper do for the NSA?'

'Development, he told my father.'

'Of?'

'I don't know. But it was big. Their lead program. That's what my father said.'

'But you don't know what it was?'

'I know he was given clearance above me, and that's high.'

'Yeah, we should talk about that.'

'What?'

'You.'

'Me?'

'Your role. Your job.'

'My job is boring. And it certainly has nothing to do with this.'

'There you are, assuming certainty again.'

Monica smiled properly this time.

'Humour me so we can rule it out. But we need to talk about it. And then we'll go back to the friend.'

'You wanted to know about Jasper. And the Army. And the NSA.'

'And you're telling me about him. Is that it? Are we caught up with his working life, up to the point of the NSA?'

'Almost. Almost as much as I can tell you. As much as I know, I mean.'

'I knew what you meant.'

'Do you? Did you?'

'I think so.'

Monica leaned forward on the island bench, tilted her head slightly to the side. 'You're trained to spot lies.'

'So are you.'

'How do you know that?'

'Because you have government clearance just below Jasper's, which would be high, as you said, which means you've done your human-resources psych work for the government. I'm guessing military-related, given your provenance.'

'You'd be right.'

'Doing?'

'Nothing related.' Monica paused, then said, 'You saw my graduation picture, at my father's place.'

'The academic colours. And I read a brief snapshot of you online, before heading here. You're a psychologist. Or psychiatrist?'

'The former. No medication dispensed.'

'Right. Then grad-school. And since then you've worked for the government,' Walker said, seeing her shoes, her outfit, her jewellery. 'You freelance, though, never just working for them, because you're too smart for that.'

'Okay. Smart, I'll take that. Plus I want certain things. And I have a daughter to raise.'

Walker couldn't hide his surprise. 'Daughter?'

Monica smiled again, but this time in a new way, a pure way. 'She's seven. She lives with her father.'

'Okay.' Walker glanced at the fridge. There were a few photos on it of a kid, a girl. He'd pegged her for a friend's child, a god-daughter maybe. She had jet black hair and slightly Asian features.

'You really know nothing of the NSA project that Jasper worked on?'

'I heard from my father that he was doing a lot of trips to a big new complex they've built.'

'Still at Fort Meade?'

'No. In Utah.'

'Utah? What's in Utah? Does the NSA have something there?'

'I suppose so. Why else would they send him there to work?'

Walker wondered. He'd had a connection with Utah in the past. Back in the early days of anthrax threats, when he'd just started out in the Air Force and was doing a security detail on a team from the CDC to send anthrax samples to be rendered inactive by irradiation at the Army's Dugway Proving Ground, near Salt Lake City. A few years later it turned out that someone had stuffed up that day, and at least twenty government, university and commercial laboratories around the country received suspected live samples of anthrax rather than inert. That place was secretive. Utah was the kind of place he could imagine the NSA hiding something away.

'Okay,' Walker said. 'How about his personal life? Was he married? Family?'

'No.'

'No-one in his life?'

'No-one that I know of.'

'Ever?'

A look of pain passed her face before she recovered herself. 'Not that I know of.'

Walker looked across at the television screen. It showed the most up-to-date image that the Department of Defence was willing to part with of Jasper Brokaw: him in his BTUs at Ranger school. The Army Ranger School was an intense two-month combat leadership course oriented towards small-unit tactics, one of the toughest combat courses in the world and the most physically and mentally demanding leadership school the Army has to offer short of what Delta are put through. Walker had been through their Mountain component. It was tough. Jasper looked tough, for a young soldier. Slightly build, wiry, fit. The picture was ten years old.

'As a head doctor,' Walker said, looking from the picture of Jasper in what had been his physical prime to Monica, who had also been watching the screen, 'what effect do you think the helicopter accident had on your brother?'

'He had to learn to walk again.'

'I'm talking in his mind.'

'It focused it.'

'Focused it?'

Monica nodded, looking back to the image. 'Until the accident, he was aimless. Angry, driven, but aimless. He'd put off military service and gone to college and finally capitulated to my father, but rather than entering an officer school he enlisted in the Army, regular infantry, then the Rangers. Probably to piss off our father. After the accident, in rehab, being in all kinds of hospitals and physical re-education with veterans from Iraq and Afghanistan, he changed. He wanted to contribute and do what he could for his country. Before that he was all short-term thinking. Reckless. The Army had lapped it up.'

'And after? How'd it focus him?'

'He was at home and in and out of rehab for the best part of a year and turned to his old hobby.'

'Computers.'

'Yes. And he became good at it. Really good. He'd found something that he could use to contribute – in a big way – something that could become his legacy, and a way to wage a war against opponents while protecting front-line troops from harm. He became obsessive,' Monica said. 'Addicted. My dad, old neighbours and friends would tell me, and a couple of times I saw it too. After the accident Jasper went into his shell, and maybe six months later a different man emerged. It wasn't just the limp – it seemed his leg didn't bother him at all. But the change was in every fibre of his being. Irrevocably.'

Walker said, 'You really think people can change like that?'

'I didn't think so.'

'But you've changed your mind?'

Monica nodded. 'I had never been convinced. In my line of work. Through all the study I've done. Twenty years and plenty of case studies and first-hand observations, and the sum of that? People evolve, they adapt, they regress. But change? Nope. But with Jasper, I saw it. Sensed it. Knew it. He became different in almost every way.'

'Better?'

'Different. Driven. Purposeful. Obsessive.'

'He made Special Forces selection and through most of Ranger School. You have to be obsessive to get that far.'

Monica nodded. 'But Jasper never was. Not even with the Army, not with Special Forces, not with anything I'd seen. He'd trained hard, sure, he wanted it. But it was nothing like what he became sitting at a screen with a keyboard at his fingertips. That accident, his new reality, it shaped him.'

Walker saw the television's ticker stating *Cyber attacks – what's next? Who is most at risk?* and checked his watch. Just under thirty minutes until the Feds came to move Monica and he would leave for Jasper's apartment.

'Obsessive,' Walker said. 'Legacy. Resourceful. Vengeful. Skilled. Capable. Wounded. Patriotic . . . Betrayed?'

'What are you doing?'

'Cut-up technique,' Walker said. 'All the factors that are making up your brother.'

'Cut up?'

'Re-ordering. Looking for a pattern that isn't obvious on the surface. My father does it. Bowie did it to write his lyrics.'

'Oh, it must be good then.'

'It helps you see things in different ways,' Walker said, looking at the granite bench top in front of him but his gaze a million miles away. 'Jasper is resourceful and smart and calculated. Driven to leave a legacy. Determined to make cyber a new frontier of warfare – to make it all that it can be.'

'You're giving him too much credit.'

Walker looked up to her. 'Could he be cooperating with his captors?'

'No chance. He may have been a misguided youth, but for all his faults, he loves this country.'

'Leaking people's personal data and communications doesn't mean he doesn't.'

'But if we're talking cyber attacks to force the President's hand to enact the kill switch, then they have to be catastrophic in nature. Lives will have to be lost before the Internet is turned off by lawmakers. He wouldn't do that.'

Walker wasn't so sure, but he didn't voice this thought because at that moment the hallway cop's phone chimed and two seconds later there was a knock at the front door.

26

'We have to go,' said the cop in the hallway. His colleague stood in the open doorway.

'Where?' Walker asked. He headed down the hall, Monica a few paces behind him. The four of them stood in a circle in the entry way, where the hall was at its widest, before the stairs started and took up half the hall's width as it continued back to the kitchen. Both cops looked torn. Walker had seen that look before: orders from on high that weren't what they wanted to follow but they knew they had no choice.

'It's a Homeland Security code,' the cop said in monotone. 'All officers of the law are to respond and report to their assigned stations for the protection of critical infrastructure and to ensure public order and safety.'

'Jasper's next attack,' Monica said.

'Must be,' the cop replied as he checked the time on his phone. 'Sorry. The Feds will still send someone within twenty minutes. Just hang tight and lock the door.'

The two cops left without another word.

Monica went to the door and watched them move quickly down the steps to the street and across the road to their unmarked Ford, which started up and tore off with a roar of rubber and the siren bleeping in the quiet of the night, the red-blue-and-white lights on the back parcel shelf and behind the front grille strobing in the dark. She closed the door and clicked the two locks, the bolt and the chain. She turned and faced Walker, but he spoke before she could.

'This isn't right.'

'Threats have been made,' Monica replied, 'it makes sense. Maybe they've even seen a pattern emerge, noticed some activity online some place that's alluding to the next attack.'

Walker was looking at the windows in the front room, and then down the hall towards the flimsy back door. 'Do you have a firearm in the house?'

'No.'

'I do,' Walker said. He tapped at the small of his back, where her father's Colt .45 was tucked.

'Great.' She brushed past him and headed for the kitchen. By the time he joined her she was seated on a stool at the bench, the side Walker had been on before. Her shoulders were slightly sagged, her forearms rested on the granite bench top, her fingers interlaced. She was waiting.

'This isn't about the next cyber attack.' Walker remained standing, facing the back window and door.

'Then what do you think the cyber attack will be?' Monica asked.

'No idea. But it's not whatever those cops are responding to, it's too soon. Too broad. I don't like it.'

'They must have received a threat. Or intercepted something. Maybe they've managed to hack into the computer Jasper is using, and seen what's coming. Or detected a penetration on a network – that's a thing, right?'

Walker remained silent. It didn't feel right. Not like this. There were still twenty-one minutes until the FBI was scheduled to show up. Unless they too had to respond to the Homeland Security threat, setting up security at LAX or federal government installations.

'Why don't you contact your FBI lady?' he said. 'The Assistant SAC, and see what's what?'

Monica looked at him, then nodded and typed a text message. She hit send and placed the phone in front of her. They both watched the screen, waiting for a reply.

'You're not going to call her?'

'She said to message.'

Walker remained silent.

Monica said, 'Who do you think has Jasper?'

'I'm working on it.'

'You really think you can figure it out?'

'I can try.'

'You know what you haven't asked me yet?'

Walker looked at her. 'Where your kid lives?'

'What – oh . . .' Monica looked at the photos on her fridge. 'She's with her father, in Shanghai.'

'It's none of my business. But it's good to know she's out of harm's way.'

'Harm's way?'

Walker nodded.

Monica said, 'I was going to say, you never asked why I haven't been worried.'

Walker heard her, but he didn't answer. He was looking out the back of the house. The yard was small, paved and just big enough to park a car in. Bordering on the back fence was another yard, and another two-storey house. It was dark. Deep shadows were thrown by street lights and neighbouring windows. He was sure he saw something there. In the dark. The darkest part of the shadow. The umbra. Movement.

27

'Walker?'

Monica was tense; she saw Walker's face and body language and she knew that things had changed.

'This place, it has an attic,' he stated rather than asked as he scanned the hallway to the front door. He could sense movement out there. A slight shift, of something. It came from being hunted before. A sixth sense. He looked to her.

Monica saw the shift in his eyes. The danger. A call to action. 'Yes.'

Walker looked down at her hands. Her phone.

Monica looked to it. Then she knew, too.

'I didn't call anyone—'

'You didn't have to,' Walker said, and headed for the stairs, taking her hand as he did, the phone clattering to the floorboards.

They heard the noise at the front door as they neared the stairs. A knock. Three taps. Thumps. A heavy fist, gloved knuckles. Purposeful. A big, strong guy with a big, heavy fist, hitting the big, strong and heavy hardwood door. It might hold up to one or two decent shoulderings. Certainly not any kind of police ram. Certainly not against one or more big guys intent on gaining entry. And they'd be approaching via the back door too, and that would last less than a second against an attack.

Walker didn't stop moving. Up the stairs, as quietly as he could, Monica close behind. He scanned the scene, the landing ahead: four doors running off a small hallway. Three bedrooms and a bathroom, he figured. Windows out to the verandah. But not high enough, not far enough away. Too easily intercepted. They needed to buy time. Seconds would do, a minute or two would be ideal.

Knocking at the door again. Louder this time.

Monica let go of his hand, overtook him and headed for a pull-down cord near the end of the hall at the back of the house. It revealed a little trapdoor, with a ladder that folded down. She led the way up, Walker a step behind. He pulled the ladder up, and the trap door, taking a moment to pull the cord up into the roof space to impede anyone following.

Inside the attic, Monica left the lights off without being asked. Smart; the light would have spilled out the louvres front and back. Instead, there was near complete darkness inside as Walker crept along a board to the louvres, which drew in a little light from outside. They were made of pine or Oregon, a soft timber, painted several times over the decades but currently light grey, like a dove. An inch thick and two deep, spaced an inch apart, maybe twenty inches square. Backed with screen-wire to keep insects out. Good enough to see through.

Walker looked down at the rear courtyard. Looking from here out on to the dark space out there was different from being in the lit kitchen and looking out. From here, he could distinguish far more detail in the shadows. And there was movement. He made out three guys. Big. Dressed in black. Paramilitary types. Like a SWAT team. But FBI tactical guys didn't wear black, not since Waco. One was at the back door, a few feet away, ready to breach, the other two scanning windows and ready to push through the door when it was blasted open. Impossible to know whom they represented, and he had neither the time nor inclination to find out.

'What do we do?' Monica asked in a whisper.

Walker said, 'We wait.'

'How long for?'

'Not long.' Walker could no longer see the three guys at the back – they'd moved in close to the back door and were now crowded under the awning that covered the rear stairs. That meant the wait was pretty much over.

Monica said, 'Who are they?'

'No-one we want to meet right now,' Walker said, shifting his weight and ripping off the screen covering. It was quiet but made a cloud of dust.

'You think they'll go away?' Monica whispered.

'No.'

'Then why did you say—'

The power in the neighbourhood went out a split second before the sound of the front and back doors being smashed in reverberated through the house. The men would be inside now, hunting them with night vision. Monica stifled a noise – not so much a scream as shock, that someone unknown would enter her house in such a violent way, figuring that she was trapped up here in the attic space.

Walker grabbed hold of two louvres at a time and pulled them out, leaving a pile of kindling at their feet. He pushed his torso through the open space and hauled himself up onto the roof. He got good purchase on the slate tiles and hung over the edge, dropping his arms down towards the access to the attic. He felt Monica reach up and he grabbed her wrists. He braced with his legs splayed wide apart as he felt her full weight; maybe just over half his weight. He used his core strength and legs and arms as one to pull her up, quickly.

'Now what?' she asked, in a crouch on the ridge-line next to him.

'I'm going to hold onto you, and you need to follow me, side by side, and keep going,' Walker said. 'When I squeeze you jump, okay?'

'What?'

'That way.' Walker pointed to the house next door. 'We run and jump and we keep going until we get to the side street.'

A second's hesitation, then she said, 'Okay.'

They ran down the slope of her roof, Walker holding her left wrist, and near the end—

They jumped onto the neighbour's roof, the void maybe two metres. Monica landed easily, light on her toes, and was already running up the slope. Walker's right foot dislodged a slate tile and got caught in the void beneath and he had to let go of her – he motioned her on.

He glanced back as he freed his foot. Nothing to see.

It took him a second to regain his balance and get up, scrambling up the roof after having to rebuild his momentum.

They met at the ridge, and this time Monica grabbed Walker's wrist. He nodded and they set off. There were six houses ahead, all similar in design and position on the block. This street and the two either side had been blacked out – street lights too. And it was radial – a circle around the entire block, as though an eclipse of all power and lights had occurred with Monica's house at the epicentre, about three hundred yards in all directions. Walker looked up. He couldn't see it, but he knew that there must be a drone up there with an EMP.

The Protecting Individuals from Mass Aerial Surveillance Act was supposed to protect private citizens from federal agencies conducting aerial surveillance, thus preserving some semblance of Fourth Amendment rights. But the sharpest end of the stick always had some leeway with such laws and rules.

That meant that these guys were federal, military or intelligence, with unfettered access to the nation's best toys.

And the gloves were off.

Walker and Monica continued their transit, and at the final house they stopped at the other side of the roofing ridge, crouching low, holding onto roof tiles.

Walker looked back – he couldn't see anyone out on any roofs. Nor the street. He could just make out a black Suburban parked out the front of Monica's; it hadn't been there when Walker arrived. And another at the far end of the street.

'What now?'

'We get to my car.'

'Yes, but how do we get down from here?'

'Drain pipe.'

Monica looked at him, and even in the darkness he could read her expression. '*What?*'

'The tubular things attached to the guttering at the corners of houses.'

'I meant you can't be serious.'

'Or I could kick out the louvres and we go through the attic,' Walker said. 'How well do you know your neighbours?'

'Not that well.'

'Okay, well, Plan A it is,' Walker said, headed for the drain pipe at the front corner. He went first. It was made of plastic, with clamps and screws into the timber cladding of the house and the timber frame beneath. When Walker was halfway down, Monica started her descent. His feet touched the roof of the front porch and he let go of the drain pipe, then dropped down to the garden bed.

Just as he caught Monica as she came down, two sharp bangs rang through the night. Flash-bang grenades. The guys were entering the attic and wanted to stun whoever was hiding up there.

'What was—'

'Come on,' Walker said. He led Monica through the front gate and along the footpath and turned up the hill, towards his car.

'Where are we going?'

'Away from here.'

Walker unlocked his door and leaned over and unlocked Monica's. As she climbed in he put the key in the ignition but didn't turn the engine over. Instead, he changed the gear into neutral and took the park brake off, then stepped back out of the car and, a hand on the steering wheel and his feet on the road, pushed. Once the inertia built up and the car was rolling down the hill he got back in and closed the door.

They rolled down the hill with no engine power and no lights. The steering was heavy but he held it in a straight line, and the lack of engine noise allowed them to avoid alerting those back at the house. They had covered four blocks by the time the hill started to flatten out at the bottom, and he pressed the brakes for the first time. As soon as the car slowed he turned the key and shifted to second and gave it gas, put the headlights on and took the first right.

Monica stared over her shoulder, only looking ahead once they'd made another turn, to the left, where Walker unwound the engine to put a bit of immediate distance between them and those at her house.

'You okay?' Walker asked her. He was driving close to the limit, observing the road signs and traffic signals, heading east for the highway.

'Who were they?'

'Feds.'

'FBI?'

'I doubt it. This has become militarised.'

'The military? This is a civilian problem.'

Walker turned the radio up high to hear over the thrum of the Cuda's big block V8. The newscaster was talking about what might happen in twenty minutes' time. Monica sunk down into her seat.

28

They were fifteen miles north when Walker eased off the gas and reached down to turn up the radio again. The newscasters were still talking about Jasper and the cyber threat. And for good reason.

It had ticked past the deadline for the second cyber attack.

So far nothing had been reported.

Monica had settled. She'd spent the ride watching out her side window, silent, still. Walker focused on the scene ahead with regular checks in his rear-vision mirrors. There was no sign of the Suburbans nor any other pursuing vehicles. Now it was past the deadline she was watching the radio, as though she could will some news of her brother to be broadcast. Walker had kept to suburban streets, presuming that any kind of dragnet would focus on the interstates. By now law-enforcement officers would have Monica's ID on file and would be on the lookout. But why?

The downtown street lights strobed above them, a yellow glow cast over the road, the shadows between them far larger than the light that spilled like stepping stones ahead, *flash-flash-flash* as they drove under them, the rhythm soothing.

As they slowed to a stop at a red light a car approached from behind. Low lights, a sedan, not one of the giant Suburbans. It changed lanes without indicating and pulled alongside. Cops. LAPD. There were no other cars around. No people. Monica saw them and then looked to Walker, and then dead ahead, as though unsure who her friends were now.

Walker ignored the cops until the light changed to green. He shifted his foot, and immediately the police car bleeped its siren. The passenger wound down his window and signalled to Walker to do the same.

Walker did so.

The cop smiled. 'Nice ride.'

'Thanks.' Walker looked at the two uniformed police officers, ogling the car for the thing of beauty it was.

'Seventy-one?'

'Yep.'

'Nice.' The cop looked to his partner, the driver, who had turned his attention to the computer bolted to the centre console.

Walker's hands tensed a little at the wheel. The cops were listening to the radio and watching their screen. These guys were a highway patrol. Headed into town for food maybe.

Still the newscasters were saying that neither the FBI nor Homeland Security had detected a second cyber attack.

The cops were on their radio. To Walker the chatter was indistinguishable, but both cops were listening intently.

The light was still green. A car approached from behind Walker, and flashed its lights for him to proceed.

'Hey,' Walker called to the cop nearest him. 'Are you guys on some kind of lookout for this next cyber attack?'

'What?'

'Like, some kind of Homeland Security protocol? Do you have to be on guard some place?'

The cops shared a look before they shook their heads and drove off, their car lit up with lights and siren, the roar of rubber and hot fumes left in their wake.

Walker eased on the gas and wound up his window.

Monica exhaled. 'What does that mean?'

'That those cops at your house got a bogus message to leave their posts.'

'So those guys in black could take me.'

'Yes.'

'Who could do that?'

'The government.'

'But I'm not the threat here!'

Walker stared out at the road ahead, and said nothing.

29

At 2.09am the radio came to life as the newscaster announced that an unnamed government source had reported a hack on a federal database. That was the extent of it. By 2.11 the White House had announced it had no comment. By 2.13 the FBI and Homeland Security had said they were investigating a possible breach at the OPM. A minute later the news radio reported that people had found sites containing data from the OPM.

'You heard of the OPM?' Walker said.

'Office of Public Management,' Monica said. 'That's nothing vital, right? Some personal data, just like the last attack on social-media sites. Nothing immediately terrible about it . . .'

Walker ran it through his mind. Sure, this wasn't an attack on Pentagon networks, or the FBI, or even the IRS. Or stealing data from defence contractors and selling the plans of future weapons systems to a nation state or dumping them online to cause havoc. The first attack exposed personal data, embarrassing secrets that would cause mass noise and panic right in the homes of Americans. And this attack had specifically targeted federal employees . . .

Walker said, 'The OPM would have names, addresses, social-security numbers, psych profiles, security clearances. All that screening that every person has been through, it's now out there. That's what Jasper meant about the major attack on government.'

Monica nodded and had a faraway look as though she was tallying the extent of this attack. 'You're right. Security-clearance forms contain people's deepest and darkest secrets laid bare. Plenty of opportunity for blackmail.'

'Not just ordinary people,' Walker said as he drove. 'Every federal employee outside of perhaps the most sensitive positions, which you'd think, or hope, would be compartmentalised. Every person working in the White House and on Capitol Hill, every staffer, all the TSA officers and agents, postal workers, every Congressman and Senator, every Department Secretary and Agency Director. Operators at nuclear plants. Safety inspectors at dams. FAA personnel in charge of the airspace and thousands of flights every day. Secret Service employees?'

'Maybe, I'm not sure. I hope that's compartmentalised. And DoE. And others. Who knows, right?'

'Well, the millions that have been affected will make noise, from the lowest in the food chain right up to their superiors and then onwards, all the way to the President. Every person investigating this hack and the abduction of your brother suddenly has every little secret out in the open.' Walker paused, checking his mirrors but seeing nothing unusual. 'Again, this wasn't about harming national security in a way that helps another nation. It's about putting forty million federal employees at a megaphone to shout to the President: *Do something about this – either find Jasper or turn off the Internet and block the access to our secrets.*' Walker paused again, then added, 'And this attack helps foreign nationals, nation states.'

Monica turned away from the window to look at Walker. 'How?'

'Every person with a security clearance has to report every contact they have with a foreign national. That's out there now. That means that China or Russia or Iran can see that some mid-level staffer in the White House has had contact with someone from their embassy – and that person will be hauled in and questioned and probably thrown in jail, just in case.'

Monica was silent for a moment, then said, 'I hadn't thought about that. Damn. We're talking forty million people *plus*. That will make this the biggest public data heist against a government network in cyber history. Their social-security numbers, family details, personal histories, passwords, fingerprints . . . all stolen from US personnel files containing the results of security background checks.'

'Your ex-husband,' Walker said, thinking back to the photo of Monica's daughter. 'He's Chinese?'

Monica nodded.

Walker was silent.

'So?'

'Just thinking,' Walker said. 'Wondering. How did he get sole custody?'

'Money,' Monica replied, not bothering to hide the bitterness in her tone. 'And laws are different in China – she's a dual citizen, born there, in Shanghai, and it's ironclad. The law, and the money. Especially the latter. It's old. From Mao's time. You understand? He's as good as untouchable. Right?'

'But your dad – your family's pedigree in the US. There'd be people and friends and favours owed. That's got to have some sway.'

'This is – politically – it's bigger than me and my daughter,' Monica said. She turned back to stare out the window. 'It took me a while to see it that way. But I can't do anything . . . it's complicated.'

'Is he in politics?'

'Everyone with power and money in China is in politics.'

'But a member of the party?'

'Isn't it sad?' Monica said, after a moment's thought. 'That that's all there is: "the" party. Yes, I'm sure he's a member and he's got sway in those circles because of his family connections – that's how the place works – that and money. But he is what we'd call a Congressman or Senator? No. He's a businessman.'

'What kind of business?'

'Government contracts. Big business. It's all the same.'

'Sounds like the same thing over there, government and business.'

'You're right. The line is blurred, there more than anywhere. It's one and the same. Business. Politics. Money. Influence. Power. You have it until you fall out of favour.'

'How did you two meet?'

'After I finished at the DoD, I did a few years at a big firm that had an office in Shanghai. We met at the US consulate there, a gala.'

'Was he intel for the Chinese government?'

'I doubt it.'

'But you don't know.'

She sighed. 'We were married for four years. I don't think I ever really knew him. I got pregnant and we got married.'

'Like that . . .'

Monica gave him a look.

Walker said, 'Sorry.'

'You know this isn't a nation state against us,' Monica said. 'It's a terror group that has abducted my brother. No demands. So, they seem like anarchists.'

'They'll have a motive of some sort.'

'Do you think this cyber attack on a government network will change anything in the President's thinking?' Monica said.

'I'm sure we'll soon find out,' Walker said. He saw a sign up ahead, lit up with a spotlight. He slowed the car. He wanted to ask her more about her husband but decided that could wait. 'But I doubt it. It will take more than information. These attacks have been well planned.'

'I mean, really, that was all?' Monica said, her thought process running along quickly. 'Not a hack on the Department of Defence or something? I was expecting a power grid to go out. Airports to go haywire. Something that was more . . . tangible, as an attack.'

'Me too,' Walker replied. 'But this is smart. He's getting the population onside. He's heaping pressure on the politicians, and on the President. It's making things easier and easier for the President to enact the kill switch. The attackers are thinking far ahead. Get the population onside with your demands, then start doing things that threaten their safety.'

'It's like chess . . .' Monica said absently. 'Jasper always liked chess. But I just can't see how this will force the President's hand. No-one can anticipate what's coming, because whoever has Jasper is making him act six steps ahead.'

'Time will tell.' Walker pulled into the car park of a chain motel five miles south-east of where they had seen the police – the opposite direction to the one he had been headed in when they had seen him. It was overly cautious perhaps, but Walker had not survived so many years in Special Operations and the CIA by not taking precautions.

He parked the Cuda away from the office, in a space near the rooms, leaving Monica in the car with the radio on and the key in the ignition. He walked to the reception with his hands in his pockets. He was tired. Another night of not enough sleep. His mind started to wander back to this morning, when he'd woken in a hotel room with Eve. His wife? Ex-wife? He stopped himself. He had to focus on the here and now, the problems that were upon them and ahead of them.

Those guys back at the house. The EMP on a drone. The flash-bang grenades.

Feds. And not FBI or Homeland Security – surely they wouldn't act out like that, turning off several blocks of power, no calls identifying themselves as they entered the house.

So, who?

The CIA didn't operate on US soil like that. The NSA didn't have armed operators like that. Either way, there were laws in place that regulated the intelligence officers from those agencies and what they could and could not do inside the United States.

That left the military. Walker thought of all the possible units that were capable, those overt door-kickers and the black-bag types that operated off the books. There were a few likely candidates, all of them a worry. It didn't bode well.

Walker knew full well that while the Posse Comitatus and the Insurrection Acts of the nineteenth century limited the powers of the federal government in using its military to act as domestic law-enforcement personnel, there was provision for the military to act as 'advisors' on matters of national emergency. And, at the end of the day, the President could do as the office pleased, signing in an executive order to plug a legal loophole.

Walker also knew that he needed to reach out to Bill McCorkell. McCorkell could look into who it could be, so that Walker could be better prepared, so that he knew who was coming and what he was dealing with.

What it meant, Walker knew, as he neared the door to the reception office of the motel, was that the gloves were off. They were trying to stop Jasper and the terror cell that had him before a national disaster claimed countless lives. Perhaps the President had authorised an executive order permitting a select group of the DoD to deal with this national threat.

But would it be just because of the threats? Or because they knew just how capable Jasper was, what he could really do?

With the Feds came Trapwire, that nifty little system that linked every camera and photo on the planet and filtered through with facial recognition to find a target. It could be a person walking by a traffic camera or the dash cam on someone's car or a Facebook selfie that showed the target in the background. If it was on the network in any way, Trapwire could find it.

The gritty car park scrunched under Walker's boots as he approached the reception block. The lights were on inside but the doors were locked. He rapped on the glass, and a head appeared from behind the computer on the desk. Dark hair, round head; just a quick look. Then nothing. Walker went to knock again but then the owner of the head stood up. It was a short Hispanic woman who shuffled to the door in slippered feet. She stopped and looked at him through the locked plate-glass door. Waited. She was a foot and a half shorter than Walker and twice his age.

'Can I get a room?' Walker asked.

She looked past him, towards the car park. Walker realised that in seeing no car she was immediately suspicious – this wasn't the kind of place that people checked into without a car, in the dead of night or otherwise.

Walker pointed to the car parked by the motel rooms.

The woman looked, and her eyes lingered, then she nodded and unlocked the door.

'Can I get a room?' he asked.

'Yes,' she said, heading back around her desk. 'Just you?'

'Yep.'

'Just the one night?'

'Three,' Walker said. He didn't plan to stay the second or third nights but figured that it would be easier later if a law-enforcement person was tasked with checking all overnight bookings in motels within a hundred-mile radius of Monica's home.

'Name?'

Walker handed over two crisp hundred-dollar bills.

'Okay, Benjamin Dos,' she said, nonplussed, tapping away at the computer. The room was probably around sixty dollars for the night, and he presumed she was either entering the false name or simply blotting out a room for a non-existent maintenance issue. Either a small tip and a false name, or a large tip and no name registered at all. Either way, they had a room, off the grid. She opened a drawer and passed over a key on a large plastic key ring.

He looked up at the camera in the corner above the woman.

'No problema,' she said, standing and putting the bills into her coat pocket. 'It is not pointed at those who come in – the boss has it pointed at the register, in the corner there, in case, you know, the staff . . .'

Walker saw the register. There was a fridge too. Drinks and some snacks, cheap booze. He took an armful, left twenty dollars behind and headed to the car.

He knew by the time he was halfway across the car park that things had changed. The car was empty. Monica was gone.

30

Walker put the armful of food and drinks on top of the Cuda's trunk and looked around. The car park was dark, the only light coming from an old yellowed vapour light above reception and the neon motel sign with VACANCY illuminated under it; the street lights were too far away to illuminate anything.

No sign of Monica.

There were three cars and a white van. All had enough miles on them to show they were road reps. All the lights in the rooms were off. It was nearing 2.30am. Zero dark thirty in military parlance, that unspecific time in the dead of night good for hunting. There were twenty-four rooms in a double-storey block. Concrete brick construction, painted some kind of salmon or peach colour; it was hard to tell for sure in the dark, when it appeared a warm shade of grey. There was a wide set of concrete stairs in the middle of the rectangle, and another at each end of the block. Steel balustrades. The centre stairs had the dull glow of a vending machine tucked under the landing, maybe even a laundry room tucked behind.

2.29am.

The road behind him, where they had entered, was a distant off-shoot of what was once a highway but had been superseded thirty years ago by a new branch of the interstate. A truck rumbled by with a blast of air brakes before making a turn. There were some stores and mechanics and fenced-up lots. No lights, no action, no movement.

She could have hitched a ride. But why?

Walker opened the car door. The keys were still in the ignition, the radio still on.

Chatter on the news.

Federal employees were going ape because of all the details leaked. The news reporters and radio host were saying that the attack's brilliance was clear.

The two data breaches and leaks had got the population talking. Complaining. Bitching. First the gen-pop, then federal government employees. And they were loud about it. It had woken America up. Maybe not here in this downtown cul-de-sac of early-morning no-where, but in the places that mattered, there were people right now logging into their accounts and deleting all those emails and messages that they didn't want out there – all too late, because either Jasper had put them on multiple massive databanks or they were already there, stored by the NSA or whoever, and anyone could read them via dozens of URL addresses.

The Director of Homeland Security was on the radio: *'Major breaches like these will continue unless the government adopts a psychology of deterrence. What we must do in the meantime is pay more attention to defence.'*

The reporter asked: *'What are you doing about locating Jasper Brokaw and those who have him captive?'*

'What we can.'

'Which is?'

'It's an ongoing operation. I'll leave it at that.'

Walker smelled cigarette smoke on the breeze.

'Crazy, huh?' a voice said. Monica emerged from behind the landing of the stairs at the middle of the building, the glow of a cigarette in her mouth. 'Habit I kicked five years ago.'

'I don't remember you smoking.'

'I didn't. I was all about sport back then. I took it up after spending a few years straight out of college doing counselling for DoD vets returning from tours in Iraq and Afghanistan.'

Walker knew that kind of counselling; he'd had a few mandated sessions after missions that he'd been out on had either lost team members or seen atrocities.

He asked, 'Ever do work for OPM?'

'Not directly, but I've done some contracts that touched them. And I'm sure a lot of people that I've placed elsewhere are in their system.'

'So, your details will be out there too. Leaked.'

She blew smoke. 'Annoying. I'll change my phone number and email if I get swamped by crazies. It's not the end of the world.'

'Your home address will be leaked too.'

Monica shrugged and pulled on her cigarette. 'Did you get rooms?'

'One,' Walker said, taking the keys and locking the car. He gave Monica the room key and pointed upstairs. She led the way. He was two paces behind her, the food and drinks in his arms. 'I thought you'd split.'

'Why would I do that? I mean, where would I go?' Monica paused at the landing and waved an arm around. 'I've never been within twenty miles of this neighbourhood. It's practically all industry. You think I'd go hang out at some closed factory?'

Walker took the stairs two at a time. He saw over the landing the glow of the vending machines, outside a small room housing a washer–dryer and a pay phone.

'Walker?'

He stopped at their room and turned to face Monica.

She said, 'One room? I mean, really?'

'We're laying low for a few hours, tops,' Walker said, shifting the food and bottles in his arms, taking the key from her and opening the door. Two single beds, updated some time in the past decade. He entered and dumped the stuff on a battered timber table with two chairs set around it. 'With two beds. If you want to sleep, sleep. Or watch the news. I'm going to get some sleep, because it's going to be a long day. But before I do, we're going to talk and figure out what we can. We keep off the streets for a bit. We'll get back out there in the morning, when it's busier, and we'll head to Jasper's apartment. Okay?'

Monica sat on the end of her bed, turned on the television and flicked through the channels to find news.

'I can't see us making much difference . . .' Monica trailed off.

Walker sat on the end of the bed opposite. 'We'll try our best though, right? To find your brother and stop whatever is coming.'

She looked him dead on, and said, 'What if your best isn't good enough?'

•

'I've got nothing on Walker's father,' Somerville said.

'Then forget him.' McCorkell leaned against the wall. 'Focus on finding Walker.'

'He'll make contact soon enough,' Zoe said.

'Until then, try and locate him,' McCorkell said. 'Reach out to contacts, and get the images of those fake TSA guys out there. Someone knows them, or knew them. Take shifts, get some rest at some point – it's going to be a busy day ahead. I'll be in my office, on the couch – call me any time.'

Zoe nodded.

Somerville said, 'We may have to assume that Walker's not going to be around for this one.'

'Until we hear from him, we're in the dark,' McCorkell said. 'But if, or when we do hear, we need to be ready to move mountains. If he's had contact with his father, he may already be moving on this.'

31

Monica turned up the television.

NBC news was playing, and a live cross to Washington had taken place: *'The true number of federal employees past and present affected could be as high as forty million,' the director of the FBI's cyber division said. 'The FBI, working with OPM officials, can confirm that the cyber attack was two separate breaches, occurring within the past hour: one of the theft of all personnel files, and one of all the security-clearance forms. Much of that data is classified and anyone who is tracked looking at it – and we are tracking all ISPs that view and share these documents – will face prosecution. To this end we suspect that those who are holding NSA employee Jasper Brokaw are bringing this unlawful cyber attack against the United States government, and we are doing all that we can to rescue Brokaw and bring to justice those who are forcing his hand.'*

'Can't they track the hacks back to a point of origin?' Monica said. 'They keep tracking cyber attacks back to Russia and China and Iran, right? How hard can it be?'

Walker remained silent as he took off his boots, then checked the sight lines out the curtained window. There was nothing to notice out there but the cars parked in the darkness, the lit-up reception, the dim overhead street light and the empty road. Then he put the chain on the door, and a chair back tilted and propped under the handle.

'That won't stop anyone,' Monica said.

'It'll buy time.'

'For what?'

'Retaliation. Close-in, in a space like this, if something goes down it's all about kinetic energy flying about and how fast you can act and react.'

He took out the Colt M1911 and put it on the table.

Monica's eyes were drawn to it. 'That's my father's.'

'He leant it to me.' Walker watched her watching the weapon. 'You know how to shoot?'

'A little. Dad taught us.'

'The safety is here.' Walker showed her the little lever, which he flicked with his thumb. 'It's a .45 so it has a kick. If you have to shoot, pull the trigger two or three times. Just in case.'

Monica fell silent. She looked from the pistol to the television. Walker did too.

The ramifications of the social-media hack were reverberating, consequences playing out. Employees were reading what their bosses really thought and said about them to others. Rivals got the inside scoop on their opposition. Diplomatic missions fell apart. Spouses were arguing over who sent what kind of messages to whom.

By the morning news cycle it would only grow louder. Tens of millions of people whose lives crashed apart overnight would be demanding the government do something about this hacker threat. This was real, to them. This wasn't some distant thing about celebrities having their phones and emails hacked and spread over the news. This wasn't millions of intelligence and diplomatic cables being cherry-picked and published by investigative journalists at the *Guardian* and *New Yorker*.

This was happening to mums and pops, kids and teachers and bosses and spouses, and it was all compounded when, at the seeming flick of a switch between 8pm yesterday and 2am today, there were no more secrets among anyone who had ever written them on a computer.

The OPM hack was still being fully realised, but caches of the data were spreading around the Internet and the FBI and NSA were failing in their attempts to play catch-up in trying to hide it.

'Whoever has Jasper planned this well,' Walker said. He went to the window and looked outside. The scene was as before: a few cars and trucks parked out on the street; the cars and van in the car park; the woman on reception watching her stories behind the counter. He looked at the door. It was hollow, thin plywood on a light frame, good for keeping the wind and rising sun out and nothing more. His bed was closest to it, and if someone came in they'd go out the way they came even faster.

'All federal employees of America are now listening . . .' the news anchor said. He had a panel of commentators in for a through-the-night special. *'And the pressure on the White House will amplify with every passing minute. Think of the forty million social-security numbers out there now, along with all the other personal details for identity theft. All the notes from the security clearances, the background stuff – the identities of all the people close to them. You want to get to the President, well, you now know where White House staffers live, details of their family and loved ones, what their potential is for blackmail and leverage with their psychological weaknesses and flaws . . .'*

'Well,' Monica said, sitting on the end of her bed and pulling off her boots. 'Maybe this, these cyber attacks, will turn out better than expected. Or rather, not as bad as expected. I mean, we're not talking loss of life.'

'So far,' countered Walker. 'There'll be ramifications from these data breaches.'

'You know what I mean – it's not like he's shut down hospitals or turned off the nine-one-one network.' She looked up at Walker as she leaned back on the bed. 'Who do you think thought of the actual attacks? Do you think they got Jasper to cook them up as some kind of gun-to-head, what's-the-best-you-can-do type of thing? Or is it them – whoever they are?'

Walker contemplated opening up to her about his father, but decided against it, for now.

'No telling,' he said, making sure to meet her eye as he spoke. He then checked out the window next to the door, a peek through the blind, a final look. Nothing had changed.

2.43am.

32

Walker took off his jacket and hung it over a chair, then his shirt. He lay on his bed, still in his T-shirt and jeans. He caught Monica looking at him. At the scars on his arms from being battered and blown every which way in two wars. At his forearm near the elbow where a bullet had passed clear through.

Monica said, 'You've lived.'

'We both have.'

'But you've been to war.'

'A couple of them. That's the official number.'

'And unofficially?'

Walker was silent.

She was still watching him as she made her way to the mini-bar and opened a tiny bottle of whisky. Walker shook his head as she held it up to him in question, and she took the bottle and a glass with her to sit again on her bed. Her voice softened now a little in the quiet of the room. 'Why did you leave the CIA?'

'We parted ways,' he said simply.

'For your wife?'

'In a sense.'

'Do you still love her?'

'Yeah.'

'No pause. Just like that.'

'Just like that,' he repeated.

'But you're separated.'

Walker looked up at the ceiling, said, 'It's complicated.'

Monica sipped her whisky. 'Does she know what you did for the Agency?'

'No-one knows what I did for my country.'

'Not even her?'

'Not even her.'

'Why don't you have a whisky?' Monica said. 'Or are you one of those who doesn't drink any more?'

'I want to stay sober.'

'So, you're one of those.'

'What's that mean?'

'Twelve steps.'

'AA? No. Why?'

'America's great gift to the world of religion.'

'I'm just trying to stay clear, so I'm ready for anything.'

'You're not a cop. And I seem to remember us drinking a lot back in the day.'

'That was a holiday weekend.'

'Oh, that's all it was?'

Walker looked over to Monica after a few seconds of silence between them.

Monica said, 'Have you thought about me, over the years?'

'I have.'

Monica let her eyes flick towards the television, but then she looked back at him. 'You're . . . different.'

'Near-on twenty years will do that,' he said.

'Is it really that long?'

'We were kids.'

'You were, what, a year younger than me?'

'I was twenty.'

'Twenty. Gosh.'

'Yep. A couple of kids.' He paused, said, 'Tell me about Jasper's friend.'

'They fell out years ago. It won't help.'

Monica fell silent. She stared at the television but he could tell that she didn't see it. Her gaze could have reflected anything: was she thinking about her brother, recalling being young, wondering about what could have been had she and Walker kept in touch after that long weekend?

Walker stood up, went to the table and passed her a wrapped sandwich, but she declined. Instead he ate it and then microwaved a hot pocket. The packet said it was a mixture of ham and cheese wrapped in pastry but it tasted like it could have been made out of old Chinese newspapers.

He said, 'This thing makes MREs taste good.'

'MREs – ration packs?'

Walker nodded. He tossed the balled, empty cardboard packaging across the room into the bin.

'Meals, Ready to Eat. Fuel, really.'

'But you ate them.'

'The military teaches you a couple of things that you never really forget,' Walker said. 'Top of the list is that you eat and sleep what and when you can.'

'They can't have been that bad, those MREs.'

'They had tiny bottles of Tabasco in them, so that helped.'

'Tabasco makes everything better.'

'I know, right?'

'Right.'

Monica smiled. 'So, you've eaten, now you're going to sleep?'

'That's the plan. The kettle's boiled, if you want a coffee.'

They each sat on the end of their respective beds, and watched the news. It was MSNBC.

The Assistant Director for the FBI's cyber division was doing a live cross from their situation control centre in DC. *'It's the biggest*

US security breach ever and we're doing all that we can to protect those who have had their privacy compromised at this time . . .'

Monica poured another whisky. She sipped it neat and watched and listened. Walker lay back on his bed. Tomorrow would be a long day, and he knew he needed rest, however short. Monica did too, but he knew better than to tell her so. He closed his eyes, still listening to the news.

'You sleeping?' Monica asked.

'For a bit.'

'Seriously?'

'Hopefully.'

'Like, right now?'

'Sometime between now and a few hours' time.'

'Because we're better off waiting here than being out there, trying to get to Jasper's?'

Walker exhaled, hearing her tone. 'Those guys are out there, looking for us.'

'Those guys in what, two or three cars?' she countered.

'They have reach.'

'Those cops didn't bat an eyelid.'

'That might have changed,' Walker said. 'And those guys back at your house were Feds, and they have all kinds of surveillance capabilities. They'll have dropped a net.'

'So what – we're not fugitives.'

He opened his eyes and looked across at her. 'You're complaining about being here and resting a few hours while they do their thing? Believe me, if they get you, you'll be babysat in a government building some place – no more home detention.'

'They can't force me to do that.'

'They can do what they want to. For your safety or whatever they want to call it.'

'The Patriot Act.'

'Something like that.'

'You sound paranoid delusional.'

Walker closed his eyes again and pinched the bridge of his nose, staving off a headache that had been threatening to knife him in the skull for hours.

'I wondered how long it'd take you to diagnose me.'

A minute of silence passed. Monica's attention turned to the newscasters, and then she spoke. 'I mean, *really*? The way these guys are talking about it – if this is all that they're going to do with my brother, stuff like this, then who cares, right? I mean, come on . . . we're the United States of Amnesia – this will be forgotten in days, if not hours. We all know that privacy is dead.'

Walker sighed and sat up. He went to the counter by the television and started the little one-cup coffee filter machine. He waited while it hissed and steamed and filled the styrofoam cup that he took and then sat on the end of his bed to watch the news.

33

They didn't show up on records other than being listed as a Special
Forces training outfit, loosely connected to Delta Force and the
Rangers. When stateside they formed a Red Team used in specialist
training operations, and when deployed they were a unit called upon
to do the Army's dirtiest jobs. They maintained among the highest
operational tempos of any unit in the DoD. They were fighters, good
at it – perhaps too good, given that each man was broken in some way.

War did that, Harrington reflected. It broke and fractured and
stressed until even the hardest of men reached a point of either no
more, or no return. Most chose the former. These guys had chosen
the latter.

These guys were ex-Delta, each busted out for psych and
disciplinary reasons. They were given a choice: you're out of the
Army, dishonourable discharge; with all the bad press that private
contractors have got over two wars, the legitimate end of the spectrum
won't touch you – you're nitroglycerin waiting to go off. But we can
help. We've spent millions training you, and we've already lost enough
of our best. We won't let you stay in your unit, but we've created a
solution: you can join D Squad. If you do that, you still get to ride
around in twenty-million-dollar Special Forces helicopters, you can
still call in air strikes and million-dollar-per-launch tomahawks from
billion-dollar submarines. You still get to play with all the best toys

that money can buy. But you do as we say, and if you stuff up just the slightest little bit – well, that's it. It's Leavenworth for life on charges not even thought up yet. If you don't go for it, you're on your own, to join some third-rate mercenary outfit in Africa. Your choice.

So far it had worked out pretty well. In the three years D Squad had been operating, the DoD arsenal had held on to twenty-four of the world's most highly skilled Special Forces operators. D Squad comprised four teams; each had six members. Two teams were currently on active duty in Afghanistan, the third was in Iraq hunting IS near the Syrian border, and team four was under his command. They had spent the last two months tasked to Cyber Command, testing the physical security of that division of the DoD.

Captain Harrington had been in the unit since its formation two years ago. Four of the five guys he trusted with his life; the sixth should be in prison, no question about it, but he recognised that the guy had proved useful on more than one occasion in the field. Harrington had been busted out of Delta after disobeying orders one too many times. A couple of his guys had been caught smuggling. Only one, to carrington's knowledge, had murdered unarmed Afghanis and staged the scene to look like they had been an armed threat. Mistakes happened, he got that, but this guy felt no remorse, and Harrington knew that there was more than they knew about – there had to be with a guy like that who'd spent five years at constant war.

These guys weren't cops. They were never tested for doping. There wasn't a guy on the team who wasn't a juicer. Each had biceps the size of footballs, could bench their body weight in sets of twenty. They seemed to never stop moving, and never stop eating. Power bars and shakes; their mess room was like genocide for chickens.

The sum of all this? Six of the most roiled-up, angry, trained and tooled-up operators in the world.

And they were hunting Monica. And now Walker.

Harrington had debriefed the plain-clothed LAPD officers who'd been on security at the house. The officers were sheepish, knowing that a basic phone hack had taken them off target. They assumed that the bad guys who were carrying out these cyber attacks had sent through the bogus Homeland Security alert to get them off station, but Harrington knew better. He'd organised that order to get the two cops out of the way before he and his men had gone in.

Who was this Walker guy, Harrington now wondered as he headed to the two Suburbans parked at the police headquarters. The file bleeped through, and Harrington speed read through the file on Jed Walker, including the notes on his activities in New York and St Louis.

Great. A goddamned vigilante was out there.

His phone rang. General Christie.

'Yes, ma'am?'

General Christie said, 'I got your message.'

'My message?'

'What you just requested. On Jed Walker.'

Harrington stopped himself from commenting. The General was monitoring his phone and email and his request for the file.

General Christie said, 'Walker is with Monica?'

'It appears so.'

'What's his involvement?'

'I'm not sure.'

'Because you lost them.'

'Not for long.'

'How will you find them?'

'You said we had any resources we needed.'

'That's true. Find Monica. Once you have her, call in and I'll have a safe location for you to get to.'

'And Walker?'

'Just find Monica, whatever it takes.'

The General ended the call.

Harrington gave a hand signal for his team to get rolling. His crew had gassed up the cars and had eaten and were ready to roll.

Caffeine tablets had been passed around. He suspected a couple of his crew may have taken something a little more aggressive in their quest to stay awake.

The driver of his Suburban, a good soldier named Kent, said, 'Where to?'

'South-east. Keep us rolling around there. We wait for an intel hit. They'll show up soon. The way this town is networked makes it a small place to hide.'

The driver took off and the other Suburban followed. Harrington turned up the radio to catch the news commentary. They were speculating about what could be driving the group holding Jasper Brokaw. But Harrington couldn't care less about motivations. He had his own mission to worry about.

•

In the motel room the news had been turned to a low whisper. The lights were off and the television gave out a glow.

Monica said, 'I'm too wired to sleep.'

'Give it time.' Walker was on his bed, on top of the bed sheets with the thin blanket over him. He could be asleep inside a minute, if she'd just leave him alone. He decided to give her another two minutes, then he was shutting her out. She could talk to his snoring.

'What is it you thought about me?' Monica said. 'Did you just reminisce? Or were you wondering about me, where I was and what I was doing, that sort of thing?'

Walker didn't respond. A minute forty-five to slumberland.

'I thought of you,' she said.

A minute thirty.

'Not often. And not for long. But the memory was there. It was a good time. A weekend. In summer. Over in four days but it felt like a lifetime, at the time. What do they call that? The summer . . . the summer of a dormouse?'

Forty seconds. To shut-eye. Not the summer of a dormouse.

'I waited, you know? That summer and nearly to the next. I thought once you finished at the Academy, that something might happen. With us.'

Twenty-five seconds.

'Then I knew I was being stupid, and then I had a career and it was busy and ten years passed and I kept asking my dad about you – where you were and what you were up to and he'd never really say but when I pressed him to at least find out if you were okay he'd do it for me and that'd keep me going for another few months.'

Monica fell silent.

Two minutes had passed.

Walker was awake. And it wasn't the coffee. He could sleep on caffeine as well as he could sleep on a Black Hawk going into a raid. The fact was, he'd thought about her, of course he had. But he'd had the on–off thing with Eve going on back then, the high-school sweetheart he married a few years after the Academy, before his first tour in Afghanistan. Had he thought about that Fourth of July weekend? Sure. On cold moments in the mountains with explosions tearing the quietude and bullets ripping the air and when the screams of men broke the night. It was one of his go-to memories when he needed to shut out the rigours of training against torture. When he had to replace in his mind's eye what he'd seen on operations that went bad. When he needed to smile. It formed part of his happy place, which all soldiers had.

'Yes,' Walker said, his voice quiet in the room. 'I remember that weekend. And I have thought about you. I'd heard from a service buddy that you'd married. And I guess that was it – the end of my thoughts about what could have been. As nice as it was, it was a summer fling, right? Between a couple of college students. Before we were married and lived lives and all that. Simple. Fun. Carefree.'

Monica was quiet. He heard her moving. The springs in her mattress as she shifted, trying to find a comfortable position, trying to find sleep.

•

Jasper couldn't sleep. He was too wired. Jittery. Wondering, about the world out there. He could hear the television in the other, larger room, and he imagined the armed men seated around it. He was on a military-style cot bed, a kind of plastic canvas material over a collapsible metal frame. Every time he moved it squeaked and creaked. He looked up at the ceiling and wondered what was next.

34

Finally, Walker heard her breathing settle into a rhythm that signified sleep. He closed his eyes. Some rest before the sunrise.

What Walker didn't hear was outside. In the shadows. Someone watching. Waiting. Not concerned about resting at all.

•

Twenty-five miles away Harrington and his crew were driving a slow loop around where Trapwire had registered a sighting of Walker and Monica.

'I'm calling it in,' Harrington said, looking at the screen shot of Monica in the Hemi Cuda.

'That wise, sir?' Kent asked. There was no formality between them. Harrington was their leader, and they respected that, but they operated as a team of equals.

Kent was a good man of a dirty bunch, busted out of the Army proper for much the same reasons as Harrington, although Kent had dropped a JSOC officer during a reprimand, breaking the guy's jaw. Harrington liked Kent.

'We need to find the car,' Harrington said. 'I'll give it to the LAPD and Feds. Get everyone looking for them.'

'They may have switched vehicles.'

'Would you dump that car?' Harrington showed the driver.

'Nope.'

'No. Me either. They're in the car, and they're headed some place or bedded down for the night. We find the car, find them, get the girl.'

'And this guy Walker?'

'If he gets in the way we drop him. But let's try and do this clean. Everyone copy that?'

Harrington waited for all five guys to reply in the affirmative.

'Right.' Harrington pressed send on an email to the tech department back at Cyber Command – the same crew who had hacked the LAPD officers earlier – to alert the LAPD to be on the lookout for the car; they were to watch but not approach the occupants. He then leaned back and looked out the window. LA may have been mostly asleep, but there were plenty of cars on the road: those headed home from parties and clubs, those with weird shift jobs, those simply passing through.

Harrington didn't really care. His mission for now was to find the sister. If it expanded beyond that – to find this group or take action against them – well, even then their motivation mattered little. His job was the sister. And he would succeed in his job.

35

Walker woke as dawn broke. The television was still on. Muted.

The news ticker read: *'The worst ever breach of US government data.'* And: *'Social media hack continues to reverberate.'*

Monica was asleep in her bed.

Walker put the subtitles on so he could read what the news heads were saying.

'The Office of Personnel Management claims the hackers accessed not only personnel files but security-clearance forms . . . Such forms contain information that foreign intelligence agencies could use to target espionage operations . . . Chinese officials have denied any involvement . . . The group that has Jasper Brokaw captive have remained silent . . . The Director of the FBI will address the President and National Security Council at eight am at the White House.'

He filled the tiny coffee maker and set two cups under the spout. By the time it had boiled and turned itself off, Walker had showered and dressed. The sound had roused Monica, and she sat up in her bed, having slept in her clothes, and turned up the TV volume.

Walker passed her a coffee and sat on the bed opposite.

When they switched over to the local NBC news, they saw that Monica was on it. She was the headline.

'The sister of captive NSA operative Jasper Brokaw is missing. Is she part of an extortion attempt to force him to work for them?'

'I should call someone,' Monica said. 'NBC, FBI, whoever. Anyone who will listen. Anyone who can help.' She stood up too quickly, her coffee spilling on the floor.

'No,' Walker said. 'This is okay. For now.'

'*What?*'

'Whoever has Jasper may now be wondering about you – about who has you, about where you are. It may, in some way, give your brother some leverage. An opportunity to do something.'

'Like what?'

'Maybe the group wants to know about you, and maybe they get him to hack a surveillance system to find where you are. And doing that, maybe he gets a chance to get a message out, to someone who can figure out his location.'

'That's a lot of maybes.'

'It's better than nothing.'

Monica looked at him sideways, then back at the television, taking in the news, flicking channels and seeing her face on half of the major networks and cable outlets.

'We should really call the police,' she said eventually.

'It's better we stay off the grid.'

'Listen!' Monica said, looking down at Walker. 'What the hell are you doing, anyway? Taking me to the world's seediest motel? How does that help Jasper? And exactly what do you propose we do now to find him? Go to his apartment with a magnifying glass and look for clues?' Walker stood, and she pushed his chest with both hands. 'How? How in the name of everything holy do you think *this* is helping?'

Walker waited a moment. The television was on Fox News. They were talking about scandalous revelations within emails leaked from West Wing staff. It was clear that some jobs would be lost that morning, and that lawsuits would be in motion. The Senate Majority Leader was being interviewed and was talking about impeachment for all kinds of perceived improprieties that were being combed through.

Monica froze as the news cut to a familiar scene.

Jasper Brokaw, in his orange jumpsuit.

•

Jasper was filmed with that day's *LA Times*, just as before. He was jittery and nervy, just as before. He was silent. The screen went black. Then the white lettering flashed up under his form – THIS IS YOUR SALVATION – and Walker thought briefly that he had left the subtitles on, but then he heard Jasper's voice.

'Guess we've got your attention,' Jasper said to the camera. 'And you're making noise, calling the President to turn off the Net. Good. Be loud. Forty million federal employees are now calling for the kill switch to be used. And that's in addition to those already shouting about their social-media blues. After the next cyber attack, sometime over the next six hours? That noise, it's going to be a cacophony. Of course, we don't have to get to that point, to move beyond what's already taken place. There's one person who can make this end. Does the President have what it takes? Time will tell . . .'

'More than the billion already affected?' Monica said. 'What could be louder—'

'An actual attack. An atrocity. A cyber-9/11.'

'They'll stop it.'

'How? How do you stop what you don't know is coming other than by pulling the plug?'

Monica stared at the screen as her brother continued.

'During his long tenure as FBI Director, J Edgar Hoover amassed a huge collection of information on American politicians, government employees, activists and anyone else he deemed important enough to probe. For decades Hoover wielded those dossiers to prolong his grip on power, impact public policy and distort American politics. That information remained tightly controlled, used only when Hoover thought it would benefit his agenda. When he died, his long-time personal secretary, Helen, destroyed most of those records before anyone else could get their hands on them.

'Now, do you really think that the government doesn't still store all your data? Of course they do. More than ever. They scoop it all up. And I'm going to prove it to you. And there'll be no Helen to stop me. In six hours, I'm giving the world access to all the stored data of US citizens and foreign nations that is currently being held at data centres across the country. And there's nothing they can do about it, because I've already accessed it.'

He paused.

'Think back to Hoover. Imagine what would have happened had Helen sent the files to Russia. That's pretty much the equivalent of the damage done by the OPM and social-media hacks. But forget Russia. Russia is insignificant. The information will be out there for whoever wants it. What's good for the goose . . . but I'm getting ahead of myself. The last hack exposed the "adjudication information" from security-clearance investigations – the raw, embarrassing intimate personal details of an untold number of government workers, including details of federal workers' sexual partners, their drug and alcohol abuse, their debts, gambling compulsions, marital troubles, criminal activity . . .'

Jasper dropped the newspaper to the floor. 'So, I ask you, the American people, to make more noise. Stop this, before it gets worse. And it *will* get worse. You have six hours.'

36

'What now?' Monica asked.

'You said there were guys in the military who have reason to harm Jasper.'

'Sure. But wouldn't the FBI already be onto that?'

'I'd like to think so. But we'll make sure it's flagged. I've got a colleague who works for them, on secondment to the UN. She'll find out.'

'Right. And what – we wait here in this crappy motel?' She waved her hand around the room. Walker felt she was being unfair. Sure, it wasn't a five-star resort, but it was clean and tidy and warm. Far better than the majority of places he'd spent outside base in Afghanistan and Iraq.

'We go to breakfast and you tell me everything about your brother that you can think of, starting with the old friend of his that you mentioned,' Walker said, opening the door and slipping on his jacket against the morning chill. The sky had that dirty silver hue of an overcast LA sunrise in March. Monica slipped past him.

He cranked the car door open and slid into the seat. As he fired it up, eight cylinders of American pride thrummed to life with a distinctive *whump-whump-whump*. It was an inherently unstable design, the typical crossplane V8, requiring all kinds of crankshaft stabilisers to keep things in harmony – but nothing beat the sound of these crossplane V8 engines with the unevenly spaced firing patterns within each cylinder bank, producing a distinctive burble in the exhaust note.

He drove them two miles north of the motel, taking it slowly, waiting until the oil and coolant warmed through. The big fat tyres banged on broken blacktop and thumped into potholes, but they were high profile and the suspension was soft and he felt like he could have done the drive at four times the speed and it would feel the same. The course he took had a couple of left and right turns, an ambling route, the kind used by people who were lost or those checking to make sure they didn't have a tail. He found a diner near the interstate on ramp, and he pulled in hard, flicking the Cuda's steering wheel and the handbrake to slide into a parking spot.

Walker checked his rear-view mirror, and then his side window and then the windscreen. He watched an old Crown Vic buzz by. It had been behind them the whole time, a few hundred yards back on the journey from the motel to here. The driver was a male in his fifties. He kept his eyes straight ahead, went through the next intersection, kept driving.

'What?' Monica said.

'Not sure. Maybe nothing.'

'We're eating here?' Monica said.

'We'll talk. I'll eat. You do what you like.'

Walker killed the engine, got out with the keys in his hand and waited at the diner's entrance, holding the door open for her. As Monica breezed by he watched her motions as she looked around at the early-morning clientele. Truckers and delivery men and people on the road, consuming fried food and drinking bottomless cups of drip coffee. There was a television above the counter, playing ESPN.

Walker sat in a booth and a waitress delivered menus and coffee. Monica sat opposite. She looked out the window, to the east.

'This will make you feel like you're back in your neighbourhood – they have a gluten-free option,' Walker said, looking over the menu. He looked up and Monica had cracked a small smile despite herself.

'I just can't see how I can help Jasper like this.'

'I don't know either,' Walker said. 'But you *can* help him, I believe that. We just need to know where to start.'

'The proverbial needle in a haystack.'

'Let's start again,' Walker said. 'At the beginning. Who would have any reason to abduct and use Jasper's expertise like this?'

She sighed, but played along. 'Any number of terrorists, foreign or domestic.'

'Sure. But what about what *you* know.'

'Personally?'

'Yes.'

Monica looked out the window, tension straightening her posture. Walker knew that thinking back about Jasper's past meant reliving her own memories. But it was necessary, it was the only way.

'Jasper had a friend, then the guy's family moved away.'

'Military?'

'Yeah. Why?'

'Just saying. They move around a lot.'

'Right. So, they connected again in college. Got really close, dormed together, did systems engineering at SOCAL in San Fran. Then they went their separate ways. Jasper never spoke about him. A year later, out of college, Jasper joined the Army, but not using his IT skills at all. It was weird.'

'And you think this friend might have a reason to hurt Jasper?'

'Reason, maybe, but he wouldn't. Paul wouldn't hurt a fly.' Monica nodded. 'I saw an email from him, on Jasper's tablet, last Christmas. It was open, on the bench, and it was just a "Hey, what's up?" kind of thing. So, they stayed in contact.'

Walker drank his coffee and allowed Monica time to tell the story.

'I Googled him. I wanted to know what had become of him – he'd been a constant around our house, years earlier. Then he disappeared completely. I wanted to know what he was doing, where he ended up. A curiosity.'

Monica looked out the window again. She was silent for a full minute, then said, 'It was his name, that drove me. The name in the email. The photo was him but it was the name that made me do the double-take and read it.'

She looked Walker in the eyes.

'He'd changed his name.'

37

'His name was Leroy Craven,' Monica said. 'That's what we'd known him as. Then years later he reappears and has a different name.'

'People change their name,' Walker said. 'Maybe he didn't like Leroy?'

'People change their name when they get a new identity because they've gone to prison,' Monica said flatly.

Walker leaned back as the waitress refilled his coffee, and he ordered scrambled eggs and bacon, and Monica ordered porridge.

'He did five-and-a-half years at Lompoc. That's a federal prison, minimum security. I searched news files and found nothing. *Nothing* was reported of him attending court or being sentenced. Don't you think that's strange?'

'Yes,' Walker said, interested. 'Federal crime, could be cyber related. Hacking?'

'I'm not sure.'

'Did you get a release date?'

'No,' Monica said. 'I know – I thought the same thing you are right now – was it something he and Jasper did at college? Hacking something and getting caught?'

'Did Jasper do that sort of thing?'

'I've no idea. But they were tight. He was always away at college. Then the Army. Then the obsession, when it came – but he was working for the NSA by then.'

'You didn't try using your security clearance to access Craven's prison records?'

Monica added milk to her coffee, stirred it with a plastic stick and sipped it, then shook her head.

'No,' she said. 'The days you could do that kind of thing are well and truly behind us, especially since 9/11 and with all the streamlining of databases that Homeland Security has implemented. My access would be recorded, along with every file in the system that I touched, every email and phone call that I'd make around it . . .'

'You'd lose your clearance,' Walker said.

'Yep,' she said. 'And as much as I want to know, it's not worth losing my job and reputation over.'

'Maybe now it is?' Walker said.

Monica sipped her coffee and smiled. Their food arrived. She added sugar to the porridge and stirred it.

'No,' she said. 'We don't need to do that. We can visit him. Craven. Or, should I say, Paul Conway, as he's now known.'

'You know where he is?'

Monica nodded. 'It's easy to find someone's address nowadays. Find out where they're registered to vote, what car and house they have in their possession, basic credit check, all kinds of info.'

'Is it far from here?' Walker said, eating a loaded fork full of eggs.

'Not far, though it may take a while, the way you drive that car,' Monica said, smiling.

Walker could see that the idea of potentially getting somewhere in the search to help her brother had brightened her mood. Progress.

'By the way,' she said, eating, 'I'm not some gluten-free-organic-flavoured-air-eating hipster.'

'Never for a second crossed my mind,' Walker said. 'You don't have the post-ironic beard to pull it off.'

•

General Christie opened the file on Josiah Walker.

Graduate of the Air Force Academy. Like all candidates he obtained a Bachelor of Science. Sub-majored in politics and history. Academically brilliant. His father had attended too. At the time of his enrolment he was nineteen, six-two and 200 pounds. On graduation he was six-three and 245 pounds. Played quarterback for the Falcons, which wasn't that much below a starting position in a low-ranked NFL team. He could have had a career in the pro league, was approached by scouts after the finals, but instead he went into the 24th Tactical and deployed to Afghanistan, the first of three tours, along with two in Iraq. If he'd stuck around, Walker could have been closing in on the rank of Brigadier General; he had the pedigree and aptitude to end up with a long and easy career, but instead he chose the most dangerous job in the Air Force, then bugged out when he was promoted to desk staff. Then he joined the CIA.

PT results were outstanding. Middle-distance awards, but not much of a fast runner. Strong swimmer. Mesomorphic body type that responded quickly to stimulants, hence the bulk gained and prowess on the football field.

Walker was proficient with all small arms, expert on the pistol. Lethal in hand-to-hand combat.

The 24th Tactical. An Air Commando, and then some. Walker trained with SEALs and Delta. He had worked with them and the CIA, and everyone else.

Postings in Germany, Japan, Korea. Wounded three times, with three Purple Hearts. Silver Star. Air Force Cross.

Retired a Lieutenant Colonel when he was being sent away from front-line duties and into training.

At least, that's what it looked like, on the surface.

But then Christie read the Agency's human resources file of Walker's acceptance. He had undertaken similar aptitude tests to those from the AFA, plus a raft of others, Agency specific.

The psychologist had made copious notes. Walker passed and was accepted, obviously, but there were notes, detailed ones, seven pages worth. War had changed Walker, was the summary. It was usual for a person's responses to change over ten years – maturity, life lived. But this was beyond that.

Walker had become obsessive, a trait he hadn't shown before.

Obsessed with justice, with seeing a task done right, with getting the job done no matter what the personal cost. Most people want to think that they can fix wrongs. Walker knew that he could.

Hence, the final recommendation was that Walker be considered as an officer in the Agent Provocateur area. An AP.

A rare – exceedingly rare – position in the modern CIA. Not just a case officer recruiting agents and running a network. His role was to seek out the nation's opponents and then destabilise, degrade and destroy.

He joined the CIA's National Clandestine Service. That file was a separate one, and Christie would read it next. She went through the last notes, the citations for the awards. The citations for the Air Force Cross were redacted, which meant it involved secrets. Probably working with the Agency . . .

Christie crosschecked that file, which included the times during Walker's ten-year Air Force career that he had worked alongside CIA officers in Afghanistan and Iraq.

Jed Walker. Ten years in the Air Force, eight in the CIA and a brief twelve-month stint in the State Department before going off the grid until the New York Stock Exchange incident. The Vice President was a close ally and friend.

So, what's he doing with Monica Brokaw?

General Christie picked up the phone and called Langley. Maybe the CIA still had a leash on this guy . . .

38

Harrington had managed a total of two hours' shut-eye. Would he call it sleep? No. He liked his sleep. He did that when he wasn't on the job. His whole crew had napped, at some point, in shifts, a half-hour here, an hour there. Now the sun was up and they were all awake and caffeinated and edgy.

Twice they'd responded to sightings. Twice it was a partial match that hadn't paid out.

He and his crew were at two locations, thirty miles apart, north and south Los Angeles.

'Change of plans,' he said to Kent. 'Head back to the airfield. We'll take to the helo. The others can keep looping around the south in their car.'

The driver nodded, pulled a U-turn across four lanes and planted his foot, happy to have somewhere definitive to go rather than driving around in huge circles.

'We haven't had a decent hit,' the guy in the back said. 'How is that even possible, in a city like LA, with cameras on people's dashboards and on security feeds at every gas station and bar, every hotel foyer – every person and their smartphone clicking away and posting shit online.'

'They slept somewhere,' Harrington said. 'Maybe even in their car. But they'll be moving, if not now then soon. They'll turn up.'

•

Jasper's old friend Paul Conway lived in Palm Springs, and they were headed there because they were already east of the city and it was closer to them than Jasper's apartment, which wasn't going anywhere. The day was turning out to be windy and bright. Walker unwound the Cuda's engine on the freeway. It felt good, and it sounded good. On the highway ramp his foot pressed the accelerator hard to the floor, all that power through the back tyres, threatening to fishtail on the way down. The force of the big engine pressed them back hard into the vinyl seats like they were leaving LA on board a fighter plane. Walker loved it.

On the flat open road he eased into a cruise, sitting on eighty-five. Again going fast enough to get booked, but not arrested. He checked the gauges and dials: all normal. He cleaned the windscreen with the washers. Shifted in his seat. Adjusted his sunglasses against the sunlight dead ahead.

He kept the Cuda nudging three figures all the way east. Monica was enjoying the ride.

The landscape became that of America from so many westerns he'd seen as a kid, the ones that didn't have the budget to go farther east than LA. The sound was nostalgic too. The soundtrack of America: the engine and rubber on the highway, slinging them cross-country. A blonde in the passenger seat. Someone to save, and people hunting them. The Colt .45 in the door pocket. A modern American take on the western, and little had changed. Death and adventure and the unknown swirling around them.

An hour into daylight and the day was turning out to be a bright one, the sun blazing in the east. The clouds had dispersed into long wisps that looked like the ripples of sand under waves on a beach. Nacreous cloud formations, Walker recalled from his Air Force days. He'd called in Close Air Support in clear skies and black skies. The weather didn't much bother the US Air Force. In fact, inclement weather was a friend of Special Forces units: there was nothing like a black night of sleet in which to hunt, bringing all their training and skills and specialised optical kit to bear upon an enemy. He'd seen A10s light up the mountains with depleted uranium rounds. He'd directed a Lockheed AC-130 Spooky to level a ridge-line humming with Taliban activity, the gatling gun spewing out 3600 rounds per minute of 25-millimetre shells, doing in a couple of minutes what his squad of sharpshooters on the ground had not achieved all day. He'd felt a MOAB, the Mother Of All Bombs, from twenty miles away, detonating in the mountains to collapse cave systems. Any closer and he would have lost his hearing, closer still and limbs would drop off from the shockwave.

Glory days.

'What are you thinking about?' Monica asked.

Walker looked across at her. She'd been watching him reminisce.

'You were far off, had the beginnings of a smile,' she said. 'You should smile more.'

'I'll smile when we're the other side of this deadline with your brother in safety and the Internet still on.'

'Avoiding my question and comment much?'

'Okay. I was thinking of Afghanistan.'

'Okay, sure, that makes sense, seems a cheerful place,' Monica said.

'There's good memories among the bad,' he said.

Monica said something under her breath, then, louder: 'You're typical of an operator who's done what you've done. Guys like you, those not burned out. To be doing what you're doing, out of choice. Addicted to it.'

Walker was silent.

'Then again, maybe it's not a choice,' Monica said. 'Those like you, plenty of them, can't let go.'

'You sound like my ex-wife,' Walker said.

'Smart lady, by the sounds of things.'

'She is. How about your guy? Smart?'

'Yeah, he was smart. Successful. Charming. I got pregnant. We had a girl. Sally.' Monica looked out her window. 'It worked for a while, and then it didn't. None of it was planned, but it's worked out now. Better, maybe. Sally goes to an international school, comes here each holiday. And we all get along.'

'Who is he?'

'A guy.'

'I thought as much. What does he do besides big business?'

'Why that question?'

'I'm wondering.'

'Wondering? Why wonder? What's my marriage got to do with anything? What – because you've already mined every part of my job history, this is all that's left to know?'

'I'm just trying to better understand you. Your motivations. Goals. Ambitions. Needs. Fears. Desires.'

'Because you're Oprah now?'

'You're the shrink,' Walker said, glancing at her. 'Why do you think?'

'Because you're suspicious.'

'That's my general disposition. It's served me well.'

'No, it's not your general disposition,' she replied. 'It was trained into you. Honed over a lifetime of work. And your work became your life.'

'The American dream in action.'

'Why do you say that?'

'Work hard, get lost in your work, you become your work, and you forget all the other stuff that's important in life, then you grow old, alone, and die.'

'Maybe you should have a talk show.'

'I'm just saying.'

'It's training. Like you train a dog. You were just smart and obedient. And you know what? You're a product. The end result. Air Force. CIA. State Department. Whatever. You're it. Probably about the best we've produced. In certain ways. In the ways we needed.

You're a tool of the state. Sharp when you need to be, blunt when required, brutal and calculated at a whim.'

'Now you're flattering me.'

'No, it's not flattery, Walker.' Monica looked out her window and stared at the landscape. 'It's sad, really. What we made you. What you became in every level of your life – because that's what it does. It's not a switch, it's not on or off. It's what they train you to become. And you can't ever let it go, because you were too adept at it. That's sad. For you, and for anyone who will ever care for you.'

'Don't be too beat up about it,' Walker said. 'That's a short list.'

'I'm serious.'

'Because people can't change, right?'

'No. People change all the time. In tiny ways. Adaptation. Learning. Evolving. You choose not to.'

'I didn't choose this. The here and now.'

'Of course you did. Come on. You're no longer CIA. You're no longer anything, really, and that's what makes this sad. You're a stateless tool of the state. Roaming around, still trying to find a purpose, something that you can fix. A knight errant of the old world, looking around for problems to solve.'

'Sounds like you may be talking about yourself.'

'You were interrogating me just before, about my life, my husband. That's not conversation. See? You can't switch it off. You'll never let it go.'

'And what's this you're doing now?'

'Conversing.'

Walker glanced out his side window, said, 'Hard to imagine why you're single.'

'It's not hard to imagine why you are.' Monica nodded, looking straight ahead, her mind and mouth racing. 'Let's see. Divorced. Took her a while, she had hope – delusional – but hope, that you'd change. But she'd had enough. She realised that you can't walk away. It's a family thing, isn't it? Ingrained. It's all you know, from your father. You've grown up with it. It's not all you know now but it's an imprinted behaviour that stuck and came easily and you followed it to the nth degree, drinking every last drop of the Kool Aid that the government was dishing out. It's habitual, addictive, and you "chose" not to let go. You chose this life over a life with her.'

Walker was silent again.

Monica looked at him and said, 'What was her name?'

Walker didn't reply.

Monica started to speak and then stopped herself.

They drove in silence for five minutes. Just the sound of the engine and the tyres on the road.

Then, Monica said, 'Look – I'm sorry, okay? Not for you, not for who you are. For what I said.'

39

The big block V8 engine was a beautiful thing, one of the great contributions to the world from the United States. But it was thirsty. Walker had pulled into a gas station and was filling up a third time in twenty-four hours. He tried to work out the mileage but gave up. It wasn't bad on the highway, but around the city it was like he could watch the gauge going down with every minute that passed.

Monica had gone to the restroom. It was the type of non-chain gas station that had a decent diner that catered to truckers and road users who didn't have company cards. And, Walker figured, less of a chance of being plugged into a network of cameras available to the prying eyes of the NSA.

'Still filling up?' Monica said. She'd brought them both coffee in styrofoam cups.

'Emptying a shale oil deposit all on my own.'

'They really should build that pipeline.'

'Or this car should just be driven around on Sundays.'

'It's a nice ride,' Monica said, leaning on the front fender. 'Yours?'

'What, you think I stole it?'

'It does look like something from *Grand Theft Auto*.'

'Well, look out hookers and pedestrians,' Walker said. The pump handle tapped out and he holstered it. He pulled out a wad of bills.

'You didn't pre-pay?'

'They'll track it,' Walker said, flicking through the cash and pausing as he saw Monica deliberating in some kind of internal reprimand. 'You paid with a card?'

She nodded, then cringed. 'It's all I had on me when I left the house,' she said. 'I'm sorry.'

'Then we have to get moving,' Walker said, heading into the gas station, where he paid for the fuel and a couple of trucker caps and a pair of sunglasses for Monica. Outside, she was in the car. She'd tossed her coffee, her distaste not at the drink but at her actions. His was on the roof of the Cuda. He took it, slung himself inside the car and started it up, checking his mirrors as he did up his belt.

Then he stopped. The silver Crown Vic with the middle-aged driver was on the shoulder of the freeway just before the gas station, doing its best to be hidden behind a road sign.

'Hang on,' Walker said. He drove out of the station and planted his foot entering the highway. The Crown Vic made a show of keeping up.

'What is it?'

'We've got company,' Walker said, checking his rear-view mirror. Monica looked over her shoulder.

'The guys from my house?'

'No.'

'Who?'

'I don't know, but I saw him near our motel. Maybe he was out there all night, watching us – there was a Crown Vic in the lot.'

'Really?' Monica watched out the back window.

Walker eased off the accelerator and sat on sixty-five. Better to see what this was about, than lose the chance. The Crown Vic wasn't government. It was ten years old and dinged up. The driver wasn't schooled in making a tail that would go undetected, or maybe he had been once but now didn't have the energy or inclination to do it right. And he was alone. So, whoever it was, he didn't fit into this scenario with Jasper Brokaw. At least, not from the outset.

Walker signalled to turn off at the next town.

40

The next town was Beaumont. The decade-old silver Crown Vic was two vehicles behind. Walker eased through the main street. This was the kind of town that didn't do or make anything, likely never did. A weigh station of old, built up slowly to cater for a community, a single option for everything. One gun shop. One grocer. One bar. One gas station. Sprung up to serve locals, and those on the road. The same shops and stores as thousands of other towns just like it dotted across the United States. Half the places boarded up. The courthouse. The lawyer's office. The video store. Maybe vibrant, once, for what it was, then the highway skipped around it and the through-traffic stopped and with it went all those who made their living from transient customers. And as each service provider became redundant, there was neither the life nor the inclination to adapt. Hence the shuttered buildings, the shutters mainly plywood boards that had been there a decade or more, buckled and bent and distorted by the elements and time.

Progress.

'He's still back there,' Monica said.

Walker nodded. He knew exactly where the car was, and what he'd do about it. He took the next right-hand turn, a side road with a hamburger joint and barber shop and ten empty places, and then pulled into an alley and told Monica to get out of the car.

•

Harrington returned to the airfield just as the message came through: a hit on Monica's credit card at a gas station.

Outside Beaumont, eighty miles east of them. No security cameras but he knew that the tech team back at Fort Meade would now be bringing to bear anything that they could to get a sighting – traffic cameras on the highway and all offshoots would have analysts poring over them to double-check any likely hits on the car.

'Wheels up,' Harrington said. 'And get the others rolling.'

41

Walker was on foot. He tucked his cap down over his eyes, and was wearing just his T-shirt and jeans and boots. He headed back up the dead-end alley, and around the block. He'd left the Colt in the car. It would be overkill to bring it. From what he'd seen of the guy, glances at a distance, he was around fifty and heavy-set, the kind of jowls that suggested a long-time desk man. Sure, he might well have a firearm, but Walker would not give him the time or room to use it. He crossed the street.

Monica was in the burger joint; trucker cap and sunglasses on, in a booth, out of sight.

Walker watched the road from a seat on the stoop of a double-storey townhouse. The Crown Vic did a slow pass. The driver clocked the Cuda parked down the lane and pulled over to park halfway down the street. He stayed in his car, the quick flick of the reverse lights signalling that the transmission had gone into park. He watched the laneway from his mirrors, waiting.

Walker gave him a few minutes to settle. The engine was running, vapour trickling out the exhaust. The guy hadn't got out of the car for at least a couple of hours, from outside the motel to the diner to where Walker had seen him near the gas station to here. He would be well formed into that seat, probably with the aircon set to a comfortable temperature: high sixties or so, for a guy of such girth.

He wore glasses, large and silver- or gold-rimmed. He squinted against the sun hitting his windscreen. No seatbelt.

Walker used that sun. The street ran east–west, and he skirted around the block and approached from the east, the guy facing him but his eyes on his mirrors, looking behind. Walker put his sunglasses on. No shirt or jacket. A different silhouette from how he'd appeared earlier this morning. The last few paces came quickly.

The driver didn't know what hit him. Literally. By the time he did, it was far too late.

Walker gripped the metal NASA key ring of the Cuda in his left fist and smashed the driver's window out with one sharp blow that made a cracking, popping sound as the safety glass shattered into a million pieces. The guy reeled to his side, away from the onslaught, hands up to protect his face. Walker opened the door and dragged him out and up to the stoop, sticking to the shadows. A truck rumbled by. The man in his grasp was five-nine and 190 pounds and Walker had him pinned up against the door of the stoop, a hand at his throat and the other patting him down. He came up with a snub-nosed .38 from a leather holster under the guy's jacket.

'Talk,' Walker said, the pistol up under the man's chin. 'Now or never. Who are you and what are you doing?'

42

'We changed our minds,' Jasper Brokaw said. 'You've seen what we've just done. The federal attack will be later. This one . . . it was just there, and we couldn't say no to it. With all that you'd been saying on the news, about us, about the threatened attack – you're all so smug, but not any more, right? What better way to get the population onside than to air all of their dirty little secrets, *right*?'

The camera closed in slightly to Jasper. His bruised cheek was angry now, his eye above the bruise swelling and weeping.

'Failure to act will have significant ramifications,' Jasper read from a piece of paper. It seemed as though his hands had trembled, briefly. 'Starting small. Every person's Internet search history is now available to be read online. Their social-media accounts are all open, readable to all.'

Jasper gave a URL address.

'Moreover,' he said, 'all Dark Web addresses, and all intercepted and stored correspondence stored at the Bluffdale complex in Utah are also available for all and sundry to read online.'

He looked at the camera. 'That's it. Our third cyber attack is . . . think of it as a warning shot. Your time is running out, Mr President, to shut down the Net. Failure will result in action being taken. You've seen what we can do to breach security and publicly release data.

By the next attack, you will know that no network is safe, no matter what you try to do. Turning off individual servers will only force our hand to something else.'

The screen went black.

43

'I can't,' he said. South-western accent. The other side of fifty. Looked like an old cop, or any number of ex-NCOs Walker had bumped into since leaving the military. A man who knew what to do in a tight spot. No-nonsense. But he was drawn and tired. Not just from being stuck in his car since at least Monica's house last night and then the motel and then the drive here; he was like someone who had not given up on life and living but had come close a few times. Too much greasy, salty food and too many cases of beer. No exercise and no compulsion to do much of anything but a dead-beat job.

Walker pulled back the hammer on the pistol. It was an old thing, well used and well maintained. The wooden stock was worn to a smooth shine. Walker could see semi-wadcutters loaded in there. A useful weapon, up close. At the base of the chin it would be devastating, equivalent to a small explosive boring up through bone and tissue and detonating inside the brain pan and exploding out the back of the skull.

'I can't, I really can't,' he repeated. 'Please – I'll go away. Give me a chance. Please. You won't see me again.'

Walker turned the guy about and pushed him along the footpath to the alley, the snub-nosed revolver dug hard into his back. He halted them a few paces before the parked car.

'Silence here isn't an option,' Walker said. 'But I will let you go, unharmed, if you tell me who you are and what you're doing following Monica Brokaw.'

The man looked up and down the alley; Walker could almost see the wheels spinning in his mind, trying for options but finding none. No chance to run. Can't outrun bullets.

Instead he said, 'How do you know I'm not following you?'

'If you were following me you'd have to be one of the greatest trailers on the planet, and I'm not feeling that,' Walker said.

'Oh.'

'I saw you from the motel. But you must have seen us sooner, which means you were at Monica's house.' Walker looked him up and down. 'There's no way you're involved with the crew who entered her house. And they'll be headed here now with their machine guns and the stun grenades, because they've made Monica, back at the gas station. So, either I tie you to the welcome sign coming into town and let them cavity search you until you talk, or you talk to me. What's it going to be?'

Monica was walking down the laneway towards them.

'You wanna talk now?' Walker said.

'I really can't. I shouldn't—' The guy looked up and saw Monica approach. 'Oh . . .'

44

'Doug Granger,' Walker said, passing the guy back his wallet. The ID was a Private Detective licence issued by the state of California. He was seated on the front fender of the Cuda, his pistol still in Walker's hand. Granger had just given a four-word answer to explain why he'd been trailing Monica. 'Your ex hired me.'

Monica said, 'It can't be true.'

'Believe me, Monica, I've heard that before. But it's the truth. Don't feel bad about it. Happens every day, and then some.'

'My ex?' Monica was shaking her head. 'He'd never do that. I mean – why? We get along. He's more than fine with the custody arrangement we have – I should be the one casing him, so why? Why would he?'

'Not mine to ask why.'

Monica took a few paces away, headed up the lane towards the street.

'How long?' Walker asked him.

'Two months,' Granger said.

'Two *months*?' Monica turned back, looking suddenly ill. She paced the alley next to the car.

Walker said to him, 'So, you do this a lot?'

'Yep.'

'Plenty of spousal stuff.'

'Yep.'

'What's her ex like? Compared to others?'

'No idea,' Granger said. He got up, pocketed his wallet, looked at the snub-nosed .38 in Walker's hand. 'I've never met him.'

'Do you do that often, with clients?' Monica said. She looked from him to Walker. 'This could be bullshit. It could be someone posing as him.'

'Don't meet clients often,' Granger said. 'Sure, if they live outta state. It's not ideal, but a job's a job, and he was paying me for 24/7 surveillance, and that's not cheap. Not for two months. I had to outsource.'

Walker said, 'You're sure it was her husband who hired you?'

'Of course.' Granger looked offended at the prospect. 'He was only interested to see if there was infidelity. A custody thing, he said. I saw all his ID, the marriage and divorce papers, spoke on the phone a few times to hammer out the details.'

'Name?'

'I can't—'

Walker spun the .38 around. He wouldn't shoot the guy, but he'd happily knock a few answers out of him.

'Dan Kong.'

Walker said, 'Monica?'

Monica looked away.

'Chinese national,' Granger said. 'Based in Shanghai. Hence no face-to-face meeting. That's it. A simple job. My bread and butter.'

'Right.' Walker looked at Monica, who was pacing at the end of the lane, looking at the ground and thinking hard.

'Look,' Granger said, 'I've got photos of you two leaving the motel this morning. But I gotta say, this isn't a relationship, is it? I'm not reading it. And you've showed no signs of being in any kind of relationship at any point – no offence.'

Walker said, 'You used to be a cop?'

'Oklahoma City, twenty-six years.'

'You were outside Monica's house last night?' Walker asked.

Granger nodded. 'I saw you arrive. I was parked down on the same road you were on.'

'Yet you saw me enter?'

'Via a camera in the bush across the road. Close-area transmitter. Then I saw those guys roll up – then the camera went dead. I was about to get out of my car and proceed around to eyeball the situation when I saw you roll past me, in your car, down the hill – and I followed.'

Monica said, 'Do you have any idea who those guys were?'

'Nope. Feds of some sort.'

'Why do you say that?' she asked.

'I mean, gotta be, with tech like that?' Granger shook his head. 'I mean, they had the means to shut down everything on the block – even my battery-powered surveillance package – *battery powered*, so it's not like they cut the grid. Who could do that? What could do that?'

'An EMP,' Walker said.

'What – like a nuke?'

'There are other ways to generate an electro-magnetic pulse and deploy it. This one was on a drone.'

'Damn. A drone aeroplane? Damn.' He looked hesitant. Looked at the .38 in Walker's hand. 'This is about you, isn't it?'

'No.'

'Her?'

'Her brother.' Walker watched Granger's face for any sign of recognition, any little tell. There was nothing. Maybe he hadn't seen the news, but it was unlikely. Maybe he hadn't heard the name Jasper Brokaw and put two and two together, but it was unlikely.

'Look, mister, whatever this is – wait . . .'

Then Walker saw him make the connection. Of the two names, one he was being paid to tail, and one that had been mentioned repeatedly on the news.

'Oh shit,' Granger said. 'Shit. Your brother? That NSA guy that's captured? Oh . . .' He looked at Walker. 'Oh. You're a Fed? Am I in trouble? Is this about – is this related to the Chinese? Oh shit . . .'

Walker looked to Monica. She was shaking her head and went back to pacing about.

'I'll drop the client, okay?' Granger said. 'Just leave me out of it. I'll walk away, right now. Just give me a chance to walk away, with my licence and reputation. That's it. I'll hand over all surveillance, all correspondence, everything.'

'You'll stop following us,' Walker said, unloading the .38 and putting the six semi-wadcutters in his pocket. He knew from the pat-down that Granger didn't have reloads; this old ex-cop wasn't in the business of drawing his gun, let alone getting involved in shoot-outs. Walker passed the .38 over. 'And you'll do something for me.'

Granger holstered the gun and moved off the fender.

'Anything.'

45

'Yes?' Special Agent Fiona Somerville said. The number of the incoming call on her cell phone was blocked. 'Sorry, *who* is this?'

Doug Granger repeated his name, and explained that he was representing a friend who could not be named over the phone but had once given Somerville a ride on a motorbike through the mid levels of Hong Kong.

'Oh, right, I know who you're talking about,' Somerville said. 'And?'

'He says you need to make sure the FBI looks into an Army case that Jasper Brokaw worked. And to look into Dan Kong. I've just sent you a link to a wireless hard-drive, and the password, and you can read up on who he is.'

'Okay.' Somerville stood next to Zoe and opened the link that had been sent through.

'The Army case,' Granger said. 'He wants you guys to look into Jasper's old Army service, the early case he did liaising with the 110th MPs.'

'The 110th?'

'That's what your friend told me.'

'Is that friend of mine still there?'

'He told me I can't answer that.'

'Right. He seemed okay?'

191

'I don't know what he's normally like,' Granger said, 'but he seemed like he could stop a freight train with his bare hands, if he had to.'

'What's your connection with this?'

'Nothing. I don't want any trouble.'

'We've just accessed the file. You've been looking into . . . Dan Kong's ex-wife.'

'Yes, ma'am. Like I said, I don't want any trouble here. Not with the government or anyone else.'

'Right. Is that all?'

'That's all he told me to tell you, ma'am.'

'That's it?'

'That's it.'

'You're sure this friend of mine is okay?'

'Ma'am, it'd take an atomic bomb to do that guy much harm. Goodbye.'

The call ended and Somerville smiled. Walker was okay, and she had work to do that would help him – and this situation – out. She tapped a text message to McCorkell stating that things were progressing, and sat down next to Zoe.

'I'll work on the FBI, see where they're at,' Somerville said.

'We just got a tap on that call's location,' Zoe said. 'Beaumont.'

'Where's Beaumont?' Somerville said.

By way of answering, Zoe zoomed out on the map. 'Near Palm Springs, about thirty miles west.'

Somerville said, 'What's near there, I wonder . . .'

'Maybe Walker made the guy travel away from LA to make that call?'

'No. I think that the caller stayed there, and that Walker has moved on. I think someone's closing in on Walker, and he knows that, so he's leaving breadcrumbs and obstacles to tie them up a little.'

'Who would be after him?'

'We need to find out.'

•

Walker gave the PI back his .38 rounds and nothing more was said between them as the older man headed away from the laneway, his mood and demeanour higher now that Walker had given him another job; clearly he was energised to be involved in something beyond following an ex-spouse around.

Monica remained silent, sitting in the passenger seat, as Walker started up the Cuda and feathered the gas, dropping into gear and taking a right onto the side street before looping back around the block to the main street in the direction of the interstate: east, towards Palm Springs.

The entire altercation with Granger had lasted fifteen minutes. Walker figured that if that team were back in LA, and they made Monica's credit-card purchase just over twenty minutes ago and were mobile, on the road, to the east of LA, then he and Monica had maybe a half-hour window. He pushed the gas pedal down.

'You want to talk about it?' Walker said as they merged onto the highway. The time for being cautious was disappearing and he shot the engine up to a hundred miles per hour in seconds.

'Not really.'

Walker let it be. For now. But he wondered. Custody was no big deal and seemingly not relevant. But something else had occurred to him in the conversation with Granger. Monica's husband, being a foreign national, raised some interesting questions about her clearance level.

Any employee of the US government, or holder of a classified and above security clearance, who came into contact with a foreign national from any country had to report it. If you travelled overseas you were quarantined from that clearance-level work for six weeks, relegated to general duties where you didn't touch anything sensitive should you be compromised.

How had that worked out with regards to their marriage? Did he travel back and forth to China during their marriage? Did she? Did she come into regular contact with his Chinese friends and associates? If she did, then her clearance was virtually null and void, because she wouldn't be able to access or use it for extended periods, while security analysts pored through all her calls and emails and looked into the background of each and every individual she met.

This wasn't necessarily a problem, but there were some questions that could have answers relevant to this situation. What did her ex-husband do for work? Whom did he work for? What was his relationship like with Jasper? Did he know who Jasper's employer was? When did they marry and when did it end – and at what stage in the relationship did he know that she had such high security clearance? Why did the marriage end? All these questions would come to the culmination of: Could your ex-husband have targeted you for a relationship to get to either your clearance or to Jasper?

But Walker let it be, for now. He gave the car a spurt of gas and overtook an eighteen-wheeler. The engine sounded good on the freeway when wound out. Heading east. Fast. Half an hour to go. They would meet this friend of Jasper's and see what he had to say. It seemed the hotter lead; whatever the guy may currently feel about Jasper, he'd have some background and he'd be a resource for the tech side of things. He might even have some good ideas about what might be coming. Maybe even how to track Jasper through the broadcasts.

Walker looked at his watch. The hours were counting down to the next attack.

46

That text message from Somerville to McCorkell went over the cellphone network via local towers.

There was nothing they could do about being clandestine. Somerville was being watched by the NSA, and they had her phones and emails monitored by computers and presided over 24/7 by a flesh-and-blood agent. That tech agent tracked the last call to her phone to the town of Beaumont.

He passed that intel along the chain.

It pinged in the control room in Fort Meade, from where copies were sent out to the NSA and the military's Cyber Command. The two-person team handling the tracking of Monica Brokaw and Jed Walker brought up the map of the pay phone's location and then tapped into Trapwire.

Footage from all the cameras and photographs taken in the town were downloaded. There wasn't much. The facial-recognition software took two minutes to scroll through several terabytes of data and come up with a match on Monica's face crossing a road. Then it found her again, a side profile, in the passenger seat of a car, the picture taken from the dash cam of a courier vehicle.

Harrington in the helo, lifted off, the nose tucked down as the Black Hawk raced east.

His starlight communications bleeped. He checked the message. The car was a black Hemi Cuda. It was headed east.

•

When Walker entered the outskirts of Palm Springs he realised that he didn't know where he was going and he slowed and said, 'You know Paul's address, right?'

'Well . . .'

Walker looked across at Monica.

She gave a shrug.

Walker pulled over at the first non-chain diner he saw and killed the engine, which was steaming from the quick sling along the highway into town. The car park was near-empty, but inside seemed a decent trade. The locals from the neighbouring businesses, in getting breakfast. He looked back at the road. He knew that those Feds would not be far away now. He hadn't noticed any fixed cameras on the highway into town. But time was running out. They needed to keep moving. The engine pinged and hissed with the heat of exhaustion.

'What do we do?' Monica asked.

'How'd you get his address before?'

'I Googled it. Crept around online for a while until I found it.'

'How long?'

'What?'

'How long was that while?'

'Several hours, over a few days until I found it.'

'Great. We don't have that time. We have several minutes.'

'It wasn't easy the first time, but it should be now.'

'Because you didn't know his new name before?'

'I knew it, I'd seen it on that email on Jasper's tablet. But I was starting from scratch – there's a couple thousand, maybe more, Paul Conways in the United States.'

'But only one in Palm Springs.'

'Yeah.'

'Okay,' Walker said, getting out the car, then talking to Monica over the roof as she got out. 'I'll order coffee, you do your best to charm some guy to use his cell phone to Google Paul. Fast as you can.'

'In there?'

'In there. You really don't like diners?'

'It's just . . .'

'What?' Walker asked, locking the car.

'Nothing,' Monica said.

'Tell me,' Walker said, walking in step next to her, headed for the entry.

'We could go to the local police,' Monica said. 'Talk to them, tell them what we're doing. They could help us.'

'They'd look you up and see an alert in the system and detain us until those armed guys in black arrive.'

'You think?'

'I know.'

'Okay.'

Walker opened the diner door and was steered by a waitress to a booth. He watched as Monica found her mark: a bald guy in a suit with a nervous energy about him. She leaned over the table, her hands on the laminate top, her head tilted slightly, her mouth moving slowly as she spoke.

The guy nodded, and passed his phone to her. She sat down opposite, and started to tap away.

Walker's coffee arrived. It came with a doughnut on the house. He cracked open the California road-map book and studied the roads of Palm Springs. Five minutes and a coffee refill passed. Monica was still on the phone, sitting across from the bald guy, who kept looking up from his laptop to steal glimpses of her. Walker looked out the window. The sky was clear, just some wispy clouds at the edges of the valley, fingers of vapour pouring over the mountains, towards them. The grip of inevitability.

'Got it,' Monica said, drinking her lukewarm coffee that had been sitting there for nearly ten minutes. She brandished a note on a napkin: Paul's address. 'Not ten minutes from here.'

•

What Monica didn't know, and what Walker didn't know, and what most would be surprised at, is that any camera on any personal digital device can be turned on remotely by those in the know and capture pictures and video. If the device has a microphone, it can grab sound too.

The cell phone that Monica had held was a popular model smartphone, designed in America and largely manufactured in China. It had enough computing power to word process documents and render images and play movies and games. Its microphone was good for conference calls, either in the car or lying on a table between a group of people. There were two built-in cameras, pointing front and back, and the one pointing to the front, to the person looking at the screen, was rated at three megapixels.

The NSA called the program Brighteyes. An evolution of the Trapwire system, which covered all fixed cameras as well as the footage on people's social-media accounts. With Brighteyes, they could turn on any camera or microphone on any phone, even if it was off. And the beauty of the program was that it would search for a facial recognition of all in its field of view.

The NSA tech had the phone's image of Monica locked and confirmed within five seconds of her picking up the phone. Her location was tagged, and all the details of that phone's owner were now being worked over by the analysts at Cyber Command. State troopers were already moving to begin surveillance of his work and his home in Anaheim. His phone would be tracked until an agent declared it no longer necessary. He would be questioned until it was proven beyond reasonable doubt that he was not involved in impeding a federal investigation.

The microphone was on and recorded whatever it could pick up, and that was sent as a digital file to the analysts, along with all of the keystroke data and details of what Monica was doing in the phone's Internet browser.

The Cyber Command heavy hitters in the form of Harrington's Blue Team were on their way, by road and air, halfway from LA to Palm Springs, rolling fast.

47

The house was a squat stone construction of a sprawling Californian Bungalow meets New Mexico stucco ... something. Walker liked it. It was homely and masculine and looked like it belonged there, and wouldn't be going anywhere inside of a century or two. The timber beams holding the roof were from big trees, reclaimed from another project, hewn maybe a century before. The split stone echoed the shades of the desert. The yard wasn't anything like those of its neighbours, with brilliant green turf and European trees that needed a small town's water supply to keep growing. This was a product of its environment but constrained by man: cacti and prairie grasses, spindly trees that grew between rocks.

'Coming?' Walker said. He was out of the car and put his head back in through the door. Monica still had her seatbelt on. She looked at the house like it was a mirage in the desert.

'Monica?'

She turned to Walker. Nodded. Undid her seatbelt.

The street was deserted. A two-lane blacktop with grass verges but no front fences, just manicured lawns and the occasional shady tree and clipped hedge. Too manicured; alien to this environment. Except for Paul's. His place seemed like it had bobbled up from the ground, a tumble of rocks and dirt and old wood and stone. They walked up the driveway. It was concrete with a pattern, oxidised the same earthy red-brown as the gravel that made up the garden beds. A double garage was set back from the cascade of the house, out of view from the front doors by a wall of yuccas, the spiky green leaves standing out in the built landscape.

Walker knocked. Waited. Looked at Monica. She was quiet, nervy at the thought of seeing an old family friend for the first time in years.

'Maybe he's out,' she said.

Walker knocked again, and then they heard noise from within. Then silence. Walker looked up and saw a tiny camera in the corner above the door. A bolt sliding.

Paul Conway answered the door. His eyes were on Walker, then Monica, then back to Walker.

He had a hunting rifle in his hands. Loose, pointed at the doorjamb but for the time he jostled back from the lock.

Walker drew his Colt .45. Aimed it centre-mass.

Paul's eyes settled on it. Then his body went slack. He looked at Monica then Walker, and back at her, searching.

'Monica,' Paul said. 'I knew someone would come – but you? And this guy? Why – how—'

'We need to talk about her brother,' Walker said. 'And time's ticking.'

His face fell. He looked from them to the street. Walker's car, clearly not government issue. He uncocked the rifle's breach, ejecting the shell into his hand, and passed the rifle to Walker, who stood it just inside the front door.

'You . . .' Paul looked to them both, and then he closed his eyes and shook his head. 'You shouldn't have come here.'

48

Paul Conway, formerly Leroy Craven, was dressed in shorts and T-shirt. Five-seven, 170 pounds, hair tucked behind his ears and ending just above his collar, beard grown out a little beyond neatly trimmed. Wired eyes like he hadn't slept in a while.

'I can't have this!' He ran inside, leaving the front door open. He opened the door to a coat-room-cum-cupboard, and reached inside.

Walker took two strides inside and caught Paul's wrist. He held it tight. Walker had it in him to squeeze hard enough to crush bones and tendons and split muscle and skin; if the guy struggled and tried to pull another firearm, he just might do that.

But Paul wasn't reaching for a gun. He pointed with his free hand. The junction box. Tucked inside the cupboard.

'The cameras,' he said. 'This house is wired up the wazoo. Everything gets recorded. Security.'

Walker let him go and watched as Paul flicked the mains switch. The television Walker could see from the entrance went black.

'You're on the run?' Paul said to them.

Monica opened her mouth but then stopped and looked to Walker.

'We're working off the grid,' Walker said.

Paul shook his head. 'Grid? What – you think not carrying a phone will keep you dark? That it will somehow save you? When's the last time you stopped and paid for gas or bought a coffee?'

Walker looked to Monica.

'In town?' Paul said.

He could see the answer in Walker's eyes.

'Shit.'

And with that, Paul was on the move. He spoke as he ran upstairs: 'We've got minutes, not hours, until they're on to you!' Paul shouted. 'Until they're here!'

Walker turned to Monica. She seemed no less tense as she crossed her arms and entered the house. She looked about, poked her head into the rec room and took in the big-screen TV, surround sound, massive leather recliner in pride of place for serious gaming time, a couple of couches against the walls, bookshelves full of paperbacks and movies and games. No photos. Walker followed her through to the kitchen and watched as she opened the refrigerator, inspected it, closed it. Finally she seemed part-way satisfied.

At the sound of noise out the front, Walker moved up the hallway, his boots squeaky on the polished flagstones. He saw the car: an SUV; huge thing – a Tucson, an off-white colour. It sped by and pulled into a driveway halfway down the street. A woman got out, went to the rear door and lifted an infant out of a capsule.

'Okay, let's move,' Paul said, coming down the stairs, dressed in jeans and sneakers and a sweater, a small backpack over his shoulder. 'Like, *now*.'

Walker was already out the door, the keys to the Cuda in his hand.

'Nope,' Paul said, heading to the side door of his garage. 'That car's burned. They'll have images of it, and of you two in it, from all over the place. We'll take mine.'

Walker looked at the car that he'd driven from Mexico the day before. He paused and considered pocketing the keys. He looked at them in his hand, the single key on the NASA key ring – and then he tossed them into the tall prairie grass under Paul's front windows.

'Sad to see it go?' Monica asked him as they went through to the garage.

'I'll come back for it, soon enough,' Walker said.

'I'm not a betting man,' Paul said, walking through his garage past a Toyota Prius and towards a big truck covered in a tarp. 'But if you guys are being pursued by the NSA, as I'm suspecting you are, then they're going to have that car impounded. And they're going to be coming after you with what might as well be the eyes and ears and wrath of God.'

Paul pulled the tarp off to reveal a jacked-up twin-cab truck that had seen far better days. The tyres were big off-road things. The windows were after-market tinted and were bubbled with age and a job done cheaply. It had a snorkel air intake, a winch on the front nudge bar, and Nevada plates.

'This vehicle's registered in another name,' Paul said, chucking his backpack in the back passenger cab seat. 'You two get in there, and stay down until we're well out of town.'

'Trapwire,' Walker said.

'That's right,' Paul replied. 'And I've heard rumours about some other mass-surveillance program too. You two will be lit up like Christmas trees right now, got it?'

He went to the driver's seat, got in and started the engine. It turned over straightaway and had the unmistakable sound of a big diesel. But a modern diesel, not original to the truck. Again, after-market drop-in. Maybe one of the VW diesels that got sold super cheap after their emissions cheating scandal. A bug-out car, ready to roll. Walker saw in the back of the truck another gas tank. Long range – they could probably get over a thousand miles if they had to.

'Twelve hundred miles,' Paul said, seeing Walker calculating. 'Far enough to get anywhere I'd need to.'

'Where are we headed now?' Walker said as he and Monica climbed in the back.

Paul hit the gas, drove out of the garage and down the drive and then headed north. 'As far as I need to go to drop you guys out of town and let the heat die down.'

'We need your help to find Jasper,' Monica said. 'You can—'

'I can't get involved. Just let this play out,' Paul said. 'Maybe it won't be as bad as you think.'

'This is legit,' Walker said. 'And your reaction to us turning up, and now bugging out, proves that you think it's worse than you're trying to tell yourself.'

'It might not pan out like the news outlets are suggesting,' Paul said after a few moments of contemplation. Walker could see that he was conflicted in all kinds of ways. 'It's basically whoever has Jasper versus the world. It can't end as big as they think.'

'Why do you say that?' Walker asked.

'These hacks? A lot of the most vital systems in this country are near-to impenetrable,' Monica said. 'Especially to one guy, in this case Jasper, working over thirty-six hours.'

'They've probably planned this for a while, whoever has him,' Walker said.

'Impenetrable,' repeated Paul. 'Nothing is. Humans are behind it. Once things go Quantum AI, sure, but that's not here yet, so there are ways in and around. You hack the right person, they become the malware. And if they're the person you need, then you're in the system you need. Right?'

Monica said, 'Then who can we hack to find Jasper?'

'No-one. I've hacked a bunch of people. Not lately, but they're still in there, in the system, higher up the food chain now. Whatever we want, I can get in. But not from back there,' Paul motioned over his shoulder towards home. 'Here's too hot. If you're here, they won't be far behind.'

'Who's they?' Walker said.

'The men in black. They go around in black cars and black helicopters. They own the night and they can make the day night too. And we can't do it in town.'

'Then where?'

Paul checked his rear-view mirror and kept his foot firmly planted on the gas pedal. 'I know a place.'

49

Walker and Monica were on the rear bench of the truck, a blanket pulled over them. The ride was choppy, side to side, as Paul navigated out of town and took corners, but on the highway it was calm.

'Five more minutes and you guys can get up,' Paul called out.

Monica was facing forward. Walker was behind her, his back against the back of the bench seat. His left arm was around her, to keep her from spilling off the seat. The top of her head was under his chin, and he felt the heels of her boots against the front of his ankles. Her left arm was looped over his, and her hand held his wrist. It was near black under the blanket. Monica felt warm. Her hair smelled of citrus shampoo. She turned her head so her face was turned up towards his.

'You think he's going to just ditch us some place?' she asked in a whisper.

'He might try, but we need to talk to him first,' Walker replied.

'He seems paranoid.'

'He's got good reason,' Walker said, his voice quiet under the blanket. 'And he's right. We were careless, with using your card before. You can't underestimate these guys. Paranoia is their default position.'

'So what if whoever is behind us catches up with us? Why can't we talk to them, work with them?'

'The guys from your house didn't strike me as wanting to sit around and have a chat types.'

'They might have wanted you, not me. I mean, they don't know your motive here. Maybe they had surveillance on me, to protect me, thought of that? I mean, if they knew you wanted to help—'

'It'd be far too late. Those guys back at your place are out to scoop up anyone they see as a threat or involved in this and they won't be persuaded to accept help from the outside. Certainly not before it's too late, and we've reached the thirty-six-hour mark.'

'But do you think that Paul can be persuaded to help us find Jasper?'

'I think he's our best and near to our only shot at making a difference, to getting to your brother, to stopping what's coming.'

'Really?'

'Yes.'

'What if you can't persuade him?'

'I doubt I can.'

'But you just said . . . oh. *I* have to do it.'

50

'You can get up now,' Paul called.

Walker flicked off the blanket. Monica scooted across the bench, behind Paul, leaving Walker behind the empty passenger seat. The car was still coasting along a two-lane highway. Blacktop, patchy. Not the interstate, Walker noted. Something north-by-north-west. The road had a slow gradient. They were going up, the truck easily doing sixty. In this particular truck they could drive all the way to Yellowstone without stopping. Probably further.

'I'd ask how you found me,' Paul said, his eyes not leaving the view ahead. 'But it wouldn't be too hard to do, even for an amateur. If one was trying to find me. If they knew my new name.'

'You weren't trying not to be found,' Monica pointed out.

'I'm guessing you could have done that pretty well, Paul,' Walker added. 'Building layers of protection around your new ID?'

Paul nodded. 'The question is, Monica, *why* were you looking for me? Before this thing with Jasper?'

Monica, silent, stared at the back of his head.

'You had to change your name, because you've got a record,' Walker said.

Paul glanced at him in the rear-view mirror.

'You needed to move on, get a decent job,' Walker said, 'so you bought or created your new ID.'

The glance became a longer look. 'Who are you?' Paul said slowly but clearly.

'Jed Walker.'

'I mean who, not a name. Who do you work for?'

'Myself. I'm helping Monica find her brother so that we can stop these cyber attacks. I'm an old friend.'

Paul adjusted the mirror slightly so he could get Monica into view. 'That true, Mon?'

'Yes.'

'And you trust this guy?'

'Yes.'

'Why?'

Monica looked at Walker, then back at Paul's reflection in the mirror. 'Because he's helping me, and no-one else is.'

'What about the FBI?' Paul said. 'Surely they'd have reached out to you straightaway.'

'Yeah, right. They did. They wanted me to stay indoors with Dad. Wait this out. Watch it, see what comes, sit on our hands. All while someone had Jasper – have you seen it? How they have him? What they make him say and do?'

Paul was silent but he nodded. He overtook a refrigerated truck without slowing. The road ahead stretched to the horizon, tilting up to a blue sky.

'Whoever has him will—'

'Monica,' Paul said firmly. 'I really don't care much for Jasper, right? I mean, he was in contact a couple of years back, and then he did the same old cut and run. Fool me once, right? Damn . . .'

'How can you say that?' Monica said, sitting forward on the bench and looking closely at him.

'Mon, do you know what Jasper and I were doing? The government was what we were fighting against in the first place. All those hours and days and weeks and months – working to dismantle what they were doing. And then he joined them.'

'And look where that got him, right?' Monica said. She let it hang in the air a moment, then added, 'Do you think he deserves what's happening to him?'

Walker waited to hear an answer but none came. Monica sat back. She was looking down at her hands, wringing them and clutching them, fidgeting with bottled-up anger and angst.

'I'll tell you this much for free,' Paul said. 'For all Jasper's faults, he's patriotic. The last time I spoke to him, he was still at the NSA. When he got there he was in the Global Communications Department. All of the covert sites and cover-sites all networked through Fort Meade and Langley. He reached out to me to do some white-hat penetration – he said he couldn't believe the vulnerabilities in the systems. And they were there – I could read comms in less than ten minutes if I knew an internal email address within the given department. The NSA were great at coding and crypto but shit at tech. They were using off-the-shelf software and hardware that had all kinds of vulnerabilities – and this is at the Top Secret level. The work I did with him got him a commendation and promotion, and he went off to Berlin for a six-month posting. He offered me an assistant role; he didn't realise that it was too late for me. Government work's out of the question. Fine for him, right?'

'Do you know what he was working on in Berlin?' Walker asked.

He nodded. 'We spoke, for the last time it turns out, four months into that tour. He rang me one night – we spoke for hours, until dawn my time. He was drunk, which was rare for him—'

'He doesn't drink,' interrupted Monica.

Paul paused, as if deciding how much to tell her. 'He did, sometimes. And over there, he told me he was doing a lot of it. They all did. It's how they operated.'

'Drinking didn't agree with him,' Monica said to Walker.

'Berlin . . . there were always big gatherings of delegates from industry. One week banking, the other mining, pharmaceuticals, tech, you name it. He made friends with a bunch of the CIA officers working out of the embassy on the Casanova Project. Heard of it?'

'No,' Monica said.

'Recruiting,' Walker said. 'Through nefarious means.'

'Recruiting for what?' Monica asked.

'Look,' said Walker. 'I worked for the government, and I mean *worked* . . .' His voice reverberated around the cab of the truck and settled like a thick fog. 'For a long time. Pointy-end stuff in all the messed-up places that you can think of. And I got out, because they burned me. I settled that score. Jasper's part of the machine, like I was. He deserves our help.'

Paul looked at Walker's eyes in the mirror and said, 'Hate the player, not the game?'

'You've got it backwards,' Walker said. 'Hate the league. The guys calling the shots. Sure, fine, I get that. But those in the arena – shit. And besides it all – whether we like Jasper or not, we need to do what we can to find him and stop him. If he melts down a nuclear plant or diverts air traffic control into chaos . . .' Walker leaned forward, his forearms on the back of the front seat, his weight making it creak and tip back a couple of inches. 'What's vital here is that we don't get to see what's going to happen at the thirty-six-hour mark. And all that happens before that. You get me? We have to give it a shot.'

Paul's hands on the steering wheel relaxed. His jaw too. He looked out his side window at the basin of the wide valley spreading out below. The highway cut through it in place of a river. Bone dry, but for the houses and their insatiable appetite for brought-in water.

Paul said, 'You want to know what I saw when I saw Jasper on the screen last night? I saw a dead man.'

51

Harrington's team cleared Paul's house. The help was hovering overhead, waiting to launch a pursuit should Walker start up the Cuda.

But they needn't have worried.

Walker, Monica and Paul had gone.

Harrington stood outside on the street, where the rappelling ropes were discarded from the chopper. Kent and his team's junior soldier, a tall lanky guy named Angelo, joined him.

'What now?' Kent asked.

'Get the ropes,' Harrington said, and pointed down the road where it widened at an intersection. 'Have the help pick us up there. They can't be far.'

•

'You thought that too, right?' Paul said. He was looking at Walker in the rear-view mirror, waiting for a response.

Monica looked at Walker. 'What's he mean? That they'll kill him once all this is done?'

'Maybe,' Walker said. He held her eye. 'Or that Jasper could already be dead.'

'But he's still broadcasting,' Monica replied.

'They may have pre-taped it all,' Walker said. 'We can't rule that out.'

212

There was silence as Paul drove on. A mile. Two. Five.

'I think he's alive,' Monica said finally. 'I think he'd have been smart enough to play this out on the technical side – make it so that they think they can't carry out the cyber attacks without him alive. Paul?'

'He might have done that,' Paul said.

'I think he did,' Monica said, more firmly this time. 'So, he's alive. So, we have to find him. And stop him. Will you help us, Paul?'

Paul glanced out his side window. When he spoke, it was monosyllabic. Unfiltered. Unemotional.

'I'll try.'

52

Paul stopped the truck at a gate on a fire track that wound up into the San Bernardino National Forest. The gate was steel, the posts treated timber almost a foot in diameter, the chain and padlock rusted. He left the truck to idle while he worked the lock open, unhooked the chain and opened the gate. The air was cold outside. Pines grew tall, reaching for sunlight, their roots finding purchase where they could in the rocky terrain.

'Does this seem like helping Jasper?' Monica said, watching as Paul trudged back over, the shaded ground frosted underfoot.

'He's got computing gear,' Walker said, pointing to the backpack on the passenger seat; the zip was undone enough to show a couple of laptop computers. 'He knows what he's doing. He's exactly what we need right now – a guy who knows your brother and his online MO better than anyone else.'

'He got arrested, remember. Caught.'

'That's to our benefit,' Walker said. 'He's extra-cautious now.'

Paul opened the door. Cold wind cut inside.

'Twenty minutes,' he said, putting the truck into low range and thundering up the overgrown track, small saplings being swiped out of the way by the big nudge bar. He put his headlamps on against the gloom. 'Keep your eyes open for bears. I'd hate to run into one.'

•

It took closer to forty minutes because the track was so overgrown. Twenty minutes in, they had to stop to repair a small steel-framed bridge that spanned a thirty-foot ravine with a raging river running through it. Monica watched as Walker and Paul fixed the section of timber planking that had rotted.

'Jasper and I started up a cyber-security company,' Paul said as they worked. 'We called it Macro Security. Banks and other corporations hired Macro to hack their networks and steal information, then tell them how to keep bad guys from doing the same thing. So, we spent a lot of time dreaming up ingenious break-ins. Sometimes we used those ideas to boost our street cred and advertise the business by making presentations at elite hacker conferences – elaborate festivals of one-upmanship involving some of the greatest technical minds in the world.'

'I remember Jasper going to one,' Monica said. 'In Vegas?'

'Yeah, DEF CON,' Paul said. 'We started brainstorming, and we came up with a tool for attacking networks and gathering information in penetration tests – which turned out to be a revolutionary model for espionage. By the end of that year, we'd written a program called Flea. Not only did Flea hide the fact that it was stealing information from penetrated computers, but its spying methods could be remotely updated, switched out and re-programmed through an encrypted connection back to a command-and-control server – our dorm room.'

'That got you noticed?' Walker said. He'd replaced the timber and stood on its centre and bounced a few times to check its worthiness. Fine for his weight. A two-thousand-pound truck . . . probably. The steel-frame bridge had seen better days. The drop was steep, eighty feet, rocky below, a tight street of white water. No guardrails.

'We got noticed in a big way,' Paul said, leading them back to the truck. 'It was good for our fledgling business, but it also got the attention of law enforcement and the military, which I hadn't really figured at the time would turn into a burden – those guys don't take "no" that well.'

'What did they want?' Walker said.

'Us. Our skills. Our thoughts,' Paul said. 'After 9/11, when counter-terrorism efforts and intelligence became increasingly reliant on cyber operations, the pressure to militarise those capabilities, and to keep them secret, increased – but those running the show are too far out of the loop. It'd be like working for a bunch of old dudes who think computers know the answers to everything, rather than what we've programmed into them.'

In the truck, Paul drove on. The bridge creaked and groaned as they crossed the ravine.

'A few years later,' Paul said, 'after Jasper and I fell out, malware now known as Flame appeared in Europe and eventually spread to thousands of machines in the Middle East, mostly in Iran. The thing was, it was just like Flea. Flame included modules that could, through an encrypted connection to a command-and-control server, be updated, switched out and re-programmed remotely – just like what we'd done.'

'That was Jasper?'

'For the government. It had to be,' Paul said. 'The Flame software offered a very full bag of tricks. One module secretly turned on the victim's microphone and recorded everything it could hear. Another collected architectural plans and design schematics, looking for the inner workings of industrial installations. Other Flame modules took screenshots of victims' computers; logged keyboard activity, including passwords; recorded Skype conversations; and forced infected computers to connect via Bluetooth to any nearby Bluetooth-enabled devices, such as cell phones, and then vacuumed up their data as well. It was good.'

'I doubt my brother would have turned down the military if they were asking him to help out,' Monica said.

'They hadn't been asking us to help out,' Paul said, slowing the truck and putting it into low gear to navigate a tight switchback in the road. 'They were asking for *everything*. And they're idiots – all that money, and that's the best they can do? Hacking military networks is like playing chess with a pigeon – no matter how good you are, the bird is going to shit on the board and strut around like it won anyway. That's how they react, when they realise people breach their stuff. They're like – we had a breach, but hey we found it, we patched it, so we won. Idiots.'

'Sounds like you were the one who hesitated,' Monica said. 'You could have joined Jasper.'

'Yeah, I hesitated. But he did too, at the start. He felt he wouldn't be able to effect any real change. And he was right, at the time. It wasn't until a few months later that we saw what the DoD did with our Flea architecture that he was sold on their vision.'

'What was that? What did the DoD do?' Walker said.

'It was small. But it led somewhere big. It was a malware virus that would be named Duqu, which targeted fewer than a hundred machines, collecting information about the computer systems controlling industrial machinery, and to diagram the commercial relationships of various Iranian organisations.'

Walker said, 'That led to Stuxnet.'

'Yep. This was when Jasper first started with the Army cyber stuff, after his training accident. The first versions of a computer worm, designed not for espionage but for the physical sabotage of machinery, began to infect computers in several countries but primarily in Iran. It was a thing of beauty – it was one of the most resilient, sophisticated and noxious pieces of malware ever produced. But then it got out. After the worm was loose on the Internet, analysis by private experts produced a detailed account of its source, aims and target. They called it Stuxnet, they tracked it back to the US and it had destroyed the uranium-enrichment centrifuges at Iran's nuclear facility in Natanz. It was the first known cyber weapon to cause significant physical damage to its target, and the first autonomous weapon with an *algorithm*, not a human hand, pulling the trigger.'

Walker looked at Monica, who was fidgeting and getting restless and checking her watch.

Just over an hour to go.

53

Not so much a hut or cabin, Walker saw, but a freight container. The small kind. Twenty feet long. Used for shipping and seen on the backs of trucks around the world. And here, on a mountain. Sitting on precast concrete footings that had been dropped in before the container. Maybe by air. A Chinook or something would do it easily enough – they were designed to drop huge artillery pieces and vehicles and tonnes of troops and supplies in otherwise inaccessible places. The Boeing CH-47: the workhouse of the US military since the 1960s. Walker missed them.

'How'd you get this up here?' Walker asked.

'I didn't,' Paul said. 'It was part of a fire-prevention thing in the eighties, when they started phasing out the watch towers. There are still a few of them dotted about. They were designed as refuges for fire crews who got separated. They've got water sprinkler systems all over to keep them cool for up to an hour, in the event of an emergency.'

He pulled the truck parallel and killed the engine. As they all climbed out they felt the cool mountain air. There was no view through the trees, which were pines and firs. Walker could make out the sound of running water nearby. The last melts from the winter, or maybe the creek ran like that year round. But he doubted it; on the track heading up he'd seen cedar and oak dying from drought.

Systems playing havoc. If it wasn't fires it was drought and if it wasn't drought it was beetles or some such.

'What can we do here?' Monica asked.

Paul didn't answer. He merely unlocked a hefty padlock at the end doors of the container and pushed aside some cobwebs. He then sprayed lubricant on spark leads and primed the fuel lines. The generator started up with a putt and cough, then he adjusted the fuel and air mix and rolled out a flexible exhaust hose. Beyond the generator were a couple of dirt bikes, which he wheeled out.

'Think you can kick these over?' he said to Walker.

Walker took the spray can and went to work on the bikes. One was four stroke, the other two. The two stroke started on the third kick-over, a puff of blue smoke belching out of the exhaust. Walker topped off the tank from a jerry can of gas and mixed in the two-stroke oil. The other bike took a couple of minutes of kicking-over, then Walker rode it around the container. The tyres were sloppy and low on pressure, but he couldn't see an air compressor. He turned off the bike and leaned it on its stand, next to the other, and went into the container.

The first room was the generator and storage area, about seven feet tall and wide and ten feet deep. A plastic water tank took up half the space. There was a wall behind that, about half a foot thick, and beyond that was another room. The door to get in was not unlike that on a battleship or submarine, in this case not to form a water-tight pressure seal but a smoke and heat barrier. This room was set up as the safe room. The floor and walls and ceiling were all half a foot less than what was a usual shipping container's internal dimensions – insulated against the potential heat of a bushfire, Walker presumed. He had to duck to move about.

The only furnishings were a stack of plastic chairs, a fold-out camp bed and a desk. There was a stash of water bottles and canned food to last someone a couple of weeks.

'I'm going to connect via a VPN account that redirects to international servers at unpredictable intervals,' Paul said, setting up his laptop and then plugging it into a power board along with an extension lead, which he took and hooked up to a fold-up satellite dish that he clipped onto the container's external door frame.

'And that will do what?'

'We'll see what we see,' he said, calibrating his laptop and typing in commands to a screen that to Walker seemed archaic: a black background with plain type, mostly white, though some was in light blue and yellow. A series of commands and requests and data inputs and answers.

'The first attack that they had Jasper do was a multi-platform hack,' Paul said. 'That'll take us too long. Like, weeks. But this morning's? One target, right? The OPM databases. I can look at that. The servers will be down but they'll be ghosted elsewhere. I can see if he's left us anything.'

'Breadcrumbs,' Walker said.

'That's right,' Paul said, his fingers working faster on the keyboard than Walker thought possible. 'Unless they had a tekkie or coder or someone as good as Jasper or me watching over his shoulder, they'd not notice it. Something small. A word or catchphrase that leads to a file. His chance to get a message out.'

'But if they had someone like that, why have Jasper at all?'

'True,' Paul said. 'But Jasper would know things about the NSA that outsiders wouldn't. So, you can bet that whatever is coming, one or more will be a cyber attack at the government or the NSA.'

'How long will this take?' Monica asked.

Paul's fingers stopped for a split second, then resumed.

'I don't know,' he said. 'Their systems are down and I'm gaining entry to other servers that acted as back-up until the time the tekkies there managed to disconnect it all. Maybe a few minutes, maybe up to an hour.'

He hit enter, and the screen scrolled with information, letters and numbers.

'I gotta go through all that,' Paul said. 'Ah . . .'

He stopped and smiled. Pointed at the screen. A familiar word among the tech babble.

'Ares,' Walker said. 'A Greek god?'

'Of war and chaos,' Monica said. 'Jasper was always fascinated by Greek gods. And he's always put them as place markers in his coding.'

'He put them into all his codes, a kind of signature,' Paul said. He reset the code running on the computer. 'In September 2011, another piece of malware took to the Web: later named Gauss, it stole information and log-in credentials from banks in Lebanon. That had his fingerprints all over it.'

'That's when Jasper was in Geneva,' Walker said.

'Right,' Paul said. 'He was losing it. Seeing all the spy crap and what we were doing. I tried to talk him into quitting, coming out to the Valley and starting something up again. But he wouldn't hear it. He wanted to work his way up, do what he could for the country. I kept telling him we could do more from the outside.'

'You always wanted more,' Monica said. 'You always wanted the best. The unobtainable.'

'I was a teenager when you knew me, Mon.'

'It's you.'

'I changed.'

Monica didn't reply.

'Look, I get it, okay?' Paul said. 'But this is it – it's who I am. I work and I live and that's it. You've seen my place. Hell. Maybe one day I'll meet a girl and fall in love and get married and have a kid or two. That'd be great. I've got the time for it, doing what I do, right? All those guys I went to college with? They're pulling eighty-hour weeks for what they earn and they've got it all in their Truman Show houses in Silicon Valley but you know what they don't have – time. Time's all I appreciate now. You would too. Jasper as well. If you'd been where I've been. It was minimum security, but still. You've got no idea. None.'

'Spare me,' Monica said.

'Well . . .' Paul flicked between screens and was running code on several sites at once. 'Where would we end up if we never changed? In this wired world we are now *all* in. You're in my world. All those people out there; social media masking as intimacy. Nope. I can't do that. I wanted to be free. Out here, I've got that.'

'In late 2011,' Monica said after a moment, 'Jasper was working on something big, he said, that would protect the country.'

'That's what he told me too,' Paul said. 'Something called Monster-Mind.'

'I've heard about that,' Walker said. 'It's an automated detection and protection system, right?'

'Yep,' Paul replied. 'It detects cyber attacks and then strikes back, all on its own.'

'You never wanted to work on something like that?' Monica asked.

'Hackers have a reputation for getting high,' Paul said. 'If I worked for the government, I could never get high again. Some of the best don't join for that very reason. Plus, what would I do – join the DoD Cyber Unit? Have to do all that PT, the push-ups and runs and shooting drills? Pfft. No thanks.'

'We'll make food,' Walker said, grabbing a small propane burner and a pot and a couple of cans of chilli beans.

Monica looked at him like he was wasting time.

'Take it from someone who learned fast and learned the hard way: you eat and rest when you can,' Walker said.

She looked at Paul plugged into his computer and capitulated. She followed Walker outside the container and watched him set up the stove on a large boulder that was half-buried in the ground. He set the stove alight and poured the contents of the cans into the pot.

'I'm going for a walk,' Monica said. Walker hadn't seen her make her way over to the truck, but she was there, leaning against the cab, hands in her pockets.

'Where?' Walker said, looking around.

'Does it matter?' she said.

Walker watched her. She was edgy again. Nervous energy. It was better to keep her occupied.

'Okay,' he said. 'Don't go too far away. We don't know what's going to happen.'

'He said it might take up to an hour.'

'You're going to walk for an hour?'

Monica shrugged.

'Are you okay?' Walker said, taking a step towards her.

'My brother's been kidnapped and beaten and God knows what else to force him to destroy the free world in a day and a half. Yeah, I'm great.'

'I know you're conflicted.'

'Am I?'

'He hurt you. Maybe this is his penance.'

'This isn't about what he did to me.'

'I'm not saying it is.'

'But you think that's clouding my thoughts?'

Walker remained silent.

Monica turned and headed down the overgrown track they had driven in on. Walker figured she wouldn't venture off the track, and that she wouldn't wander far. A wind from the north fluttered the first leaves of the fir trees. There were no other obvious paths, but he knew there would be more fire tracks snaking through the mountains, and that none would take her to a dead end. He found the continuation of this track on the other side of the container. It was more overgrown than the lower section.

He turned down the gas stove as the chilli began to bubble and went back inside to look for bowls. He found some near the jerry cans in a stack of junk on the shelves. There were a few bottles of cheap-label booze as well. And a cash box. He pulled out the box and opened it. It contained a small bag of weed, some cigarette papers and little foil packs. The dust on the box told Walker it hadn't been touched in a long time. But maybe that just meant that Paul hadn't visited here in a long time, which seemed probable with the overgrown track leading up the mountain.

'That you, Walker?' Paul called out.

'No, it's a bear,' Walker replied. He put back the box and went to the computer room.

Paul said to him, without looking up, 'I need more speed – gotta try a different sat link. Can you tilt the dish ten degrees up and thirty to the right?'

'On it,' Walker said, heading outside.

'My mistake,' Paul called out a minute later. 'Another ten to the right!'

Walker made the shift. 'That good?'

'Checking . . . little more . . . yep.'

Walker returned to the stove and turned it off. He looked around and saw a world of brown-grey-greens around him with a light blue sky that punched through the trees. No sign of Monica.

54

Paul and Walker ate chilli and drank water while the computer screen ran down lines of code. Paul was in his element, fingers and mind working fast whenever the terminal needed his input.

'I'm piggybacking off the network at the University of California in Berkeley, giving us more grunt to slam through all this,' Paul said, eating and watching the code run on the screen.

'It's been twenty minutes. Are you seeing anything in there?' Walker said as he finished his food.

'All kinds of things,' Paul said. 'Where's Monica?'

'Out there. Clearing her head. What do you see?'

'Good place for it. Out there.'

'Better than in here.'

'What's wrong with here?'

Walker leaned forward, into Paul's space. 'How long have you been coming here?'

'A while,' Paul said, edging away as he resumed eating. He watched his food and then looked around the spartan space. No windows, just the light from a bank of fluorescent tubes above and what spilled in from the open doors. 'Before I got my house. A guy inside told me about these places. How he camped out in one when there was heat on him, and that he was only found when he went to town a few too many times.'

'But you were out, not on the run. Or were you hiding from someone?'

'Not anyone in particular. But I was used to being in a small space. Away from out there. Away from home.'

'Home, in San Fran?'

'Yeah. I tried that. My parents turfed me out after two years – I couldn't get a job and I was using. That's something I can thank prison for, right? I went in a guy against the system, never took anything stronger than beer and whisky; came out of the joint chasing highs wherever I could. Anyway, my parents sent me to rehab a few times. I ran from the last one, some place in Pasadena where they think if you just eat bananas and talk about Jesus you'll be cured of all your sinning.' He exhaled, put his food down, leaned back. 'I took all I had and put it into that truck, and a computer and generator, and I drove out here. I set up for . . . four, five months. Did some online trading. All legit. Made some coin and used it to get my new ID. I checked into a motel in Palm Springs, showered, shaved, bought a suit, and got the first job I went for. Of course, the economy being what it was, I picked up that house for near to nothing. I feel more guilty about that than anything, you know? That someone got screwed out of their life savings and lost their house because of stupid decisions that rich guys in Wall Street and Washington made.'

'You could track them down online, transfer some cash to their account, if that's how you feel about it.'

'I did. And I quadrupled their money over the past five years. They'll be okay now.'

They were silent for a moment, and Walker watched as Paul checked over his machines.

Walker said, 'Tell me about Jasper.'

'There's not much to tell.' Paul picked up his food again, glanced at the computer screen, and continued to eat as he spoke. 'You know it. Tekkie. Obsessive. A guy who started out like me and went a different way.' Paul looked away from the screen briefly to Walker, then back again. 'Nine-eleven changed him,' he said. 'He believed in the anthrax. Believed in what was being said and that we had a duty to take a stand and band together to work for America.'

'So, he changed before you got busted.'

'Yep. He started spending time hacking Iraqi shit – emptying Ba'ath Party bank accounts, donating the funds to the veterans, that sort of thing.'

'No surprise that they offered him a deal – and that he took it.'

'Right.'

'Did you resent him?'

'For not doing time? No. He . . . turns out he never grassed on me. He just said he'd work for them. I had that deal on the table too. I declined it.'

'He told you that?'

'Yes. I asked him. When we first met up after I got out. I turned up at his place full of rage and instead I found the brother I'd known when we were kids. He was still okay then.'

'Okay?'

'He changed for good around 2010, 2011. He was . . . how can I put this . . . wrecked? Beyond disillusioned.'

'Because of the work they had him doing?'

'That, and what he'd seen others do. I mean, with 9/11, he was all for making us the biggest and best on the block. He had no qualms hacking other governments and dropping in malware to watch their every move. So long as it took America forward, protected us. But then in 2010 he did his first overseas posting. He'd already done about a year and a half in Hawaii, some big data centre run by the NSA in a former torpedo bunker from World War Two. But in 2010 they sent him off to Berlin. It was a plush posting, on paper. Meant to be a reward for him. I visited him there. Man . . . that apartment he had? It was badass. His expense account, the girls, the bars . . . that's when he started drinking. Not for fun. Because of what he saw.'

Paul sat up as his computer stalled and he typed in a new request over a couple of lines and it resumed its search.

'Jasper was working closely with CIA officers in recruiting agents in business and governments that would pass through town – it was a mecca for all kinds of summits and conferences. Jasper was tasked with intercepting all local comms in and out – reading all emails, putting local cell-phone traffic through keyword filters, hacking networks and getting the inside on trade negotiations and inter-consular chatter. But it was the human targets that got to him. The CIA officers' usual MO was to get the targets drunk and – well, you probably know all this, right? They'd get them in compromising situations, like caught with hookers or drugs, and arrested, and then they'd come in using some kind of diplomatic cover and pull strings and it'd go away – in return for all kinds of secrets.'

'Right. Though not just a one-off – ideally you want to run agents to the limit of their clearance, until they're no longer useful.'

'Did you do much of that in your time at the CIA?' Paul's tone was somewhere between condescending and knowing.

'No.'

'What *did* you do?'

'I destroyed things.'

'Like what?'

'Whatever needed to be destroyed.'

'Right.'

Walker watched as Paul checked his screen. The lines continued to blur by.

'Did Jasper know about you and Monica?' Walker asked.

55

Walker looked at Paul. Paul looked back, his blank stare quickly fading to one of being caught out.

'She told you?'

'No,' Walker said. 'But you just did.'

'Damn.' Paul turned back to his screen, and stared absently at the running code. 'Yeah, he knew. Kind of. He knew I liked her. He knew we'd hooked up. It was – it started out a kid thing, you know? We hooked up once in high school, at a party – I mean, she was a freshman, I was a senior, there was booze, and I was a teenage guy, right – I had sex on the mind the whole time. And, well, she was bangin'. Still got it, too, but I don't think about that much any more.'

Walker let that slide. He didn't much care what Paul felt these days. He wanted to know as much as he could about Jasper, and the relationships that he had. Walker was looking for patterns. Behavioural traits. Choices made in the past that might influence decisions taken in the present and the future.

'Then,' Paul said, snapping back to reality, 'a few years later, in college, we went out for a semester. She was doing her masters in psych. Jasp and I were doing computer engineering. It was before our stuff took off. Before we ditched college. It didn't work out.'

'What was Jasper's reaction?'

'He didn't know about that.'

'Just high school?'

'Yep.'

'You kept a six-month thing secret?'

'Yep.'

'And you were dorming with him?'

'Yep. I'd visit Monica.'

'What did he think you were doing?'

'Going to the gym.'

'Really?' Walker didn't see it.

'Fencing, okay? I was pretty good too. I sparred with the Olympic guys and had my share of wins.'

'And you're sure he didn't know?'

'I never communicated with her electronically.'

'What – you think he'd keep tabs on your comms?'

'Not mine. I know he watched hers. He'd read her emails and phone messages. This was pre-Facebook, right? Times were simpler, it was easier to be discreet. Now, no-one can hide anything.'

Walker nodded, not quite believing that Paul had managed to have a covert affair with his best friend's sister right under his nose with no way of traditional communication. If Jasper really hadn't noticed it, either Monica and Paul had been very good, or Jasper wasn't as good at deciphering patterns and behaviour as his job and clearance would suggest.

'How did you communicate?'

'We had some set times. Plus we'd made an arrangement to go to the library each day, between two and three, I think it was; if the books in a certain section were arranged a certain way, it'd mean a day and time and place to meet up. And I'd ride by her apartment off campus late most nights, and if there was a lamp on in the window . . .'

Paul sat up. The code had stopped. He tapped away at the computer.

'Oh . . . oh,' he said, smiling. 'Oh, you're good.'

'What is it?'

'It's Jasper. He's left crumbs – and chucked a few in front of him.'

'You know the next target?'

'Not yet, but I will. I think.'

'Where?' Walker said, leaning forward. The random letters and numbers meant nothing to him.

'When the—' Paul stopped.

'Is it . . .' Walker prompted; all he could see was that the data had stopped streaming down in a ceaseless waterfall of information.

'Yes,' Paul said. He highlighted a number at the end of the code. 'This is it. It doesn't belong here – it has no purpose. Numbers.'

'And?' Walker said. 'It could be random.'

'It means he's leaving us crumbs – breadcrumbs, you know, like the nursery rhyme.'

'Fairytale,' Walker said. '*Hansel and Gretel.*'

'He was obsessed with fairytales,' Paul said. 'That and Greek mythology. Anything where the forces of evil were big and complex but overcome often by an everyman-type character.'

'Where do the breadcrumbs lead?' Walker asked.

'I don't know.'

'Can you track them?'

'I wouldn't be as good as I think I am if I couldn't.'

Fingers whirred over the keyboard.

Paul hesitated, then said, 'You want me to find where Jasper is being held captive?'

'I doubt they'd have let him see where they took him,' Walker said. 'It's more like where the next planned attack is occurring – whether they're keeping him alive to stop the attacks, or they made him code them all and then they killed him, he's letting us know where the next is. It's somewhere on the west coast.'

'Look it up on a map of—'

That's when he heard the scream. A woman. Monica.

56

Walker was outside the shipping container in seconds. The screaming had stopped the moment he'd emerged into the clearing around the site. He couldn't see Monica, but from what he could figure from the direction of the sound, she was down the path.

He ran. Paul too. They were both unarmed. Walker wondered about the kind of threat they might encounter – Monica didn't seem the type to twist an ankle or fall. And the scream was different from that; it was a scream that cut into the skull and spelled *danger* and *help me* and *save me*.

'Could be an animal,' Paul called out behind Walker. 'I've seen bears and snakes around here.'

Walker trekked down an overgrown bank to cut off a switchback in the road, and saw a flash of Monica's pale skin where she lay on the road, curled in a ball, her arms around her head. By her side was an e-cigarette.

'Oh, shit,' Paul said. '*Shit*. Damn. Look, she'll be fine. It'll just take time.'

Walker picked up Monica, put her into a fireman's carry and started up the road as fast as he could. She was limp, and sweating, and murmuring. Paul was next to them, sniffing the e-cigarette.

'What did she take?' Walker barked at him.

'DMT,' Paul said. 'Hallucinogen. She must have found it in my truck. It's an odourless powder. There wouldn't have been much in there, residue maybe, but even tiny amounts of it can produce extremely strong effects. It was from months ago, I'd forgotten about it – I'm clean now.'

'What's it doing to her?'

Monica was squirming in Walker's arms, her limbs moving slowly, as though she were swimming in thick fluid.

'Right now, her whole world is dancing,' Paul said. 'She's seeing fantasy. She's going through something very serious. Beyond consciousness – but she's conscious, if you get me. She's trying to flee this physical realm. I . . . I used for a couple years, and went through so many dreams and so many scenarios. It's basically a concentrated dream. She'll be okay, it's a clean come down and then it's just over. She's spinning geometric shapes like a screensaver, or cartoons. Her reality is running 4D, time and space bending. She's moving like that because of a falling sensation.'

'How long is it going to last?'

'An hour, maybe. Maybe more.'

'We don't have an hour.'

'I have a needle in the truck – Narcan, for ODs. Sublingual injection will work fastest, or in a muscle it'll take maybe twenty minutes. It's in the glove compartment.'

'Is that safe?' Walker caught sight of the cabin and the truck. He picked up the pace. 'Sublingual? Like, under the tongue?'

'Yep.'

'Have you done it before?' Walker asked as they neared the truck.

'Never tried it.'

Great.

'She'll be okay. Let her ride it out. She can't make the dreaming stop. She feels physically heavy. She can't do or say anything until it passes. Time has slowed down for her. But it'll be a little less intense and then a little less intense until she's not high any more.'

Walker carried Monica into the container and laid her on the camp bed.

'Sorry,' Paul said.

Walker nodded. 'Okay. We need to keep an eye on her, and in the meantime you tell me about the hacks. Social media. Why?'

'Social media? Nope. The hell with that. That's just a means for them to get all of your data. Whatever they want. It's a good thing for Jasper to hack to make noise, that's all.'

'What if the Net's shut down?'

Paul looked at Walker. 'Do you know how the Net works?'

'Not really.'

'Well, you know about search engines, right? Well, they show maybe one per cent of the Net. The rest is hidden. Deep Web. You need specific URLs to find those sites. Or Tor networking to keep the servers anonymous. Jasper and I started off by hacking a gym teacher at high school. He was running some perverted thing, broadcasting pictures from the change rooms, using a Deep Web address to share them around. We made it so that his and his buddies' computers' cameras turned on them. This was early days of everyone having cameras that were an add-on to their computers, but it was easy enough for us to do. That was the first thing. No-one ever knew who did it. The teacher and two of his sicko buddies went to jail, and they were all placed on sex-offenders lists. It felt great. We wanted more.'

Walker looked back to Monica moving around; she was slow and languid but seemed content to remain on the bed. At least it was low to the floor if she decided to get more active.

'Then we hacked a place just near USC, a business that made no sense in terms of their computer power,' Paul said, pacing around in front of his computer screens. 'Why would that place have such fast-speed Internet? We looked closer. It was a front. It was government. The more we dug into their network and came up against secondary and tertiary firewalls, the more addicted we became. It turned out to be a manufacturing plant, some kind of chips we use in cruise missiles, designed and owned by an Israeli outfit.'

'That's what got you busted?'

'No. They never knew we were there. They knew someone got in – we watched them, from afar, online, snooping around the edges. We watched how they recoded and re-tooled their security. We had malware in there, tracking keystrokes, listening to all the conversations via the computer's built-in microphones. We learned a lot. Even made ourselves security passes; we took images from the computer cameras of the tech crews IDs. We went in and out of their server headquarters each week and started taking surplus supply. Soon we'd built enough computer crunch to move on, and we did.

'We felt untouchable. We set up a legit company doing cyber security for the little guys akin to what only the big boys could do. It paid our way to keep up our other online interests. And it was our downfall. People give stuff away for free, or next to, which is what we were doing. It gets noticed by the big boys in cyber security. They start to wonder why some mom-and-pop outfit has better online security than their own subsidiaries. Competitors probably complained long and loud enough for some big players to hear. We got all kinds of buyout and job offers, and turned them all down, of course. We were saving the world, Jasper used to say, one corner store at a time.'

'But the big guys didn't like it.'

'Nope. They started losing business – to us, a couple of punks still in grad school. We outsourced and set up a lab with thirty undergrads hot-desking 24/7 for decent pay and great experience. Not in the Valley; in San Fran. We were rolling along. That's when we got busted.'

'And you went your separate ways?'

'We split. It was something I was doing, so I got busted. I did the time, got the new ID. Cyber-security engineer. It's what I do best. It's a small firm and it's a fraction of what I could earn if I worked some place else, but it's all I want, all I need.'

Walker looked to Monica. She was on the cot, waving an arm around in the air and looking unfocused in middle distance, like maybe she was seeing something in the air that she disturbed. Walker was now split – if he got a break via Paul to Jasper's location, or the location of an attack, should he leave her behind? He had thought the three of them could travel together – three might make a better group, if police were now on the lookout for them. And Paul would be a handy addition. But Monica was now a liability – she'd slow him down, and he didn't have time for that.

57

Paul was silent. He stared at the screen in front of him.

Walker could see that something had changed in him. In his eyes. It was as though he was seeing something clearly for the first time.

Walker said, 'What is it?'

'It's a message,' Paul said, looking at the file open on the screen. 'From one person to another.'

'From Jasper.'

'Yes.'

'To who?'

'Me.' Paul looked to Walker. 'He wrote that to me. Not to anyone else. To me. He knows that others would be looking into this code. Dozens, hundreds of coders and analysts at the NSA and the Cyber Warfare centre would be looking at this same server right now, and he wanted to get this just to me.'

'He doesn't trust them.'

'But how would he know I'd be looking here?'

'Maybe he knew Monica would find you. Recruit you. And that you'd do all you could to help out.'

'But she wouldn't have sought me out, not without you. You're driving this. So, how would he know?'

Walker looked to the screen. 'What's it say?'

'I'm thinking,' Paul said, looking back at the numbers. 'It's a key. A cipher. We used to do these back in college.'

'And what does it mean?'

'I'm thinking . . . it's a long one. The longest I've seen. It'll take a while.'

Paul's eyes stayed on the screen. There were three lines of numbers. Seemingly random. Single digit, then double, then followed singles, doubles and triples. Repeated, over three lines.

Walker said, 'That's just gobbledegook.'

'It just needs . . . dashes. And dots. And a key.'

'Can you decipher that?'

'This stuff, I don't know,' Paul said. 'It's either random shit, or it's leftover code from something already in the server, maybe a test they'd run once. It's nothing. But this . . .' he tapped a line above the twenty lines of trash. 'That's it – that's the proof that Jasper is alive. That he's made it so that they need him for every coming attack; he's convinced them that without his final keystrokes, they can't go ahead, so that they won't kill him.'

'And they'd buy that?'

Paul nodded. 'It's what I'd do. They might have cooked up their laundry list of targets and he's worked them into the system, ready to go, but as the government and private industry responds to the threats and starts fire-walling and disconnecting servers, they can pull the trigger on what remains, but it requires further work by Jasper. So, he's definitely alive.'

Walker looked at Monica, who was still lying down but was now watching her hands above her face. Her mouth was opening and closing.

'She's seeing little green men,' Paul said. 'An hour, maybe – she'll be fine, you'll see.'

Walker looked back to the screen.

The numbers weren't random. And they weren't trash.

They couldn't be.

A code.

Latitude and longitude?

A set of possible targets?

'I need a pen and paper,' Walker said.

Paul looked at him. 'You really think I have pen and paper? I'm digital, man.'

'Check your truck.'

Paul lingered a moment and then left.

Walker looked at the screen. Four lines of numbers.

It was time. The next cyber attack.

58

Walker had paper – an old road map from the truck, and the inner part of a broken biro. He wrote down the code, number by number, replicating how it was set out. Paul was scanning the Web for news of the next attack.

'Here . . . There's been a global hack of flight plans,' Paul said, tapping a screen. 'News sites are saying this is it.'

He opened a browser and pulled up a news site to run in the background so they could listen in.

'Interesting . . .' Paul said.

Walker continued transcribing the code.

'I don't think this is Jasper.'

'The code?'

'No – the code, whatever that is, that's Jasper. But the airline thing. I think it's someone else, taking advantage of an already crazy situation.'

'Why?'

'It's too low tech.'

'Like leaking data?'

'No, the way it would have been done,' Paul said. 'That kind of thing is like eighth-grade hacking – it's just brute forcing the flight plans to bump them out for a few hours, a day tops, while tech teams reset.'

'And you think someone's out there just adding to the chaos?'

'It happens all the time. It's like when there's a riot going on and everyone starts to go out into the streets and loot and create more havoc. You know how many attacks there are every month on US government networks, let alone private? Billions.'

'You may be right.' Walker put down the pen and ripped off the corner of the code, pocketed it, and passed a copy to Paul. 'Reading material. You never know – a pattern may jump out at you.'

'What are you going to do with it?'

'I'm not sure. I'll think about it. Maybe get it through to my friends, see if they can make something of it.'

'You're wasting your time.'

'Makes me wish my father was here,' Walker said, staring absently out the door to the woods.

'Why? What does he do?'

'He – he's . . .' Walker looked at Paul. 'Nothing. He does nothing. But he's always seen patterns in places where others can't.'

'Well, in the meantime, every major airline in the world will be grounded,' Paul said. 'It might take the big Americans an hour to get back up, and others up to half a day to reboot and purge their systems.'

'How do they do that?'

'By using guys like me.'

'And how many guys like you are there?'

'Plenty . . .' Paul stopped himself. He looked at the screen. 'Not enough. Not for something like this – every tech security firm in the country will already be clocking overtime to secure networks. To retest and get them on this? It'll not only take time, it'll keep them from doing the security work. Think of the money involved in the total shutdown of global airspace for a few hours.'

'Maybe whoever has Jasper wants them tied up,' Walker said. 'Think about it. All the tech heads working for the airlines for the next, let's be conservative and say six hours – there's no-one there building the walls, certainly no-one there manning the walls.'

'It'll take up all the time until the next attack, maybe longer.'

'And that's what they want. They want to exploit that vulnerability.'

'So, we get a warning out now?'

'It won't matter. They can never plug the security gaps in a couple of hours. They don't know in what form the attack is coming, and how much of the code is already inside their servers – and if they try to do a measured shutdown and purge and reboot, it might just trigger the event early.'

'So, we move on to what's next,' said Paul. 'What's the next event?'

'It's in those numbers. They'll start with the biggest ticket item. Start looking at possible targets and then—'

'Damn!' Paul slammed his hands down on the keyboard. 'The sat link's dead.'

'But the generator's still going,' Walker responded, suddenly on the alert. 'I'll check it.'

He went outside. The dish was still connected, the angle remained how he'd set it.

Then came two sounds, almost simultaneously: the generator dying and a buzzing noise, in the sky.

A drone aircraft.

59

The drone was flying a wide arc a few hundred feet out. Walker scanned the woods and the scrub. Nothing. He raced back to the cabin, where Paul was trying to hand-start the generator.

'They're here!' Walker said. He picked up Paul's rifle, put a round in the breech and moved to Monica, who was still doing her hands-in-the-sky routine.

'Where?' Paul said.

'I don't—' Walker stopped. He saw them. A HALO drop. High Altitude, Low Opening. They were coming in from the north, with the wind at their back. Maybe 10 000 feet out. Falling at around 250 feet per second. Four of them. Tiny dots. Growing bigger.

'The bikes—' Paul started to say.

'Split up!' Walker ordered. 'Put Monica in the back seat of the truck and I'll take her – you take a bike, meet at Jasper's apartment in Palo Alto. You know it?'

'Got it.'

As Paul lifted Monica and made his way to the truck, Walker took up position outside the container and dropped to a knee, lining up the drone through the scope of the rifle. *Crack!* Miss. He followed its arc, his mind working out the drop with gravity that the bullet's trajectory would take, and the wind resistance that would sheer across its path as he fired east—

CRACK.

Miss.

He reloaded.

He took a deep, measured breath as he continued to follow the drone's flight. It was executing a circle, maybe a thousand feet in diameter with the container at its centre. It was now almost to the south. The wind would be behind the bullet, not sheering across it. He exhaled and his finger tightened—

CRACK.

Hit.

The bullet struck a wing. The drone lurched to the side, a tight banking. The aileron control on one wing was severed, forcing it away on an unsteady flight path.

Paul zoomed past Walker on one of the bikes. Walker ran to the other bike and kicked it onto the gas-bottle stove.

The intruders were ten seconds out. Almost in range of pulling their chutes, then they'd open up with weapons.

Walker checked that Monica was secured in the back seat of the truck and then started the big diesel engine and dropped into gear. With the rifle next to him he drove, his hands tight on the wheel, doing a big loop back down the track. He stopped a hundred yards out, just in sight of Paul's bike as it disappeared.

PING PING.

One of the group in the air had a long rifle. A sniper. They'd just deployed parachutes. But shooting from an arrested fall was harder than shooting from the steady ground.

Walker lined up the gas bottle under the remaining bike.

CRACK.

Boom.

60

Walker drove the truck down the track towards the ravine and stopped when the tiny steel-frame bridge spanning it came into view – along with a car. A black Suburban, stationary on the other side, blocking any hope of crossing. Walker stopped the truck, put it in park and pulled on the brake.

'Monica, I'm sorry about this,' he said, looking at her, syringe in hand. 'But you need to be in the here and now.'

She didn't hear him, didn't understand, or maybe both. Her head was leaning heavily against the back seat. Walker thumbed the cap off the syringe, turned it around and jabbed it into her chest. She let out a gasp, and her hands started to shake.

Walker looked across the ravine. Thirty feet.

Two men.

The driver, who stayed behind the wheel. And the passenger, who was half out of the car, propped against the open door, pointing an HK416 assault rifle. At Walker.

Walker put his hands in the air, clearly visible and empty above the dash.

'What are you doing?' Monica mumbled, trying to sit up but clearly still spinning.

'He'll shoot us before we can get past them.'

'But—'

'Out the car, now! Let me see your hands!'

Walker climbed out slowly, leaving the Colt and the rifle on the seat but shoving a screwdriver that had been in the side pocket into his boot.

The guy looked at Monica, who was swaying in the back seat.

'What's with her?' he shouted.

'She's drugged.'

'With what?'

'I don't know. She took it by accident.'

The guy watched, his eyes raking over Walker and then Monica. Then he stepped around his door, his assault rifle still aimed at Walker's centre mass. He was big; one of the biggest Walker had seen. Then he smiled and put the assault rifle on the hood of the Suburban. He removed his thigh holster and the utility belt on his black paramilitary uniform, and then his tactical webbing vest and body armour. Walker knew from vast experience the type of knives and other lethal and non-lethal weapons that now sat on the bonnet of the Suburban.

The guy started to move across the bridge, heading towards Walker. The veins in his thick neck pulsated with every movement, and were visible at thirty feet away. The skin on his face and knockout hands and forearms was flushed red with adrenaline and the exertion that came with moving such bulk around. His head was close-shaved, a bulbous thing, a basketball. Beady eyes. Madness in there. At least six-five, well over 300 pounds. Steroid bulk. This man was strong, angry, sure of himself.

Walker decided to meet him halfway.

'You're that Air Force punk, Walker. You've given us trouble. And it's my lucky day.' He chuckled and looked back to his friend, who was less than impressed but clearly was not going to interfere with this animal. 'You're nothing to us, Walker. It's Monica we've come for. So, you're surplus. Redundant. A gift, really.'

'What about our friend? He's a good technician. Has insights to the situation with Jasper.'

'We'll find him.'

Which means he got away. Which means the other guys would be headed down here. Which means they would be on foot, and if they skipped the winding road and went over the terrain in a straight line, homing in on the GPS location of their buddies, they would be here in under twenty minutes. Which made sense, now. This brute was like a cat playing with a mouse for the benefit of pleasing its master. Walker wasn't a fan of cats; they strutted about like they owned the joint.

Like this guy.

Twelve feet away. Walker stooped moving. The giant did too.

Walker said, 'Who are you?'

'I'm a whirlwind.' The guy chuckled. 'You're not going to know what hit you.'

'Funny man.' Walker stared at him, then looked over the edge of the ravine.

'You won't think so,' his opponent said, his maniacal smile replaced by blind fury, 'when your teeth hit those rocks down there.'

Walker liked blind fury: it clouded judgement. This guy was former military, and Walker knew all about that. He said, 'What do you want with Monica?'

The guy started for Walker, taking big strides. 'You'll never know.'

Walker shook his head. Wrong answer.

•

Harrington stood and looked at the charred remains of the computer gear and cabling, the fire still melting away in blue–green flames at the plastics, the smell of kerosene in the air.

His three guys came running back. They stopped short, hands on their knees, sucking breaths, shaking heads.

'Have the helo search for him,' Harrington said to them, then into his tactical mike: 'Team two, report?'

There was a moment's pause, then the driver of the team-two vehicle replied. 'We got them. Repeat, target acquired and detained.'

Harrington smiled, told his man they would hoof it by foot and be at their GPS location in fifteen minutes.

61

The target had been acquired, yes, but not detained. Not yet.

Walker knew that this huge guy was ex-Army because of his stance. You could pick them, in hand-to-hand combat, the differences between Army, Navy, Air Force and Marines. Even within the four branches of the military, there were differences; and then further differences in what the Special Forces outfits like SEALs and Delta used. This guy was Army. And probably good at the job, once.

New soldiers begin their Combatives training on day three of Initial Military Training at Fort Benning, at the same time they are first issued their rifle. That training begins with learning to maintain control of your weapon in a fight. Keep your weapon, you have a much better chance of survival.

The three basic options taught for encountering a resistant opponent are to disengage to regain projectile weapon range, or gain a controlling position and utilise a secondary weapon, or, as a third option, close the distance and gain control to finish the fight.

This guy had just voluntarily given up his firearm, figuring he had the bulk to do the job, probably assuming his colleague would take action should the unexpected transpire.

That was his mistake.

It was the colleague in the car that Walker was concerned about, not the slab of beef in front of him. In Walker's experience, it wasn't so much the bigger they are the harder they fall, but the bigger they are the harder the blows on impact. Smaller guys were faster, they could get in close and dart out again, slip out of mounts and grapples and chokes. Bigger guys had longer reach, and in this case a lot more mass and strength, but this meant a bigger target and surface area for Walker to play with. But the guy behind, at the wheel of the Suburban – he was the trouble. He had firearms and a vehicle at his disposal.

Walker glanced back over his shoulder. Monica was moving about in the car, slowly remembering who and where she was. Over the giant's shoulder, the figure in the car was watching passively, his hands still on the steering wheel of the Suburban, as though he were ready to drive onto the bridge and roll over them at any given moment. If that were the case, good for Walker – it was easier to dodge a car than a bullet.

So, back to the task at hand.

The giant was a pace away and he shaped up to fight.

Walker recognised the stance and motions and knew that he was a similar vintage to Walker's service, for surely things had changed in the past ten years that he had been out of the DoD. As the years and decades passed, more and varied martial arts had been added. Joint locks and choke holds became more technical, more useful, more efficient.

Entirely serviceable. Walker had learned them too, the abbreviated Air Force version, then he'd learned further techniques when training with the 24th Tactical. Then he went to the CIA, to the Point, which is where he learned all kinds of improvised weaponry outside of what the DoD taught. Useful, that level of knowledge.

The initial techniques are simply a learning metaphor useful for teaching more important concepts, such as dominating an opponent with superior body position during ground grappling or how to control someone during clinch fighting. They are taught as small, easily repeatable drills, until they master techniques of escaping blows, maintaining the mount, escaping the mount, maintaining the guard, passing the guard, assuming side control, maintaining side control, preventing and assuming the mount. The drill can be completed in less than a minute and can be done repeatedly with varying levels of resistance to maximise training benefits.

'Okay, whirlwind, or do you need me to buy you a drink first?' Walker said. He gave this guy a minute, tops.

The giant attacked hard and fast.

Soldiers are then taught how to gain control of a potential enemy at the farthest possible range in order to maintain their tactical flexibility, then assess the tactical options and how to implement them.

Walker let the blow glance by, spinning around him, so that he could see Monica over the guy's shoulders. She'd steadied now. She was watching dead ahead, at the scene in front of her, as though seeing the world for the first time and comprehension still a long way off.

The giant stepped in and threw his right arm around Walker's neck, while Walker braced against the guy's chest with one arm and grabbed his wrist with his other hand, while the giant pulled Walker in for a head-butt.

Walker didn't resist. But what he did do was let go of the guy's wrist and raise his elbow. The crack on impact of elbow and head was spectacular, the guy hit between the eyes with his own vicious pulling motion being a harder blow than Walker could hope to land on his own inertia.

The giant stumbled a step backwards.

Monica was sitting upright in the seat. Walker saw her glance down in front of her to where the Colt lay, and then back up to the window, and down again, as if she was thinking but her brain was still a while away from drawing concrete conclusions.

A trickle of blood ran down whirlwind's nose from where he'd been split open on his neanderthal-like brow ridge, the crimson running into his mouth where he smiled with now bloodied teeth.

'Ha!' he said. 'Good . . . good. Now I'm angry. Puny Air Force man.'

'Yeah. And you know what?'

'What?'

'You're as useful in a fight as a fart in a whirlwind.'

The smile dropped from the giant's mouth.

Walker figured this guy hadn't been in a real fight since he was about fifteen, when, pre-steroids, he would have already been about six-three and a couple of hundred pounds. The other kids on the high-school football teams would have been smart enough to give him a wide berth.

This was fine by Walker. He enjoyed training people, had always enjoyed it. And if this guy survived the fall, then he too would learn a valuable lesson. Even if he didn't survive, the last moments of falling through the air would be his schooling in physics and a reflection on all that he'd done to get to that point of inevitability.

Walker rushed him.

The two men grappled, arms locked, each trying to make the other turn and drop and submit into a mounted choke hold.

Pound for pound, Walker was stronger.

But the giant had too many pounds on Walker.

Walker gave up fifty per cent, just for a half-second, letting the whirlwind get in close, fast. Then Walker switched positions and pulled his arms out of the hold, twisted his body and used all of his weight to turn the guy around. The brute pulled a knife from his boot and as he came up Walker pulled the screwdriver out and put it into the guy's neck, right into the half-inch-thick pulsating carotid artery, and kicked him off the bridge. As he fell his hand went to his neck and he dropped the knife and he stared up at Walker, wide-eyed. Lesson learned.

Suddenly Walker's attention was drawn away by a roar to his left.

The Suburban, racing towards him, both the driver's hands at the wheel, the vehicle so wide that the edges were almost hanging over the bridge. Walker had nowhere to go but over the edge and to hold onto the steel structure underneath or to try to jump onto the Suburban's hood—

BANG! BANG! BANG!

Walker ducked for cover and looked behind him.

Monica was standing next to the truck, her father's Colt .45 in her hands, holding it double-handed in a steady A-frame braced position.

BANG! BANG! BANG!

Walker looked left and dropped down lower in case of a round going astray.

BANG! BANG! POP!

The Suburban's windscreen was shattered by the heavy .45 rounds, the ninth bullet had gone close enough to the driver to penetrate and explode on impact with the laminated glass. The driver's face erupted in blood and he put his hands to it, the Suburban careening to the right, hard and fast. It flew off the bridge and dropped like a stone, hitting the side of the canyon with a crunch and falling, tail first, down the tight ravine, smashing onto the body of whirlwind.

Walker, still standing, saw the driver's face, scratched up more than anything serious, lock in a look of surprise as the car's gas tank caught alight on the rocks and a plume of fire engulfed the car. Black smoke ballooned up past the bridge and into the sky.

62

Walker guided the Colt from Monica's hands and led her to the truck. She settled on the front bench seat and he climbed in behind the wheel and took off. He drove across the bridge, through the billowing black smoke, navigating by instinct, and then he was through the smoke and across the bridge and he sped down the mountain trail.

'I just—'

'No,' Walker said to her, checking his rear-view mirror before taking a turn down the track, not seeing any men or vehicles in pursuit. 'You shot at him. You hurt him, sure. But he killed himself.'

'You think?'

'I know. And you saved me – and yourself. You did the right thing.'

Monica was silent.

Walker downshifted and took another tight turn down the steep track, then glanced to Monica holding on to the dash and said, 'You okay?'

'I don't know what happened.'

'You tripped out.'

'How? Did I fall?' She put a hand to her head but felt nothing. No bump, no graze, nothing that could account for the blackout and woozy feeling. Then she looked down and saw the syringe on the floor of the truck. 'Did I . . .'

'That? No. That was me.'

Monica looked to him. 'You?'

'You had an e-cigarette, and it wasn't loaded with tobacco. Or weed, or any other kind of soft recreational drug.'

'I – I don't remember. I remember seeing it, on the floor back there.' Monica looked into the footwell at the back seat and saw only trash. 'What was in it?'

'Some kind of hallucinogen. You'd have to ask Paul to be sure.'

'Paul – where's Paul?'

Walker sped up as the track started a long sweeping decline along the side of the mountain.

'He's out there somewhere.'

•

Harrington looked down at the burning wreckage of the Suburban. He could see a charred corpse in the driver's seat. But not his other guy. He sent Kent down to take a look. He waited.

Kent saw something down there that confirmed both team members were dead and he looked up and shook his head.

The soldier next to him said, 'What now?'

'Get the helo to pick us up,' Harrington said.

'It's tracking the contact on the motorbike.'

'Our mission is Monica. Re-task the helo.'

'Copy that.'

63

Walker drove east on the interstate, and eventually they would head north, to Palo Alto. It had been twenty minutes since they'd left the fire track. Twenty minutes of Monica's silence.

'We need to change cars,' Walker said.

Monica said nothing, merely stared out her window.

'We'll take Granger's Crown Vic. Actually, we'll get him to drive us. They're looking for me and you. Not him. Not three people.'

Monica remained silent.

'We'll get to your brother's apartment and see what—'

'What's the point?' Monica didn't look at him as she spoke. Her voice was flat, tired, losing hope. 'Paul was our lead. What can we do?'

'I got some intel from Paul. A code. We'll find your brother.'

'Really?' Now Monica was looking at him. 'What kind of code?'

'Numbers.'

Monica was quiet long enough for Walker to look across at her.

'What kind of numbers?' she said finally.

'In series of three. Single and double and triple digits, then singles and doubles, singles and doubles.'

'Do you have them written down?'

'Yeah,' Walker said. He fished into his jeans pocket as he entered the outskirts of Beaumont. He handed over the folded piece of paper.

Monica held it, and her hands began to shake, but not from the drugs or the adrenaline.

'What is it?' Walker said. 'Are you okay?'

'Did Paul see this?'

'Yeah. Of course. He found it. He thought it was trash code at the end of the first couple of attacks. But I transcribed it. I think it's something. There's a pattern in there, somewhere.'

'He said it was trash code?'

'That's what he said. But there's a pattern in there, I'm sure of it.'

'It's not a pattern,' Monica said. 'It's a book cipher. The numbers refer to pages and lines and words in a book.'

'You're sure?'

'Yes.'

'Which book?'

'I have no idea.'

'But you're sure it's a book code?'

Monica looked out the window, the paper loose in her hands. 'Yes.'

'Maybe Jasper left the book at his apartment?'

'Maybe.' Monica looked ahead.

'There were hundreds of books in his apartment.'

'Yep.'

'But he'd probably need to have a copy on him, of this particular book.'

'No. He'd have memorised it.'

'Memorised the location of every word in each line on each page of a book? That's impossible.'

'Not for Jasper. Not if he knew the placement of the letters, memorised them. He deals in numbers all the time – he's a freak with them.'

Walker found the second motel on the highway, where the decade-old silver Crown Vic was parked. Granger had followed his instructions.

'You look worried,' Monica said.

Walker glanced at her as he slowed the truck but continued past the entrance.

'What you said about Jasper,' he said. 'If he knew the letters and memorised them . . .'

'What about it? What are you thinking?'

'I'm not sure yet.'

'Well, I am sure.' Monica nodded. 'He used to do book ciphers as a kid. Obsessive. My father taught him. So, he has a favourite book, or two, or ten, and he's memorised letter positions in them. Simple as that.'

'You use that word a lot with your brother – obsessive.'

Monica didn't answer.

'So, he used a book cipher to get a message out. To whom? How could he be so sure someone – Paul – would look into the hacks? Would he have, if we hadn't got to him?' Walker pulled the truck to a stop a block from the motel and parked around the corner. When he killed the engine, Monica was still silent, so he said, 'Our next step is to find the book he used to crack it. The exact edition, right?'

'Yes.'

'And you have no idea what book he'd use.'

'No. He never did book ciphers with me.'

'Just with your father?'

'No. Not since . . . not for a long time.'

'Then who?'

'Paul. He used to do them with Paul.'

64

Harrington and his now four-man team were picked up by the hovering helo from the roof of the container. The rectangular steel structure was the closest area the helicopter could come in close to, given that the bridge was swamped with the acrid black smoke of burning vehicle and fuel and bodies. They had evacuated the site as magazines from their fallen team members' weapons started to cook off and high-velocity rounds pinged against the steel bridge structure and surrounding rocks.

'Back to base,' Harrington said over their tactical radios. His crew, as hardened as they were, fell silent and sombre at the loss of two comrades. 'We regroup, get better intel, find out exactly who the third person was. He was a tech head of some sort. I want to know what they were looking at. What servers, what databases, what files they touched. Make sure I have that intel by the time we're on the ground.'

Kent said, 'What are we doing about finding them?'

'They'll show up soon,' Harrington said. 'Aside from Trapwire running their facial rec against every picture and video in the country, I'm declaring a state-wide man-hunt for the three of them. Who was that guy on the bike?'

Kent flashed Harrington a picture on a tablet. Harrington took the device and showed their sniper, who had scoped the scene as they'd parachuted in.

'That's him,' the sniper said. 'Hundred per cent.'

'Good.' Harrington scrolled down. 'Paul Conway. Works in IT security in Palm Springs.' He passed the tablet back. 'We need to know everything there is to know about him. In the meantime, I want roadblocks on every interstate. Start them a hundred miles out of here. Have county deputies cruise every B-road. We'll get them. They'll get theirs.'

•

The private detective drove the Crown Vic near the speed limit, which was annoying because Walker wanted to get to Jasper's apartment as quickly as possible, but it did give him time to think and decompress.

Walker and Monica sat in the back; the rear seat was as comfortable as a plush sofa. Walker had his window cracked, and the radio was turned to the news, and they listened as they drove north-east on the Interstate 5. They were thirty minutes beyond Beaumont.

Walker couldn't figure out why Paul had not said anything about the book cipher, but he did know where Paul would now be headed: Jasper's apartment. He would need the book that matched the cipher, and even if he had the exact copy and edition back at his own house in Palm Springs, he knew well enough that it would now be crawling with cops and Feds. They just needed to get there before Paul, or while Paul was still there.

'Maybe just a little faster?' Walker said.

The PI picked up the speed by five miles per hour and seemed reluctant to go much beyond that.

Walker imagined the trip taking five hours, best case. If they hit any traffic in or around LA, people headed back into town after a weekend away, or headed into San Fran for the same reason . . .

The passenger headrest was all the way down and Walker could see clear over the top of it. The road ahead was a ribbon of blacktop largely devoid of cars on this Sunday lunchtime. The back of the PI's head was bulbous and there were scars in the bald patches that signified he'd had a tough time of it at some point, either in a fight or maybe even a car wreck.

Granger had been genuinely happy to see them. Walker assured him that there was no heat coming down on him from any kind of federal authorities, though Walker was happy to maintain this illusion as a possibility to keep the guy in check.

In turn, the PI had told Walker that he'd followed his instructions to a T. He'd booked the motel room with cash, had not contacted anyone, and had sat and scoured the news and made notes about anything that seemed pertinent about the cyber attacks.

He'd spent the past twenty minutes recounting those notes, which he summed up as: the President seemed unlikely to use the Internet kill switch legislation because it would be too big a blow to the economy, local and global; the General in charge of Cyber Command was now running quarterback – and she was a no-nonsense woman; and basically no-one in law enforcement had any idea who had Jasper or where he was being held hostage or what might be coming in the next attack. Nothing had been reported of the ICANN members being abducted, and Walker made a mental note that he should ask McCorkell to look into that when he next rang and checked in. He'd have Granger do it.

'Oh,' Granger said, 'and you should hear the world bitching on about all their social-media accounts being hacked. I mean, you'd think they'd be smart enough, right, to figure out that anything written or spoken in the world is out there for all to see. I mean, really, has nobody heard of the Patriot Act? That thing's been in place since 9/11, right? Idiots. Tell you what, though, this is going to mean big business for me. Since that Ashley Madison hack in 2015, my phone's been running hot. Now, with all this out there? Damn. It's Christmas in March and will be into April and May and beyond for the next five years for guys like me. I'm gonna need staff. I'm gonna need a bigger office . . .'

Walker tuned out. Monica had already done so as soon as they'd sat in the car, cradling a bottle of water and leaning back in the seat. She'd closed her eyes and may have been sleeping. Walker checked over his shoulder and looked up into the air out the back window. Nothing showing. No Suburban, no helicopter.

65

'There's a state-wide man-hunt in California for Walker and Monica and this guy.' Somerville brought an image up on the screen. 'I've just run him through Homeland Security and he's clean, but look what happened when I ran his image in the DHS database.'

'Paul Conway,' McCorkell said.

'School friend of Jasper's,' Somerville said. 'Went to college together, all the usual. Did five years for hacking and fraud. Created a new ID, now does a regular IT security job at a pharmaceutical company based in Palm Springs.'

'Can you make some calls, get the heat off Walker?'

'No. This is military now.'

'General Christie.'

'Yes. I've tried contacting her office all morning to liaise.'

'But?'

'I've not heard back.'

'Where's she located?'

'Cyber Command. Fort Meade. But she could be set up in the Situation Room of the White House for all I know.'

'I'll find out,' McCorkell said, picking up a phone. 'And when I find out, you and I are going to pay her a visit.'

•

Walker checked over his shoulder again. He was feeling a little better now that they had put nearly a hundred miles between them and the paramilitary team in the mountains. But he was unnerved that there was no police or military presence of any kind on the road – it was like any other Sunday, perhaps a little quieter than usual as people lived through the fallout of all their data being hacked, and sat glued to their television sets wondering what was next.

'Relax, I've got eyes in the back of my head,' the PI said, seeing Walker's actions in his rear-view mirror. 'Anything shows, I'll let you know. And this old girl won't let us down.'

He patted his dash, as though knocking on wood in the hope that the Crown Vic would, indeed, not let them down. It was a good model of car, a reliable rear-wheel-drive sedan, big and roomy, used for years by police agencies country-wide until production had stopped around 2011. Walker knew that plenty of detective departments and federal agencies still hung onto them, preferring the steel frame and bodied sedans over the newer and more efficient vehicles in their fleets; the plastic jobs in the car pools were preferred only by the younger and newer members rolling through. It was more than nostalgia – it was clinging to a piece of technology that you knew worked, and that you continued to trust. Like Granger with his .38 revolver. He'd probably learned to shoot on the same model, and over the decades as all the other guys had moved to polymer-framed automatics with high-capacity magazines and better accuracy and ergonomics, he'd clung to the thing. A comfort blanket as much a talisman of protection and justice as a reminder of all that he'd done.

Walker glanced again. Still no pursuit. No Suburbans. No helicopter. He looked forward. Monica was still asleep. Granger was quiet. The news was on the radio.

So, Walker thought, Jasper has used a code that would only make sense to Paul. Did that mean he knew Paul would look into the hacks? There was no other reason. No other, unless there was another person to whom he had sent book ciphers after his friendship with Paul had petered out.

So, what did that mean? If the message was aimed at Paul, perhaps they'd been in touch more than Monica was aware of, more than Paul had admitted. Considering Jasper's personality, was it likely that he would share such a code with a new friend, rather than one he'd known since childhood?

Maybe. Maybe, yes. Or no.

Walker looked to Monica, and he realised he was looking at this the wrong way.

Jasper knew that Paul would look at this, because he knew that his sister would get involved and force Paul to help.

Which led to the real question: if Paul knew what those numbers meant, why hadn't he said anything?

Walker couldn't help himself. He checked over his shoulder again, out the back window. Nothing back there but an eighteen-wheeler and a couple of soccer-mum SUVs, probably loaded with kids.

'Walker . . .' Granger's voice was accompanied by the car slowing.

Walker looked forward. Traffic had banked up. And suddenly Walker knew why this section of the interstate was not rolling with blacked-out Suburbans and helicopters.

The flashing lights of a police roadblock.

66

'Those federal guys have reached out to state police and are looking for us,' Walker said.

'Then put these on,' Granger said. He reached across to the glove compartment, pulled out two sets of old-school metal handcuffs and passed them to Walker. In the next motion, he took the service lane, plugged in a magnetic blue flashing light and put it on the roof of the Crown Vic.

Monica, suddenly awake, looked to Walker, uncertainty in her eyes.

Walker put his cuffs on. He clicked in one wrist, and made the other sit on his lap, as if closed. He motioned to Monica to do the same, but she looked apprehensive.

'Just do it,' Walker said.

Monica put her cuffs on. CLICK CLICK.

Just as Granger rolled up to the state police cars, an officer moved over from where he was inspecting a vehicle and held out a hand for them to stop. He was a motorbike cop: leather jacket, boots, sunglasses, his helmet on the handle of his bike parked by the emergency lane.

'Tell them you're taking us in,' Walker said into Granger's ear. 'Tell them to keep the roadblock set up, that there's a third man they're looking out for.'

Granger was silent but he gave a tiny nod as he brought the car to a stop, and the cop moved around to his window as it wound down.

'Officer,' Granger said. He flashed his wallet. Or a wallet. Walker couldn't see it, but it must have been his old badge, for Granger said, 'Burbank PD.'

'Detective. We're screening for three fugitives, sir.'

'Listen to me, son,' Granger said in a low voice. 'I'm taking these two in.'

The cop looked into the back seat and went a little wide-eyed at the faces.

'That's right.'

'Where's the third person? Conway?'

Walker was not surprised to learn that their names and images were out there; the cop had recognised them and distinguished who was missing.

'No idea,' Granger replied. 'But it's imperative that you keep this roadblock up and continue to look for him, and that you keep this under a tight lid.'

'Sir?'

'If Conway finds out his accomplices have been taken in, he'd go to ground. If he thinks he's got a chance for escape, he'll keep running.'

'I'll need to talk to my sergeant.'

'Son, you've seen the news? The cyber attacks?'

'Yes.'

'This is the captive's sister.'

'His . . .' the cop looked into the car. 'For real?'

'That's right. This isn't a man-hunt to apprehend them. It's to locate and detain them until this ends – for their own safety.'

'But . . .' The cop had his hand on his radio.

'Chuck, right?' Granger said, looking at the name plate pinned to the cop's jacket. 'I'll remember that. I'll tell your sergeant and your captain how professional and thorough you've been. But I have to get these two back to LA. Just look out for the third guy. He's out there, won't be far off.'

'I—'

'Son, if you put this over the radio, then the people who have this lady's brother might well just come for her. And they're a hell of a lot scarier than you or me or all your buddies here. This has to be quiet. I have to get them into town.'

'Sir, okay.' Chuck looked over at his colleagues and tapped his watch to signal he was off. 'I'll do as you say. But I'll escort you.'

'Chuck . . .'

'That's the best I can offer, sir. You follow me right on in, and I'll drop you to where you need to get to, and I'll make sure you're all there safe.'

Granger glanced ever so slightly at Walker in the rear-view mirror. 'Okay,' he said. 'Lead the way.'

67

'We need to get off the road,' Walker said as soon as the window was up and the motorbike cop was on his machine and taking off, lights flashing. 'We can't go through to LA. We have to keep moving, to Palo Alto, but not like this. We haven't the time.'

'What do you propose?' Granger said.

'We're going to have to make a phone call,' Walker said. 'At the next gas station. Pull in, pump gas, have the cop watch over us, and you go in and use a pay phone. And you're gonna need to buy a road atlas.'

'Road atlas?' Granger said.

'They'll track us,' Monica said to Walker. 'The phone call, I mean.'

Walker said, 'It's the best chance we have.'

'But they're watching your friends at the UN,' Monica said. 'They'll track that call.'

'We won't contact them,' Walker said.

'Then, who? Who can help us?'

'Your father.'

•

'Yes?' General Brokaw answered the phone.

The man on the other end said, 'You have a friend from Colorado

Springs. He asked that you write this down and refer to that book on your desk, the one you've been meaning to use this year.'

'But I don't—'

'Just write this down.'

Then the voice delivered a sequence of numbers, with dashes between them, and that was that. The call ended.

General Brokaw looked at the numbers he'd written down.

He looked at the road atlas on his desk. Then back to the numbers. Then he remembered a game he'd taught Jasper as a child. Page, line, word . . .

And he smiled.

•

Harrington and his crew landed at Los Alamitos Army Airfield in southern LA and immediately prepared to head out again.

'Roadblocks?' Harrington asked his team member that he'd tasked with communicating with the Californian police departments.

'Nothing yet, sir,' Kent said, 'but I've got full details now on Paul Conway.'

Harrington took the tablet to their kit tables and poured coffee from a big thermos. He sat and scrolled through the data, taking in everything he needed to know.

'Get this back to General Christie's office,' he said after ten minutes. 'Make sure they're aware.'

'On it.'

'So, where does he head? Where . . .'

'Sir?'

'Conway's part of this,' Harrington said, draining his coffee and filling another. 'Either from the start or because Walker and Monica Brokaw got to him. They've split up. Where does Conway head?'

'I thought we only cared about finding Brokaw's sister.'

'And until we do that, we work all the angles. Conway's part of this. We have to figure out what he's doing.'

'Sir, Cyber's on the line.' Kent held out a satellite phone.

'Harrington. Yep. Okay, good, send it through.' He hung up and looked at his tech guy. 'They're sending through all the traffic, all of what went from Conway's computer that piggybacked a network at UC Berkeley and bounced it all off one of our communications satellites.'

'Is that even legal?'

'Them hacking or us getting their hack? You know what, it doesn't matter. The General was very specific. Today, we're the law. Whatever we need, they'll get it done for us.'

68

The Air Force helicopter organised by General Brokaw was a UH-1Y, out of Vandenberg Air Force Base.

It met Granger's car at a country club north of LA, in a grassed area created especially for the purpose of providing helicopter transport for the exclusive membership. The motorcycle cop had been sceptical when given a new destination, but when he saw the light grey of the Air Force chopper and heard the unmistakable *whoop-whoop-whoop* of the Huey and saw the door gunners out each side, he knew that this operation, like he'd been hearing via snippets of news all day, was fast becoming a military one.

'Thank you,' Walker said, shaking Granger's hand. 'You did a good thing.'

'Don't mention it,' he replied. 'Anything else I can do, aside from the phone call?'

'I've got your number,' Walker said, patting the guy's card in his jacket pocket. 'If I can think of anything in the future, I'll let you know.'

Monica climbed aboard the chopper. Walker was close behind.

'Sir, I'm Master Chief Doolan.' He passed over two sets of earphones with mikes attached, and helped them into the bench seat against the rear wall, then plugged in their headsets, and said, 'General Brokaw has put us at your disposal.'

Walker nodded. He liked Airmen like Doolan. Good people. Family. Loyal.

'I'm Lieutenant Colonel Walker, retired,' he said. 'This is the General's daughter, Monica Brokaw.'

'Pleasure, ma'am,' the Master Chief said. 'I'm sorry for your brother's situation.'

She nodded.

Doolan said, 'Where to?'

'Palo Alto,' Walker replied. 'As central as you can get. As fast as you like.'

'We can do that,' Doolan replied, and he held the mouthpiece close to his mouth as he ordered the side doors closed and moved to a jump-seat behind the pilots and strapped in. The aircraft took off, nose dipped loose as the pilots belted north-west.

'You understand this mission is completely dark?' Walker said into the mike, looking at Doolan as he spoke.

'Yes, sir,' Doolan replied. 'The way I see it, someone's messed with Air Force, and we're doing what we can to even things up a little.'

Walker gave a thumbs-up.

Monica looked out her window as the green grounds of the country club and golf courses made way for housing estates and strips of desert and highway and the hills and mountains that stretched all the way north. Her hands were clasped in her lap, and when Walker leaned over and put a hand on hers, he was surprised to see they were relaxed. But then, he figured she had been on plenty of flights, on all kind of aircraft, in a lifetime of following her high-ranking father around as a military brat. She let his hand remain there but she neither took it nor squeezed it.

Walker looked dead ahead as the next question rolled around in his mind: why did Paul Conway remain silent about the code? *Why* . . .

69

'Touchdown in thirty seconds,' Doolan called.

'Okay,' Walker said. He'd studied a map of the streets surrounding Jasper's apartment building and memorised the route from where they would be landing, on a commercial helipad near Stanford Medical Center. Palo Alto stretched from San Francisquito Creek to the north to San Antonio Road to the south, from the San Francisco Bay to the Skyline Ridge, a mess of houses and buildings and monolithic homes that formed the bulk of the world's tech companies.

Monica had said nothing during the trip other than to recount Jasper's address. Walker thought her reticence was caused by the drugs that still coursed through her. She'd finished a bottle of water but had not eaten. Her whole form seemed in a funk, as though the adrenaline had drained through her and she had no energy left. He knew what that felt like. He'd been there many times, after breaching doors and engaging an enemy and things going to shit – and afterwards, a flat funk. A SEAL buddy had got him onto magnesium supplements, which seemed to help a little. Walker didn't know the medical reasons behind it all. But it worked.

The helicopter pivoted and hovered down to a light touchdown. The engine spooled down. Doolan unclipped Monica and helped her out. The two door gunners waved goodbye. Walker stood next to Doolan, far enough from the Huey to be clear of the wash of the still-turning rotors as the engines idled.

Walker said, 'Master Chief, I'm going to need one more thing from you and your two boys here.'

'You name it.'

•

'Got him!' Kent passed the tablet to Harrington and pointed to the Trapwire screenshot of Paul Conway. 'He used another ID to book a charter flight out of Palm Springs, light aircraft. This is from the reception's camera, hundred per cent facial recognition match.'

Harrington said, 'Destination?'

'Flight plan has him headed for San Francisco.'

Harrington nodded. 'Gotta be Brokaw's apartment. He's headed there. That server he touched, all that extra text that our tech guys at Meade said was on there – that's a goddamned code.'

'A code for what?'

'Get the team in the air in five minutes,' Harrington said, already loading up his gear. 'And get the drone over Brokaw's building.'

70

The favour that Walker asked of the Master Chief worked. The Air Force man, with his two NCO door gunners from the Huey, were dressed in their Airman Battle Uniforms, the Air Force equivalent of the Army's BDUs, complete with their body armour and helmets, secondary weapons of holstered 9-millimetre Beretta pistols, and M4 assault rifles. They looked a mean, serious outfit.

They approached the two uniformed Palo Alto police officers who were standing sentry on the footpath by the stairs that led up to the front door of the four-storey apartment block, and Walker watched from a block away as Doolan did as instructed.

'You really think this will work?' Monica asked, standing next to him and watching intently.

'Yes,' Walker said. And it did work. Doolan had instructed his two guys to stand sentry, with M4s at the ready across their chests in a defensive stance. They stood at the top of the stairs, by the wooden doors into the block, while Doolan spoke to the two cops and walked them up the street towards their cruiser, keeping in front of them so that the cops looked forwards, towards him.

'Go,' Walker said to Monica, a hand on the small of her back to guide her in front of him. They crossed the street and made for the apartment building. He could see that Doolan was keeping the cops facing the opposite way, keeping their attention as he explained how this was becoming a military situation, at the very least buying some time for Walker and Monica to enter, look around and find the book, and bug out.

Up the stairs they ran between the two Airmen standing at attention, and then took the lift to the fourth floor.

'What if we can't find the book?' Monica said.

'We'll find the book.' Walker was confident, but this feeling faded as the old lift clanged and banged its way up the shaft and the door rattled open onto the fourth floor. The building was old and dank, and the light at the end of the hall, above Jasper's apartment, 408, was flickering and blinking. There was police tape over the door. Walker tried the handle – it was locked. He gave it a shoulder and the wood splintered from the jamb and the door gave in and yawned open.

He reached in and flicked on the hall light. He went inside, Monica close behind him. The wall was painted light blue, maybe thirty years ago, and that paint covered several other layers. The floor was made from the same worn floorboards as the passageway outside. The apartment was dark. All the blinds were drawn, and the sun was almost set.

The first room, to their right, was a bathroom. It was empty – devoid of everything but the toilet and basin and shower over a bath. There were no towels, no toiletries, nothing. The next doorway was to their left and was a bedroom. It contained a mattress on the floor. No sheets, no pillows, no wardrobe, no side tables or lamp or books or clothes. Nothing but a small window, the blind drawn.

Next the hallway opened up into a kitchen and living area. The only furniture was a beanbag, a tall lamp and a small television on the floor. Nothing in the kitchen but a small bar refrigerator. The only thing suggesting any form of a home was the wall the door was set into, lined entirely with bookshelves, and on those bookshelves were not hundreds but thousands of books. Rows stacked neatly, standing up, spines out, and then above each were stacks of books in every possible nook of space.

Walker held the note containing the code in his hand. 'Where do we start?'

Monica shook her head. 'I have no idea.'

•

General Christie placed a call to her team. It was a secure satellite link, protected by the best cryptography that the NSA could create.

'Sit rep?'

'All good here,' her guy said. 'I'll have good news for you soon.'

'There's just over four hours to deadline.'

'Will the President order the kill switch?'

'Maybe. Maybe not. Better for us that he does, so make sure you get done what you need to get done. But the plan is playing out – that guy is headed there. Be ready for him.'

'Yes ma'am, you can count on us.'

There was a knock at General Christie's door. Her secretary entered and said, 'Visitor, ma'am.'

'I'm not to be—'

The door behind the secretary was pushed open and Bill McCorkell entered. 'General Christie. We need to talk.'

'Continue with your mission,' General Christie said into the phone, then hung up and turned to McCorkell. 'Okay, Bill, take a seat. I'll give you exactly two minutes of my time.'

Walker looked out the window of Jasper Brokaw's apartment. He imagined someone watching the place, casing it, looking for the patterns of his trips home. Maybe they had him flagged at the airport in Utah, when he got on a plane and headed here. If Walker had more time, he would talk to the neighbours, see what they noticed back then and now. The witness to the abduction. Find out exactly how it had happened. There was no sign of a struggle in here. Nothing was tossed. The books were neatly stacked. The futon mattress was neatly tucked against a wall.

It didn't seem right. What time was Jasper taken? Did his abductors drug him? Walker thought back to the needle in his neck back at LAX yesterday. They were missing something. It wasn't right.

But he didn't have the time.

The books.

Monica found a can of peaches in a cupboard and ate them with her fingers because there was no cutlery. She sat on the floor in front of the television. 'Another attack coming in . . . six minutes.'

Walker was looking at the shelves for patterns. But there was no obvious pattern. It was a mix of fiction and non-fiction, recent and old. They were not ordered alphabetically. Nor by genre. Not colour coded by spines. There seemed to be no obvious hierarchy of organisation. Autobiographical, maybe? Stored in the order in which Jasper bought them? Walker lifted a book. *Foucault's Pendulum*.

He imagined the books off the shelves and scattered over the floor. Cut-up technique. Look for a pattern in there. A favourite book. Something worn? Or something preserved, well kept? It had to be popular and generic enough to be used for the code. Something that each man had, Jasper and Paul, the exact same edition, so that they could use the same . . .

'This isn't right,' Walker said.

'What's not right?'

'I don't think they have the same book.'

'That's impossible. That's how a book code works. Like the particular edition of the road atlas that you told Granger to get, to match my father's.'

'I think it's a book that's here, and here only. I think he wanted Paul to come here to decode the message. And like you said, he already had it memorised.'

'How? And why?'

'It makes the code even harder to break.' Walker tapped the novel in his hands. 'Think about it. If someone saw it as a book code, then they could crosscheck which books were at both locations – here, and at Paul's house.'

'I didn't see any books at Paul's house.'

'Me either. But I think it's here. And while your brother might have remembered them, Paul wouldn't be able to. And because they've been out of contact for so long, there's no telling, from Jasper's knowledge, if Paul still had that book in his possession. So, the code has to be cracked here. He wanted Paul to come here. And I bet Paul knows exactly which book to look in.'

'Okay . . .' Monica leaned back, her hands behind her on the timber floorboards. 'So, what do you look for? There's got to be three or four thousand books on this wall.'

'How about a book that they had enjoyed together. One that they would have used back in junior high. A favourite.'

'Okay, okay. So, that rules out anything published since.'

'Right.' Walker looked at the spines. He recognised many of them. 'Okay, that takes out about a third of them.'

'That's a start.'

Walker nodded as he kept looking.

'When did they meet?' Walker said. 'When did they start the book codes?'

'High school.'

'Years?'

'I don't know. Jasper'd been doing it for years with Dad . . . but I know they were doing it by university. And probably before. I think anything from 1999 to 2003.'

'You're sure?'

'Sure.'

'Okay. So it could be anything pre then – but let's concentrate on that range first, as a sweet spot. A book they enjoyed together, and probably used back then for codes.'

'Ah, okay, let me think . . . you know what, I have no idea. Why would I know that?'

'I thought you might remember it . . .' Walker trailed off, then turned to Monica. 'Sorry.'

'Greek myths!' Monica said, suddenly animated. She sat forward and started to tap the floor with one hand while making a whirling motion with the other. 'He was obsessive back then. He brought Paul into it too. They read them all. Let me think . . .'

Walker scanned the shelves. He came up with three titles. '*The Odyssey, The Iliad* . . . there's texts on Achilles, the Trojan War, Alexander the Great . . .'

'Publication dates?'

Walker opened each to its imprint page.

'All in the right time frame,' he said. 'All have his name written in the front. Same handwriting, seems like a young person's writing, messy and unsure.'

'He's always had terrible handwriting.'

'Does that mean something, psychologically?' Walker asked as he took the piece of paper with the code written down.

'It means he has crappy handwriting.'

Walker began to go from page to page through *The Iliad*, matching the pages and lines and words and reading them out.

'Not that,' Monica said. 'Next.'

Walker moved on to *The Odyssey*.

Cut-up technique. How Bowie wrote his lyrics. Look for new patterns.

Then, Jasper came on the screen.

72

'So, the GPS system is down,' Jasper said. 'And that's just the start. Now, I'm going to conduct hourly cyber attacks, and you have just four hours until the main event. And I'll tell you what . . .'

The camera zoomed in to Jasper's face.

'If you think you can stop me, you can't. It's happening. It's happening and I'm showing you just how vulnerable you are. For all the protections you've put in place over the years, for all you've done over the past twenty-four hours, you can't keep me from doing it.

'Well, there is one way. One.

'So, I ask you, will the President do what must be done?'

The camera's view widened out again, showing Jasper sitting in his orange jumpsuit.

'Three more hours, three more cyber attacks. First, GPS is down. Then, you know those drone things you like to fly about and kill people with? News flash – I'm now commanding them. How many are there over US air space? Where will they be flying? Are some of them armed? How will you stop them? What will you use to intercept them when every weapons system you can deploy, whether jet aircraft or missiles, are redundant, because I can own their computer systems. If you aim a missile at my drones, I will redirect that missile at a hospital. If you launch jets to fly sorties to gun down the drones,

I will commandeer the controls of those jets and smash them into the ground – or maybe fly them at the fading sun or the moon, just to see how far they can go.

'Ask yourself: at what point do you pull the plug? You have a solution to this. Use it. I dare you.

'You have less than four hours. Tick-tock.'

•

Walker still had a book in his hand as they watched the latest threat. Monica had finished eating. Her hands seemed steady, the effects of the drug mostly abated with the adrenaline and the time and the food and water.

'What do you think?' Monica said, her eyes still on the tiny screen.

'GPS is a big deal. It's going to wreak havoc on all kinds of transport and logistics. It'll hurt in all kinds of ways.'

'Surely they can work around it.'

'In the next few hours?'

'They'd have contingencies.'

'Would your brother have factored that in?'

'You talk like he designed these attacks.'

'I think he did,' Walker said, voicing the thought that had been building. 'The way he's been talking. From the first presentation to what we just saw. Much heavier with the "I". "I'm now commanding them." "I will redirect." He's owning it, don't you think?'

'You're saying they took him and forced him to make all this stuff up, or else?'

'Or else . . . what?' Walker said. 'What kind of leverage could they be using? He's not tight with family or friends, and those he was close to are you and your dad and Paul and none of you were taken. Unless he has a significant other you don't know about, who is being held captive.'

'I really doubt that.'

'Okay.'

The newscaster crossed to a correspondent on Pennsylvania Avenue, the most famous landmark in the world behind her. With a gaggle of other news crews jostling for real estate, the reporter gave a serious précis of the events that had just transpired, as well as those threatened, and then crossed to inside the White House, to the Press Room, where the President stood with the Director of Cyber Command, General Christie.

'We are confident that the Department of Energy,' the President said, 'in conjunction with the Department of Homeland Security, have made every effort and taken every measure they can to safeguard the national energy grid. We ask for calm as we work towards fixing this. And given the global severity of this situation, I have authorised an executive order, giving the military, under the direction of General Christie of Cyber Command, authority to act on US soil in this matter of national security. General Christie.'

The General nodded to the President and took her place at the lectern, and then—

A noise, in the apartment. Someone was in the bedroom and the door to the living area pushed open.

Paul. He was wearing a climbing harness, and held a silenced pistol in his hand.

He said to Walker, 'Put the book down.'

73

'Don't do anything stupid,' Walker said to Paul. He kept the book in his hand.

Paul looked from them to the television. The General was fielding questions.

'What did she say?' Paul asked.

'Who?' Walker glanced at the screen. 'The Cyber Command Director?'

Paul nodded. The pistol was still in his hands, and he was jittery, looking at the screen, occasionally glancing at Walker.

'She was responding to the latest threat,' Walker said, gauging the distance between them. Three paces. Too far. Paul's pistol was a Glock 17. Walker could try to draw the Colt from the back of his jeans where it was tucked into the small of his back, but the time it would take to clasp the weapon, take off the safety, aim and fire . . . too long. Paul may or may not know how to shoot, but as inaccurate as pistols were, at three paces it was an irrelevant argument.

'How'd you get here so fast?' Monica asked.

Paul said to her, 'You okay?'

'Fine,' Monica said. 'As well as I can be. How'd you get here? We had serious help.'

Paul again glanced at the television. The President had joined the General in taking questions from the press.

Walker inched closer to Paul.

'I flew,' Paul said. 'Like you two obviously did.'

Monica asked, 'Where'd you get the climbing gear?'

'Same place I got this gun,' he replied. 'The Internet's good for things like that, if you know where to look.'

'On your Tor sites,' Walker said. 'The Deep Web.'

Paul nodded.

'Why didn't you tell us about the book code?'

'I—' Paul caught himself. 'You two should go.'

Walker said, 'Where would we go?'

'Anywhere,' Paul said. 'I've got this.'

'You'll let us leave?' Monica asked.

Paul said, 'You shouldn't be here.'

'What are you going to do?' Walker said. 'Translate the code? Then what? Go find your old buddy and shoot it out with whoever is holding him captive? You think you might have this, but no matter what you can do on a computer, at the end of the day we're talking guys with bullets. Trained guys. You haven't got *that* covered.'

Paul was silent.

'Solve the code,' Walker said, sitting down next to Monica and tossing the book at Paul's feet. 'Solve it and tell us and then do whatever you want to. But we're not going anywhere without knowing what's next, and you're not going to be able to do anything to help Jasper on your own, so pretty soon you have to realise that we're in this together.'

Paul looked to the book by his feet. 'You won't do it with that book,' he said. He tucked the pistol into his climbing harness and looked at the shelves. He went from left to right, top corner along, then the next shelf down, right to left, scanning, then the next down, left to right . . . and stopped.

'This,' Paul said. He retrieved a copy of *Jurassic Park* by Michael Crichton. 'Our favourite book. I went to two second-hand places before coming here. And besides, think about it: if he's left a message about the hacks or cyber attacks, you're not going to find references to computers in those old things.'

Walker looked at the stack of books on Greek myths he'd piled up.

'Okay, start reading out numbers,' Paul said. 'It's page, line, word.'

Walker was about to and then stopped. 'First, why didn't you tell me about the book code, back at the container?'

'First, read out the code, and we get out of here and help Jasper,' Paul said. 'Then I tell you.' He motioned to the television, where General Christie was still briefing the press. 'It's because of her.'

•

'How did you get on with General Christie?' Somerville asked McCorkell in the reception area of the White House.

'I got nowhere,' McCorkell said. 'She's cagey. Stonewalling. It's not right.'

'The whole world is looking to her on this,' Somerville said. 'And you know what – she loves it. If she succeeds, this might just be what Cyber Command needs to become its own branch of the DoD, alongside the others.'

McCorkell paused a step and resumed, falling in step with Somerville to the car. It would mean Army, Navy, Air Force, Marines . . . and Cyber Command. As a fifth branch. Cyber warfare – the new battlefront. Why not? He'd heard it debated and proposed over the past couple of decades. This meant General Christie had everything on the line. She would become a Joint Chief of Staff. She'd always been politically ambitious – maybe her ambitions went beyond that.

'Bill?' Somerville said, holding the door open for him.

He nodded and got into the back seat of the town car.

Bill said, 'See if Zoe can get anyone to hack General Christie's system.'

'Hack? You're not going to be able to—'

'If Chinese hackers can get every secret we have, I'm sure we can hack in on the General. Try her phone. Let's see who she's been speaking with.'

74

'*The grid is the key*,' Monica said, reading the words they had transcribed. '*You can stop it. Come to me, not online. I'm at the place we always wanted.*'

'What's that mean?' Walker said. '"The place we always wanted."'

'I'm thinking,' Paul said, looking absently at the television. 'I'm thinking.'

'What's "the grid"?' Monica said.

Paul's gaze didn't move.

'Power grid,' Walker said. 'That'll be their end game. Shut the country down – but not until we've all seen and heard about their previous attacks.'

'Jasper could be anywhere,' Paul said. 'We used to talk crap about all kinds of places.'

'We should move,' Walker said. 'Think elsewhere.'

'I was going out the window to the back,' Paul said.

'We can't all do that,' Walker replied.

'How'd you guys get into the building, past the cops?'

'Some friends helped, but they'll have moved on by now,' Walker said, knowing that Doolan's bluff would have only worked for so long and that they would have had to leave their post by now. 'We'll head out the front door, one at a time. Right past the cops. A minute apart.'

'I can go out the window and send the harness back up.'

'We can sound the fire alarm,' Monica countered. 'Evacuate with the rest of the building. It's Sunday evening, there are probably a hundred people in here.'

Walker nodded, but he didn't like it. And it had to be the front door, because he'd had Doolan check the service door at the rear and it had been locked and alarmed by the police. The idea of spending time using Paul's climbing gear and going up and down from the roof or out a window had little appeal, especially because he was unsure if Monica was fully functional.

'If the fire alarm goes off, the cops will be suspicious,' Walker said, 'and they'll scan every face. If we go out one at a time, we're each just a person leaving. They never suspected that someone is up here.'

'Okay, so we go out the front,' Paul said, unclipping his climbing gear.

'Wait,' Walker said, catching Paul's arm. 'Before we leave the building, tell me: what do you know about the General of Cyber Command.'

•

'Listen up,' Harrington said over their tactical radio earpieces. 'I know you're all pissed at what happened to our boys. You've every right. But revenge will come later. This isn't just about Monica Brokaw any more – we need to get Paul Conway alive too. He's now priority number one. Got that? He knows something about Jasper Brokaw's abduction, he's an asset.'

'What about Walker?'

'You do what you have to do. If he's a threat, drop him.'

•

Jasper punched in the commands. His fingers hesitated a moment. He knew what would happen. The attack was routed through servers in eastern Europe and eventually stopped in Russia. He hit enter.

The US response to the cyber attack on a critical government system would be instantaneous.

Monster-Mind.

The nation's first and last line of defence for dealing with cyber attacks. It detected an attack, and retaliated with a greater than proportional response, most often completely crashing the attacker's computer networks, wiping data and creating back doors in firewalls for future remote access. Sometimes it even crashed entire ISPs, even national Internets, as it did in Syria.

Jasper knew it because he had helped develop it.

But what now? What would the Russian response be, when Monster-Mind hit back?

And would that finally be enough to force the US President's hand in using the kill switch?

75

'It happened in my own home,' Paul said as they clambered down the stairs. 'Two weeks ago. I walked in from work and they were there, waiting for me. I was sat down. They'd found me. General Christie – she came to my house, sat in my living room, waited until I got home that day. And she gave me an ultimatum.'

Walker stopped at the second-floor landing and checked the view below through the handrails. He kept the others halted and silent, tucked against the wall, as an occupant entered her apartment on the next level down, oblivious to their presence.

'Okay, go on,' Walker said, leading the way down. He moved slowly and quietly, the others following his actions.

'The General said they'd help create a better ID for me, steer me into better jobs, gift me my choice pieces of tech, and a bunch of other sweet-deal kind of stuff, if I helped them out in a security exercise. She sold it to me, and, I mean – what wasn't to like about it? A legitimate government-issue clean slate, the most serious hardware money could buy, just for a help-out in the exercise.'

Walker said, 'What kind of exercise?'

'A war-game, they called it. Run by the Cyber Mission Force. General Christie said it involved a virtual-range environment for its personnel to conduct training exercises and obtain certifications, while fighting a series of live, adversary-mimicking "Red Teams". She wanted my help because I was on the outside and had no connections within Cyber Command.'

'And you're sure this was General Christie?' Walker said.

'Yes. She showed up with a group of heavy-set guys, a paramilitary-type outfit. Serious. Almost carbon copies of what we saw before. Maybe the same exact crew. Six of them. And the General. She was in charge. She told me to just call her General – she was in plain clothes, never gave me her name. But I did some digging after they'd left. There's not that many female Generals in the US Army. I found her image online, saw that she's the head of US Cyber Command's offensive team.'

'And what did she want from you in this exercise?' Walker stopped them on the first-floor landing. He wanted to hear this before they left the building.

'I had to reach out to Jasper, ask for his help.' Paul looked to his feet. 'She said he was the best operator she'd seen. She wanted him running a Red Team unit to test out her guys. It was all about sharpening Cyber Command, giving them a unified command-and-control platform for fast-moving and large-scale cyber operations, particularly for offensive operations. When I told Jasper, he jumped at it. Loved the idea of doing an off-books deep probe to test out what the US military could do in the face of skilled cyber attacks.'

'You . . .' Monica said, her voice low, and she was right up in Paul's face. 'You've been lying to me this whole time. You gave Jasper up? To what end? Are you saying all this isn't real? It's all just some kind of war-game?'

'It's real,' Paul said. 'I know it's real because of that code he sent out. He wouldn't have done that unless he was in trouble. He needs me to help stop the attack on the grid – he needs us to get him out. And there's no way – no way in hell – that the cyber attacks so far would have been sanctioned for a war-game, right, Walker?'

'Right.'

'So, what?' Monica said. 'You're saying that General Christie is what, exactly? Corrupt? A traitor? She lied to you to get Jasper involved in a situation that had him abducted and forced to attack his own country? Why?'

'We'll find that out,' Walker said as he started walking down the stairs again. The others followed. 'But it's happened before. Happened a few times, and been proposed many times. It's not just endemic to the US, or to recent history. When you have a military, it's going to be made up of all kinds, and they're going to have all kinds of motives. It's always been that way. For some, self-interest trumps all.'

'Paul,' Monica said, 'why does Jasper think you can help him stop the attack on the power grid? Because you're the one who got him into this?'

'No,' Paul said. 'He's reached out to me because I worked on the security patches. If anyone can attack the grid, it's me. In fact, only me.'

Walker stopped at the final landing, said, 'But he can get around them, right? Hack the DoE servers? Overload the grid or shut it down?'

'He can't, not that way,' Paul said, looking to Monica. 'A year back I was tasked with what my company does – penetrating networks. When I led the team testing out the DoE's new security, I got in. They patched it. We got in again. They asked me what I'd do – and I made it secure for them. They had two other firms try to break in, but they got nowhere. I'd made it as unbreakable as a crypto can get.'

'You said no crypto was unbreakable,' Walker said.

'Technically, that's true,' Paul replied. 'But this one is different. It's unique.'

'You created your own code,' Walker said. 'A human code, like what Jasper sent you.'

Paul nodded. 'Like that but advanced. When I set up the security, I put a code in there. It's got a human-made code, just like the book code – it's simple, but you need the key to unlock it.'

Monica said, 'What's the key?'

'Not what,' Walker replied, 'but who.'

'It's me,' Paul said. 'I'm the key.'

76

Walker shook his head. He didn't like this. Not at all. Paul was set up to bring Jasper in, and now Jasper had penetrated the Department of Energy's network, seen the code that he recognised, and was now calling Paul in. To Walker's mind it was simple: keep Paul away, stop the attack on the grid.

'Jasper knows that you're the key,' Walker said.

'Yes,' Paul said.

'How could he?' Monica said.

'He's already been in the DoE systems,' Walker replied, 'he's seen Paul's code, recognised it. So, he knows that he needs Paul there to unlock it.'

'That's right, and I can,' Paul said. 'I can get in there and do the job. At least, I can go there and offer up a trade – me, for Jasper.'

'Why would you do that?' Monica said.

Paul looked at his feet. 'When your brother and I were caught, it was worse than you know. The deal he made, working for the NSA? That got me five years. It was me, Monica, who did the crime, and I deserved to do the time – I was the one who pushed and pushed, always wanting more. Deeper penetration, more sharing of classified information. I could have been a Manning – should have been – doing life in a Leavenworth-type place. But he did the deal and agreed to work for the government to commute my sentence, and I did five years in what was essentially a white-collar resort. I owe him for that.'

'So, what?' Monica said to Paul. 'You're just going to go in there and do the work of the terrorists, of General Christie? You think they'll even trade him for you?'

'Like I said, I'll offer the trade,' Paul said. 'Me, for Jasper. I can finish what they want. And I owe it to your brother.'

Monica shook her head. 'Why should I believe you now?'

'Is there any way that without you they can get into the energy grid?' Walker asked. 'Any way at all?'

'It's unlikely, but I can't rule it out. If Jasper tries to get into the Department of Energy's servers, he'll be Trojanised,' Paul said. 'He'll go in hiding behind a packet in a firewall. It'll appear that he's got a legitimate header, like an ID number, in order to pass through detection. But hidden within that is a separate, hidden packet, and that's the Remote Access Tool. A RAT. And that RAT is going to sneak around, de-cloak, scoot off and scurry around like a rat – and open a door. But the thing is? No matter what, he can't open it. Because the lock on that door was made by me, and can be opened only by me. Every attempt to hack it just makes it more impenetrable. Any malware he enters to worm its way around gets frozen out by the program's code – I designed it so that it changes the code of legitimate applications as they run, starving the malware by denying it the system resources it needs to operate, killing it.'

'But there's a way in,' Walker said. 'A code you put in there?'

'Yes.'

'Like a book code.'

'Like that, and given that he knows me . . . he just might be able to get in there without me.' Paul reached into his pocket and retrieved a die. 'It's a random sequence of twelve words intersected by a series of numbers twelve digits long. It's impenetrable because it was created by a human, and I set it via rolling a die, and only I know the sequence and the words involved.'

'Why did you do it?'

Paul looked at Walker for a moment, clearly wondering if Walker really needed an answer, then he said, 'It's the hacker in me. I couldn't not create a back door into the DoE.'

Walker merely nodded and headed down the final set of stairs. 'I need McCorkell to get to General Christie,' he said. 'If she organised this from the start, she's the one who has got Jasper some place.'

'Somewhere he and Paul always wanted . . .' Monica said, walking alongside him.

'It wasn't meant to be real,' Paul said, falling into step behind them. 'The General said it would help. Help me, help Jasper, help them, help defend the country. It wasn't meant to be real . . .'

Walker said, 'Does the General know of your work on the DoE?'

'Probably.'

'Because of the coded back door?'

'No. I told no-one about that. But Jasper would recognise my work. So, I figure he's buying time with his captors, so that I can come in and help out.'

Walker stopped inside the entry hall by the mailboxes; double doors ahead led to the street. 'When we drove in here, there was a gas station next to a bar, around the block to the south-west. We go out the front door here, a minute apart, and we meet at that bar. I'll head north and go around. Monica, head south, then cross two blocks down to head west. Paul, go out the door and straight across the road and take whichever route you like. We meet in that bar in ten minutes. Got it?'

They nodded.

Walker said, 'Show time.'

77

Walker was the third out the door of Jasper's apartment block. On his way by the rows of mailboxes he lifted some junk mail and flicked through it as he passed the cops on the footpath, his cap down low and the visor covering his face as he turned and headed up the street.

He walked a block and rounded back towards the gas station and bar. There was a string of shops, each more hipster than the last. A French patisserie that sold macaroons. An organic butcher. A cafe that either served gluten-free wi-fi or something else entirely – hard to tell. A florist that specialised in mosses and prairie grass for fifty bucks per bunch or ceramic cup full. And at the corner, next to the gas station, was the bar: Firewood. Another hipster hallmark: taking an unrelated noun and repurposing it as a business name. Walker passed the front window and glanced in; he saw Paul and Monica sitting at a table, and he continued on to the gas station, where for three dollars forty he bought the best map of the area available. He headed back to Firewood.

Inside was dark; the only windows faced east and the sun was already setting, and the lamps, though plentiful, were in green shades and low wattage. Walker thought that the dim atmosphere combined with the beaten-up old wood panelling suggested what once might have been an Irish bar before it started serving cocktails out of mason jars at fifteen dollars a pop. It was empty but for a group of hipsters in a far corner, dressed in lumberjack shorts presumably made of organic cotton and discussing things so obscure no-one outside their clique would understand.

Walker dropped the map on the table between Monica and Paul and headed for the bar.

'You believe this cyber shit?' the barman said, not looking up from his phone. 'You should read what they're saying on Reddit about all this. No way will the Internet go down – or the power. It's all a big load of BS, the government's got all that protected.'

'Pay phone?' Walker asked the barman.

'Pay phone?' the barman said, looking up, a wry smile on his face.

'Phone. Put money in it. Make a call.'

'Oh, yeah, sure, back there,' the guy replied, looking at Walker strangely. 'About a decade ago.'

'Right.' Walker pointed to the phone in the guy's hands. 'May I please use your phone?'

'Do I look like the telephone company?'

'Two-minute phone call,' Walker said, putting fifty bucks on the counter and keeping a couple fingers on it. 'Consider yourself the modern equivalent of a payphone.'

'Apparently that's what I am now,' the guy replied, passing over his cell phone and holding the other end of the offered bill. 'Two minutes.'

Walker saw that the guy had a cigarette lighter on top of a packet of tobacco and rolling papers.

'And I'll take your lighter.'

The hipster bartender looked at it and hesitated. Walker was still holding onto the fifty. The hipster tugged at it and felt the resistance. Then he reached with his other hand and passed over the lighter.

'Use that to get yourself a haircut,' Walker said as he let go of the money. 'And a shave.'

'So I can look like you and everyone else? Yeah, right.'

Walker sat in a booth next to Monica, opposite Paul.

'Some place you always wanted to see . . .' Walker said, tapping in the number for McCorkell's New York office.

'I still don't get it,' Paul said. 'We've just been talking it through.'

Walker said, 'Where did you always want to go?'

'Going to the moon was my first aspiration,' Paul said. 'And later, with Jasper, we talked about going to Stanford – they were developing the precursor to the Internet there when we were kids. It's still a world leader – and close to here.'

'But we've seen crosses to there since this started,' Monica said. 'Stanford's computer labs are leading university teams across the nation to try to trace back the hacks, so it can't be there.'

Walker said, 'I missed that.'

'I didn't,' Paul said. 'It crossed my mind to go and join them, then you two showed up.'

'Well, Jasper reached out to you,' Walker said. 'You have to know what he means, even if you don't think you know.' He tried McCorkell's cell phone.

'Maybe I will remember, or figure it out,' Paul said. 'With time.'

'We don't have time,' Walker said, the phone to his ear as the call connected and started to ring.

'They'll track that call,' Paul said.

'We'll be out of here in a couple of minutes,' Walker said. Two rings. Three. 'Jasper's message – it has to be something easy for you to recall. He would have made it the first thing to pop into your head.'

'Stanford was the first thing. We wanted to go there,' Paul replied. 'Neither of us got in.'

'I'll mention that to my guy if he ever answers,' Walker said, looking at the screen to make sure he'd punched in the correct number. 'I'll make sure they've done a search.'

'If he's there, they'll have a physical connection into the computer networks, so, somewhere on campus,' Paul said.

Walker nodded.

'Jasper . . .' Monica said. She motioned to the television over the bar. 'Look at him, in that last broadcast. He's changed.'

'How?' Walker said. Four rings.

'His expression. The way he spoke just before. It's like he's delirious.'

'They may have drugged him,' Walker said. Six rings. Seven. He looked down at the map of San Francisco. He found Jasper's apartment and started looking at concentric rings out, at one-mile intervals. *Where? Where would they take him? It's close . . . near here. What's near . . .* Eight rings. Nine. Walker hung up and re-entered the number and tried again. 'And kept him awake – maybe he's been awake for more than twenty-four hours. He's desperate and running on empty. It could be the gravity of the cyber attacks he's had to complete, and he's degrading and destroying the nation that he signed up to defend.' He looked to Paul. 'Where else? What's near that you could do this kind of thing from?'

'Wherever they have Jasper, it's somewhere with access to big hardware,' Paul said. 'I'm talking serious grunt machines, because the computing power he's using is bigger and meaner than the systems he's hacked so far.' Paul tapped the map. 'So, Silicon Valley, or a university, maybe something government. You could tap into any number of super-computers, servers, whatever you want. There's a lot of that in the vicinity.'

'Let's narrow it down, then,' Walker said, staring at the map. 'It's got to be government. Has to be.'

'Why?' Monica asked.

'Whoever has Jasper has to have control,' Walker said. He tried another phone number, Somerville's cell. 'To have no-one around to see it. If General Christie is driving this, she'd make sure it's somewhere she can keep controlled for the duration of the operation. And it can't be shut down. All that points to military. There's redundancies there, too, because the General is thinking like a military commander and she wants the option of defence if it comes to it. She knows that she has to hold the fort for the full thirty-six hours.'

'Defence?' Monica said.

'First and foremost, she'd take it over.' Walker ended the call and looked at the phone. Something wasn't right; he hadn't even reached McCorkell's message service, nor Somerville's. 'They'd have it scheduled for maintenance or something, so no-one is around. That's the first step. Then she'll want safeguards in place. It has to be off the grid. Generate its own power – not just as a back-up power plant, but its own power station, separate from the grid, if they're threatening to take it down.'

'A government response would have been to turn off power to any possible location,' Paul said. 'But all these places around here – Apple, Google, Yahoo, you name it – they've all got their own power generation, big gas turbines to ensure that they've got reliable supply no matter what.'

'Power . . .' Walker stared absently. Then he dialled another number, this one a cell phone, a number that hadn't changed in all the years he'd known it. 'It needs defence from power. From shutting it down, I mean.'

Paul said, 'That's what I just said.'

'No. You're thinking macro. I'm thinking micro . . . an EMP.' His attention returned to the map, to those one-mile rings out from their location. Within just a few miles of where they were in Palo Alto was virtually the centre of the Internet and all that ran it. 'Though it doesn't have to be military, it could just be government. Christie could pull strings to take over anything federal she wanted or needed.'

'That narrows it down.' Paul looked at the map. 'Where's a government-owned site that has its own power plant, and has an EMP-resistant super-computer? Cheyenne Mountain in Colorado? That place ticks all the boxes. It's literally designed to survive anything.'

'But it's too far away,' Walker said, tapping an imaginary point at the far edge of the table, way off the map. 'And there are too many people around there for the General to do something like this and keep it under wraps. It can't be a part of vital national security infrastructure.'

'Maybe she sold it to them as an exercise as well?' Monica said. 'Sucked them in, made them leave? Locked them out of part of the complex?'

'She sold the exercise lie to Paul, sure, but that was before all this started,' Walker said. 'But it wouldn't work now, not since it's been getting airplay, now that the world believes a terror group is actually doing all of this. To me that rules out anything military, because there's too many people and bureaucracy involved in any place that would have the type of computer power we're talking about. She may be head of Cyber Command, but no Admiral or Air Force General is going to turn over his entire base, empty it of all personnel, for her to use for at least thirty-six hours.'

'You really think it's close to here?' Monica said.

'Yes,' Walker said. 'From the time they nabbed Jasper to the first broadcast and hack, what was that – an hour? Less? We know they put him in a vehicle and then changed vehicles. Maybe another car, maybe a helo. But even if they put him on a helo to somewhere, they couldn't travel far before landing and getting him to a video and then a computer terminal. It all happened inside of an hour from the abduction. That tells me they're holding him somewhere here, in Silicon Valley.'

Paul's eyes scanned the map. Monica's too.

And then Walker saw it. He saw it and he felt a weight in his gut, a pit of sickness that was instantly roiling and bubbling, because he thought of the car that his father had given him yesterday and the key ring and he knew, then, that his father knew far more about Zodiac and how it was playing out than he had admitted.

'Here,' Walker said, his finger on the map. 'Three miles from Jasper's apartment. Government owned and operated, and I bet you a section of it is closed off right now for some reason or another.'

'NASA,' Monica said, reading the map. 'Ames Research Center.'

'Yes, and—' Walker brought the phone's mouthpiece up to his lips. 'Eve – it's me. Listen, I need you to do something. What – no, I'm fine. Eve, I can't get hold of McCorkell or Somerville. You have to keep trying for me, every number you can try, for him or Somerville or anyone there who can get you through to them, but you need to say that they have to get General Christie. She's the one driving this: she got to Jasper Brokaw via Paul Conway, and Jasper is being held at the Ames Research Center in Silicon Valley. It's part of NASA. Got all that? Yes, Ames. Good. They'll know what it means. Thanks. Talk soon.'

Walker ended the call before Eve could go on, because he knew that she'd be worried and would want to know where he was and what was going on and in what capacity he was involved in the cyber attacks, and he not only did not have the time but he wanted to keep her in the dark as much as possible. *Because that's worked so well all these years . . . Do people change? Can they? Can I? Will I?*

'It will have the computer gear, the power station, and the EMP protection . . .' Paul trailed off. 'That's NASA's super-computing centre. And we used to talk about being astronauts. That was the first thing we ever said – we did an assignment together on going to Mars. That's when we became friends.'

'Ah, my phone?' the hipster bartender said, his arm outstretched to Walker, but he paused mid-action.

Walker tensed.

The barman had the same expression on his face as Monica and Paul. What he didn't have was a red laser dot in the middle of his chest like they had.

Walker knew, before he saw them. He turned slowly, keeping his hands flat on the table.

Four black-clad paramilitary guys stood in a tight huddle, their faces hidden behind black ski masks, their silenced H&Ks aimed with laser pointers.

No way out.

78

'This is Harrington,' he said into an encrypted satellite phone. 'We've got them. All safe and sound.'

There was a pause, and then Harrington said to General Christie: 'Sorry, can you repeat that? Okay. Okay. Right. Copy that, moving now.'

The call was ended and Harrington said to the driver: 'NASA's Ames Research Center, eastern gate.'

•

Eve tried another landline, then another cell number, and they all ended in the same result: nothing – not even voicemail.

Eve paced her room. She saw on the news that the Russian President had ordered a proportional military response to a US cyber attack on their nation's communications network, and that it would be swift justice against the perpetrators. Columns of Russian armoured vehicles were crossing the border into Eastern Ukraine, and NATO announced that it was mobilising its rapid reaction force so that all options were on the table. The news feed cut to the White House for commentary.

Eve stared at her phone.

When she thought of McCorkell and Somerville, she also thought of the first person who she had met out of that UN team: Andrew Hutchinson, an FBI Special Agent on secondment to the unit. She had his cell-phone number in her phone, and she rang it.

Nothing. Not even voicemail. The phone just rang and rang.

Then she saw the Vice President of the United States on the television, and did a double-take. She dialled the operator for a call-connect.

'The White House, please. Yes, *the* White House. I don't know – is there a press number? Or how about general enquiries? Okay, that's fine, put me through. Thank you.' Eve waited as the call connected, and when it was answered she said, 'This is Eve Walker, and I need you to listen to me: I have an urgent message for the Vice President, from Jed Walker . . .'

•

Walker was in the back of a transport van, his back against a side wall, a black hood over his head and his wrists bound behind his back with plastic cable ties. Paul was seated to his left, and Monica to his right, each identically subdued. He knew from the sounds and motions inside the van that two of the paramilitary guys had climbed in and sat opposite, watching them. The leader, Harrington, whose name he caught one of the guys saying as they were loaded into the van, was talking – Texas accent – on the phone in the passenger seat. And the fourth guy was at the wheel, driving through Palo Alto.

To NASA's Ames Research Center.

Did these guys know that Jasper was there? Judging from the way Harrington took the information during the call, Walker figured he was in the dark about the location; Harrington had seemed surprised that they weren't heading to a DoD site. Unless of course his surprise had actually been connected to what he had been instructed to do with his prisoners once they arrived at Ames . . .

79

'Okay guys, listen up,' Harrington said.

Walker listened closely, trying to glean as much information as he could. He knew he could bust from his cable ties, but the two guys opposite would be on him fast. He wouldn't have time to remove his hood before attacking the man immediately in front, so he would be reliant on how that guy reacted before deciding on a course of action with the second one. Still without seeing, fighting blind. Not a good option.

'Our orders,' Harrington said, 'are to hand over these three to another group who have set up security at the computer hub at Ames. In and out. Got that?'

'Why there?' the guy opposite Walker asked.

'That's above our pay grade,' Harrington replied. 'But I assume the General's got a tech team from Cyber Command holding station there in case the DoD needs to use the computer facilities. It'll be a safe place for these two – while they work out what to do with Walker.'

'We can't keep him?' the driver asked. 'The son of a bitch killed—'

'For what purpose would we keep him?' Harrington said.

The driver was silent.

'Justice will come,' Harrington said. 'The General will know what to do with him.'

'There's DoD at Ames?' the second guard in the back of the van asked.

'Yes,' Harrington said. He paused, then said, 'Team Black is set up there.'

The men in the van fell silent. Walker sensed all kinds of opportunities and dread in that silence.

•

'Damn!' Special Agent Fiona Somerville said. She indicated and started to slow the car, just a few miles out of Dulles where they had a jet waiting to take them back to New York City.

Bill McCorkell looked over his shoulder.

'It's DC police,' Somerville said. 'I'll flash my badge and we'll be on our way.'

'You were speeding?'

'A little. Nothing to make any trouble.'

'No, wait,' McCorkell said, looking again out the rear window. It was impossible to make out the markings on the squad car in the dark and with the flashing lights strobing at them, but the uniform he did now see, as the officer started running from his car towards them. 'It's Secret Service, uniform branch.'

80

The vibe in the van had changed. Walker felt it in the air without a word being spoken.

Team Black is set up there.

That's what had changed the mood. Tension. Apprehension.

First, it meant that this team was surprised that DoD had people there at all. So, they weren't in the loop on that. Nor why they were headed there – certainly not on Jasper being there, either. But did they know of the General's involvement? And the silence that followed Harrington's mention of Team Black – these guys knew Team Black. It wasn't like they were saying Delta were there, or a Ranger platoon. It was specific, and therefore small, part of the same black-ops outfit as them, in this case working for the General out of Cyber Command.

Walker summed it up: a small blackball outfit of the DoD, operating on US soil. Split into six-man teams? And the General was bent. And, it seemed, these guys in the van weren't privy to Team Black's operations or intentions.

Walker had to exploit that.

•

McCorkell stood on the shoulder of Interstate 66 and used the Secret Service officer's phone to call Eve Walker.

'The Vice President got your message,' McCorkell said. 'And it turns out that someone has put blocks on all my team's phones so that they're no longer connected to a network.'

'It's General Christie,' Eve said. 'That's what Walker told me to tell you. That she's driving this – that she has Jasper.'

McCorkell was silent.

'Are you still there?' Eve asked.

'Yes,' McCorkell said. 'I'm here. Was that all he said?'

'He said that Jasper is being held at Ames Research Center.'

'He said that?'

'Yes.'

'Okay, okay. That's it?'

'He said this all started with General Christie.'

'Okay. Thank you, Eve. Are you safe?'

'Yes I'm at—'

'Listen, do me a favour,' McCorkell said. 'Wherever you are? Leave your phone behind, take cash, no cards, and hole up for the next few hours until this blows over. Things have been said on this call that may get flagged and then tracked back to your cell phone and your location can be found. Do you understand?'

'Yes.'

'Good. Watch the news. You'll see when this ends, and after that – well, then all will be fine. Stay safe.'

'Thank you.'

McCorkell ended the call and asked the Secret Service agent to escort them directly to the White House.

81

Jasper could tell that things had changed. He'd counted six armed men over the course of his time at Ames. Never all in the one place, never more than three of them down in the computer network centre, as though the other three who rotated through were on sentry duty. One was in charge, that was clear. His name was Webster. Jasper had never seen their faces, because they wore ski masks when they brought him out of the computer room to film the demands that were beamed around the world. He could tell things had changed, because they were animated now, moving about, quickly, not measured and laconic as they had been up until now.

From where Jasper sat at a computer terminal, he could see out a glass wall to where two of the guys were pointing and directing, as though they were expecting someone to come to the compound.

Jasper felt a flush of heat rise up his neck. Had Paul got the message? Was he on his way? How would these guys react? Jasper stood and paced. He felt he had to tell these guys that Paul was not to be harmed.

'Stay in there!' a black-clad guard shouted.

•

The van pulled to a stop. Walker heard an electronic gate opening. Another stop. Another gate.

The guy opposite Walker said, 'Where are we doing the handover?'

'Up here,' Harrington said.

'You sure you want to do this?' Walker called out. 'General Christie won't be too pleased.'

Silence.

Then, the guard opposite Walker said towards the front of the van: 'How's he know about General Christie?'

'He saw the news,' Harrington replied. 'Nice try though, fella.'

'It's no try,' Walker said. 'Ask Paul here. General Christie and Team Black visited his house two weeks ago, asking about Jasper, to get him to come out to his old apartment this weekend. Why would she do that? Why, if she wasn't driving this whole thing herself?'

'It's true,' Paul said through his hood, his voice calm. 'She came to my house. Sold me a lie, about getting Jasper there to be picked up and taken away to do an exercise against Cyber Command.'

'Shut up,' the guy opposite said.

'She told me what would happen with Jasper,' Paul went on. 'Well, in a sense. She told me it was an operation, that you were all in on it.'

'Did she stay for dinner?' the guy asked, and his buddy laughed with him.

'No,' Paul said, 'but she drank a mocha with four sugars, which I thought was weird. Who drinks that, right?'

There was a beat of silence, then Harrington said, 'Stop the van.'

•

McCorkell strode into the White House like he owned the place. To be fair, he had as much stake as anyone and much more than most, given that his career there as a National Security Advisor had spanned three administrations, and a couple of others on an advisory basis.

He took the stairs down towards the Situation Room. Somerville was by his side, although she would have to wait out in the aide staffing area.

McCorkell could tell by the protective detail outside the closed doors that the President was still away, probably still on board Air Force One, where he would remain until all this was over, and that the Vice President was residing. Good.

82

Harrington said, 'You had General Christie in your house?'

'Yes,' Paul replied.

'In Palm Springs?'

'Yes.'

'What date?'

'Exactly two weeks ago. A Sunday. Just after lunch.'

The guard opposite Paul said, 'That's the day Team Black rotated back to 'Stan.'

'And how is it they could get taken from the field over there and placed here within twenty-four hours?' Walker's opposite number said.

'Look,' Walker said to them, and his face was pointed, under the hood, to the leader in the front passenger seat. 'You know my name, so you've read my file. You know I'm ex-Agency. I know a set-up when I'm in one, and you guys are about to get burned. We're your only bargaining chip here, and if you go in with the three of us and hand us over, then you've got nothing to negotiate with, and there's little chance that you're walking out of here alive.'

'This cracker's talking bullshit, Harrington,' the driver said. 'No way would the General think like that. No way.'

'Harrington,' Walker said, 'if your buddy here is right, and I'm wrong, then why didn't you know about this? Why isn't it adding up? How is it that Team Black is here, where Jasper Brokaw is being held, and you're only just now arriving? And why did the General use Paul here to make contact with Jasper? This whole thing stinks.'

'Yeah, how's that?' the guy opposite Walker said. 'No way they could have got stateside and jumped ahead of us on this.'

'And the fact is,' Walker continued as if that man hadn't spoken, 'if I'm right, and you do nothing about it and just hand us on over, we're all dead, because you're walking into a set-up. If I'm wrong, and you hand us over, then it's just the three of us and Jasper that are screwed. Your call. But if you do something about it, be smart about it. Damn. You save the day, along with your lives and ours.'

There was a long pause, then Harrington said abruptly, 'Change of plans.'

'No way—' the driver said but Harrington cut him off.

'We're not taking a chance, because this doesn't add up,' Harrington said to him. Then, towards the back of the van he said, 'Take these two, and wait back here. One stays with them, one sets up with eyes on a scope of the drop zone. Change comms down two bands to keep Team Black in the dark. And get the drone overhead.'

Paul said, 'This place is EMP-proof.'

'The drone's still handy,' Harrington said. 'Await my orders. We'll go in with Walker and see what's what. If it checks out, I'll tell you to bring them in, and we've done nothing other than be cautious for a couple of minutes.'

The guy opposite Walker said, 'And if it doesn't check out?'

•

The door was opened for McCorkell and he entered and scanned the Situation Room.

Seated at the table was the National Security team: the heads of the FBI and Homeland Security, the Secretary of Defence, the Attorney General, two of the Joint Chiefs, the Director of National Intelligence, and the Vice President. There were a few National Security Advisors and senior military personnel at the end of the table and at chairs against the walls, taking notes and collating data and responding to questions that they could either answer straightaway or defer to those outside the room for clarification. That channel was a two-way street, with orders from the room being dispatched down the chain and implemented around the nation and the world.

And on the large screen at the end of the room was a face, speaking to the room. The main screen was actually made up of three dozen smaller screens that could be tasked on different images and video feeds, but at this moment it displayed only one visual: General Christie.

'Sir,' McCorkell said to the Vice President, who looked up upon McCorkell entering. 'A brief word?'

The Vice President, seated in the middle of the board table, nodded, got up and walked over to join McCorkell in the far corner, away from the large screen.

'Sorry – what is this?' General Christie said. 'What's McCorkell doing? Someone turn up the audio at your end.'

'Sir,' McCorkell said, his voice low, ignoring the General and talking to the man who trusted Jed Walker quite literally with his life. 'Walker has intel from the field.'

83

Walker was now alone in the back of the van as it drove over concrete. The hood was still over his head and his wrists were still tied behind his back with the plastic cable ties. The seams in the road where the concrete slabs met acted like a trundle wheel and told him that they were driving about twenty miles per hour, and he figured they were headed west, because of the compass in his head. They were almost at the NASA super-computing lab.

'Any chance I can get this hood off?' Walker asked.

Silence from the front.

'Is there anyone around?' Walker asked. 'Employees?'

'It's a Sunday. This is NASA,' the driver said.

'There's no security?' Walker said. 'There's always security; there's billions of dollars of tech sitting around here. Don't you think that's weird?'

Silence.

'What did General Christie say to you before, Harrington?' Walker said. 'Did she mention Jasper Brokaw being here? That Team Black had liberated him from his captors – or that they were waiting for your arrival to use Paul Conway to covertly hack the systems here and override Jasper's commands, then you boys would have to deal with the terror group?'

No response.

'Do you know for certain that Brokaw's here?' Walker said.

Harrington remained silent. Then, as the van started to slow, he said, 'The drone's just coming overhead now.'

'I'd use it,' Walker said. 'The EMP.'

'You said before this place was EMP-proof,' the driver said.

'But Team Black's communications systems aren't,' Walker said. 'What are there, six of them? They're your enemy here, don't you see? And they're set up. Defensive. They've got a kill box all organised. It's a trap. It won't affect what Team Black are doing with Brokaw—'

'Would you shut up?' the driver said. He pulled to a stop. 'This is it.'

'Can't see them,' Harrington said.

'These guys have that reputation,' the driver replied. 'Especially in the dark. You heard what they did in Syria, right? Shit. They hunted down half of IS's hardest operators, and none of it was reported. I heard they even—'

'You need to use the EMP to shut down their comms, now,' Walker said. 'It's a—'

'You need to shut it,' the driver said.

'The EMP is a smart move,' Walker said. 'Put them on the back foot for a spell. I'd leave two on Brokaw, send four out here to mop you guys up. Maybe just three, if they think they're so good and there's four of you.'

'Seriously,' the driver said. 'I'm going to come back there and knock you right the fu—'

WHACK.

It was two sounds, a millisecond apart. First, the unmistakable sound of a high-velocity round as it punctured the windscreen, to the top left. The second sound came when the bullet hit the driver. It must have deflected on the laminated glass because while it was still a head shot, the driver was now gurgling. The sounds of death, before the silence. Walker imagined a .300 round, probably fired by an M2010 sniper rifle since these guys, Team Black, were US Army. The twelve-gram projectile, travelling at 3000 feet per second, deformed on the windscreen and hit the guy a little lower than aimed, then spun its way through the side of the driver's skull and tunnelled down and across through his face, tearing out the back of his neck. Air sucked and hissed as the guy's final breaths expanded and deflated his lungs and escaped out of all kinds of new orifices. He slumped forward and came to rest on the van's horn, which sounded long and loud and incessant in the still night air.

'Put your hands up!' Walker said to Harrington. 'Show them you're capitulating – and start bargaining!'

'Okay,' Harrington said. 'Okay.'

Walker's breath was fast inside the hood. He felt his heart topping out and immediately forced himself to relax.

'Make them take you inside,' Walker said, feeling his heart rate slowing a little. 'Me too. Tell them the others are ten minutes out, that you had to separate in taking the three of us, and that you have to greet them when they roll in.'

'They won't buy that,' Harrington said out the corner of his mouth, barely audible over the horn's blare. 'Okay, I can see them approaching – two of them. Team Black . . . Sons of bitches. Traitors.'

He rattled off a few more choice words.

Walker said, 'Your comms still up?'

'Yes.'

'Your team heard all this.'

'Yes.'

'Okay, good. Tell them to put the EMP overhead in five minutes. And have them tell Monica: Paul Revere, one for come, two for stay put.'

'What?'

'Just tell them that. She'll know.'

Walker heard Harrington whisper into the microphone that was taped around his neck and picking up his vocal vibrations, and then he heard the front door of the van being opened, and then the rear doors.

'We can't let the grid shut down,' the Vice President said. 'How realistic is this?'

'Sir,' said the Secretary of Homeland Security. 'The national electric grid is comprised of three smaller grids, called interconnections, that move electricity around the country. The Eastern Interconnection operates in states east of The Rockies, The Western Interconnection covers the Pacific Ocean to the Rocky Mountain states, and the smallest is the Texas Interconnection system.'

'No BS now,' the Vice President said. 'Can it be brought down by a hack?'

'It should be fine.'

The Vice President looked exasperated. He said, '*Should* be?'

'Since 2010,' the Secretary of Homeland Security said, 'we've deployed a wide range of advanced devices, including more than thirty thousand automated capacitor feeder switches—'

'Damn it!' the Vice President banged his fist on the table.

Then, another voice came over the speaker on the table. The President of the United States. 'We've spent hundreds of millions to make a resilient grid infrastructure that can survive a cyber incident while sustaining critical functions. Are you now saying that it's all been for nothing?'

'Mr President,' the Secretary of Homeland Security said. 'Most Internet attacks just affect users of one particular site or service. This one, however, will be aimed at breaking the whole thing. The fact is this: Jasper Brokaw is an insider. If someone can wreak havoc, it's him.'

The room fell silent.

McCorkell looked around. 'If I may,' he said. 'We've got an option here, in Jed Walker. Give him time.'

84

Jasper heard the gunshot. It was a dull, muffled sound through the concrete walls of the computer lab, but his time on the range in Fort Benning in Infantry training and then all the hours of shooting he'd done at Ranger School told him what it was: a high-calibre sniper's rifle. The thing he didn't know was, who was shooting at whom? Was someone here to liberate him, and were they under attack? Or was it the armed guys here, defending the position? Either way, it wasn't good – not now, not like this.

I need more time.

And help.

He entered the final commands for the next attack and set the RATs to work. Networks that he had infiltrated weeks ago were now doing his bidding.

One more attack remained. The power grid. And he couldn't do it, not alone. His palms were sweaty. He stood and paced then went to the stack of snacks, popped an energy drink and it fizzed and spat at him. He wiped the sticky red liquid from his hands to the front of his jeans. He looked across at the orange jumpsuit lying over the back of another chair, thought about how he would have to put it on one more time and sit in front of the camera.

In the meantime, chaos would reign. And the President just might buckle under the pressure.

•

Walker was forced to his knees next to Harrington, beside the van, and his hood was pulled off. Then Harrington's ski mask. The guy had a shock of red hair, a mess of it, and a beard to match. This black-bag outfit was clearly not like other Army units, Delta notwithstanding. They were designed to be able to operate outside regular Army units. Probably specialists in assassinating High Value Targets. If this guy Harrington was sitting next to you in a cafe, you wouldn't notice him as a potential threat until he'd stuck a knife between your ribs.

Two operators, clad in black and ski masks, were standing over them. They were identical to Harrington's team but for the weaponry. These guys were eclectic. They had the best of the US arsenal, plus the more exotic. Heckler & Koch HK416 assault rifles, as used by Delta and SEALs. One had a battle-scarred AK74 carbine strapped to his thigh, the other a long curved kukri-style knife. The type of stuff they would have acquired from the field while on operational deployment. Trophy hunters.

'This is Walker,' one of the guys said. 'Where are Paul Conway and Monica Brokaw?'

Harrington was silent.

Good. Buy time. Walker calculated the distances between the two men standing over them. The closest, the speaker, the one who had unmasked them both, who had stripped Harrington of his weapons, was a pace away, directly in front of Walker. The other stood sentry four paces back, his primary weapon, the HK416 assault rifle, action-ready in his grip. Walker knew he could snap out of the cable ties, but making the distance and disarming and subduing the man before his partner acted was near to impossible.

The guy crouched down and pulled up his ski mask. He was a hardened nut. Burn scars marked his face and neck, probably from an IED blast a decade back.

Harrington said, 'Why are you doing this, Jones?'

'Where are they, Harrington?' Jones said. 'Where are your team?'

'My team's gone,' Harrington said. He gave a nod to Walker. 'Thanks to him.'

Jones's eyes darted to Walker. 'That right?'

'They started it,' Walker said. 'Some big bald oaf, on a bridge. Who knew trolls walked on bridges?'

'Well, you always were the B-Team,' Jones said, looking back to Harrington. 'You guys never deserved to be part of this outfit. You're far too soft. And unless you cooperate, right now, you're going to die here, tonight, by my hand. So, I'll ask this just one more time. Where's Conway? The computer guy?'

The computer guy . . . Walker watched him closely. *And he's dropped any concern over Monica's location. Why?*

'Why'd you sell out like this?' Harrington asked him. 'What did the General promise you? How'd she sell it, to attack your own country like this?'

Jones was silent. Then, he looked at Harrington, drew the sixteen-inch kukri blade, which glinted under an Ames Base street light above, and held it towards Harrington. 'This is the last time I ask, while you're still in one piece. Where are Conway and the woman?'

Walker heard a noise. A faint buzzing.

The drone.

Walker could tell that the EMP had just been deployed, because Jones's expression changed.

'Idiot,' Jones said, pulling out his earpiece. 'You think cutting our comms is going to save you?'

Then there was another noise. This one was closer, and louder. A wet splat, or clap, like someone dropping a watermelon off a roof and onto the ground at your feet. Just behind Jones. His reaction was priceless.

'No,' Harrington said, 'but that might.'

Jones had heard the noise at the same time he heard Harrington speak – and he knew what that noise was, and that his fate was sealed as soon as he looked around, but he couldn't help it – human instinct. Just a second, not even, but he had to glance back to see how his squad mate had died.

Harrington used both hands to grab his knife hand and he pushed up from his knees, driving the long blade up through the bottom of Jones's chin and out the top of his head.

The next sounds were the lights shattering above them, again from Harrington's sniper, then—

WHACK! WHACK! WHACK!

85

A Team Black sniper was firing in the dark. The only thing he hit was his own man; Jones, still with the knife through his head, was now performing the role of human shield for Harrington and Walker. They shuffled around, then stopped.

'Okay,' Harrington said into his mike in response to the news relayed to him. He dumped the body. 'Their sniper is down,' he said to Walker.

He retrieved his weapons from the ground near the van, and Walker flexed, bringing his arms, still behind him, up in a fast x-motion, snapping the cable ties. He picked up the H&K rifle from the headless ex-soldier.

'You turned off the EMP,' Walker said.

'Just for a moment,' Harrington replied.

'No, it's good,' Walker said, joining Harrington and scanning the dark and the shadows of the buildings for the remaining three members of Team Black. 'Let me talk to the other team, on the open channel.'

Harrington unclipped the mike from the guy he'd stabbed and passed it over.

Walker said to him, 'What's their team leader's name?'

'Webster.'

'Okay.' Walker wrapped the mike around his neck and velcroed it in place, put the earpiece in. 'Webster,' he said clearly. 'This is the end. You've got two minutes to exit the computer lab, with Jasper Brokaw, in the open. If you fail to appear, you will be met with extreme prejudice. By that, I mean that you will be shot, several times, and your name will forever be mud in this fair nation as the truth comes out. One minute fifty . . . one minute forty five . . .'

Webster replied, 'Who is this?'

'Consider me a whirlwind,' Walker said. 'And you're about to have a house dropped on you. You let Brokaw go now. One minute thirty. You can do a lot in a minute and a half. And it's time for you and your team to decide which side of history you want to be on.'

Harrington stood and pointed his rifle as a black-clad figure emerged from the shadows. One of Webster's Team Black men.

'Gun down!' Harrington said, stepping around the van and keeping a line of sight on the surrendering—

WHOOMPH!

Harrington snapped back, his head turned to a puff of vapour.

•

'Okay,' the Vice President said to McCorkell. 'Thanks. Good work.'

'We're a hundred per cent on this?' the Secretary of Defense said to McCorkell.

'One hundred per cent,' the Vice President answered for him.

'Okay,' the Secretary of Defense replied. He left their four-person huddle, the Secretary of Homeland Security with them, and went to an aide, a full-bird Colonel, and whispered instructions.

'So,' the Vice President said to the screen, where General Christie had been leaning back in her chair for the past three minutes, watching but unable to listen. 'General Christie. Is there anything you want to tell us?'

'You're up to date, Mr Vice President,' the General replied. She'd crossed her arms, looking unfazed as they talked.

'I mean, General,' the Vice President said, leaning on the end of the table with the knuckles of his fists, his eyes straight down the video conference camera like looking down a barrel, 'what do you have to say about a team of yours being at Ames Research Center, having Jasper Brokaw there under guard? Interesting and pertinent information, wouldn't you say?'

McCorkell smiled when he saw General Christie's face drop. It was just a split second, then she gained composure and started to try to spin her way out of it. The two Joint Chiefs went a little red in the face, and pulled in their aides to get options rolling to deal with this shift.

'That's preposterous,' Christie said. 'Sure, I have a team there conducting a training exercise, but there is nothing that is remotely—'

'General!' the Vice President said. 'Enough! In under two minutes you are going to have a squad of MPs kicking down your door and you will be in cuffs, so talk now and start undoing this!'

'It's too late,' the General said calmly. She sat back in her chair and un-crossed her arms, staring at the camera in front of her.

86

This sniper fire was very different from the earlier shots. This was the report of an anti-materiel weapon, a .50-calibre rifle capable of punching holes through walls and light-armoured vehicles with its depleted uranium shells.

Walker ran towards the entrance to the computer lab. One thing about a .50-calibre sniper rifle was that it was big and slow to task and track and acquire a fast-moving target. Walker hit the front of the building; behind him, huge chunks of the concrete road and sidewalk had been blown out, until the sniper's clip was empty. He thought in the silence that remained he could hear a new mag being clicked into place, four storeys above, at the top of the computer lab, but he may have imagined the noise just as he imagined the action. The .50 sounds rang in his ears. The thing he couldn't know was whether the new sniper was alone up there; or did he have a spotter, watching his back?

'Okay, Webster,' Walker said. 'You've got fifty seconds. Last chance. There are now three of you. One on the roof, and I'm guessing two inside, with Brokaw. What's it going to be, Webster? Live like whatever it is you think you are, or die a lonely traitor's death? Forty seconds. Tick-tock.'

Silence.

'Okay, good,' Walker said. 'Harrington's boys, watch for my signal and then bring Conway in to do his thing.'

'What's the signal?' a voice replied, a voice Walker recognised from inside the van, the guy he guessed was their sniper.

'You'll see the guy with the point-fifty-cal hit the ground, head-first,' Walker said, already moving into the building.

'Copy that.'

'Remember,' Walker said, 'when things go dark, you'll be able to see my signal for your location to enter. Monica will tell you.'

'Copy that. Get some.'

The radio went dead as the EMP was again deployed. The four-storey glass and steel computer-lab structure wouldn't be EMP-proof, but the basement floors were, inside what was effectively a giant Faraday Cage to stop electronic emissions getting in or out of the massive server rooms. Walker found the stairs that led up and took them three at a time, the H&K rifle out front, the way ahead completely dark.

•

'What have we got on the ground near Ames?' the Vice President asked the room.

'Air Force guards out of Travis,' the Chairman of the Joint Chiefs said. 'Navy has armed NCIS personnel at the Naval Weapons Station in Concord. They can all be airborne and inserted inside of thirty minutes.'

'Palo Alto PD can set up roadblocks. Their tactical units can be in place in fifteen minutes.'

'Have them start a perimeter well outside so we can control the area,' the Vice President ordered. 'Where's all the NASA security?'

'General Christie had them all cleared out by six am yesterday for the so-called exercise. They're all on leave.'

'National Guard?'

'They can be there over the next half-hour. They've been gearing up all day in case of civil unrest, and California has already activated them in a few areas.'

'Admiral?' the Vice President asked the Chairman of the Joint Chiefs.

'Do it. Palo Alto, start locking down the whole area. It gives us time and options, and minimises civilian casualties should we need to take things further.'

'Further?' McCorkell said.

The Admiral nodded. 'We know where they have Brokaw. We'll get all the intel we need from General Christie as to who exactly is holding him. If they won't see sense and drop arms, we can strike the computer facility with JDAMs.'

'It's hardened,' an aide said, reading over schematics on a tablet. 'Underground redundancies for power generation.'

'We've got options for that,' the Admiral said to the Vice President. 'I'll make sure they're all at your disposal within the hour.'

'This has to be surgical,' McCorkell said to the room. 'There's Jasper Brokaw and other hostages. SWAT teams and cops and National Guard troops will create a siege-type situation.' He looked to the Director of the FBI. 'Hostage Rescue Team?'

'On standby in LA,' the FBI Director replied.

'They should be airborne,' McCorkell said. 'Forward deployed.'

The Director nodded, and got an okay nod from the Vice President to put the order through.

'We've got a total of an hour and ten minutes to their final deadline,' McCorkell said. 'We'll get one good shot at this and it has to be right.'

'That's ten minutes until the next attack, God knows where or what,' the Secretary of Homeland Security said. 'We need it to end as fast as possible, before things go too far.'

'We've got Russian tanks rolling into Eastern Ukraine,' the Admiral said. 'This went too far hours ago. Mr Vice President, we need to patch in the President on this and have a strike on Ames on the table, ready to go, should we need it. I can have F22s in the vicinity within fifteen minutes.'

'Okay,' the Vice President said. Orders started to be replayed. Everyone in the room was talking on phones or to aides, getting options rolling. He turned to the Secretary of Homeland Security. 'Are you certain the energy grid is secure?'

'Mostly, sir,' she replied. 'Just five minutes ago I would have said a hundred per cent certain. But now . . .'

'But now?'

'But now I wouldn't bet the house on it,' she replied. 'Not with how events have been unfolding. I don't like it.'

'We have to make General Christie talk,' McCorkell said.

'You do it, Bill,' the Vice President said, looking to the veteran security specialist. 'You've been at the forefront of this the entire time.'

'Because of Walker – and he's there at Ames.'

'Then he has twenty minutes, tops,' the Vice President said. 'Marine One is outside, take it to Fort Meade. Get to Christie, make her talk. What's at play – how's she getting to the grid? She talks or there's fire and brimstone for her, and for those at Ames.'

87

Walker knew he was four storeys up, at the roof level, because the stairs had ended. By the flickering glow of the lighter, he saw a door handle, and the security tape that had been broken at the latch to signal that the door had been used since security had done its last sweep of the building, presumably before General Christie had had the site evacuated almost thirty-six hours ago.

What was on the other side? The sniper's spotter, with an H&K rifle of his own, ready to turn Walker into ribbons of flesh and bone and gore? Or the sniper, lying on the roof, the business end of the barrel pointed at the centre mass of the door, waiting for it to open?

Walker kept his back to the wall. The wall itself was precast concrete, which would have metal reinforcing bars running through it, and was at least eight inches thick given how the steel doorjamb was set in place. He wasn't entirely confident it would stop a depleted-uranium round from a .50-calibre rifle, but it felt good to have that mass there, even as a placebo.

Walker pocketed the lighter and exhaled. He reached out his hand and opened the door by pushing the bar and flinging it open.

Nothing happened. He got as low to the floor as he could and peered out, then crawled out.

Nothing happened. He got up on a knee, his eyes down the sights of his H&K, scanning the scene.

And then he saw the sniper's position. The huge gun, a Barrett M107, was at the parapet, still aimed out at the car park below and resting on its bipod. The mat that the sniper had lain prone on was empty. A stack of spare mags sat next to the long gun. Walker saw all of that in a second but it was too little, too late.

Hands grabbed the H&K. Strong hands, twisting the weapon from Walker's grasp. Walker twisted with the motion and caught his attacker a little off balance, enough to separate.

The drone buzzed so close overhead he could feel the exhaust of the engine.

Walker spun around and kicked the guy's legs out. His finger found the trigger of the H&K and Walker stitched him up as he fell backwards, the 5.56-millimetre rounds hitting him at a rate of fire of 850 rounds per minute until the entire magazine of thirty rounds had been expelled in two seconds – they nearly all had hit home, from the dead man's groin to the top of his head.

Walker dropped the empty assault rifle and snatched up the guy's weapon, a Sig pistol, and dropped to one knee to scan the roof.

Deserted.

So, two members of Team Black remained below, guarding Jasper.

Walker tucked the Sig into his belt, then picked up the corpse of the sniper, hefted him to the side of the building and dumped him over, where he landed with a dull thud, head-first, because the head is the heaviest part of the body, even when partially emptied by high-velocity rounds.

He then held the lighter up in the sky and lit the flame.

•

'Change of plans,' Webster said, entering the room and standing next to Jasper, a Glock pistol in his hand. 'Activate the power outage now.'

'I can't,' he replied. 'I've instigated the drone takeover, and the traffic system—'

'We've run out of time. Bring it forward,' Webster said. 'Now.'

'That's what General Christie wants?'

'Yes.'

'I mean – now? Not an hour from now?'

'There won't be an hour from now.'

'Well, I can't do it,' Jasper replied, sitting back in his chair.

Webster's voice was gravel when he said, 'Can't, or won't?'

'I can't do it, you know that, not without Paul – he knows the code to get into the back door of the Department of Energy override. As soon as you get me Paul, five seconds after that we're done. He's everything – I told you that right from the start.'

'Okay,' Webster said. 'I'll get him. You make sure you're ready. Take this.'

He left the room, leaving Jasper to stare at the Glock pistol in front of him.

88

Monica saw the light. It was one continuous flame, holding for five seconds, which meant *Come on in*. She was standing next to Paul. On her other side was Kent, a member of Team Blue who had been manning the drone's controls on a tablet and using it to buzz close to Walker's attacker – the drone that was now doing its EMP work via an autopilot circuit above.

The other remaining Team Blue member, doing sniper overwatch a few yards away, called out, 'What's Walker's Zippo mean?'

'It means he's going in,' Monica said. 'And that we should too, so Paul can get into the servers and cut Jasper out of them while Walker finds them.'

'Okay. Kent will go with you,' the sniper replied, getting down from his post. 'I'm going after the base's power supply.'

'Where's that?' Kent called out as he helped Monica down from atop the guard box.

'Far eastern corner of the base.'

'Good luck,' Kent said, then passed Monica and Paul a pistol each and said, 'Stick close to me. You see anyone dressed like me who isn't me or him, shoot them until they drop, got it?'

•

335

Walker made his way downstairs with the dead man's Sig in his hands. He stopped at each landing, looking and listening before turning and leading the way with the pistol held out in front in a two-handed grip. Two levels below ground, the stairs ended at a solid door. He used the lighter to read the sign. 'Caution: computer servers – electronic protected area. Door must close before next opens.' He knew he had reached the part of the building the EMP could not affect, the heart of the server system.

He opened the door and entered a small airlocked space. The door behind him closed, and then he heard an electronic click as the door ahead unlocked. He pulled it open – it was a big, heavy blast door, designed to be sealed against any kind of fire or explosion outside by pushing it tight into its heavy steel and concrete frame.

The corridor ahead was lit by tube lighting, and he moved slowly forward.

No sign of Jasper, or anyone else.

Glass walls ran along either side, and beyond them were lit-up computer labs. One side held server banks, rows and rows of six-foot-high black stacks, each with hundreds of tiny little lights blinking and flashing. It was cold down here, and there was the sound of powerful airconditioning systems working hard to keep all that hardware cool.

Walker heard a noise and stopped. A door to his left was open. He could not see anyone beyond, but he did see something familiar – the video set-up. It was in an area of the computer lab that had been cleared of desks and consoles so that there was room enough for the chair that Jasper had sat on and the blank white wall behind and the tripod and camera pointed at the chair. Yesterday's newspaper was on the floor amid bottles of water, some empty, some full. Packs of MREs. Four military cot beds: one for Jasper, three for the team members to hot bunk.

Walker scanned the room.

Nothing. No sounds. All the computer terminals seemed to be on, the screens each displaying different sets of programming codes, and a few showing news sites. This was their command-and-control centre.

'Drop the gun,' a voice behind said. Webster's voice.

89

Walker turned, slowly, immediately thinking, *At least they didn't just cap me, which means they want something from m*e.

Jasper Brokaw was there. As were the two remaining members of Team Black. One held a pistol to Jasper's head. The other pointed a customised sawn-off shotgun at Walker.

'The gun,' Webster said. He was the man with the gun to Jasper's head. 'On the floor.'

Walker crouched and placed the Sig on the tiles.

'Kick it over,' Webster said.

Walker did so.

'Where's Conway?' Webster said, still holding the gun to Jasper's head.

'Outside,' Walker said.

'Why?'

'Why not?'

'You're lying,' Webster said. He looked to his comrade. 'Guard the stairs. Don't kill Conway. We need him.'

The guy left the room, headed for the stairs that Walker had just come down.

'What do you want with Paul?' Walker asked.

'Get his gun,' Webster said, suddenly letting go of Jasper.

Jasper bent down, picked up Walker's Sig, and took it to a terminal where he sat down and went to work at some code.

Walker looked from him to Webster, then back to Jasper again.

'Amazing, how little you know about what's going on here,' Webster said, striding the few paces towards Walker, his pistol raised and pointed one-handed dead at Walker's heart. 'And how you're never going to know.'

A gunshot rang out.

•

McCorkell was in the air, talking over a secure radio link to the Vice President in the Situation Room of the White House.

'The President wants to act,' the Vice President said to McCorkell. 'And I have to say, I agree with him – we can't let them shut down the national energy grid.'

'Give Walker some more time.'

'We're entering the final hour any minute,' the Vice President replied. 'And their threats so far have come to fruition. I'm sorry, Bill, but we have to shut this down.'

'If you shut the Net down, it's down for weeks, you know that, right?'

'Shutting down the Net has just shifted to Plan B.'

'And what's Plan A?'

'We've got a sortie of F22s headed for Ames. They can wipe the site in fifteen minutes.'

'Killing Walker, and Jasper Brokaw, and Monica Brokaw, and Paul Conway. Not to mention destroying billions of dollars of government—'

'We have to act,' the Vice President said with finality. 'The President is making a call on it in eight minutes. Plan A. Then, if needed, Plan B. He's not going to sit here and do nothing while a terror group cripples this country forever.'

'Give Walker more time.'

'I'm sorry, Bill. I really am. But we're out of time and options.'

'Send guys in – you've got FBI and National Guard units—'

'And if they see that they'll act early, crashing the power grid.' The Vice President paused, then spoke in a tone that brooked no argument. 'Bill, America without electricity is a billion dollars a second down the drain. The site is being wiped in fourteen minutes.'

90

The gunshot Walker heard was from the shotgun, and its boom echoed through the computer lab. He closed his eyes.

Webster smiled.

Jasper's fingers didn't skip a beat.

Then, more gunshots sounded.

The *pop-pop-pop* of 9-millimetre pistols, at least two of them, shooting rapidly, then the louder boom of the shotgun, then once again, then another volley of 9-millimetre shots – and then silence.

Two things happened at once.

Webster's finger tightened on the trigger of his Beretta.

And Walker dropped and dove.

The pistol belched out three rapid-fire shots and destroyed computer terminals as Walker landed behind a partition. Two more shots blasted holes either side of where he lay.

Walker heard the man run away, towards the stairwell, only turning to yell, 'Jasper – cover him!'

•

Monica and Paul looked at Kent, who was dead, a close-quarters shotgun blast having turned his chest into a bloody pulp as soon as he'd opened the secondary door. Then Monica looked at the gun in her hand, and the form of the dying man with the shotgun.

Bang.

Paul put another round into the guy's body, and he went limp.

'Wait,' Monica said, catching Paul's arm. She pointed down the hallway, and aimed her gun.

•

'Jasper!' Walker called out. 'Jasper – I don't know what you think you're doing, but you can stop this. If you ever thought this was just an exercise, you can still get out of it. Paul's here. Your sister's here. Yesterday I was with your father. They all care about you.'

No answer from Jasper. No shooting either. He could hear that Jasper was no longer typing.

'Jasper – be realistic about this,' Walker said, speaking up towards the ceiling, loud enough to be heard across the room. 'We're here. And they know – the government knows, that you're here. They'll have cops and Feds and the military all forming rings around this place. You have to think about how you want this to end. It's not too late to come out of this. But if you take it further . . .'

Nothing. Not a sound.

'If you turn off the energy grid, think of all the hospitals that will be without power. For how long? How long will their emergency generators last? What about the people at home who rely on power to survive on medical equipment? What about all the hell-raisers who are going to be combing the dark streets tonight? Or America's enemies, deciding to make what they can of the situation. Think about it, Jasper. Think of it all, and of your involvement.' Walker paused, then added, 'No-one has to know. I can get these two guys. And we can get to General Christie. You help us out here, no-one has to know of your true involvement. Jasper . . .'

Silence. Nothing. Nothing but the gush of the airconditioning and the hum of a few hundred computers.

Walker got to one knee and looked up, over the partition, towards where Jasper had been seated.

Empty.

91

Monica followed Paul down the corridor. The floor was tiled with white ceramic tiles, the suspended ceiling clad in white acoustic tiles and lighting panels, and the walls either side were made of thick clear glass. To her right were rows of black servers, like library-book stacks, though these were all black and sleek and lit up with blue LEDs and labelled at each end with NASA logos.

'This is NASA's Advanced Super-Computing Division,' Paul said, walking slowly and holding his pistol ready, as though waiting for another threat to emerge like the guy with the shotgun who had blasted Kent away as soon as he'd opened the airlock. 'Their Pleiades system is in the top five most powerful super-computers in the world.'

'And they have Jasper in control of it,' Monica said, walking close to him.

Then, ahead, two figures emerged.

'Guns, now,' a deep voice said.

As they took another pace forward Monica made out her brother, next to a man dressed in the same black paramilitary gear as the others, and the same full-face ski mask. The man was holding a pistol to her brother's head.

'Drop the guns!' the guy said.

Paul bent down and put his gun to the floor then raised his hands.

Monica held her pistol steady. She remembered how her father had taught her and her brother to shoot a 9-millimetre when they were kids. Like pointing your finger at the target, he'd said. Point and shoot.

•

Walker stood. There was no sign of Jasper. He went to the console where Jasper had been seated. There was no pistol there. No weapon.

The screens were all running data that meant near to nothing to him.

He looked around the room. Nothing much of any use. On the desk opposite was a small tool-pouch. He took two small screwdrivers, put one in his back pocket and another in the palm of his hand. He slid off his boots, then crept from the room, his footfalls silent on the tiled floor.

•

'Monica,' Jasper said, the gun to his temple. 'You shouldn't have come here.'

Monica held the pistol steady. The 9-millimetre Sig was similar to the Beretta she'd learned to shoot with, but a little bigger and more plasticky. It had a three-dot sight system, and she lined them up at the head of the man who was pointing the pistol at her brother. They were maybe twenty paces down the hall. The target was small, his head partially obscured by her brother's. She knew she could not guarantee the hit. Her finger pressure increased on the trigger.

'Mon,' Jasper said. 'Please. Put the gun down. No-one has to die here.'

Monica kept the pressure up. The man holding her brother was taking half-strides towards them, narrowing the distance, increasing her chances of a shot.

'Please,' Jasper said, his shoulders hunching. 'Put your gun down. Please? There's no need for that. We're going to walk out of here – it's nearly over. See? We can walk out and go home and go see Dad. Make things right. I – I can make things right. Once this is done – you'll see. I promise. I'm . . . I'm – I'm sorry, Mon. Okay? Please . . . I'm sorry. I'm so sorry.'

Monica's hands started to shake and tears ran down her face. She saw Paul watching her and nodding, and she lowered the pistol. He took it from her trembling hands and placed it on the floor, then stood up and held her.

The guy took the gun from Jasper's head.

Jasper smiled. Then, he reached into the back pocket of his orange jumpsuit and pulled out a pistol of his own, pointed it at Paul and walked towards him. 'Now, it's time that you did the job you've always been preparing for.'

92

Walker moved quietly up the hall. He'd seen the back of Webster holding the pistol to Jasper's head. They were twenty paces away, and slowly moving towards Monica and Paul. He kept crouched down, out of sight of Monica and Paul by the two standing bodies between them.

Walker watched them trying their play of hostage-and-captor again.

He saw it work on Paul.

Then Monica hesitated.

Then Jasper said the words that Monica had always been desperate to hear.

Then she passed over her pistol and Paul put it on the floor.

As Jasper headed for Paul, Walker knew he had a second, maybe two, until Webster turned.

Walker moved fast.

Webster turned, bringing his pistol up.

•

'You always were the better coder,' Jasper said to Paul, standing over him. 'But you never were much use at chess.'

Paul was silent.

'*I* organised your new ID via that Tor site,' Jasper said to Paul, his pistol pointed at Paul's head. 'And *I* got you that interview and made them take you on at the security contractor that looked at the DoE and other government agencies. That's been the exercise. Not this. Don't you see? This was all preordained, by someone far, far smarter and much more insightful than you, and many, many steps ahead.'

Paul's face fell.

Monica's hands balled into fists and she screamed as she launched at her brother.

•

Walker jumped the final few yards, his fist outstretched.

Webster brought his pistol up to fire before Walker's fist found its mark – against Webster's head.

Walker fell.

Webster stood over him, smiled, and brought the pistol to aim.

•

Paul caught Monica and held her back. He could see commotion over Jasper's shoulder, and recognised Walker.

'See,' Jasper said, a smirk on his face. 'That's the girl. Always needed a little . . . direction.'

'The hell with you!' Monica screamed. 'This was all you! You're attacking your own country? You're pathetic! A monster!'

Jasper shook his head. 'You have no idea. This will make us all so much stronger – so much stronger. We need a Cyber Command that is equal to the other branches of the military – and this will bring that, you'll see. People will thank me. Play your part, and they may even remember you.'

•

'This is where you—'

Webster was standing over Walker, pointing the gun at him, and stopped mid-speech. His left hand went up to the side of his head, where Walker's right hand had landed the blow. He felt the impact point, and touched the end of the screwdriver that had imbedded through the temple, that point where the skull is at its thinnest. Webster's mouth opened and closed, once, twice, three times, then he fell back and landed with a thud.

Dead.

The sound alerted Jasper, who turned around and took in the scene. Webster on the floor, killed silently but for the fall. And Walker, on his back, scrambling away, towards the door to the server room.

Jasper shot at him. The glass wall shattered but held – huge panes of laminated tempered glass, each sheet an inch thick and made up of plastic sandwiched between layers of lead-free glass.

'No!' Monica yelled.

Walker got to his feet behind a server. He ran down the row, took a right turn and doubled back. It was dark in here, and Walker thought he was onto a good thing until he realised it was about as bad as he could imagine: the lights overhead came on as he ran, motion sensors lighting the way. Wherever he ran in this room, it would be lit up for a predetermined period of time. Nowhere to run, nowhere to hide.

Another gunshot rang out.

Then – darkness.

93

Team Blue's sniper was at the power plant and realised that it was not deserted. With billions of dollars worth of technology on the Ames campus, unless there was a severe natural disaster or emergency, there was no way every staff member would leave.

There were two staffers in the power generator, a gas turbine unit with a couple of wind towers recently added. He had been fully prepared to use his two thermobaric explosive grenades, and if that didn't work he was considering piloting the drone into the place to shut the power down.

He didn't need to do either. What he did do was point his rifle at the two NASA contractors, who were only too willing to follow his orders to shut down all the power on the base. Within a second of seeing the streets and buildings go dark, he saw the emergency generators kick in, with muffled dim lights springing up here and there. Figuring the worst, he tied up the staffers and ran back towards the super-computing lab.

•

The emergency lighting lit the room at intervals.

Walker was still. He was listening. The sea of tiny blue lights of the servers were on but the sound of the airconditioning had disappeared. He moved two rows over, closer down the hall to where Monica and

Paul and Jasper had been. He peered down the row and saw beyond the glass wall that the emergency lighting in the hall had kicked in, and that Jasper, Monica and Paul were there, and that Jasper was herding the other two at gunpoint towards the computer lab.

Walker crept down the alley between the servers, his footfalls still silent on the tiles. The room was already heating up, and he wondered if there was a thermostat that would override the system and shut the computers down once they had reached a peak temperature. But even if this were the case, it was no kind of fall-back plan, not in the time frame that was now upon them. He had to get to Jasper and stop what was coming.

•

Jasper sat Paul in a chair at the terminal he'd been using and held the gun to his head.

'Enter your code, and start your RAT,' Jasper said. 'Get into the DoE's server and shut the grid down.'

'I can't,' Paul said. He looked across to Monica, who had her arms crossed over her chest and was shaking her head.

'You can and you will and you have one minute,' Jasper said.

'Why?' Monica said. 'Why are you doing this?'

Jasper pushed the pistol hard into the back of Paul's head, so that he was stooped closer to the computer screen.

'Just do it.'

Monica said, 'It's not too late to change, Jasper . . .'

•

Walker stayed in the shadows, near the camp cots and the camera on the tripod, watching the scene. Jasper still had the gun to Paul's head; there was no way to get in there and disarm him without Jasper painting the screen with Paul's head. But Jasper needed Paul, for his end game, which meant that as long as Paul stalled, Walker had time.

Paul was typing commands.

Walker moved to the camera, flicked it on and pointed it at Jasper, all without making a sound. He zoomed in to capture the scene: the three of them; the gun to the head; the microphone picking up the conversation from ten feet away. Broadcasting the scene to the world.

94

'You can't do this,' Monica said. 'Take a higher road. For once in your life, be a better—'

'Shut up! Of course I can, I can do whatever I want!' Jasper replied without looking at her. 'Well, *he* can – but I'm the one with the gun, right? And look, it's really quite easy. Right? People make mistakes, Mon. Have I? I don't know. But you know what? It was human error that caused the blackout in August 2003 – more than fifty million people without power for two days. That was a high-voltage powerline in northern Ohio that brushed against some overgrown trees. It shut down and caused a fault. Normally that problem would have tripped an alarm in the control room, but the alarm system failed. You know why? It was hacked.'

'By you?'

'No. By someone with malicious intent, I'd say.'

'And your intent is what?'

'Patriotic duty,' Jasper said. 'Many steps ahead of this moment here. You'll see. At any rate, that blackout from a single source forced other powerlines to shoulder an extra burden – and in turn they cut out by tripping a cascade of failures throughout south-eastern Canada and eight north-eastern states, making it the biggest blackout in North American history. What I'm doing will become just like that. It will make us stronger. Make the system stronger.'

'And you want to do that to the whole country?'

'Oh no, nothing so primitive,' Jasper said. 'See, the US power grid consists of three loosely connected parts: eastern, western and Texas. That's our first problem – it's just three connected pieces. So, what we're about to do, in the long run, will make our country better. And I'm not just talking about the power grid – I'm talking about all these attacks. It's like losing a war: you learn from it, improve and adapt for the next one – and there will be a war, a big war some day, and we have to be prepared. It's people like me and General Christie who get that.'

'You want this cyber attack to result in the government implementing a smart grid capable of monitoring and repairing itself?' Paul said. 'Why don't you just spend your time programming for that?'

'You're thinking too small, as usual,' Jasper said, pressing the Glock harder into the back of Paul's head. 'This is one of many attacks I've performed since yesterday, each needing attention. Every hack that I've implemented over the past thirty-five hours has been about highlighting what we need to fix. Secure our networks. Crypto our information. Protect our infrastructure, from GPS to the energy grid. Fire back at attacks at the source. Have safeguards on our automated weapons systems. Admit when we are attacked by a foreign national and fire back a proportional response. And pre-emptively strike. We can now – why not? Why not wipe out the economies of our adversaries? Why not let the world read all about them, every little private detail, to show what kind of corrupt hypocritical despots they really are?'

Walker kept the camera rolling, never letting his eyes leave the gun in Jasper's hand.

'It's not too late . . .' Monica said. She had tears running down her cheeks. 'If you want the country to have learned a lesson, you've done it. Now stop it.'

'One of our greatest threats are those people here who are being radicalised and inspired by the propaganda that groups like ISIS put out there on the Internet,' Jasper said. 'These home-grown violent extremists are inspired from overseas but they often act alone, and it's not easy to track them down. This is the profile of the enemy within. This will give us a chance to root them out, starting from scratch, starting with an Internet where everything is monitored.'

'You've changed, man,' Paul said.

'I'm the hero this country needs right now,' Jasper said. 'You'll see.'

'People will die, Jasper,' Monica said. 'All the hospitals without power? All those traffic lights stopping people slamming their cars into each other? Accidents will happen. People will riot and loot.'

'It's like ripping off a bandaid,' Jasper said. 'Or consider it a bit of Darwinism. We'll be fine. Well, at least I will be. I can't speak for Paul here.'

'You're a real hero,' Monica said, not hiding the spite in her voice. 'Dad would be so proud. Mum too.'

Jasper turned and pointed the gun at her. His expression was deadpan. 'Paul, you have ten seconds, and if you're not done by then, I will shoot my sister. That would make you sad, I would think. Unless you've changed? Your choice. Tick-tock, old friend.'

95

Jasper had dressed in his orange jumpsuit for the last time. He tucked the Glock into the back pocket and took his seat in front of the camera. With its viewfinder facing him, he used the remote to zoom a little, so that it framed him tightly, from the chest up to an inch or so above his head, and a couple of inches clear either side. The background, this time, was the background of the NASA computer lab – and Walker knew then that this was for keeps. Neither Monica nor Paul would be getting out of here alive. Jasper too – this seemed like he was about to admit to the world what he'd done and why, and Walker could not see a way out for him if he did that.

'Let's see where we are,' Jasper said to the camera. 'And let's see how I can take you away from the edge of this abyss . . . When I was in the Army, I saw things that shook me to my core, that changed my view on how our country is governed, and where we have arrived, as one people, as humanity.

'This is my chance to set things right. But let me tell you what I saw, the thing that made me then change direction, inspired me to join the NSA and work from within, which has brought me to this point, where I am on your screens right now.'

Jasper took a breath, then said to the camera: 'In 2008, something quite extraordinary occurred in the United States, something that – despite its clearly controversial nature – went almost entirely unaddressed by mainstream media. On the first of October 2008 the US military assigned the 1st Brigade Combat Team of the 3rd Infantry Division to the United States Northern Command. This meant that American soldiers were operating on US soil, seemingly in direct contradiction of our constitution.

'The 1st Brigade was there so that it could be called upon to help with civil unrest and crowd control or to deal with potentially horrific scenarios such as massive chaos in response to a chemical, biological, radiological, nuclear or high-yield explosive attack. But our Posse Comitatus Act, passed in 1878 following Reconstruction, prohibits federal military personnel from acting in a law-enforcement capacity in the United States, except if authorised by constitutional amendment or Congress.

'I ask you, where does it stop?

'Since September 11, 2001, the executive branch has been slowly chipping away at civilian protections against martial law, possibly rendering both Posse Comitatus and the Insurrection Acts impotent. You know what?' he tugged at his orange jumpsuit. 'We're all prisoners, in this country. And that's gotta change. It's time for us all to rise up and take control. It's our constitutional right.

'We will have a cyber equivalent of Pearl Harbor at some point, and we must not wait for that wake-up call. Through my actions, I'm giving our nation a chance to adapt. Social networks and other online services are the command-and-control choice for terrorists and criminals; my work has highlighted that. Massive networking makes the US the world's most vulnerable target. We need to be aware of that. The question for us is not what new story will come out next. The question is, what are we going to do about it?'

96

Walker had watched Jasper's speech.

And now, Jasper had signed off and moved back to Paul, who was taped to the chair, and he held the Glock to the back of his head.

'Enter the code,' Jasper said. 'Do it now, or . . .'

Jasper lowered the gun at Paul's leg. Walker reached up and pressed the record button, and the feed started to transmit to the world.

'The code,' Jasper said.

Paul's hands didn't move.

'You always were slow to realise what needed to be done,' Jasper said to him. 'Don't you see what I've done? Don't you see what you could have been a part of?'

Paul was silent and still.

'The code, bitch!'

'Leave him alone!' Monica said.

'Oh, my little sister is sticking up for this guy?' Jasper said to her in a mocking tone. 'Why? Why would you do that? We're supposed to be family . . .'

Walker made sure that the camera took in the whole scene. Right now, hundreds of millions of screens around the world, perhaps in the billions, were seeing this live feed.

And they were seeing Jasper for who and what he really was.

'Come on!' Jasper screamed at Paul. 'I've done it this far! Me! All on my own – I've stood up to make this nation a stronger place – and now, at the end, you're going to stand in my way?'

Paul was silent. He just stared at the screen in front of him.

'Okay,' Jasper said, his tone was defeated. He pointed the Glock down towards his sister. 'Paul? Paul . . . look here Paul.'

Paul looked.

'You enter that code to shut down the nation's energy grid, or first my sister loses the use of her legs, and a lot of blood, and then her life, and then the same will happen to you, only slower.'

Paul looked to Monica.

'Ignore him,' Monica said. She was composed and calm. 'They'll be here soon. This will all be over.'

'One,' Jasper said.

'Leave her be,' Paul said. His voice shook. 'You—'

'Two,' Jasper said. 'Just enter the code.'

Walker moved around the room, crouched low, so that he could come up behind Jasper. Without a weapon, he would be reliant on crash-tackling him, and doing his best to not allow the Glock to go off in Monica's direction.

'Three.'

97

In General Christie's office, McCorkell and Somerville watched the screen in detached incredulity. General Christie had not yet said it, but it was clear to anyone in view of a screen that Jasper was a part of this, a willing participant rather than a hostage being forced to do the will of others.

It took a while for Monica to start screaming. By the time she did, Paul had entered the code, and suddenly Walker came into view, running across the room.

Jasper saw Walker and brought up the Glock. He started firing—

And then the screen went dead. As did the lights in the room, until the back-up power system took over.

McCorkell looked to General Christie.

'See?' she said. 'I win. You lose. You need to wake up. We're in a cyber cold war. You think this ends now? You're a fool. People will rally behind me. We'll get our cyber arm of the military. I'll be pardoned. I'll be honoured. And then where will you be? We'll see who comes out on top after—'

Somerville punched General Christie square in the face, and she slumped unconscious in her seat.

'Thank you,' McCorkell said.

'We have to get help into there, for Walker.' Somerville was on the phone and calling in everything that was on hand at Ames.

McCorkell looked at the time. 'We might be too late.'

•

Walker felt the bullet tear into his left triceps and his arm exploded in heat and heaviness, as though he could no longer control it.

But it didn't matter. Two hundred and thirty pounds hit Jasper side on, and it would have made his football coach back at the Air Force Academy Falcons proud. He heard the air crash out of Jasper as he was hit, and then Walker landed on him with all his force and weight, which slid them both across the tiled floor, slippery with blood mixing from both Monica and Walker. Jasper's head hit the tiles with the satisfying sound of a coconut cracking and he was out cold, and the Glock clattered across the floor. Walker sat up and inspected his wound. Not bad – not much blood compared to what was on the floor.

That was from Monica. Her leg shot was in the thigh and it was arterial blood.

'Pressure!' Walker said. He removed his belt in the three strides it took to reach her and looped it around her upper thigh and pulled it tight as he elevated the limb above her heart, her torso and head now on the ground.

Her shock was abating and she screamed – the kind of scream that ripped through the air and sliced into the walls, the sound destined to forever echo in the concrete bunker.

'Paul?' Walker said as he watched Monica's bleeding start to slow to a trickle.

'Rebooting . . . now.' He left his chair and crashed down onto the slippery floor, next to Monica, and held her hand.

Monica said, 'The power went down?'

'And will stay down, until the local power company manually restarts all their mains switches,' Paul said, helping stabilise Monica, putting his folded shirt under her head and keeping hold of her hand. Blood was everywhere. 'But the grid is back up, Mon. And it's over. Hear me? Jasper is over. This is all over. We won.'

Monica nodded. Her face was white.

Walker stood and went to try one of the phones to call for an EMT—

And stopped.

Jasper was gone.

98

Walker looked back to Paul, who was holding Monica and talking softly to her to keep her awake. They both saw the expression on Walker's face and knew, without even looking around, what had transpired.

Walker said, 'I have to—'

'Go,' Monica said. 'Go. Get him.'

'I've got this,' Paul replied. He squeezed Monica's hand. 'We've got this.'

Walker gave Paul a landline phone from a desk and then he ran.

•

'We've got San Francisco SWAT and EMTs rolling into Ames now,' Somerville said.

On cue the television news feed went from the talking heads discussing their shock over Jasper's involvement to a live feed from a news chopper above NASA's Ames Research Center. The entire area around Ames was blacked out, but the campus itself had a few building lights on, generated by its back-up power.

'What's that?' McCorkell said, pointing to the east. 'Fires?'

Somerville looked closer at the screen. A few blocks out from Ames were residential streets. Then the helo tracked its cameras at the SWAT and EMT vans rolling through the streets towards the super-computing lab. The EMT vehicles stopped. The SWAT van rolled closer and stopped and then its members fanned out. Another helicopter came into view and landed – a ghost in the night, painted black and visible only for its navigation lights. An eight-man team dressed in combat fatigues.

'That's HRT,' Somerville said. 'They'll go in first.'

McCorkell nodded, watching the FBI's Hostage Rescue Team move quickly towards the super-computing lab, the members splitting up and heading for two entry points, while the Palo Alto SWAT unit set up fire positions outside.

The news helicopter did a wide circuit, and the cameras were now pointed away from the Ames Research Center, towards the glowing fires a mile out.

The images showed the National Guard at their checkpoints, a three-mile diameter bubble around Ames, and beyond the Guard troops and their big bright lights was the darkness of a city with no power. But that darkness was punctuated, near the Guard units, by fires. First one, then a few, then several, and now more than a dozen, glowing and burning hot and bright. Some fires were cars, others were molotov cocktails burning against the ground.

'People are rioting,' Somerville said. 'The power being out, all cell phones being out – they're losing it.'

'Wait until they get the power on and find out what kind of guy Jasper Brokaw really is.'

•

Jasper ran. His prosthetic leg below his knee was loose but he ignored it, ignored the pain and the way that it was wobbling and slowing him down. He kept checking over his shoulder, the Glock in his hand, trying to think how many rounds he had left, if it came to it.

He was in the sub-basement level. He had studied the schematics for the building and he knew that this was part of an emergency escape network twenty feet beneath the base, with concrete tunnels and ductwork and piping overhead, weaving all over a couple of square miles, with egress points dotted all about the base and beyond. Blue stripes and green stripes were painted on the floor. He knew that the tunnels with blue stripes led to exit points on the base, and that those with green stripes led to points outside of the NASA compound.

He followed green.

There would be cops at the exit, he figured.

Emerge, plead for help, they'll give it – shoot them, ditch the jumpsuit and keep moving. Blend into the crowd—

'Jasper!' A voice cut through the tunnel. Walker. 'Jasper! I'm coming for you!'

99

Walker stopped at a cross junction in the labyrinthine tunnel system beneath Ames. He stood still and listened, trying to make out which way Jasper had gone. He kept a hand tight on his arm as blood poured over his fingers, the flow faster than before from the exertion of running. Movement, shuffling, the echoed pitter-patter of the uneven gait of Jasper running away. The tunnel to his left, with a green stripe painted on the floor and ductwork and piping above, and every fifteen feet a small neon light overhead.

Walker set off in pursuit.

•

Jasper stopped. He was panting hard. He propped himself up at the turn in the tunnel; the construction of the tunnels included lots of thirty-degree turns so that if there was a blast or a fire it would not flush clear through the tunnel like a chimney and the fire-suppression systems in the pipes above could stand a chance to extinguish it.

Ahead was a clear 200 yards. He held the Glock with as steady a hand as he could muster.

Deal with Walker. Get to the exit. Kill the cops. Blend in. Get a vehicle, get away, find a phone, call the General, replay and reboot. Maybe what they'd done was enough. Maybe it wasn't. Either way, so long as he got out. He saw a shadow at the bend behind him.

Jasper fired twice. The sound of the 9-millimetre Glock in the confines of the concrete tunnel was near deafening, and he worked his mouth and jaw against the sounds that were crashing through his head. Seeing Walker go down, he turned and ran.

•

Two hundred yards of travel for a 9-millimetre bullet was not a problem. Aiming and hitting a target, a moving target, over that distance, was near-on impossible. The fall of the round over that distance was extreme as gravity worked on the projectile. There was no wind sheer to factor in.

The two slugs from the Glock were travelling at 1200 feet per second down the corridor and Walker dropped as he heard the shots, thinking in that split second that Jasper would be aiming high, for a centre mass, while at the same time his mind told him that any action was useless and likely just as dangerous as taking no action at all, because the two lumps of metal headed his way would likely hit the concrete wall or ceiling and ricochet around and spit up bits of concrete that would act as shrapnel. In the same moment that he hit the concrete floor he knew that by the time he heard the shots the rounds would have been on him already, so it was a moot point as the speed of sound was around 1200 feet per second. Hear the shot – and the shot is at you.

The shooting stopped. The sound echoed. Walker got up and checked himself over. His hands were covered in blood, but it was just the blood running down one arm and trickling down his fingers, and it was the blood from that same wound now on the opposite hand as he'd used it to clamp the wound.

He started up the tunnel and his leg nearly gave out.

He fell down.

A small entrance tear in his black jeans, in his mid-thigh, at the front, slightly to the side of his femur. He opened it a little more and saw the wound. It was either a bullet or shrapnel, he couldn't tell which. There was no exit wound. It bled but it was nothing like Monica's arterial wound.

He looked up the tunnel and ran as fast as he could, but by the time he'd made 200 yards he was feeling dizzy. He saw a door, another 200 yards ahead. No Jasper. He ran for the door.

•

Jasper held the Glock in his right hand, behind his back, and he used his left hand to hold onto the handrail as he made his way up the concrete stairs. It was a narrow staircase, and steep, and there were thirty-six steps. At the top was a steel door, and it had a bar across it that said to 'Push to exit'. He paused, composed himself, and pushed.

100

Walker got to the door at the end of the tunnel. It was a fire door made from laminated sheets of fireproof sheet-rock and had a small wire-mesh glass window set in it. There was no sign of Jasper beyond, but there was no-where else he could have gone, so Walker pushed open the door and started up the stairs. Pain shot up through his leg and he felt light-headed.

There were thirty-six steps, and at the thirty-second Walker slipped; his leg couldn't carry all his weight, so he shifted his weight to the other one and used his wounded arm to support himself. His hand, coated in thick, tacky blood, repeatedly slipped on the handrail, but he dragged himself forward to the steel door that had a 'Push to exit' bar. He pushed it gently and put his weight behind it to force it open.

It stopped about a foot away. It was noisy outside – very noisy, like a giant street party and a sporting match rolled into one. Walker pushed harder and opened the door enough to slip out, and he immediately saw why it hadn't opened.

Two uniformed police officers were on the ground, dead, each shot twice through the head. One had fallen against the door.

Walker bent down and picked up his Glock and cell phone from the closest. The phone was powered on but there was no signal.

Walker looked around. No sign of Jasper.

Then he saw the orange jumpsuit, crumpled on the ground. His gaze was drawn further out, to the street, which on this side of the NASA block was a mixed-use residential and business street. Then he saw where the noise was coming from: at the end of the street a full-blown riot was taking shape. There were two Humvees, and numerous National Guard troops, under the only light around, their own big strobes.

Walker saw the glow of fires and the fury of people throwing bottles and stones at the Guard troops. The opposite end of the street had a similar scene, but further away, and with fewer people.

Walker headed towards the busier area. If Jasper wanted to disappear, a big crowd was better. And he would be in the open for less time, hobbling along.

Walker too was hobbling. And struggling. And he nearly slipped on something – a cell phone.

Then he saw more of them. People had been throwing them at the Guard troops, and as Walker scanned the people's faces, he saw their anger and frustration directed towards what they saw as representatives of a government that had let them down through inaction against a terror threat. Everyone, young people mostly, massed there, facing the Guard troops. A few hundred people were acting as one, chanting and yelling and full of fury, fire burning in their eyes. The Guard had a front line of men with riot shields and a second line with M4 assault rifles, maybe loaded with riot rounds, maybe not. Walker headed into the crowd.

•

Jasper was pushing his way through the mass of protesters. The Glock was tucked into the pocket of his jeans. He wore only a T-shirt and thin cotton hoodie with jeans, so he was cold, but that didn't bother him. He had the hood pulled over his head, so he was near invisible as he made his way towards the back of the crowd. It was hard going, with the mass moving against him, but he was just over halfway through and already thinking about how so many of these idiots, so quick to get to the action and add their pitiful voices to their cause, would have left cars double- and triple-parked on the streets beyond, with doors open and keys in the ignition. In an hour he would be in his safe house north of the city, and he would stay there until he felt it was safe to venture outside. That may take months, but he was prepared for that. This was his opus. The sum of all his work for the government. All that disappointment he'd ever encountered and felt. All the bullying from his father about doing his service. All the crap he'd gone through during boot camp, in the infantry, and the cyber division and the NSA. Now the whole world would know just how capable he was.

Then, he looked back, over his shoulder. Human instinct. He had to be sure that he was not being followed.

101

Walker saw Jasper's face. A figure in a black hoodie, glancing back over his shoulder, for a split second, and then there was recognition there, in his eyes, and Jasper turned away and tried to move faster.

But he couldn't. If you move rhythmically through the mass of an oncoming crowd, filling spaces and having people weave around you as you move your own way, you'll get somewhere. But try pushing and muscling your way through, and you'll end up bumping and knocking and bouncing into people – people who then bounce and knock and bump into others, and then things get tense, and angry, which was where things were now headed.

Then, the whole world changed.

The street lights came on.

Flickering, one by one, linking up and illuminating the streetscape. And then the building lights.

Walker kept moving. Hobbling his way towards Jasper.

A noise started up. At first a chime, then a cacophony. Cell phones. It started with a few, then several, and then dozens and more. The sound of people trying desperately to call loved ones and reach out to anyone in the darkness that had covered the country for the past fifteen minutes.

'Hey!' someone shouted up ahead as Walker made up some ground in his pursuit of Jasper Brokaw. 'It's him! It's the guy from the TV – the captive!'

'Look!'

'It's him!'

'Help him!'

'That's him!'

'Hey, man!'

'Look!'

The crowd changed. Changed mood, changed direction. It was fast becoming an inward-looking, swirling mass, a school of fish swarming around a middle point, encircling Jasper.

Walker could see and hear the hubbub start to die down as he moved against a tide that slowly stopped. The crowd started to thin. People were picking up cell phones and answering calls and seeing news feeds on social media and videos of what and how Jasper really was. Suddenly the night was near silent, for the briefest of moments.

And then it changed again.

102

'We've got Monica and Paul,' Somerville said, hanging up a phone. 'Monica's in bad shape but she was stabilised on the scene and they've started transfusions – she's being medivaced as we speak. Paul is unharmed.'

McCorkell nodded, watching live footage of the riots at the National Guard lines near Ames Research Center, followed by a cut to an anchor who reported that power had been restored across the country, with some states and counties having to rely on workers to manually throw circuit switches in certain areas of the grid to reset. The anchor then put a finger to his earpiece and spoke.

'This, just in, breaking news from outside NASA's Ames Research Center in Palo Alto, where the now confirmed terrorist, Jasper Brokaw, has been staging his own capture and . . . and I believe we have footage coming in live, we'll – yep, we'll see the scene now in a live cross . . .'

•

Walker had moved to within reaching distance of Jasper when the terrorist stopped and pulled out his Glock. He fired up into the air to spook the crowd, who were now leering and heckling and throwing things at him – and nothing happened. Emptied, on those two cops earlier.

Walker watched.

'That's him!' someone shouted, pointing at Jasper.

'That's the son of a bitch there!'

'He's the terrorist!'

'Get him!'

Soon it was dozens of voices. Then hundreds. Chaos.

Jasper looked to Walker as the first cell phone was thrown and hit his head. Blood trickled down. Then a rock. A bottle. A shoe. More phones.

Walker gave him nothing. He backed away.

The crowd moved in. Punches were thrown, people were yelling and shouting.

Those outside the first couple of rings of people were holding their cell phones up, filming the scene, the sight like a modern-day rock concert where people experienced the act filtered through tiny screens and crappy audio quality to play back again at a later time on a tiny screen with crappy audio. History was being made and it was being recorded, but those present were less participants than conduits.

That footage was being streamed live, being grabbed online and being played on social media; memes were already starting to spread like a virus. The world knew what Jasper Brokaw really was.

Countless people were filming Jasper getting his butt kicked. Walker didn't need to do anything more; Second Amendment and all that.

Walker turned and limped away.

103

Walker hobbled down the road. He saw a phone on the street, discarded or thrown earlier when it was still useless.

He picked it up and touched the screen. It was locked, but he needn't worry. He looked at the ground and the discarded cell phones like leaves in the fall, littering the ground, tossed away in some kind of mass movement against all that was happening. He picked through them until he found one that was not locked.

Walker rubbed the blood from his hand and dialled a number he knew by heart. And on the third ring it was answered and he heard the voice that he never wanted to forget, never could forget.

'Hello?'

'Eve . . .'

'Jed?'

'I . . . I'm . . .' Walker stumbled from the loss of blood and the phone clattered to the ground. The world started to spin as he tried to focus on the phones around him, to locate the one he had used. Sights and sounds began to blur and dim.

'Are you okay? Jed? Jed? Walker – Walker!'

Walker could hear Eve's voice as he bent through doubled vision to retrieve the phone. Blood coated his hands and he fumbled until he wiped them on his jeans, and then he grasped the phone and brought it to his ear and sat down on the footpath. He lowered himself down, gently, onto his back. The ground was hard and cold, the sky was dark, most of the street lights still yet to come on, a sea of stars above.

'I . . .' Walker said into the phone, his voice rasped breaths. 'Eve, I'm sorry.'

'Where are you?'

'I just wanted you . . . to tell you . . .'

'Tell me where you are.'

'I wanted you to know that . . .' Walker blacked out for a second. He saw two National Guardsmen running towards him. 'You – you need to know that I – how I . . .'

'Jed?'

'I wanted to tell you, Eve, I . . . that I . . .'

'I know. I know. Me too.'

EPILOGUE

Walker was in a bed in Stanford University Hospital. A nurse checked him over, helped him sit up and left the room. McCorkell and Somerville were standing by the foot of the bed.

'The ICANN members?' Walker asked.

'They were housed at Los Alamitos Army Airfield in LA,' McCorkell said.

'The same place Harrington's crew used,' Somerville added.

'They were taken there by Team Black?' Walker asked.

McCorkell nodded, said, 'Apparently they were told it was a forty-eight hour security exercise.'

'And if the Internet had been shut down?' Walker said. 'What then?'

'Team Black would've been free of safeguarding Jasper and all that, so who knows?' Somerville said. 'Bullet to the head? Locked away somewhere a little more permanent? We may never know.'

'Only General Christie could answer that,' McCorkell said.

Walker said, 'Ask her.'

'We have,' McCorkell said.

'Repeatedly,' Somerville added.

Walker said, 'Be more persuasive.'

Somerville said, 'She's pleading the fifth.'

'Makes you appreciate the good old days . . .' Walker said. 'An extraordinary rendition flight to Egypt or Syria would do the trick.'

'She'll talk, eventually,' Somerville said.

'When she talks, we need her trigger,' Walker said. 'What made her start this when she did.'

'Does it matter after the fact?' McCorkell said. 'It's too late. We have to keep moving forward.'

'You won't find patterns if you only look forward,' Walker said. 'What was General Christie's Zodiac go-signal. We find that out, we may start getting ahead of this, maybe preventing what's next before it starts playing out.'

'Perhaps there is no pattern,' Somerville said.

'There's a pattern,' Walker said. He winced as he shifted his bandaged leg. 'My father's involved so there had to be. The NASA key ring and where it played out. He knew what was happening, and where.'

'On that . . .' McCorkell looked to Somerville.

'They've found your father,' she said.

Walker said, 'Where?'

'Malta.'

'What's in Malta.'

'Nothing much.'

'Who found him?'

'Interpol hit. We got lucky. They're surveilling him. The government here knows. FBI wants to be there on the ground, they've just sent a snatch team. They want to bring him in.'

'When?'

'This time tomorrow,' Somerville said. 'I'm on a flight in an hour. I'll be there when it goes down.'

'I have to get there.' Walker made to get out of bed.

McCorkell waved him down.

'Book me a flight,' Walker said. 'Fastest you can get.'

McCorkell watched as Walker steadied himself on his feet. His thigh was wrapped in a tight bandage. The colour had drained from his face with the exertion.

Walker said, 'My father is Zodiac, right? He has to be. And I'm the one who's going to bring him in.'

Walker took a step. His leg gave out and he caught himself on the bed.

McCorkell said, 'You can't do this.'

'Stop me,' Walker said, trying to stand un-aided and failing. He steadied himself on the hospital bed.

'There's another way,' McCorkell said. 'I have a contact on the ground there in Malta – an old friend. And he can get to your father. Get him moving, buy some time. Maybe another twenty-four hours.'

'Do it,' Walker said, sitting down on the bed. 'Get us another day. I leave tomorrow. This ends with my father. This ends the day after tomorrow.'

If you enjoyed *Kill Switch*, read on for the beginning of the next book in the Jed Walker series . . .

DARK HEART

PROLOGUE

Freeing herself from under the bodies would not be easy. It would take all the strength she had. The blood made it harder. She closed her eyes and pictured a different time and place. The tangle of lifeless arms and legs, the weight of leaking torsos and heads, became friends playing a childhood game of stacks-on. *Move*, she thought. *Get out of here.* She slipped, and shifted, and slid. Got nowhere.

It's useless. I'm trapped.

She could smell the death around her. Could taste the coppery blood, like an old penny in her mouth. Hear the silence. She couldn't move her arms enough to be useful – they were pinned beneath hundreds of pounds of dead weight. She squirmed and wriggled. The blood was tacky and thick. Gallons of it. Multiple gunshot wounds. High-powered assault rifles. New weapons, nothing like the ones the militia used. The cacophony still rang in her ears; the screams echoed. Otherwise, it was silent. She moved fast and shuffled on her back, but she was getting nowhere on the slick ground, and a body above her shifted, blood pooling onto her face, forcing her to cough and gag and start to hyperventilate.

You'll die like this.

Rachel Muertos kept her head tilted to the side and closed her eyes and slowed her breathing. *Something else. Anything else. Somewhere happy. Another time.* She pictured her mother, a career librarian in

1

San Francisco elementary schools, and it worked better than the image of the playground. Her mother had been through hell to get into America, and she'd survived. She'd thrived. Thinking of her mother's smiling face took her away from the reality around her as she lay still. Her breathing relaxed. Her senses settled. The screaming, black silence gave way to actuality. First came noises. She heard dripping, and the wind that blew through the long-ago bombed-out warehouse. The dripping sound was blood. Rachel fought to stay composed. She pictured her mother's face, that familiar smile, and thought back to being in bed as a child in Los Angeles when they'd first arrived in the United States. It was a few months before they'd moved north and settled and she'd started preschool and she could remember her mother reading her books in English. It was like they were both still there, in that moment long ago. The memory calmed her. She felt hope.

Move, bit by bit.

She started to roll her shoulders; her arms were pinned to her sides. She tried her feet; her heels moved up and down like paddles. She shifted and slipped and tried to move, just a little, away from the blood that now drizzled onto her neck. In her mind's eye it was like trying to get out from beneath an avalanche of bookshelves, all that mass, all those words not spoken, her mother cheering her on. The reality seemed made-up, unreal, but she knew what happened. She'd seen it. Heard it. Real-time. Hyper real, really, because when the killing had started, everything had amplified.

Stop. Rest. Relax. Try again.

She managed to move just enough to keep her face clear, and then stopped moving to regain her strength. The heat kept the blood slick and viscous, even now, almost two hours after the event. Drip-drip-drip. The heady funk of body fluids created a humid environment. Rachel breathed through her mouth to avoid the smell. She heard a noise. A bird, perhaps, or a person. Far off. Like shuffling. Rachel made a noise. Not a call for help, but a faint hello. She felt it was safe now. To make noise. To create movement. To try to emerge from the tangle of death that had kept her alive. To find safety. But her fright and initial reaction, which was to play dead as the bodies piled around and then upon her, was proving her downfall. The strength had gone out of her. All that mass. Her arms and legs tingled. The weight pressing on her body meant her chest could only rise and fall in small, rapid motions. She knew that if she breathed out fully, her lungs would not have the power to inflate again. She was hot and tired and getting more and more light-headed.

You have to keep trying. You have to save yourself.

It took her ten minutes of wriggling and paddling and shifting to realise that she couldn't get out. Not on her own. She didn't have the strength. She'd spent too long in the one spot, with five, or six, or more, bodies piled on her. Then her breath started to quicken as she thought that maybe she'd been shot and couldn't feel the pain of the wound for the numbness of the weight upon her and the time elapsed. Maybe her spine was compromised. She started to scream but knew it was useless because she could barely let any sound out. No-one had heard the gunshots and carnage and thought to investigate it. No-one would hear her scream and investigate it. But it was all she could do, and she had to do something. She screamed. The sound was pitiful. Her lungs could inflate maybe halfway, and she could only expel half that. The sound was of a small child, and she again pictured herself sitting up reading with her mother not long after they'd arrived in the United States to make a new life.

Your mother went through hell. Get out of this, for her.

She yelled. A little louder this time. Stopped. Kept still.

Movement. A noise. Hope. Or a threat.

Then, one of the bodies shifted. Slid right off. Thumped as it landed. And then another. The release of pressure was like being born again. She could breathe, and see, and hear, and move. Another body fell to the concrete floor. And another.

And then a face, above her. One of the other Americans. He'd come back, to help her. He shifted the bodies and helped her up to a seated position, and looked her in the eyes as he spoke.

'Find Jed Walker.'

Seven thousand miles away, Jed Walker took his first unaided steps in four days. The nurse was close by, as was the physiotherapist, and he waved them away and gave a thumbs up. This was nothing. A nick. A ricochet of a pistol round. Through the quad. Along it, actually, a groove half an inch wide and three inches long. Surface muscle damage, some skin grafted from his hip to make the cosmetic repair. Plenty of physiotherapy to regain full functionality. Walker was prepared for that. He'd been shot before, twice in fact, and he'd got through both those rehabs just fine. This was nothing on those instances. Besides, being shot wasn't the worst that had happened to him. He stopped and turned and headed back down the corridor of UCSF Medical Center in San Francisco and he knew that even with the full weight on his leg he'd be fine to go home soon. He'd be slowed down for a while, sure, but as long as the stitches held and the wound heeled, he'd be up to speed in no time. He wouldn't be anywhere near full capacity for a few weeks, then he might have a slight limp for a couple of months after that while his muscles adjusted to their new arrangement, but he'd be fine.

Which is fine, Walker figured. *So long as nothing urgent comes up.*

•

Rachel Muertos woke to the beep of intensive-care equipment.

'Good morning,' a voice said. 'Do you remember your name? Where you are?'

She saw that the speaker was a man in military uniform. ACUs, to be precise – the US Army Combat Uniform, all patterned and baggy and ready to see action. He was a veteran from the campaign in Afghanistan, because he was wearing a legacy camouflage pattern that had since been replaced. Officer's rank sewn on his bib, but she didn't know what it meant. Army Surgeon's patch attached above his name plate and on his left sleeve pocket flap. She knew that symbol. He stood next to her bed. Close. Her eyes lingered over the medical patch, which depicted a modified caduceus, with snakes entwining a winged sword rather than the conventional staff. The sum of it all was a relief to see, and she smiled inwardly at the recognition. Being here meant she was no longer in Syria. *But where?*

'What do you remember?' he asked.

'Your medical patch,' Muertos said. 'It's wrong.'

'What do you mean, wrong?'

'It's not your fault; it's the Army's mistake, from way back. In the US Army context, the staff is replaced by a sword. But the caduceus symbol is the wrong symbol: it has nothing to do with medicine. The Rod of Asclepius, that's what should have been used. That has a single snake, rather than the two-snake caduceus design; it has ancient associations with trade, trickery and eloquence.'

The army doctor was quiet, watching Muertos. Beyond the surgeon and his pen light that was following her eyes, she could see a building. Not a field hospital. There was airconditioning. The bleep of medical equipment. Overhead lighting. A sterile smell.

'Your name?'

'Rachel,' she replied. 'My name is Rachel Maria Muertos.'

'Do you know where you are, Rachel?' As he spoke he pocketed his pen light and then made notes on her medical chart.

'A hospital.'

'Specifically?'

'Specifically?'

'You've been told.'

'Told? When?'

'We had this same chat yesterday,' he replied, taking a step closer, again shining the light in her eyes, then moved back. 'I told you where you were. Do you remember that? Do you recall what I told you?'

Rachel paused, then shook her head. Then went still. She became aware of another presence in the room. Another man. A big man. In the far corner. In shadows. Dressed in a suit. Official.

Rachel said to the surgeon, 'Where am I?'

The doctor moved away and turned towards the other man. 'She's not ready for questioning. She needs more time. Her memory, it's coming and going, but she's not ready yet.'

The suited man stepped from the shadows. Rachel could just make him out. Unfamiliar. Beyond big. He was huge. Broad shoulders. When he got closer, she looked away. There was something about him. He was aged about forty, his head shiny under the lights. Strong jaw. A nose that had been broken more than once. Wide-set dark eyes. A brute.

'Two minutes,' he said to the doctor, who shrugged and moved back to give him room. The suited man's voice was deep, gruff. American, but unspecific. Maybe west coast. But he had no tan, and there was nothing relaxed about him, which were things Muertos associated with her adopted home state of California. This guy looked like he had a high degree of Neanderthal in his DNA make-up. He was easily as wide and tall as a door. No fat. All muscle. His suit bulged at the biceps. He didn't wear a tie, because there was no tailor in the world who could make a dress shirt to button up around a neck that size, let alone a tie long enough to wrap around it. A chill ran through Muertos as she felt the man staring at her.

'Rachel, I'm with Homeland Security,' he said. 'We spoke yesterday, you and I.'

'We . . . did?' She looked up at him, and forced herself not to look away. She searched his face, and though she saw nothing familiar she now knew why there was something odd about him. He was bald, completely bald – no eyebrows, no eyelashes, no shadow of a beard. Just dark eyes set in a big face. The eyes were calculating. Fixed on her, like a predator.

'Yes,' he said. 'What do you remember?'

'Where am I?'

'You're at Ramstein, Germany. Military hospital. You were told that yesterday. What do you remember about how you got here?'

'How'd I get here?'

He paused, his eyes searching her face, then said, 'You remembered all that crap about the US Army medical patch, and you don't remember what brought you here?'

'What? No. No, I don't. How'd I get here? Please, tell me.'

He looked around the room like he was frustrated. She could see a pulse ticking away at a thick vein in his temple.

'You showed up in hospital in Damascus, Syria, two days ago,' he said. He looked at her. His eyes, set back below a big boney brow, searched her own for any sort of telling sign. 'When you were brought in, you were covered in blood.'

'Blood?'

'Yes. A doctor from Médecins Sans Frontiéres thought to run checks on it. It was the blood of at least six separate people.'

'I . . .'

'Whose blood was it?'

'I don't know.'

'What do you remember about Syria?'

'I don't remember.'

'Don't play with me.'

'I don't remember. What did I say yesterday?'

He watched her in silence. Five seconds. Ten. Then he said, 'That doctor from MSF said that you were talking, in some kind of a delirious state, from the time you were brought in to when he had to sedate you. You were saying the same thing, over and over.'

'What was I saying?'

'You can't remember?'

'Could I remember it yesterday?'

The man watched her, as though her question were a test. The vein ticked away, the pulse escalated, as if Muertos's lack of memory was making him angry.

He eventually said, 'You were in severe shock, but you're otherwise unharmed. Delirious, they said. But I need you to think, Rachel. Do you remember anything of what happened in Damascus? Anything at all?'

'Why was I in Damascus? How did I get there?' She looked across to the doctor. 'How – how did I get here?'

'Look at *me*,' the Homeland agent said. 'Rachel, look at me. That's it. Now, think. Do you remember anything that can help us?'

Rachel Muertos was silent.

'Find Jed Walker,' he said. 'Over and over. That's what you were saying. *Find Jed Walker.*'

Rachel's eyes were blank. 'Find . . . Jed Walker?'

The Homeland agent nodded and leaned closer. Then, in a tone that suggested she should summon an answer, said, 'Who is Jed Walker?'

'I . . . I don't . . .' Muertos started to breathe fast, and the heart-rate monitor spiked. 'I don't . . . where . . . How am I . . . Who . . .'

'Agent Krycek, she's not ready,' the doctor said, moving back into the light and taking Muertos's wrist in his hand. Her heart rate started to calm. 'She needs more time.'

Agent Krycek stared at the army doctor.

The doctor looked down to Muertos. 'Rachel, we'll give you more time. You need rest. And time.'

Rachel was silent. She watched the Homeland agent, Krycek, as he stared at the doctor. The doctor was unflinching amid the weird, close to volatile, tension.

Krycek's face turned to Muertos and he gave her a look that could have been read as wary. Certainly serious. Curious. Suspicious.

'I'll be back, same time tomorrow morning,' he said to her. 'We'll talk more then. You will remember.'